Chapter One

"YOU KNOW I HATE THIS, RIGHT?" MASHA SAYS, RIDING shotgun in my Nissan LEAF as I squeeze into a parallel parking spot two sizes too small. It's a brilliant blue morning in Los Angeles, but Masha doesn't know that—she's blindfolded with the faded green bandanna my mom used to wear to weed her begonias.

"You've made your thoughts on bachelorette parties clear," I say, squinting to read the four different parking signs through the fronds of a palm tree—if there's a way to get towed in this town, I'll find it.

Damn. Thursday street sweeping.

"Luckily," I tell Masha as I throw my car into reverse, "twenty years of friendship has taught me to read between your lines. What you hate are penis-shaped plastic straws, male strippers, and Sex Position Bingo—"

Masha gags.

"Because," I continue, "you're still scarred from your sister-in-law's bachelorette."

"The stripper sat on my lap," Masha says. "And *grinded*."

"I know, babe—"

"Then my sister-in-law sat on *his* lap. And grinded."

I glance at my watch—three minutes to eleven—then boldly swerve into the marina's paid lot.

It's like there's a hole in my bank account.

But what's an additional thirty dollars for parking, compared with your best friend's happiness? When I tug off Masha's blindfold in a minute, the view of the Pacific will make a much better reveal than a side street dental office.

I park the car and reach into my back seat for the rusty green tackle box I stocked this morning with plastic lures and fishing line.

The cold nose of my terrier, Gram Parsons, nudges my hand. He loves to fish and is eager to get out of the car and consider the subtleness of the sea. Me too.

I place the tackle box on Masha's lap and take a breath.

"Here's what you don't hate," I say. "Intimate gatherings, Pabst Blue Ribbon, beef short ribs, nineties R & B . . . and fishing."

I reach for the cooler, borrowed from my friend Werner, who owns a Greek-fusion restaurant in West Hollywood. Since I'm perennially short on cash, sometimes Werner gives me lunch shifts at Mount Olympus, and recently . . . there may have been some lighthearted petting in the walk-in fridge. But that's neither here nor there. What's here—what's now—is my best friend on the eve of her wedding; my favorite pup, decked out in the turquoise life vest that makes him look like a doggie briefcase; my dad's old tackle box; and this cooler, complete with Bluetooth speaker.

I crank Toni Braxton's "Breathe Again" and undo Masha's blindfold.

ADVANCE PRAISE FOR

What's in a Kiss?

"A heart-stoppingly romantic exploration of all the what-ifs—told with so much humor and heart that you will lose yourself in the fantasy. Beneath the joyride of electric tension is a thoughtful commentary on friendship and the consequences of our choices. I loved it!"

—Annabel Monaghan, national bestselling author of
Same Time Next Summer

"[A] completely captivating, heartfelt, and humorous rom-com that explores the ever-present question of *What if?* With her signature wit and characters I want to be best friends with, Kate will make you believe in soulmates. . . . I loved every second!"

—Falon Ballard, author of *Just My Type*

"A sexy and romantic delight about parallel lives, what-ifs, and kisses that cross a multiverse."

—Abbi Waxman, author of *The Bookish Life of Nina Hill*

"Funny and sexy, *What's in a Kiss?* spins a slip of fate into an utterly charming rom-com, full of delightful surprises and nuanced family and friendship dynamics. A sweet and smart story of the love found in every lifetime and the destiny we make for ourselves."

—Emily Wibberley and Austin Siegemund-Broka,
authors of *The Roughest Draft*

"Heartfelt and appealing, *What's in a Kiss?* is the perfect read for anyone who adores swoon-worthy romance with a touch of magic." —Lily Chu, author of *The Stand-In* and *The Comeback*

What's in a Kiss?

LAUREN KATE

G. P. PUTNAM'S SONS
New York

PUTNAM
— EST. 1838 —

G. P. PUTNAM'S SONS
Publishers Since 1838
An imprint of Penguin Random House LLC
penguinrandomhouse.com

Library of Congress Cataloging-in-Publication Data

Names: Kate, Lauren, author.
Identifiers: LCCN 2024004194 | ISBN 9780593545171 (trade paperback) |
ISBN 9780593545188 (ebook)
Subjects: LCGFT: Romance fiction. | Novels.
Classification: LCC PS3611.A78828 W53 2024 |
DDC 813/.6—dc23/eng/20240205
LC record available at https://lccn.loc.gov/2024004194

Printed in the United States of America
1st Printing

Book design by Ashley Tucker

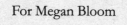For Megan Bloom

No one can predict the present.
—Sophocles, *Antigone*

"Mrs. Morsova," I say grandly, because I love how Masha and her fiancé are making a legal mash-up of their last names— come Saturday Eli Morgan and Masha Kuzsova will be Mr. and Mrs. Morsova. "Your deeply personalized, two-woman bachelorette party awaits. So, let's fucking throw down!"

Masha blinks in sudden sunlight—then screams like she won the Powerball. She lets fly her beautiful, massive smile and throws her arms around me.

"BBS, Liv," she says.

"BBS, Mash."

BBS is a code that calls back to the beginning of our friend-ship, to the day Masha and I met.

We were eight years old, in third grade, each of us the only girls on our respective Little League teams. It was the playoffs. I was catching for the Yankees. Mash was batting cleanup for the Braves.

In the bottom of the ninth, Masha drove the ball to the center field fence. She was rounding third when our shortstop threw the relay to me. Masha charged the plate. I held my ground. We collided—and by some thunderclap of destiny, both of us broke our left fibulas. The same orthopedist reset both our bones.

I was in agony, physical pain compounding my grief at hav-ing dropped the ball, at the memory of the umpire calling Ma-sha safe. But when she signed my cast (red, like hers) with *Broken Bone Sisters*, a lifelong bond began.

Now we clamor down the dock at the port of Marina del Rey, tackle box, fishing poles, and boom box cooler in hand. We're laughing like we're eight again. It's a typical mid-May morning in Southern California, the kind of day that dazzles tourists, but here we take our midseventies, slight breeze, and periwinkle sky just a little bit for granted.

Even though I've spent my entire life in LA, the smell of sea air still makes me buzzy, primed for adventure. It's a feeling I realize I haven't had in a while. I've been wasting a lot of recent time stuck in other people's traffic, or holed up in my bungalow, doom-scrolling job boards on my phone.

I push all that aside today. Today's about being in the moment with Masha.

We head for the whitewashed tackle shack at the edge of the dock, where a couple of bored teenagers pass out paperwork and boat keys. While Masha slathers on sunscreen and checks out the boats, I slip two of the finest credit cards from my collection to the kid at the counter and suggest splitting the rental fee down the middle. I call this going Schizophrenic Dutch.

The kid sizes me up: cutoffs and flip-flops, no makeup, hoodie with a hole in one sleeve, long dark hair tossed into a messy bun. I've always looked young for my age, which my mom swears will someday be a blessing. But for now, at twenty-eight, it means that absolutely no one—not even this pimply stoner—takes me seriously.

He looks down at Gram Parsons in my arms. "There's a fifty-dollar pet fee."

"This isn't a pet," I say.

"What is it, then?"

"Haven't you read *The Call of the Wild*?" I say. "This dog is my equal. This dog is—"

"You didn't reserve a crew," the kid says. "Just the boat."

I look over his shoulder at our rig for the day. It's a modified forty-two-foot sportfisher, circa 1965. In tall black letters someone has hand-painted her name on the hull: *Tongva*. My kind of boat.

"We're the crew," I say, enjoying his incredulity. My dad taught me to helm a 120 footer when this punk was in utero, but I don't waste my breath bragging.

"The security deposit kicks in if you—"

"We'll be fine," I assure him, taking the boat keys.

"Where are you going to fish?" he asks, following me down the gangway to the boat.

"I was thinking we'd try the water," I say with a wink as I climb aboard. "Come on, Mash."

By eleven fifteen, I'm steering us out of the marina, standing at the wheel with the sun on my shoulders and a smile on my face. Gram Parsons pants in the captain's chair behind me, and Masha's got her feet dangling over the edge, wake kicking up and tickling her toes. Her floral sundress hugs her curves as she lays back and closes her eyes.

This peace is what I wanted for her today. Ever since she got engaged, it's been a struggle for Masha to stick to her vision of her dream wedding: tiny and personal. Both Eli's and her family have been pressing them to expand the guest list, to include cousins, colleagues, cat-sitters.

Masha's big and opinionated Ukrainian family knows only one way to host a wedding, with factory settings for the DJ, catering, and decor. I've attended three such parties for Masha's relatives in the past six months alone—and honestly, they're fun. But they're also the very last kind of celebration Mash would ever want for herself.

When she put her foot down at her bridal shower brunch—capping the reception at eighteen guests and trimming the rehearsal dinner to only the actual wedding party—Masha's family was horrified. Babushka stormed out of the Ivy so fast the restaurant rattled. Ever since then, quietly and on the cheap, Mash, Eli, and I have been planning a much smaller version of a wedding that's truer to their style.

I'm proud of the way my favorite introvert has held her boundary. Tomorrow's rehearsal dinner and Saturday's celebration are going to be precisely as the bride and groom want them, if I have anything to say about it. And, though Masha's still not convinced, my money's on her family showing up to the reception, taking one look at the happy couple, and putting all this pettiness aside.

I snap a picture of Masha in her sun hat, coastline receding behind her, her adult life zooming into view before her. I flip the camera to selfie mode and take a picture of my smiling self. Even though my own adult life may still be a little out of focus, it cannot blur how thrilled I am for Masha.

When you've been friends as long as we have, it's impossible not to see yourself—every aspect of your identity—in relation to each other. Drop us into any situation and it's a safe bet Masha's instinct will be the opposite of mine. While she's compassionate, contemplative, conscientious, and femininely curved, I'm impulsive and outspoken in my baggy boyfriend jeans. While she's known Eli was The One since high school, I remain open to all the infinite possibilities future romances shall bring. Masha is the Sophie to my Frances Ha, the Lenù to my Lila, the Constance Wu to my Awkwafina. We couldn't be more different, and there's no logical reason we should get along so well, but we do. Chalk it up to two decades of history, plus our enduring love of baseball and Korean BBQ, and of course, each other.

When Masha went to Pomona to get her art history degree, and I got my teaching credential at Cal State, we wrote snail mail letters to each other twice a week, even though we were only an hour's drive apart. When she landed the assistant docent job at the Getty Villa the week I started teaching drama at the local middle school, we surprised each other with congratulatory tickets to the same Dodgers game.

Three months ago, when I got furloughed from my teaching job, Masha actually cried. I held out the tissues, preferring the wineglass-half-full approach: if the school district hadn't gutted its arts program, I wouldn't be free on this fine Thursday morning to host her bachelorette.

I do miss my students. I miss that moment when I'd see it click in a kid's eyes that they could channel their own emotions into a character completely unlike themselves and bring a role to life. I'm bummed those awkward eighth graders only got through half of *The Glass Menagerie* before the school ran out of funding, but I'm also trying not to let the layoff get me down. Because what good would that do? I'll find another drama teaching job. If there's one thing this town is full of, it's parents who dream they're raising Hollywood's next big star.

I steer the boat toward the *Star of Scotland*, the sunken wreck of an illegal gambling boat that sank off the coast of Santa Monica eighty years ago. Now it's a diving and fishing paradise, a double down on a good time. By the time we've made it through TLC's first album, I'm dropping anchor and reaching for our poles.

"I haven't done this since your eighteenth birthday," Masha says. "Remember you caught that big blue fin? Then your dad dropped it back in . . ." Her smile fades as she locks eyes with me.

"The classic 'one that got away,'" I say, making sure my tone stays bright. It's not that my father's death is still raw—it's been ten years since his heart attack, and I've done my due diligence in therapy and broken dreams. The fact that losing my dad upended my one-time college and career plans isn't even something I think about anymore.

Most of the time.

I'm the kind of person who likes to believe things have a way of working out for the best. And the proof is in this moment, right now, sharing a brilliant boat-ride bachelorette with my oldest and best friend.

"I hope you're hungry for some *galbi*." I go low on the penultimate syllable to sound like Oprah. Mash loves Oprah.

I kept the ribs warm using the partition in Werner's luxury cooler, but I dressed the presentation down by tossing two of my mom's old heating pads on top.

"You didn't." Masha reaches for one of the hot, floppy sacks and gives me a thwack with it. "These bring back so many memories."

"PMS Eve," I say, referring to the once-a-month holiday my mom invented when I got my period. Throughout my teen years, Masha, my mother, and I were all on the same cycle. We were that close.

"Remember when Lorena used to make us those awful vegan nachos?" Masha says. "She'd insist we lay on the couch in your den with these heating pads over our laps, while she force-fed us the entire John Hughes catalog."

"For all our bitching and moaning," I say, "that *was* an important cinematic education."

"But we didn't understand any of it." Masha laughs. "We thought the Valium scene in *Sixteen Candles* was just what happened when a woman got married."

I laugh, then realize Masha's gone quiet. And a little pale. She slides her pole into one of the holders attached to the stern and pops open a can of PBR. "That's going to be me two days from now."

I feel the window narrowing before Masha wedding-spirals. I've got to make her laugh. I slump against her, impersonating Molly Ringwald's wasted on-screen sister walking down the aisle: "Looovve the teapot."

Masha cracks a smile, indulging me, but she's clearly on her way to the fetal position. Her eyes clamp shut as she hugs her knees. And she's rocking.

"What if it's a disaster? What if my mom makes a scene? What if I fall apart?"

I put my pole and beer down, take her shoulders gently, and look into her hazel eyes. "Masha. My love. I'll be at your side. No matter what. You can do this. You and Eli are beautiful together. Your future sparkles with enthusiastic, introverted love."

"But what if . . ." She trails off and we gaze at each other.

"Yeah," I say quietly. She means the rest of it, the life that comes after *I Do*.

Divorce, infidelity, sudden death, unemployment, depression—every wrecking ball in the book found our nuclear families at some point while we were growing up. There's no use pretending we'll escape adulthood unscathed. But where Masha can take to her bed on these subjects, I become defiant, like, *Life, do your worst. I dare you to flatten me.*

I know a huge portion of my strength comes from having Masha and my mom in my corner. Without them, a flat tire would lay me low. But with their support, I could navigate a four-tire-blowout on the Autobahn, backward and upside down. Lucking into having Lorena as my mother and Masha as my BBS are the great gifts of my life.

Which is how I know that right now, my job as maid of honor is to dish out every support Masha needs.

"Do you want to do a visualization?" I ask. Mash and I got in the habit of doing these last year, before our intramural baseball playoffs. Since we won the championship, I know the technique works.

"Good idea," Masha says, casting her line again, watching her lure vanish into the sea.

"Okay." I close my eyes, feeling a nibble on my line. I jerk the rod, but the fish escapes. I wait for the right visualization to come to mind, and smile when it does. "Imagine: Eli's in a white studio, alone . . ."

I pause as the details find me. Masha's groom-to-be is a ballet dancer with the Los Angeles Ballet. The way the man looks in his tights ought to be illegal.

"The curve of flesh," I intone. "The tension in the fabric of his tights—"

Masha laughs, breaking my focus. "First of all, Eli would die if he heard you right now. Second, you're doing really well, but I think I need a more immediate visualization. Like, Saturday? The ceremony? Me standing before the altar, not pulling a *Runaway Bride?*"

"Yes, I see it!" I close my eyes and reset. "You're standing at the altar. Your veil rests perfectly on your hair, which isn't too poufy. The eccentric yogi officiant is fashionably late, enough to give you a thrill. Oh, but look, he's here now. In the warm Santa Monica sand, Eli stands beside you—"

"No tights."

"Completely tightless," I say. "His tux looks great, and he's gazing at you like Kenneth Branagh's Hamlet looking at his dad."

"You're so weird."

"I'm right behind you—"

"Yes, boo," she says. "I see you."

"I'm holding your bouquet, and I've got your back. Always."

I feel Masha reach for my hand and squeeze. "Thank you, Liv. This is good. Maybe I can do this."

Never one to be left out of group love, Gram Parsons barks and kisses both our hands.

"You can totally do this," I say, smiling behind my closed eyes. It *is* a good vision, and in two days, it's about to be real. I can see it: Masha's elated. Eli's lucky AF and knows it. I'm happy for them.

And, when I glance across the imaginary aisle of this imaginary ceremony . . . there is Eli's very real Best Man.

Damn it. Glasswell strikes again.

Who let Jake Glasswell into my visualization? I did not order his famous smile or green eyes, and I would like to send them back. I was doing just fine, thank you, right up until he showed up.

But he won't leave. He sticks in my mind, because . . . oh right, he just does whatever he wants. He just gets whatever he wants. He probably doesn't even want half the stuff he gets, he's just that lucky.

It's not that I'm delusional. I know I'm going to have to face this guy at Masha's wedding, but I intended to put off thinking about him for as long as possible. Like, until tomorrow's rehearsal dinner, when—glowed-up and dripping in my legtastic mini dress—I'll feel a tap on my shoulder and I'll turn, slowly, casually, like whoever's on the other side can wait.

And there he'll be. After all these years. I'll be ready for him. My tone and body language will be the essence of nonchalant when I say, *oh hey,* and *yeah, I guess it has been a minute.*

But I don't need to think about Glasswell now.

As I will my brain to kick him to the curb, the boat rocks, and I realize Masha's on her feet.

"Bite!" she shouts. "Big bite!"

I gasp and see Masha frantically reeling in her line, her pole bent like the Arc de Triomphe. I scramble to grab a net and get my phone out of my pocket. I video the bride-to-be lift a fat halibut from the water.

"Beautiful!" I say as Masha lowers the wriggling fish into the net.

I run to my tackle box, find my pliers, and remove the hook from the fish's lip. Its scales glisten like diamonds.

"This is a good omen," Masha says, as she tosses the fish into the tank attached to the deck. Then she gives me a hug that *almost* casts Glasswell from my mind.

Chapter Two

———

AN HOUR LATER, OUR BEERS ARE DRAINED, OUR GALBI reduced to bones. Gram Parsons dozes on a cushion at the bow, and I'm fileting the halibut as Snoop raps and Masha steers the boat nice and gentle toward home.

"I can't tell you how much I needed today." She sighs, facing the sea.

"You really thought I was taking you to a male strip club at eight a.m.," I say, throwing fish guts overboard.

"Thanks for knowing me," she says.

"I haven't solved the mystery," I say, "but I've uncovered some clues."

"I love you, Liv," Masha says, gazing into the horizon.

"I love you, too." I give our words the space they deserve, then I say, "Is now a good time to discuss some maid of honor logistics?" I've got one gloved hand on the fish, the other pulling up the Notes app on my phone. I'm still unsettled by how easily Glasswell slipped into my visualization before and am glad to shift my focus to my many more important tasks.

"Sock it to me," Masha says.

"You have one last dress fitting, tomorrow at two," I say. "Eli's tux is being dropped at his studio by noon. You're confirmed for a manicure at three, then microblading at four."

"Can you meet me for the manicure tomorrow?" Masha says. "My treat."

"I'd love that, but . . ." I say, glancing at my chewed cuticles, which are presently covered in fish scales. "I can't. I'll be at Lorena's."

"Right." Masha nods. "Of course."

During the pandemic, my mom and I started a podcast called *The Reader's Daughter.* Lorena is so avid a reader of self-help books that she lectures innocent strangers in the checkout line at Ralph's. Now, thanks to our project, she has the perfect forum for expressing her zeal to the abyss.

And I do mean abyss. Our subscriber numbers are lower than the last round of a limbo line. But we love it because it's fun. And an unexpected way to bond. I do the production and sound editing in the makeshift studio in her garage. We joke about our nonexistent sponsors, but it's no joke that the pod is how we survived the pandemic. I didn't think I could get any closer to my mom, but our podcast proved me wrong.

"Last week's episode was amazing," Masha says.

She truly is a fan. All our listeners' love is sincere. All four of them.

"I particularly liked when Lorena called you out for not reading *Why We Dream.*"

"We were reading two different editions! Mine might have been . . . abridged."

"Classic. Your dynamic with Lorena is gold. You should look into sponsors," Masha says.

"Ha."

"*Olivia*. The podcast could *be* something. Take it more seriously."

"I take it seriously."

"As seriously as you take messing around with Werner?" Masha knows about my walk-in fridge rendezvous with Werner, and she doesn't exactly love it.

"Olivia," she says. "Werner brought *CliffsNotes* when he came to see your middle schoolers put on *A Midsummer Night's Dream*."

"He's a chef, not a renaissance scholar! Come on. Werner's fun. He's laid-back, no-drama, and even you had that sex dream about him in his chef whites."

"Which I swore you to secrecy about!" she reminds me. "Werner's . . . fine. On a scale of one to deserving you, he's like a four."

"Harsh!"

"I'm just saying, you have a pattern with guys like him. Very quickly, they bore you to tears. You're two texts away from throwing your phone at the wall. Which means you're four hookups away from ending things."

I pretend to be offended. "I am not that predictable."

"If you don't believe me," she says, crossing her arms, "check the top row of your bookshelf."

Oh no she didn't.

The top row of my bookshelf is where I keep my diaries. There are fifteen of them, one for every year of my life since eighth grade. Color coded in rainbow order.

"You know I never read those," I say, though I can't help suspecting that Masha is right. Not like I'd peruse my past to find out. "Purge and shelf. Purge and shelf." I mime the act of diary writing, then flinging them away to gather emotional dust.

"What about Evan, from the mint green edition?" Masha says. "Or Jonah, from your periwinkle pleather book? Or . . . what was his name, that punk rock guy who went down on you in his nasty old truck—"

"*Tristen!*" I recall with a smirk. "And that truck was only nasty in the very best sense of the word."

"Tristen," she says. "Teal journal, spiral bound."

"Shut up. You don't actually—"

"No, Liv, I don't read your diaries while you're taking too long to get ready, tempting as it is. It's just that I've been with you on many of the occasions when you've been filling those books up—with accounts of attractive, forgettable men you'd never actually want to be with long term." She nods at me. "And I'm right about the path you're on with Werner."

As I stack halibut filets on the cutting board, I reflect on my recent romantic history. I'd met witty but emotionally unavailable Evan when we were canvassing door-to-door for the last presidential election. That *would* be the mint green volume. And Jonah taught music—I think—at one of the schools where I taught drama. We'd had a few bland dates the year I was writing in the periwinkle journal, but, if Masha hadn't remembered his name, I don't think I would have. Tristen I remember—our chemistry had been worthy of more than a few diary entries. But if I'm honest, our best sex happened via FaceTime when his band was on the road.

Which is . . . pathetic.

But so what if my love stories thus far aren't worthy of a Pulitzer Prize? What Masha's not giving me credit for is this: each time one of my relationships ended, I've *survived*.

I know what real heartbreak looks like. I've seen it up close and way too personal: my mom after my dad died. I know all the things it can wreck.

No thanks. I'm good with guys like Werner—here today, whatever tomorrow.

"Liv, I love you," Masha says. "You light up my life. And you deserve a bronze statue for how much you've boosted your mom's last decade. You go out of your way to help other people like it's your job. It's beautiful. But you know—you do know—that you're avoiding your own heart?"

"Can we put a pin in my love life until after we've celebrated yours this weekend?"

"Fine," Masha says, wagging a finger at me. "But don't think we're done with this subject."

I ignore her and return to my list. "We need to be at Mount Olympus tomorrow night by seven. The menu's finally set." Planning a rehearsal dinner for only five guests may sound easy—and it was certainly simpler than it would have been had Masha's and Eli's overbearing families been invited—but adhering to Eli's dietary restrictions was no small feat. "Everything's vegan, gluten- and dairy-free."

"Bless you," Masha says. "Eli's nutritionist won't kill me. Yet."

"And," I say, proud of this surprise, "I sweet-talked Werner into giving us the Treehouse for our party of five."

The food at Mount Olympus is great but simple—Werner's

not winning any Michelin stars. His roof deck, though—it silences the snobbiest of LA haters. Two of whom will be in attendance tomorrow night.

Not that I care what Glasswell and his over-the-top celebrity girlfriend think. I'm still not entirely sure why she's even invited.

"Oh wait, it's now a table for four," Masha corrects me. "Didn't I tell you?"

I blink. "What?"

"Jake's not bringing Aurora."

"Oh?" I cough, feeling a tightness at the back of my throat. I suddenly wish I'd packed a few more PBRs. I feel Masha's gaze on me. Even though I've barely said a word.

"Be nice," she warns.

"Since when is *Oh* a derogatory word?" I use my filet knife to slice too hard into the fish's spine.

"You know," Masha says. "If I'd told sixteen-year-old Olivia that *the* Aurora Apple was canceling an RSVP, there would be hair-rending on the level of Greek tragedy."

It's true that in my younger days, I was a massive Aurora Apple fan. I internet-deep-dived her enough to know her real name is Allison Applebaum, and she was born two years before me to two schoolteachers in Topeka, where she starred in every musical production her high school put on. When she played Caligula in the teen rom-com *Oblivious*, her aesthetic took over my vision board for the rest of high school.

But last year, when Aurora started cohosting Glasswell's internationally syndicated morning talk show, *Everything's Jake*, rumors swirled that the cohosts were in fact a couple. I quit my intrigue with Aurora cold turkey. I started to see her for what she really was. Another fool duped by Glasswell's phony charm.

I don't ask why Aurora is gracing us with her absence to-morrow night, and I can't know whether having one less snob at dinner is a good thing, or whether a table for four will force me into additional interaction with Glasswell. Either way, none of this is enough to spoil a successful day of friendship and fishing. I drop the ziplocked filets into the cooler and decide not to ob-sess. It's that simple. Mind over madder.

"It'll be fun," Masha says as I literally bite my tongue. "I don't think the four of us have hung out solo since, wow . . . prom?"

"Has it been that long?" I say, my voice suddenly tight. I start hosing down the boat's cutting board so I don't have to meet Masha's eyes.

"Liv?" she says. "You okay?"

"Absolutely!"

I feel her squinting at me. "You're not feeling weird about seeing Jake this weekend, are you?"

"Of course not!" I sputter. "That'd be ridiculous. Why would *I* feel *weird*?" We're near the marina now, so I take the tiller and putter to a slower speed. I wave at a passing boat full of kids and grandparents, hoping Masha doesn't notice the sud-den heat in my cheeks.

"Hmmm," she says, because of course she noticed.

We've taken a wrong turn in this conversation, and I need to get us back on track. I am (was) a drama teacher! A professional. Paid to understand the art of acting. If I can't do this now for the sake of my best friend's happiness, then what is wrong with me? I meet Masha's gaze and commit:

"You're right. The whole weekend's going to be a blast."

And somehow, just like that, Masha smiles and leans back on her bench, convinced. Hell, maybe I'm convinced, too. Maybe I'll be fine seeing Glasswell tomorrow night.

Chapter Three

"THIS IS BULLSHIT, JOY!" I YELL INTO MY PHONE AT THE teenaged girl whose YouTube tutorial—*Foolproof Box Dye at Home!*—is now a failed hypothesis.

While Joy shows off her fabulous glossy highlights from the comfort of what looks like a very soothing pink bathroom, I'm squinting into my phone from a folding chair in my slanted backyard with dye oozing down my forehead and dripping into my eyes.

I toss the bottle over my shoulder in frustration. Then I wince and start crawling through the dirt, squinting my burning eyes in search of the busted bottle's plastic pieces before Gram Parsons gets his underbite on them and I'm out another five hundred dollars at the vet.

And that's when a jackhammer shudders into earsplitting action at the top of the hillside abutting my backyard.

"You've got to be kidding," I shout at the sky.

The guesthouse I rent on a narrow crevice of Laurel Canyon backs up against a steep and rocky hill. At the top of that hill, some half acre above my backyard, lies a mansion that's been under construction ever since I moved in three years ago. I've never seen the mysterious celebrity living the high life up there, but I've heard enough to form a strong opinion. The daily power saws and Bobcats and jackhammers, the troop of tree trimmers and various other burly men have come to dominate my aural landscape, and many of my nightmares.

And today, I'm less than in the mood.

I've fantasized about mounting a projector screen to that rock for outdoor movie nights. Now it sounds as if my neighbor might be breaking ground up there to put in a pool.

I grit my teeth. I can already hear that pool's construction taking up the next nine months of my life, piercing like a diamond arrow through my skull, through my tranquility, my hillside. I know this space isn't *really* mine, but I live here, and I need it.

This stamp-sized rental—and I say that as a fan of postage—is the best deal in the canyon. It's tiny and quirky, the carpet is older than me, the doors stick, and the kitchen's built into the hill so that its window is level to the ground. It makes Masha claustrophobic, but I love the fact that when pasta night strikes, I can open the window, reach out, and pluck fresh basil from the ground.

This house is cool in the summer, cozy in the winter, and smells like night-blooming jasmine for three solid months in the spring—always during my birthday. I love this house, and so does Gram Parsons, who has a real tight crew of puppy pals up and down the block. So as long as I can scrape together the rent to pay my slightly batty landlord, I'm not going anywhere, and I demand some peace.

I'm already past my breaking point, juggling all my maid of honor duties this weekend. Trying to primp and prep and prime myself to show Glasswell what a non-hot mess I've grown up to be. To pull that off, I need things to go smoothly for two days. I cannot deal with the ceaseless earsplitting scream of a jackhammer, or a singed eyeball from this cheap dye, or one more thing going to hell right now. I cup my face in my hands . . . and catch a whiff of something foul.

"Oh no," I groan, becoming aware of the chemical burn spreading through my scalp. I race to the garden hose and turn it on full blast.

I scream as the water nails me, hard.

I'm afraid to survey the damage I've done to my head, but for Masha's sake, I summon the strength. I find my phone, open my camera app, and shriek at the view in selfie mode. It's worse than I feared. My hair is fried and slightly . . . blue. Everywhere *except* for my prematurely gray roots. I'm at the point where I'm contemplating Sharpie . . . when I imagine Glasswell gasping at the sight of me at the rehearsal dinner tonight.

Not happening.

A brick-like throb builds in my chest. When I think of showing up at Masha's wedding, it's not *her* judgment that worries me. It's Glasswell's. The Best Man. The guy who always managed to make me feel like a loser, starting way back in high school, when I was rather cool.

I can't let him see that he was right about me all along.

I need professional help. I'm going to have to shell out at least a hundred dollars, probably more, for someone to properly fix this. I sigh and open my least favorite app on my phone: my bank. My balance laughingly informs me that my debit card will not quite carry me through a hair rescue at a salon.

I flop into my creaking hammock and curl into a ball. I pull out the stale bagel I've stashed in my sweatshirt pocket and take a bite. I will fix this problem like an adult. Which means I need to make some dough ASAP if I want to avoid asking my mom for a loan. And I do.

I text Werner to see if I can come in for the brunch shift. He writes back right away:

Shift's covered, but the walk-in fridge is open.

Ugh. I start to type back a no-nonsense rejection when I remember yet another irritating fact: I have to tell Werner that our party tonight is down from a five-top to a four-top. I had to beg him for the Treehouse, usually reserved for parties of twelve. I even used Aurora Apple as a bargaining chip, swearing to snap some social media pics of the famous actress loving Werner's small plates.

Glasswell is *nearly* as good in terms of social media currency, but any pic I'd take of him would have to look like an accident, lest he think I think he matters.

Werner texts: You there?

I sigh. In person, Werner's gorgeous, like a less symmetrical Ansel Elgort. But today his texts are just one more thing I can't deal with. I feel an urge to throw my phone at my hillside—then I remember Masha's words yesterday on the boat:

You're two texts away from throwing your phone at the wall. Which means you're four hookups away from breaking up with this guy.

Two texts = phone very nearly thrown at cliff.

Four more hookups and . . . honestly, I doubt we'll get that far. The thought of ending things with Werner doesn't bother me so much as my own predictability, at least according to Masha.

If you don't believe me, check the top row of your bookshelf.

Not like I have time to do that today.

Instead, I silence Werner's notifications and open my Lyft driver app. A moment later, there it is, that ding telling me a rider's in need, and a very small amount of money will soon flow my way.

Gram Parsons whimpers hungrily. I give him the rest of my bagel. "This isn't forever," I say. "Just make it through the weekend."

Inside my bungalow, I grab my Catalina Wine Mixer trucker cap and tug it over my wet, blue head. I search in thirteen places for my keys. I stare for half a minute at my calming visual mantra: a framed poster of the balcony kiss from Zeffirelli's *Romeo and Juliet*. Finally, at the door, I encounter Gram Parsons, who gives me side-eye and a disgruntled growl. I forgot I'd promised we'd hit the canyon dog park today.

"I'm sorry, buddy," I say, giving him a scratch. "Mama's gotta work."

He changes tactics, to a mewling whine. I kneel to meet him at his level.

"Would you feel better if you came with me?"

He wags his crooked tail.

"Fine." I swoop him up, praying none of my riders will be allergic.

We're halfway out the door when I remember I've barely opened the book my mom's reviewing on the podcast today.

Since I always have extra time while I'm waiting for my Lyftees, I circle back to my bookshelf. But instead of reaching for *Get Out of Your Inner Hero's Way*, my gaze travels up. To the top shelf.

There they are. My color-coded row of diaries, all fifteen of them.

If you don't believe me . . . I hear Masha's voice again.

I run my hand along their spines, tracing my life. A shiver passes through me as I let myself remember the girl I used to be, and the woman I used to dream I would become. She's all there, in those pages.

I touch the first diary, a red one, given to me on my thirteenth birthday. It's the book that documents my first period, the summer I got braces, the paranormal romance novels I used to be obsessed with, and basement rounds of Spin the Bottle.

Next to it is the spiral-bound salmon-colored notebook from freshman year of high school—the year when my life kicked into a higher gear, when I started to see my future like a path that I could pave myself and follow. My first of many report card 4.0s. And the year Mash and I made school history by being the only girls to have made Palisades's varsity baseball team.

Orange diary for sophomore year, when Masha got her license. I remember writing nearly all the entries in the front seat of her car. I was starting catcher by then, and a rising star on the debate team. That book holds the summer my parents took me to New York and we saw a new, life-changing Broadway play every night for a week.

Junior year is glittery gold—college tours and my first lead in a school play. It's the year I got serious about acting, the year

New York started calling my name. I wore a Juilliard sweatshirt like it was my capsule collection.

When I reach the fifth book on the shelf—pale yellow, senior year—I smile. I'm an accidental genius. I need to make a toast tonight to Masha and Eli, but I've been blocked on what to say. Nothing I've come up with yet has felt momentous enough. For all of senior year's many peaks and valleys, only one matters today. This book contains the story of the first night Masha and Eli got together. Senior prom.

Call it instant inspiration. Call it a sentimental miracle.

I pull the journal from the shelf and slip it in my bag.

Chapter Four

NEAR THE BOTTOM OF COLDWATER CANYON, JUST before I reach the smooth, flat streets of Beverly Hills, there's a 9:48 a.m. logjam Waze did not anticipate. I find myself sandwiched between a school bus and a party bus on a two-lane road. I can't see in front of or behind me, but judging from the sustained honking up ahead, everyone stuck here should probably accept that this is where we live now.

On the bright side, I've got a passenger, so at least I'm being paid. I feel a little guilty about the traffic surcharges, but a glance at his suit in the rearview mirror tells me he's probably expensing this ride anyway. And his soft snores say he could use the extra winks before I drop him at his office in Century City.

The sun glares through the window, threatening to burn his sleep-craned head if we're stuck here much longer. This gnaws at me. Suddenly, this guy's possible future sunburned scalp is all I can think of. I reach behind me, careful not to wake him so I can quietly tug down the sunshade.

Of course, because I'm me, I forget to put the car in park, and when my toe lifts off the brake, we creep forward until we almost fender bend the school bus up front. I slam on the brakes just in time. Thank God Gram Parsons was wearing his seat belt.

My heart pounds as I recover from the near-collision, but at least my passenger's scalp has been spared.

Is there something very wrong with me?

Masha jokes that I can't pass a stranger on the street without intuiting a need in them that only I can fill. Since we started our podcast, my mom has quoted from all manner of self-help books about how my compulsion to help others gets in the way of reaching my own goals. But I wasn't always like this.

When my dad died at the end of my senior year of high school, my mom and I fell into a kind of grief that felt like drowning. A few weeks after we buried him, I was driving to baseball practice when I cut off a silver Audi on the 101. The driver changed lanes, caught up to my window, and then, for the next three miles, he rode alongside me, laying nonstop on his horn while flipping me the bird.

I lived ten lifetimes in those three miles. Anger turned to shame to resignation to bewilderment, and finally, I got there—to gratitude. Because yeah, dickheads gonna dickhead, but this one came swinging with a life lesson, writ large:

My suffering—blinding and radioactive to me—was *invisible* to him. Audi Man didn't have a clue my dad just died. Audi Man didn't know that my future had disintegrated because my family could no longer afford tuition at Juilliard. That, moreover, there was no way I could leave my mom and move across the country to New York. That, suddenly, so much of what I'd envisioned for my life after high school . . . simply wasn't going to be.

I'd looked around at the other cars on the highway that day, imagining the millions of people in my city.

And ever since then, I've proceeded as if everyone around me could use a little extra grace.

Everyone except Glasswell.

Maybe it's because my problems with him started right *before* Dad died, but Glasswell seems to have been grandfathered in, reserving the lone parking space of antipathy in me ever since.

Gram Parsons resituates himself so his paws push my yellow journal into the center console. I take the hint and open the book. My dog may not have any idea what's going on, but I like to think he has my best interests at heart.

It's strange: even after all these years, the book still opens automatically to the longest entry, a record twenty-seven pages. Holding the book open in my hands, the memory of writing it rushes back so vividly it makes my stomach hurt.

May 25, 2014

Dear Princess Di,

About last night . . .

All I can say is I've been sold a bill of goods. By adults. By eighties movies. By the universe.

What was supposed to be a magical evening became mortifying. And now, for the rest of my days, whenever anyone says the word "prom," I'll be stuck thinking of <u>him</u>.

I laugh, because I brought this diary to read some vintage Mash and Eli romance, not to trip into a Glasswell wormhole.

The years have dulled the acute humiliation of that night, but as I read on, unexpected sensations tiptoe across my chest. I feel agitated, on high alert.

Like I'm suddenly on a collision course with shame.

The dress—my mom's yellow tulle, debuted at her own senior prom.

My date—Eli Morgan, whom I asked as a friend, because Mash was too scared to ask him as a crush. And too worried that if I didn't take him, he'd go with Natalie Planco, and the next thing you'd hear would be wedding bells.

The plan—to go in a group. The plan was fun. But then Sumi got mono, and Alina and Duke had a fight, and soon our whole limo was dropping like flies, until it was just Masha, Eli, me, and—

Jake Glasswell.

Yes, Di, that Glasswell. He's haunted these pages before. Remember when he joined Debate Club (see p. 58) and made verbal sparring with me his national pastime? Remember when he walked onto varsity baseball as starting pitcher (p. 63), right up-mound from my catcher's mitt? Remember when he capered into the auditions for Romeo and Juliet (p. 69), took one look at me atop the balcony and—mercifully— walked right out? Or, just last week, in homeroom (p. 89), when we received the same slip of paper, notifying us we'd each been named Most Likely to Succeed?

Why Glasswell decided to single me out as his lone high school rival, invading every one of my spaces, is a mystery. The boy has been enrolled at Palisades for only one year, but the two of us have enough rivalries to last at least three lifetimes.

That ends tonight, Di. Mark my words. I'm going to tell you this sad story, but let it be the last time I give Glasswell page space in my life's unwritten book.

What is up with my writing style in this journal? I must have been reading *Dangerous Liaisons* at the time. It has that breathless epistolary feel. I just hope I don't pull out the terms *blackguard* and *alas*.

I skip ahead, scanning for references to Masha and Eli. Surely I documented their first kiss? I can see it so clearly in my mind: The two of them at the center of the dance floor, under the disco ball, her hand on his butt as they swayed to Alicia Keys. She gave him her incandescent whole-soul smile, and then she rose on her toes to kiss him. It was the cutest. Full stop.

But somehow, it seems I didn't get around to documenting their first kiss here. Maybe I didn't feel that moment's sweetness suited the style of my apocalyptic outrage?

Instead, I wrote twenty-seven angry pages . . . about Glasswell. I let it rip about his snug-fitting tuxedo and his long legs taking up the limo's back seat. I wrote about how, on the way to prom, Glasswell made the limo pull over because he couldn't pass a Baskin-Robbins without ordering a rum raisin. Then tried to get me to share it with him.

What kind of person likes rum raisin?

After that, I waffled, detailing moments when Glasswell had seemed almost deceptively . . . cool. How we'd bantered about my dad's Nikon 7, which I was wearing like an accessory around my neck. How the two of us spent a fun fifteen minutes furtively snapping artsy shots of Masha and Eli flirting.

But then, I wrote about discovering that Glasswell's coolness had only been an act.

I wrote the entire shameful scene in which Glasswell showed his true colors.

Here's the thing I can't get over, Di:

I <u>almost</u> made it out with my dignity intact.

It was eleven forty-five—probably three songs left in the DJ's bank—when I stepped out of the gym for some air.

I tell you this next part only because you're physically bound to secrecy. Outside of you, I'll never breathe this to a soul.

"What'd <u>The Bodyguard</u> do to you?" came the voice over my shoulder.

I startled and spun around. Why had Glasswell followed me outside?

"What?" I asked.

"You walked out when 'I Will Always Love You' came on." He tipped his head toward the gym, the distant music playing inside. Our eyes met, and his narrowed slightly, like he was seeing something he didn't expect. "Or maybe . . . you like the song <u>too</u> much."

I blinked at him, tongue-tied. Because I <u>love</u> that song. When Whitney sings it. When Dolly sings it. I love it so much that I couldn't <u>not</u> dance to it in the gym. But I couldn't dance to it, either. Because my date was dancing with Masha, and it's not a solo number.

The thing is, I hadn't realized any of this—not consciously—until Glasswell said those words. I'd just thought it was hot in the gym.

"What if I asked you to dance?" Glasswell said.

And now it was hot outside, too.

"Here?" I laughed and shook my head. I wasn't going to dance with Glasswell on a curb. No matter how good he looked in a tux.

Why would the two of us dance? So he could try to out-sway me? Like he'd tried to out-everything me from the first day he showed up at our school?

"Or we could just talk," he said, sitting down next to me. "I saw the Wednesday performance of <u>Romeo and Juliet</u>."

And there it was. The signature Glasswellian dig disguised as an innocent comment. But he'd gone out of his way to make it clear he saw the <u>Wednesday</u> show, known as Ye Olde Clusterfuck among our cast and crew. It was the night the spotlight burned out in Act Two. And the Nurse's understudy knew exactly none of her lines. And Trevor sneezed on me while parting with such sweet sorrow. And here was Glasswell, rubbing it in.

"So?" I said, not looking at him.

"So, your performance was nothing to sneeze at."

"Puns are the lowest form of comedy."

"Fine," he said. "I have other notes."

I groaned. Why was rich and fancy, son-of-a-mogul Glasswell determined to pick apart our meager high school play? Then I remembered: He almost tried out for Romeo. He'd walked into the audition, saw that he'd be playing the balcony scene opposite me—and walked right out.

Like he was too good for it.

So, of course, he had to put down the whole show.

"Too much instalove?" I deadpanned.

He shook his head, then after a moment, said: "'Who ever loved that loved not at first sight?'"

I rolled my eyes. "What didn't you like?"

"Act Two, Scene Two."

The balcony scene.

"'So thrive my soul—'" he said, quoting Romeo.

I looked up at the stars and filled in the next line without a thought. "'A thousand times goodnight. A thousand times the worse to want thy light . . .'" I trailed off when I realized that I was getting into it. I didn't want to get into it with Glasswell.

For several moments after that, neither of us spoke.

"Olivia," he whispered.

"What?"

"How'd you do that?"

"Do what?"

"<u>Become</u> Juliet in a single line." His eyes ran over my face. "That's why you got into Juilliard."

"I'm waiting for the punch line," I said. But I was thinking: He knew about Juilliard? How?

Glasswell shook his head. "No punch line. Congratulations. I've wanted to tell you that all night."

I raised my eyebrows, still waiting. This was Glasswell, after all.

"What was the audition like?" he said.

"Like a dream," I answered unconsciously. But I didn't want Glasswell to know about my trip to New York, my Juilliard audition, my big, bright, crazy dreams. I stood up, needing to tighten the walls around myself. The song was over by then anyway.

"Congrats to you, too," I said, turning toward the door. "Columbia will be great."

"You heard?" he said. "I mean . . . I guess we both can't wait to get out of here."

Why was he rising to follow me?

I glanced inside the glass doors of the auditorium, where I saw my history teacher, Mr. Coates, stacking folding chairs. "I think it's over anyway."

"I didn't mean prom," Glasswell said. "I meant . . . high school. This town. Our parents' houses."

I shook my head. "I just want to act."

"You're lucky," he said. His eyes studied my face in a way that made me shiver, like he was seeing things I prefer to keep hidden, even from the people I like. "What about your parents?"

I lifted one shoulder, looked away. "Most people's parents don't want them to leave home, right?"

But I got the feeling Jake saw something more specific in my eyes, like he'd been a fly on the wall for yesterday's epic argument with Mom (see previous page). Like he could tell I was still tender from it.

"My parents can't wait to get rid of me," he said.

"No way."

Our eyes met. I knew his were green, but this was the first time I saw them look vulnerable. I couldn't help being a little bit curious.

"My dad thinks journalism is 'for losers,'" Glasswell said, looking down at his shoes. "That I'm a loser for wanting to go to New York, for not staying here and working immediately for him."

I knew, indirectly, that Glasswell's father had an empire of luxury condos up and down the state. Like I knew, indirectly, that Glasswell got into Columbia. The reputation of his family was one of deep wealth . . . and moral shadiness. But it had never occurred to me that Glasswell might not fit in perfectly with that reputation. I wasn't sure what to do with this new information.

"You know best what's right for you," I found myself saying.

"Maybe." Glasswell stepped closer, until we were almost touching. Until I noticed I was holding my breath. "It'll be worth it, Olivia."

"Studying journalism?"

"No, I mean, you."

"Me?"

His cheeks flushed. He seemed to struggle with the words.

"Whatever it takes for you to get to Juilliard," he said. "To New York. On stage. It'll be worth it."

"Okay . . ."

"I'm serious," he said, his gaze sharpening on mine. "You light up when you act. I think when someone's lucky enough to love something that much, they should shape their life around it. No matter what." He rubbed his jaw. "And you deserve a better Romeo than Trevor."

"Let it go, Glasswell," I teased, because what he'd said before that Trevor comment felt too surprising to respond to. "It was just a school play."

"But if I'd gotten that part—"

"Oh!" I laughed. "There it is!"

"What?" he said, glancing around us.

"Your ego! It weirdly vanished for almost four seconds." I turned to him, feigning interest. "You were saying, Romeo?"

His eyes grazed my lips and I felt a shiver run through me.

"I could have kissed you better, and you know it."

I should have laughed, but I didn't. Couldn't. It was strange. Squared off with Glasswell, gazing up into his eyes, I felt suddenly like I had a fever.

"Here's what you don't understand," I said as heat pulsed up and down my body, centering in my cheeks. "When Romeo and Juliet kiss, it's symbolic. It's cathartic. Not a flex."

"If you'd been my Juliet—"

"Your Juliet?" Like I was something for him to own.

"If I'd been your Romeo. Is that better?"

Not in a million years, I thought . . . but something inside me was heating up to suggest an opposite idea. Something inside me wondered, *what about now?*

A current coursed through my body, urging me to get closer to him. I stepped toward Glasswell. He stepped toward me. He put his arms around my waist. The touch of his fingers, warm though my dress, held me still. I found myself . . . not slapping him. I breathed in his eucalyptus-scented soap as he touched my mother's yellow tulle. I held my breath, waiting to see what he'd do.

"I know there's another world, Olivia," he whispered. "One where we . . ."

"Where we what?" I stared at him, and something happened in my chest. It was like my body knew what he was talking about. Something in me—something all the way down there—was leaning into him. Into this. Whatever this was.

He put his hand on my face and I wanted to stay there. I wanted to study there and get a job there and make babies there and be buried there. I wanted to not move from Glasswell's hand for the rest of my life.

But then Glasswell said: "This would be a waste."

I think I choked. Or maybe died. A heat wave of humiliation coursed over my body. Whatever ensued in the five seconds I spent effectively blacked out . . . the spell was definitely broken.

And thank God for that.

Who pulled away first, I don't know.

As soon as we turned from each other, an unspoken vow was sworn: we would both pretend this never happened.

I close the book with a thump and shove it into my glove compartment.

This is why I do not read these diaries. This is why they are purge-only affairs. Why hadn't I grabbed the podcast's self-help book on my way out the door? Why hadn't I left this distorted version of my past to molder on my shelf?

In the school bus parked in front of me, a kid smashes his face against the back window, locking eyes with me. In my rear-view I see a woman in pink sunglasses lean out the party bus's tinted window and take a swig of champagne. No one in this traffic jam has stopped honking.

In my back seat, my rider emerges from dreams, blinking and rubbing his face.

"Hey," he says. "Are we almost there?"

Chapter Five

I NEVER GOOGLE GLASSWELL. BUT, OVER THE PAST ten years, that hasn't stopped his face from sliding into the Explore tab of my IG, or the banner ads of my favorite feminist substacks, or the landing page of the *LA Times*. Thanks to his hit talk show and devoted fan base, the man is a meme, ubiquitous online. Usually I scroll along—pretending he's just another celebrity, cultural wallpaper that doesn't do it for me—but not today.

And it's my own idiotic fault. In the hours since I opened my pale yellow journal, civil war has broken out. The part of my brain charged with keeping me mostly functional is taking heavy ordinance from the part of my brain projecting a perfect memory of senior prom.

I'm trying to stay in my lane along Sunset Boulevard's curves, but it's like I can *smell* Glasswell's eucalyptus soap in my unchanged air filter. Like the Southern California sun *is* the heat of his palm against my cheek on the night we never kissed. And the lights turning green at Sepulveda are Glasswell's eyes, and I'm locked in their gaze, and he's talking about another world, and his lips part, and his head tips—

I need to shut these memories *all* the way down. The fate of my best friend's wedding depends on it.

I remind myself that I feel . . . blank about Glasswell. I released my mortification years ago. Hindsight clearly shows me that what happened between us one night ten years ago was No Big Deal. Which means tonight can be totally casual.

Then why do I feel like I'm trapped in the dream where I'm back in high school and forgot to study for the big exam everyone else is prepared for?

Probably because my hair is fucked, my maid-of-honor toast is nonexistent, and I'm nowhere near the version of me I want to show Glasswell tonight.

"I need to cram!" I shout in my car, forgetting I've got a passenger. In the rearview, she's Korean American, about my age, dressed Coachella-chic. It's possible I follow her on Instagram. "Sorry, forget I said anything—"

"No worries, babe," she says, not looking up from her phone. "You good?"

Her overwhelming disinterest feels like a safe forum for me to keep on talking. "It's just . . . I'm seeing this guy from high school tonight. An acquaintance. Barely. You know what I mean? It's nothing. But for some reason, I feel really unprepared."

"What's his insta?" she asks, still looking at her phone.

"No. I can't—"

"Because he's like, off the grid?" Now she meets my eyes in the rearview. One brow arches in intrigue.

"Um . . ."

"What's his name? I'll find him, no matter what dark corner of the web he's hiding in."

There's no way I'm breathing a syllable of Glasswell's famous name, which occupies all the internet's brightest places. But

maybe this woman's right about confronting him online before
I have to confront him tonight in person. Practice. So that I'll
be primed—relaxed—by the time I'm face-to-face with Glasswell.

"Thanks," I tell her. "Google is a good idea—I'll try that."

"Good luck," she shrugs before going back to her phone.

By the time I drop her off at LAX, my thumbs itch to google
Glasswell. I've even landed on the best key words. I barely make
it to the airport waiting lot before I'm typing *JGlass Climbing
Wall* in the YouTube search bar. It autocompletes after the third
letter. Of course it does.

I don't watch *Everything's Jake*, but one could not inhabit the
Milky Way and not have heard what happened on his show's
season finale last year. It happened during a rock-climbing stunt
temporarily built into the middle of the show's set. For some
reason, Glasswell and Aurora were supposed to race to the top
of the structure, then rappel down, but something went wrong.
Glasswell lost his grip, and, despite being strapped into a harness, he panicked on live TV. Apparently, his body flailed so
hard his face knocked one of the climbing holds—chipping off
an eighth of his perfect left front tooth.

For a solid forty-eight hours, Glasswell was the only meme
in the universe. Thousands of fans posted videos attempting to
knock a chip out of their own left front tooth. Every time I see
someone missing part of a front tooth, I still wonder if it's an
homage. People went so nuts that Glasswell never got his tooth
fixed, making his smile perhaps one of the world's most recognizable.

I try not to know these things, but I think they get absorbed through the LA air—a hybrid of smog, envy, and self-consciousness.

Today, I get the feeling watching Glasswell biting it on camera might be just the thing I need to settle my nerves, to take the mystique away from the man.

I put my LEAF in Park, drop my sun visor, and hunker down in the concrete pond of gig workers. We're all waiting for a ride from purgatory, though some of us think we're driving.

Barely overhead, an Airbus screams in for a landing. I prop my knees against the steering wheel and hold my phone in my lap. Anticipatory calm flows through me as YouTube loads. The first clip is called *Jake Glasswell Blooper Reel*.

I smirk at Gram Parsons, who puts his chin on my arm for a better view.

From the second I press Play I have to check myself. Because unfortunately, from certain angles—like head-on, in profile, or from behind—the man just really is beautiful. He's a handsbreadth taller than I am, with thick dark hair and broad shoulders, usually accentuated by tightly tailored pin-striped suits. But for this climbing stunt, he's changed into all black athletic gear that highlights his lean, muscular physique and makes him look like he's about to go out for a casual half-marathon. He has the kind of lopsided grin—even in his pre-chipped-tooth era—that makes camera flashes pop. *Adorable* is a word used in proximity to his name. He looks like Harry Styles's tan cousin, plus freckles, minus the pearls.

But for me, the worst part is Glasswell's eyes. They're a

sleepy, grassy green, and deceptively, cruelly kind. On this You-Tube clip, when he looks into the camera, it's like I'm back on the curb outside prom.

I know he isn't looking at me, just a teleprompter and a camera lens. But a woman could be forgiven for forgetting it isn't more intimate than that.

Is *this* what it means to be photogenic? This effortless relationship with the camera? It occurs to me suddenly that maybe the whole world feels as unkissed as I do.

Standing before the climbing wall, Glasswell addresses the camera and, with slightly ominous levity, says, "What could possibly go wrong?"

I haven't mentioned Glasswell's voice.

Instantly recognizable. Full of contradictions—warm yet gravelly, playful yet almost monotone. It's been like that at least since I met him at eighteen, and now the rest of the world has noticed. Once, when I was buying my mom a Powerball ticket at a gas station, I saw a *People* magazine headline fretting over Glasswell's recent bout of laryngitis. Glasswell's voice is practically a national treasure.

Before I can watch Glasswell tumble from great heights, the YouTube clip cuts away from the climbing wall to a different clip of Glasswell on the couch of his talk show, accidentally spitting a mouthful of champagne into the face of a nonplussed Al Pacino. I laugh as I'm then dropped into a series of graceless Glasswell stumbles and some quick-cut stutters where he really struggles with the letter P.

Gram Parsons sighs, and we both know this is beneath me,

that I'm clinging to my self-possession like my dog's fur clings to everything I own. But this isn't merely for me. I'm also doing this for Masha, for the good of her wedding weekend.

I may be a furloughed former public school drama teacher with Lyft decals on my budget car, but Glasswell's merely mortal, too. And he's made an ass of himself on national TV at least a dozen times more than me.

I can't help laughing as the reel rolls into an *Everything's Jake* monologue where Glasswell's fly is open and his boxers are printed with Minions.

That one's so nice, I think I'll watch it twice, but as I'm about to scrub backward, it cuts back to the scene I wanted to see: the infamous rock-climbing fail.

By now, Aurora, dressed in her own sleek black athletic wear, is high above Glasswell on the wall. Glasswell looks good, there's no overstating what that harness is doing for his ass, but he's also not more than six feet off the ground. And he's not moving.

"Your ass is glass, baby!" Aurora's voice taunts from above, in such a canned manner that I can tell this is one of the show's lowbrow catchphrases. "Better catch up."

Now the camera pans to a close-up of Glasswell's face. And he looks . . . terrified. His skin is ashen, his jaw is tensed, sweat beads at his hairline. His eyes bore into the wall like he's looking through the gates of hell.

This image of him does something to me—something I don't expect. I lean closer to the screen and feel, in the lowest part of my stomach, a cringe on his behalf.

"You don't have to do this," I find myself telling him, wanting to swipe out of the app because this is too intimate. This is not the detached research I came for.

"I—I don't have to do this," Jake's voice rasps, barely audible. And I know he didn't *hear* me, since that's not physically possible according to any laws of time, space, or technology. But for an instant, it feels like he did. It feels like my words reached him in another realm. Like they were *supposed* to. Like they were just what he needed to hear.

All at once, his arms release their death grip on the wall. For an instant, his expression relaxes completely. Then the video goes into slo-mo as Glasswell's mouth connects with a fluorescent-green hold. Bloody mouthed, he cries out, "Ohhhhhhh sheeeeeeeeit" in 960 fps as his body rebounds off the wall. This was the meme. This was what social media seized on and made into a million jokes.

This and the next shot of Jake crumpled on the floor in the fetal position, Aurora at the summit, covering a laugh with her hand.

I stare at my phone, feeling an inexplicable desire to pass through my screen and go to Glasswell, to help him up off the ground—

I jump when I hear the Lyft chime that asks if I want a new passenger. I do, but I feel a little nauseous as I put my car in Drive. I want to stop watching. I've seen too much already. But YouTube auto-plays a second video. This one is a recent interview between Glasswell and Oprah.

I'm about to swipe to the Lyft app so I can focus on my passenger, my driving, and the safety of the world at large . . . but Oprah's first words have me hooked.

"We've gathered a group of *Everything's Jake* viewers whose lives were changed by Jake Glasswell's fall off the climbing wall. Jake, can you tell us a bit about this very special group of people?"

Car horns blare. I hardly hear them. "Give me a break, Oprah. All he did was chip a tooth," I mutter, even as a part of me knows this isn't true. There was something else that happened in that clip. Something essential.

"The stunt was meant to be a challenge," Jake says, indulging Oprah. "For me to face an old fear of heights, dating back to when I was a child. I knew there was a risk of my panicking on air, but I wasn't opposed to exposing myself in that way."

"Let's give him a Nobel," I say to Gram Parsons.

"For the first week or so after that fall," Glasswell continues, "I was just the butt of an internet joke. It comes with the job, and I'm used to it. I get that what happened was funny. But soon, I started getting letters from people who responded—not to the moment I spazzed out on the wall—but to the moment right before it."

"'I don't have to do this,'" Oprah feeds him the line with gravity.

"That's it," Glasswell says. "And Beth, who's sitting right there"—the camera cuts to a beaming blond woman, nodding as she fiddles with a gold chain at her neck—"she wrote to me that these simple words inspired her to leave a job where she didn't feel valued."

"Amazing," Oprah says. "In fact, every person we've invited here today incited a major life change after watching you say those words and *surrender* to the climbing wall."

"We call it *hashtag JGlass Falling Up!*" an older woman in a floral blouse chimes in from the panel.

"It's remarkable," Glasswell says with fake humility. "People began to share so much with me after that episode that I found I wanted to share even more of my own truth. That day on the wall, I wasn't just letting go of my fear of heights. I was also letting go of some old pain. From my father."

"Your father?" Oprah says.

Glasswell takes a breath, folds his hands over his lap. "I lost my father when I was eighteen."

Now I slam on the brakes. Eighteen? *I* was eighteen when my dad died. *I* had my identity purged at that tender age, two weeks before my high school graduation. *I* missed out on my bright future because I stayed home to help my mom pick up the pieces of her life.

Glasswell didn't lose his father then—I watched them pose stiffly with a private photographer at graduation. The memory is burned into my brain because it made me sick with envy that he had a dad who was still alive. What the hell? Is Glasswell lying? To *Oprah*? Against my will, against my subconscious, against traffic, I'm intrigued.

So's Oprah.

She grips Glasswell's knee. "Go on, Jake. When you're ready."

My car falls in line behind the other drivers in the rideshare lot, but my focus remains on my screen. On Glasswell. He's good at this, letting the moment build around him. The camera zooms in on him and waits.

It's hard not to notice how well he's aged. Boyish manhood suits him. He's grown into his height, while maintaining his gangly high school angles. He still exudes the vibe of someone you want to get into trouble with, braided with a guy you'd give all your secrets to.

So maybe he's a better actor than I gave him credit for back in high school.

Glasswell broods, gazing into the middle distance. His eyes pool with tears. I hold my breath. Seconds pass. He doesn't say a word. Like a shooting star, a tear flashes on the surface of his cheek.

"He's faking it," I say to Gram Parsons.

Then, completely out of nowhere, a gigantic sob spumes from my chest. It bursts past my lips and eyes and suddenly I'm Old Faithful, wiping my eyes on my sleeve and trembling.

Glasswell might be fake, but he's released something real: When you lose a parent as a teenager, on the brink of your own adulthood, not only their death hangs over you. It's also the death of who you might have been before they died. So when your life doesn't look the way you wanted, every day gives you something more to grieve.

But Glasswell doesn't understand this. He's lying. To Oprah. I need to turn off YouTube. I need to get a grip. I need another life.

My back door opens.

I scream and clench my grip on the phone, shooting it into the back seat like a salmon over a waterfall. It lands face up, still playing the Oprah interview, as my passenger slides in.

My passenger—in his low-slung Yankees hat and aviator sunglasses, clutching a vintage green duffel bag—is a dead ringer for Glasswell.

Thankfully, Glasswell doesn't take economy rideshares from the airport.

"Olivia?!?" Dead Ringer says with bizarre incredulity for a Lyft passenger. My name *is* on the app, right next to *Red 2012 Nissan LEAF.*

Which makes it especially strange when my reply is: "Nope."

Anyone but me, anywhere but here.

I take a deep breath, and the scent of eucalyptus fills my nose. No. No. No. No. I look at Gram Parsons. He smells it, too.

Fate isn't *this* much of a fucker, right?

The Oprah interview is *still playing* in the back seat.

"Give me that," I say, reaching for my phone.

Dead Ringer holds the phone out to me . . .

On which we both now watch Glasswell say somberly: "It's not just losing my father that hurts, it's losing who I might have been—"

"Shut up!" I beg the phone, at last clicking off the video. The horns of a thousand cars surround me like I'm the walls of Jericho. I've got my passenger. It's time to get out of their way.

Gram Parsons puts his paw on the gearshift, as if to say, "Drive." It's what a reasonable person would do. But I have no idea where I'm going. And I'm terrified that if I click my phone back on, Oprah will be waiting.

In the rearview mirror, Dead Ringer lowers his sunglasses to reveal multi million-dollar grassy greens. He smiles crookedly and says, "Well, well, well, if it isn't Olivia Dusk."

I clock the chipped left front tooth. I register the honeyed-gravel voice. I note my running mascara. I understand that I'm in hell.

I hit the accelerator. In this most hideous of all possible moments, the only thing I can think is that at least my yellow journal is safe in my glove box, that I didn't leave it open in the back seat.

"This isn't happening," I say under my breath. I was not supposed to see this man until I was ready. Until I was dressed to kill and professionally blown out and *not* driving a Lyft and had spent at least half an hour pretending to meditate this afternoon.

"Maybe it's a dream." I hear the smile in his voice, the click of his seat belt. "Though it feels fairly real. I thought I heard you were back in LA."

Back in LA? Does Glasswell still think I ever *left* LA? That I went to Juilliard after graduation, like the yearbook said I would? Oh God, he thinks I went to Juilliard and *still* ended up driving other people for a living in my piece of crap car? That's even worse than the truth.

"All these years, I kept waiting to see your name in lights in Times Square," he says.

"Nope," I say, tight-lipped. "That'd be you."

"Ah yes, you're right. It is me, isn't it—"

"Stop talking," I say, waking up my phone and using cheetah speed to kill YouTube and open my Lyft app. When I see his destination—a residential street in Silver Lake—and Glasswell's name—terrifyingly surreal—I'm certain my life has ended. *Murdered by humiliation.*

I tug down my trucker cap, because what's going on with my hair isn't fit even for a corpse. I'm trying to drive and wondering about the state of my back seat and praying for an earthquake when he leans forward, his face between the seats, and says in that fucking voice:

"You used to have a sense of humor."

"Noël Coward is funny," I argue. "Dogs dressed as people, playing poker, are funny."

Gram Parsons growls Glasswell back into the back seat.

"What's your dog's name?" Glasswell asks.

"Gram Parsons."

Glasswell laughs under his breath. "That's *so* Olivia. Let me guess. You stayed in the motel room in the desert where the real Gram Parsons died?"

"Maybe."

"I knew it!" he says. "Did you sense his stylistic presence? Did you *feel* rock and country becoming one?"

"Look, pal—"

"I always wanted to stay there," he says.

"Don't do that. Don't mock me."

"I'm not . . ." he says, before seeming to concede. "What'd you think of my blooper reel?"

"Your *what*?" I say in my best liar voice. Which is pretty bad.

"It rolls into Oprah," he says, like he knows I was deep-dive googling him.

"I wasn't—"

"It's fine," he says. "I get it."

This humblebrag is infuriating enough that I accidentally take the on-ramp for the 405 when I very clearly should have gotten on the 105. I'd like to say I haven't made this mistake before. Some of us are born rideshare drivers, and some of us probably shouldn't have a license.

The highway is a hellscape straight from central casting: ten jammed lanes of parked cars, fanning out for miles. As I realize we're completely trapped on the endless curving on-ramp, my phone says this slowdown will add twenty-five minutes to the trip. Suddenly the half hour it should have taken to get Glasswell out of my car doubles.

I'm supposed to meet my mom in fifty minutes to record the podcast. There's no way I'll make it all the way to the east side and then back to Santa Monica in time.

If I exit now . . .

If I take surface streets . . .

If I kick Glasswell out of my car . . .

Can I leave Glasswell in a vacant lot in Inglewood?

This idea thrills me . . . until I imagine Masha catching wind of it. I bang my head against the steering wheel, causing my horn to honk, causing horns around me to honk, causing Gram Parsons to howl in tune.

"Maybe your being my ride is lucky," Glasswell says from the back seat.

"Like when a bird shits on you?"

He doesn't clap back right away. I glance over my shoulder. He's looking out his window, one long leg folded over the other in a figure four, hands clasped in his lap.

"I was worried things might be awkward," he says. "Between you and me. I think it's good we're clearing the air."

"Is that what you think is happening?"

"I'm sure we can both at least agree we don't want to mess up the rehearsal dinner tonight because of some old—"

"Don't flatter yourself," I say, not wanting to hear Jake describe how he rejected me a decade back. "Nothing will ruin Masha and Eli's happiness this weekend. I'll make sure of that."

"And I'm happy to help."

"And the only way you can help is to stay out of my way." I slam on my brakes, narrowly avoiding a collision with an Aston Martin SUV. "That guy came out of nowhere!"

"You are a terrible driver," says Glasswell, checking his seat belt. "Do you enjoy this line of work, Dusk? I suppose striking fear into strangers' hearts does seem on-brand for you."

"I should be asking why you're slumming in a Nissan LEAF?" I crane my neck to confirm that this traffic does indeed stretch beyond the horizon. "Is some intern getting fired for not booking your black car?"

"That's a boring story," he says.

"Your specialty," I say, which actually makes him laugh. "And just so you know, I'm only doing this because—"

"There's no shame in being a rideshare driver," Glasswell says.

My knuckles on the steering wheel turn white. I could wring Glasswell's face like a sponge. He's always had a gift for condescension. "My life," I say, "is one hundred percent, absolutely great."

I think of my mom, and of Masha, and this feels essentially true. But saying it out loud to Glasswell makes it sound like a lie. It's as if, from the moment he got in my car, Glasswell has been holding up a mirror to me that says, right above my face: *Your life is a shitstorm.*

"No judgment, Olivia. I swear—"

"I have a real job, okay? I'm a podcast producer for a very demanding host, and if this traffic doesn't clear, or you don't evaporate, I'm going to be late for an important recording session."

"You produce a podcast?" he says. "Wow, that's cool."

"I really think I'm going to puke."

"What's it about?"

I pause. There's the version I tell everyone, which is true, about my mother's compulsive need to discuss the self-help books she reads, and how I channeled that into something fun and useful for us to do during the pandemic. And that we've had exactly twenty-one downloads, our two reviews are mixed, and Mom and I don't care.

Then I glimpse Glasswell's arrogant face. "Book reviews."

"What genre? Classics? Sci-fi?" He leans in and drops his voice. "*Erotica?*"

Gram Parsons growls. Glasswell retreats. I eye him in the rearview mirror and say, "Never utter that word to me again."

I don't know if it's Glasswell's husky voice that's gotten me so flustered or the fact that he still seems to expect an answer, but suddenly my mom's taste in self-help books feels dubious. Why is it that so many things I feel good about become embarrassing under the gaze of this particular man?

"You're not going to tell me?" he says. "Just because I said *erotic*—"

"Contemporary, okay? Mostly nonfiction." It's not an

outright lie, but it's enough to inspire a disappointed glance from Gram Parsons.

"I'd love to do something like that," Glasswell says.

"Is there an Off switch to your pandering? You're not on the air."

"Thank God."

We fall into miserable silence. I hate the downward tick of my battery meter. I hate the NPR blaring out the open window in the Tesla next to us. I hate that we've covered less than half a highway mile.

I turn on the radio. Chuck Berry's voice fills the car as he sings "You Never Can Tell." It's a beautiful song about a wedding, and I take this as a sign to center myself. I imagine Masha's wedding going gorgeously tomorrow, bright smiles and joyous dancing, good food and great romance and ocean waves crashing in the background—

"I can't believe our best friends are getting married," Glasswell says, shitting on the vibe.

Who does he think he is? *I'm* permitted to feel that brand of wonder, because *I'm* an actual best friend to one of the people getting married. *I'm* the best friend who drives Masha to get her IUD put in and has a cherry Slurpee waiting when it's time to wheel her from the procedure because she's feeling faint. *I'm* the best friend who buys two pistachio muffins when they're in stock at Sprouts because they're Masha's favorite—one to freeze! *I'm* the best friend who waits to watch *The White Lotus* season finale when Masha gets Covid and her power goes out the same weekend, because we've yet to miss a live-texting session, and some traditions are sacrosanct.

Does Glasswell even count as Eli's friend?

As far as I can tell, Glasswell's the buddy who has his assistant send a generic gift basket at Christmas. Who invites Eli at the very last minute to join a pre-planned trip to Vegas, probably when someone more important canceled, to watch something dumb like a fight he got free tickets to.

Okay, men show their love in idiotic ways. But I take BBS with Masha as seriously as I take anything. Our bond isn't something Glasswell gets to touch.

Then again, this weekend, friendship means giving Masha the loveliest, least dramatic wedding of all time. The friend of my best friend's fiancé cannot be my enemy—at least from rehearsal dinner through Sunday brunch.

"I can't believe it either!" I force myself to say, but I sound like Moon Zappa in "Valley Girl."

"You're worried," Glasswell says.

"I'm not. The wedding will be perfect."

"I mean about your podcast. You're going to be late."

"Welcome to LA."

"Yeah, this place never felt like home," Glasswell says. "Maybe the second time will be the charm."

I cough in shock. "You're not—"

"About to flip coasts? Unfortunately, the network tells me I am."

"That's *not* funny."

I lay on my horn for no particular reason other than I'm trapped in a car with Glasswell, who's moving back to LA.

"Don't worry, Dusk," he says. "Something tells me we don't run in the same circles. You won't even know I'm here."

"Can we try that now? This is already far more time with you than I signed on for this weekend."

Glasswell slaps his knees. "Let's abbreviate it then."

I unlock the doors. "Cool. Bye."

"Ha," he says, seeming unsure if I'm joking. "I mean, if you skip my stop, and go straight to your recording studio—where is it?"

"Santa Monica. Way out of your way—"

"I can catch another ride. The only drawback," he says, "is you won't be able to blame me for making you late."

"Au contraire, derriere."

"Olivia. It's one less hour of your day spent suffering my presence," he says. "Don't overthink it. Just say yes."

Chapter Six

"THIS IS ME," I TELL GLASSWELL, PULLING UP TO MY favorite Japanese teahouse. I'm dizzy with exhaustion. Fifty minutes in traffic with Glasswell has frayed my nerves beyond repair.

He takes in the Santa Monica strip mall, with its upscale pot dispensary, robotics school, and cryogenic therapy center. I sense his question before he asks: "Where's the recording studio?"

I don't tell him it's in the residential neighborhood two blocks south of where we stand. More precisely, that it's in the garage of my childhood duplex, where my mom still lives. And since I'm also not saying that my boss is my mother, this is where our two roads must diverge.

I nod at the teahouse. "First, I drink a gallon of gyokuro. Then I go and dominate the faders." Clearly, I've crossed over into delirium. I tap the Lyft app to end our ride, then I scoop up Gram Parsons, and climb from the LEAF with a stretch.

Glasswell's out of the car, too. He looks at the teahouse. "They have matcha lattes in there?"

My heart sinks. They have miraculous matcha lattes in there. Lazarus would rise from the grave to get one. But Glasswell is not invited to my favorite teahouse.

"The matcha's better across the street," I say, pointing.

Glasswell squints into the sun, shading his eyes with a hand.

"*Starbucks?*" he says like the word is made of broken glass. "Morally unacceptable."

"You have morals now!"

"Are you this way with all your riders?" Glasswell asks. "Is this what you consider . . . five-star service?" He holds up his phone to display the screen that rates his ride, his finger lingering above the lowly single star.

"Don't you dare," I say, my voice rising. I may not be the world's most graceful driver, but I am friendly and accommodating. I do my best to offer the right ride for every passenger I pick up—Glasswell excepted. My five-star rating is a rare point of light in the dark night of my penury.

"Don't worry," he says, and taps the five stars. "I can tell this matters to you."

We stand there, facing each other. I'm steaming inside, and he won't even meet my eyes. It's like he can't see down this far.

"I'm *going* to have a matcha latte," he says, then makes an *after you* gesture toward the teahouse door.

When I don't budge, when it feels as if my jaw has welded together, Glasswell adds: "Let me buy you a drink, Olivia."

"Why? Because I'm a broke Lyft driver?" I shout-whisper in the parking lot.

"Because you gave me a ride from the airport."

"Purely transactional."

His eyes flick over mine for the briefest instant. I await his next insult, but instead Glasswell reaches out and scratches under Gram Parsons's chin. Gram Parsons is about to go into his pleasure pose—the chin-clamp, designed to lock the chin-scratcher's hand in place. And when the clamp happens Glasswell's hand will be locked against my left breast. Sans brassiere. The unexpected touch will cause my nipple to pop up like it's trying to tear a hole in the ozone layer. Which will broadcast absolutely the wrong message.

I lurch away hard, spinning a full 360. Gram Parsons whines dizzily. "Enjoy your matcha, Glasswell."

He catches up to me, circling to block my path on the sidewalk. "Olivia."

"Why can't you leave me alone?"

He sighs. "If it's that big of a deal to you, I'll go to Starbucks."

"Don't do that," I say. "You won, okay? At lattes. At life. First prize goes to Glasswell."

"You're right."

I scoff.

"I mean . . ." He runs a hand through his hair. "You're right to point out it's absurd to make this—or anything—a contest. It's just, you've always . . . ever since high school . . . you bring out something in me. Something that wants to—"

"Be a dick?"

"*Compete.*" He meets my eyes. I wonder if the fumes from the pot dispensary next door have found their way into my blood. Because now I'm frozen in place staring into Glasswell's green eyes. My body warms, centering in the area just below my navel.

What the hell?

Glasswell looks away, and everything neatens back to normal.

Everything but my racing heart. I push past him toward my mom's block.

"See you tonight, Dusk," he calls.

. . . . . .

WHEN GRAM PARSONS and I reach the house where I grew up, my mother is puttering around the garage. She's facing the storage rack with my duffel bags from summer camp, my rolled-up Jonas Brothers posters, the box with every Halloween costume I've ever worn. When she hears the door open, she waves to me over her shoulder:

"How was the bachelorette? Did you trick Mash into thinking you were taking her to get twerked on?"

"Mom," I say, hoping to communicate *everything* to her with that single grounding word.

She turns to look at me, concern practically tattooed on her face. Dressed in pink and orange ombre jeans and a matching flowy shirt, Lorena looks like a human mai tai—a comparison that can't be lost on her, seeing as she has a purple orchid tucked behind her ear.

"Liv. Baby," she says tenderly. "What is it?"

"I'm sorry I'm late," I say, a tremor in my voice. "And full disclosure, I come sans latte. This morning has been an absolute—"

I break off because suddenly my mom comes forward to place a fragrant, steaming gyokuro latte like a miracle in my hand.

There, her smooth familiar caress tells me. *You are loved, and everything's okay.*

I close my eyes and take a sip, swallowing the lump of relief in my throat.

My mom lifts her own latte and takes a luxurious slurp. "It's my week to pick up the drinks. Did you forget?"

"I guess I did."

"What's the matter? Did you accidentally take the 405 again?"

I nod. "And that's not the worst of it."

"Honey!"

Gram Parsons yelps his impatience at not being greeted yet by his grandmother. Lorena remedies her oversight and picks him up.

Part of me wants to be Gram Parsons, blanketed in my mother's embrace. Part of me just wants to move on, to feel the weight lifted from my chest now that Glasswell's gone.

But I don't feel lighter. I feel *loser*, which is how Glasswell always makes me feel. I picture him inside my teahouse, generously tipping my favorite barista, firing texts to former high school friends.

You'll never guess who my Lyft driver was . . .

"So," my mother probes. "What happened?"

"It's just . . . the wedding."

"No. It isn't." Lorena shakes her head. "You've had that wedding locked down for months. This"—she points at me—"is something else."

When I don't answer, because I cannot lie to my mom, and because I wouldn't know where to start, I feel her gaze run over my body, my face, my head.

She grabs my hat—then gasps in horror.

"You left the dye on too long, Liv! I told you to set a timer because you always get distracted. Ever since you were a toddler. Your father used to say—"

"I have an appointment to fix it, okay?" I say with more hostility than I intend.

"Thank God," she says. "Now, you don't have to take my advice—"

"Here we go," I tell Gram Parsons.

"But your dad, may he rest, loved curls for a wedding."

"Curls, great. On it."

She takes my shoulders in her hands and studies me. "You're not going to tell me what's really going on?"

I don't keep secrets from my mom. We're the kind of close that talk on the phone multiple times a day, picking up in the middle of things. She hears about every bad date, recalls the names and personalities of my favorite former students. She knows which dogs bark at Gram Parsons when I hike with him at Runyon Canyon. She knows all my regrets. Except this one.

It was a timing issue. I devoted my post-prom life to the darkness of my room, and then my dad died four days later, and the force of gravity doubled overnight. After that, things were different. My mom and I suddenly had so much to deal with, and somehow the disaster of Glasswell and prom night never came up.

I sit down at the mixing board and put my headphones on. "Let's just do the show."

My mother doesn't press—for the time being anyway. She moves to her desk and puts her own headphones on. But her eyes never leave mine as she takes a long sip of matcha and then flips on the mic.

"Helluva Friday to you, Future Listener of the Past," my mom gives her standard greeting, but her eyes are watching me.

"Helluva day, Lorena," I say my line. It was my idea to have a second mic, for chemistry and banter. Over time, my role on the podcast has evolved to something of a droll hypewoman, Tig Notaro meets Flavor Flav. But today, I'm having trouble staying inside my skin, let alone inhabiting a character. And my mom knows it. She's had my number since before I was a twinkle in her eye.

All I'd wanted to show Glasswell this weekend was a passable facade of me. Then I'd gone and been an asshole to him on the ride from the airport. But he'd deserved it, hadn't he? For catching me off guard like that? For invading my space and seizing every opportunity to condescend to me? For making me feel inferior in the special way only he can do?

I rub my eyes and banish him from my mind. Why am I thinking about Glasswell when I only just got rid of him? Is my guilty conscience gnawing away at my mind?

"Have we got an absolute treat for you this Friday," Lorena interrupts my thoughts. "Our very own Olivia, my daughter for those who don't know, vowed that she would actually read this week's *fabulous* selection, *Get Out of Your Inner Hero's Way*—"

"Mom." My voice breaks and I take my headphones off, resting my head on my desk. "I can't do this."

My mother hits the button to stop recording. And waits.

"I. Hate. Jake Glasswell." There. I've wailed it. And I don't feel any better.

"The talk show host?" my mom says, and then, catching up, "Oh, the boy from high school?"

"He's the best man at Masha's wedding," I croak. "The worst best man."

Slowly I lift my head up to meet my mother's eyes. She's waiting for me to go on. She's in no rush to ferry me out of my discomfort the way Masha's mother does. I used to envy the way Mrs. Kuzsova would rush to coo over the smallest scrape or hurt feeling Masha felt. My mom would never do that. I've come to learn it's both a strength and a weakness, her ability— sometimes her tendency—to sit with pain.

"You're going to ask me what's fanning the flames of my hate?" I say, quoting one of Lorena's favorite self-help lines.

She nods. I sigh, and so does Gram Parsons.

I think for a moment, heat building in my core. I try to think of every smug thing Glasswell said to me today, but all that comes to mind are the insults I slung at him.

"Envy," I admit. "Resentment. Ugly things he has a special skill for bringing out in me."

I see a light go on in Lorena's mind. Then she's on her feet, moving toward her bookshelf. "This might call for Brené Brown. She has an atlas of the heart—"

"I don't *want* Brené," I say so forcefully that my mom stops and turns around. "I want *you*."

"Oh honey." My mom comes to me, padding quickly in socked feet. We meet halfway across the garage. "I'm here," she says and takes me in her arms. "I'm right here."

And I cry.

She helps me toward the beanbag chair, which is the only place to lounge in the garage. I collapse on it. She folds around me. Gram Parsons hops up, and sits in both our laps.

"What did Jake Glasswell *do*?"

I have to think before I speak, because can I really still be *this* mad about what happened ten years ago at prom?

"He . . . got everything he wanted."

"Everything you wanted, too?" my mother asks.

I wipe my eyes. "A version of it, maybe."

"He went to New York," she says. "He got discovered. You stayed here and gave up your dreams to help me."

"Don't say it like that. I couldn't have left you. I didn't want to. You know that."

She nods. "I also know that if things had been different, if Dad were still here, you would have gone. And who knows what would have happened? I understand. Here Jake Glasswell is, big fancy boy, flying in for your best friend's wedding, rubbing his success in everyone's face, that he's the one who gets to show the world his light."

I cringe. "You did not just say *his light*."

"I watch the show sometimes," my mom says. "He's good. Though I don't trust that sexy baby Aurora."

I snort.

"Jake's always had that spark," she says, softer than before.

"We hate him, Mom, remember?"

"Sure, honey," she says. "But . . . do we need to? This weekend? Aren't there bigger things to feel?"

I snuggle closer to my mom in the ridiculous beanbag, not

yet ready to say she's right, but we both know she is. And this, right here, is the support I'll call upon tonight if Glasswell dares pull any shit with me.

My mom snickers. Then she breaks into a proper laugh.

"What about this is funny?" I ask, even though I'm already halfway smiling.

Practically in stitches, my mom says, "I knew that all I had to do to get you to open up was to hold you accountable for this week's reading!"

I elbow her, and she elbows me, and we laugh until finally, I'm crying the right kind of tears.

Chapter Seven

"CORNER!" A VOICE SHOUTS ABOVE ME ON THE STAIRWAY to the roof.

This is restaurantese for *Coming through with something heavy.* I flatten myself against the brick wall—harder to do in a tiered gold dress than in my usual server's uniform—just in time for Joy, our best busser, to pass with a crate of clanking cocktail glasses.

"Livvie D, looking fine," she says, noting my curled hair as she descends.

I know I look good, with my hair saved by Pierre and the dress Mash helped me pick out to accentuate my legs, but do I look good *enough* to blot from Glasswell's mind the pathetic mess I was earlier today?

Not that I care.

"This your party tonight?" Joy asks.

"My best friend's." I smile. "She's getting married tomorrow."

Since I got rid of Glasswell this afternoon, time's been flying. I've got a list of thirty things to check before Masha gets here in half an hour. I glance roof-ward and ask Joy, "How's the Treehouse looking?"

"It's not the worst place to watch a sunset," she says as she backs through the downstairs kitchen door.

I take the stairs two at a time. We call the roof the

"Treehouse" because instead of tall chairs, it's got rope swings hanging from rustic wooden beams around high marble tables. And tonight, when I come upon it, empty and an hour before sunset, it takes my breath away.

The space is rectangular, bounded by waist-high baby citrus trees—yuzu and kumquat and funky, fragrant Buddha's-hand. Their branches are draped in white twinkly lights, and they're pruned tight, so they don't interfere with the 360-degree views. No matter where you sit atop Mount Olympus, you face majesty, from the spires of downtown to the ever-edging shadows of the Hills, all of it perfumed by the buds of exotic early summer citrus.

To the east, landmarks fan out like postcards from the spinner rack: the opulent mansions of Beverly Park, the Hollywood Sign in profile, the grand white dome of Griffith Park Observatory. And to the west, when it's clear like it is tonight, you can see out across the ocean to Catalina Island and beyond.

The Treehouse legally seats twelve, though if Shonda or Tarantino calls, Werner will cram in thirty-five, fire codes be damned. I've never seen it set for a party of four, and I have to admit, it's never been more enchanting.

I check my list. Incredibly, everything seems in order. Coral ranunculus rest in a dozen scattered vases. Candles on the bar cast shadows on Mendocino seashells carried from the beach where Eli proposed. Sonance speakers softly stream my Rehearsal Dinner playlist—Angel Olsen and Darlene Love for Masha, a spray of MC Yallah and gospel songs for Eli. Here and there I've hung photos of the happy couple through the years.

Behind the bar I find the case of wine I selected of rare yet

inexpensive Mount Etna-region wines, in honor of Masha and
Eli's imminent honeymoon to Sicily. The whites are chilled, the
red's decanting, the rosato's blushing like a bride.

Having nothing to fix makes me nervous. Because when I
stop moving, stop doing, stop fixing—I see Glasswell in my
mind. Sliding into my back seat. Gloating in my rearview. Trying to pet Gram Parsons. Telling me I make him want to *compete*.

I hear footsteps on the landing and turn to see Werner hauling in the firepit, his muscles manifest beneath a tight white tee.

"Hey, mama," he says, carrying the pit toward the rattan
sectional where we'll retire after the meal. Werner's hair's a little
sweaty, and he smells like sautéed garlic. He has a burly virility
that can be alluring, but tonight, I'm finding him and the predictability of our recent history a bit embarrassing.

I definitely don't want Glasswell sniffing us out tonight.

Werner releases the firepit like a barbell, unfurls his frame,
and winks at me.

"Who's serving us tonight?" I ask, skirting his outstretched
hands, realizing the server assignment is the one detail I neglected to secure.

"Alastair."

I groan. "Someone else, please."

"He's the best up here," Werner says.

"He's an *aspiring actor*. He won't leave Glasswell alone all
night." Not that Glasswell will mind, of course. But I'm in no
mood for celebrity worship.

"This is Hollywood," he says. "Every server *except* you is an
aspiring actor."

I've never told Werner about my scholarship to Juilliard,

about the dreams I used to have. I'm lifetimes away from that girl. Is it weird that Werner doesn't know this side of me at all?

No. It's not like we're together.

"What about Silas?" I say, opening the Contacts on my phone.

"He's in that new T-Mobile commercial."

"Fucking *actors*!" I give up.

"Fine," Werner says, wiping his hands on his jeans. "I'll do it myself."

"*You?*" I swallow. Werner spends most evenings in the back of the house. Why does the idea of him waiting on Glasswell make me queasy?

"I know how to handle celebs," Werner says, giving me a wink. "I got this."

"Thanks," I say like a volcano after an eruption. "That means a lot."

Werner steps closer. "Did you do something different to your lips?"

I think about the curls Pierre styled with six different curling irons. It's hard to say, given my financial position, that this was *worth* three hundred dollars, but honestly, it probably comes pretty close.

"I got a blowout," I tell Werner.

"Hot," he says. "I'm digging this dress, too. Very flimsy."

I clamp my hands around my skirt. "Colleagues, Werner. That's all we are tonight."

"I love it when you shut me down," he breathes against the back of my neck.

I step away. "Hands to yourself. Okay?"

"You seem tense," he says, backing me up to the railing that overlooks downtown. "Anything I can do to help you relax?"

"Nope. Down boy." I have my hands on his chest, warding him off, when I hear the desperate plea of a paparazzo below.

"JGlass! Over here!"

"Really, Werner?" I say, annoyed. "You had to tip off *TMZ*?"

"What's the problem?" he says, his hands draped around my waist. "It's good press!"

Cringing at how much this surprise photo shoot will feed Glasswell's ego, I look down to the street and see him stepping from a black Chevy Suburban. His hair is coiffed and his gray suit gleams. He holds out his hand for someone behind him—

"Is that Aurora?" the lone paparazzo calls, and I feel a hitch in my chest.

But a second later, out steps Masha, laughing at the cameraman's mistake. I let out my breath. She looks adorable in her flouncy white sundress, a tiny silk tiara in her curly hair. After her comes Eli, who grabs his fiancée by the waist and dips her so deeply the ends of her hair touch the sidewalk. When the lovers kiss, Glasswell Blue-Steels his lips and pretends he's not posing for the cameras.

I'm trying to pry myself from Werner's arms, but just before I do, Glasswell looks up at the roof. And locks eyes with me. Three stories separate us but I'm instantly back in his green-gaze-tunnel, feeling my blood pulse through my limbs. Then Glasswell's eyes shift a millimeter. To Werner's mouth at my neck. I bat Werner away and seek sanctuary behind a veil of Buddha's-hands.

"I need Mel to decant more wine," I tell Werner, shifting modes. "Amuse-bouche at 7:15, then let's pour the spumante, explaining its terroir to the bride and groom before I toast."

"Yes ma'am," Werner says.

Footsteps sound on the stairs.

When Masha bursts onto the roof deck, her heels clack like castanets and a smile flares across her face. I beam back at her and feel grounded. That smile—that's why I'm doing this.

"Liv!" She squeals, squeezing me and taking in the scene. The sky's gone orange and gold. "You didn't say it was *this* good."

I hug her. "Nothing but the best for you."

"Your hair," she exclaims. "It's so . . . I've never seen it so—"

"I'll wait."

"You look beautiful."

"Not as beautiful as you," I say, and it's true. Masha radiates peace from somewhere infinite within. She's happy-beautiful. I'm overdrafted-bank-account-bewitching.

"Can I tell you this bullshit my cousin tried to pull this afternoon," Masha says, tugging me aside.

"Tell me every little thing," I say, clasping her hands and finding so much comfort in an ordinary conversation with my best friend. But even though I'm huddled up with Masha, I'm also acutely attuned to Glasswell behind me, smelling like eucalyptus and looking somehow naked in his suit.

I can't stop my mind from wandering, wondering what he might have said to Eli and Masha on the ride over about our unfortunate encounter at LAX. I'm trying not to eavesdrop on what he and Eli are saying now, trying not to wince as T-shirt-wearing, garlic-wafting Werner sashays in. Whom Glasswell just observed nibbling on my neck like Mexican street corn.

I feel a tap on my shoulder.

I turn to face him. Eucalyptus scent, green gaze, and the slow smile ever-curving on his lips.

"Dusk," he says and leans toward my cheek. Masha's watching, so I give it to him.

"It is indeed."

His kiss is soft, but there's an edge in his voice. "Nice hair. Compared to earlier."

I run my eyes over his broad shoulders, his trim waist . . . and snicker. "Barn door."

He looks down at his open fly just as the cork of the spumante pops. Behind us, Werner's placing flutes of bubbly in the hands of the bride and groom. He pours a third for me, a fourth for Glasswell. As Werner passes me my flute, he garnishes it with a smoochie face.

"A real catch," Glasswell says, somehow at my side again.

"Is that why you couldn't get your zipper up? A catch?"

"You're grasping at straws, Liv."

"Not *that* straw, thank you."

The two of us watch Werner lick spumante foam from his fingers.

"I see," Glasswell says, "because this guy's your type."

I stall, torn between saying Werner's nowhere near my type, and that my type is nowhere near Glasswell's business. But that's the pattern we've been captive to all day. I want to disrupt this downward spiral.

Werner clinks a fork against his own spumante flute.

"Ohhh, we're getting a toast . . ." I say, more than slightly panicked. "You don't have to make a speech, Werner . . . I can take it from here—"

"But not before I give an Olympus-sized welcome to the beautiful bride, Masha, and her lucky dude, Eli!" He snaps, makes a gun with his fingers, and shoots Eli before whirling on Glasswell. "And my man over here—I don't think I've yet had the pleasure—"

"Jake."

I notice how curtly Glasswell answers, how closely he studies Werner. It makes me see Werner through Glasswell's eyes. How essentially SoCal Werner is. It's not like this is foreign territory for Glasswell, who moved to LA from San Francisco our junior year of high school. Plus his job probably makes LA a regular stop for business lunches. But in all the time he's spent here, Glasswell clearly has not acquired affection for LA's downlow chillax.

Usually, Werner's casual, surfer-guy cool feels comfortable to me, but tonight, trying to charm Glasswell, he seems like a cartoon.

"You look so familiar," Werner says, wagging a finger at Glasswell, and I almost love him for pretending not to know who Glasswell is. "Did you hang out at Hyde back in the day?"

Eli coughs a laugh. Masha winces. Glasswell says, "Not that I recall."

"Hey," Werner says, "if you remember, you probably weren't there!"

Werner actually just made that Boomer joke with enthusiasm. Glasswell makes a show of faking a fake smile.

"Well, any friend of Liv's is a friend of mine." Werner puts his arm around my shoulder. "Please, kick back and enjoy that sunset." When he turns and crouches to assume his three-quarter profile pose, I know his signature line is coming: "We ordered it especially for you."

"Aw, thank you," Masha says.

"So sweet, man," Eli adds.

Werner winks at Masha. "I'll be right back with some virgin vegan bites."

As Werner disappears, Glasswell approaches, a glint in his eyes. "Did I forget to tell you?"

"What?"

"I'm allergic to virgin vegan bites. It's the virginity—can't tolerate it."

"I'll let Werner know you require standard vegan bites—"

"I'm imagining the pillow talk you two must share," Glasswell says. "Is it a lot of 'knock-knock, who's there'?"

"We can't all be geniuses putting bras in napkin holders," I say, referencing one of the dumb memes from a gag Glasswell did with Aurora on his show.

"That bit—" he starts to say.

"Oh please, defend that bit, Glasswell."

"It makes people happy!" he says so loudly Masha and Eli look at us. Darlene Love's "(Today I Met) The Boy I'm Gonna Marry" fills the tense silence that follows.

"Take it easy, guys," Eli says.

Masha adds, "Yeah, tonight's more *Sixteen Candles* than *Saw*."

"Sorry, everyone," I say, trying to be playful. "Glasswell, behave!"

"What do I have to do, Olivia?" he whispers once Masha and Eli turn away.

What is he talking about? I stare at him, wondering what he means.

Before I can ask, Masha clinks her fork against her flute. "Gather 'round! Bridezilla's gonna *toast*."

We join her on the couch overlooking the western view. The ocean shimmers golden in the distance, and it's hard to believe Mash and I were out there fishing only yesterday, cranking tunes and cracking jokes.

If I could go back and redo today, land a different Lyfter out of LAX, and prevent Glasswell from crossing my path until this moment—would I feel less vulnerable?

I sit in the center of the love seat, across from Masha and Eli, forcing Glasswell to take a solo chair. Except he doesn't. He sits himself next to me, and when his hip nudges mine, he has the nerve to apologize. "Sorry, you weren't saving this for the chef, were you?"

I scoot over, conserving the energy it takes to brawl with Glasswell. I need to focus on my favorite couple.

Eli holds Masha's hand and twists her antique ring around her finger. He kisses her shoulder, and it makes her laugh and blush. I love their pet names for each other—Burton and Taylor—and that when Eli's performance season finishes next year, they're taking off six months to teach English in Sri Lanka.

My mom has made offhand remarks about how she thinks I idolize their relationship at the expense of my own romances. It isn't true. I don't want what they have—their idea of a wild night is wading through a Netflix queue. I don't think they're perfect.

He's got a jealous streak, and she has no idea, literally no idea, how to handle trash. But I know each of these two souls has found a worthy partner. And I take pride in having played a small role in bringing their love into the world. Plus, I can't wait for the babies. I'm going to kiss my godchildren's cheeks so much they'll think that's all life is.

"So listen," Masha says, holding her flute aloft. "I know we're saving the formal speeches for the wedding, but I must thank Olivia. For everything." She beams at me. "BBS, babe."

"BBS, Mash," I say and raise my glass.

"Tomorrow," Masha continues, "some crazy shit might go down. My babushka is threatening to bring her rabbi because our officiant isn't 'real.' But tonight?" She looks at each of us. "It feels good to float inside this bubble of love."

"I'll drink to the bubble of love," Eli says, lifting his spumante flute. "And to Olivia, who planned this party, and who kicked off this love affair ten years ago when she ditched me at senior prom."

"I sure can pick 'em," I say as I raise my flute.

"It was an equal opportunity ditching." Masha laughs, acknowledging Glasswell's role.

"Well, here we are," Glasswell says and dutifully lifts his flute aloft. "I couldn't be happier for you two."

Since it's all about your happiness, I think. I can feel myself going off the deep end. I'm in a maze of mirrors, the loser version of me that Glasswell saw earlier today reflected back at me into infinity. He got into the wrong car, at the wrong time, on the wrong day. He saw the wrong version of me.

And I can't seem to move past it.

I drink, but as I do, I reflect on how much I've compartmen-talized my prom night humiliation over the years. I thought I'd outgrown it, but it turns out I'd just built a wall around it. I promise myself I'm not going to ruin Masha's wedding weekend by spiraling now.

A promise I promptly break.

Eli clears his throat. "And I'd like to say thank you to Jake. For making the time to be here this weekend. I know it wasn't easy."

When Masha coos her agreement, I can't help myself. I stick a finger in my ear like I can't be hearing right.

"What, uh, what do you mean *not easy*?" I laugh. "I feel like Delta makes first class pretty easy."

Masha kicks me under the table. When I look at her, she mouths—and not discreetly—*Au-ror-a.*

I roll my eyes. "We're supposed to feel bad for him because his girlfriend couldn't make it?"

"It's her loss, man," Eli reassures. "There are many brighter days ahead."

Does he mean Jake and Aurora broke up?

"Thanks, man," Glasswell says, sounding fake and tired. "Not everyone is destined for 'till death do us part.'"

"Maybe she dodged a bullet." This comes out louder than I intended. Masha's face registers real shock.

"Olivia!" Masha gasps.

"I'm sorry," I say, "but—"

"You're sorry . . . but?" Masha's amazed.

I open my mouth to explain that yes, there is a "but." It goes like this: I put my heart into this wedding. I scoured the internet

WHAT'S IN A KISS?

for weeks to source palo santo scented fire-resistant candles to line the aisle Masha would walk down. I booked the flowers and the music and the catering, planned the bachelorette and this rehearsal dinner. I held space for Masha's extended family's robust opinions about the right way to wed time and time again. I stood by Masha's side every step of the way because I actually fucking care. In this war with Glasswell I may have lost at Life, but I've won—I'll always win—at Best Friend.

Moreover:

"Why isn't anyone getting on *him*?" I demand, pointing at Glasswell. "He thinks he's so much better than everyone else and goes out of his way to show it. Am I supposed to be so grateful for his presence that I also have to bend over and say—"

"Party people in the place!" Werner exclaims, appearing with Alastair. "Who's ready to get unglued with gluten-free hush puppies?"

"Way ahead of you, Werner." I throw down my napkin and rise from the table, unable to meet Masha's eyes.

What have I done? Why do I let this man get the best of me over and over again? I'm so sick of Glasswell, but I'm disgusted with myself. I've lost sight of what matters and scratched the perfect off my best friend's night.

"Olivia," Glasswell says, edging past Alastair and Werner to follow me for the second time today. "Wait."

But I'm already down the stairs, halfway to locking myself in the bathroom. How long can I hide in this stall before anyone cares? A year? A decade?

Long enough for Masha to forget what I just said?

Chapter Eight

PHONE TO MY EAR THE NEXT MORNING, I PACE THE bridal suite at the rustic-chic Santa Monica inn, Shutters on the Beach. On the far side of the room, Masha's aspiring makeup artist cousin jams to Vagabon, using a soft brush to really push the boundaries of a neutral palette, while Mash watches me in the vanity mirror through a single open eye.

"It's ringing," I tell her. She nods.

The frozen shoulder I received upon returning from the bathroom last night has somewhat thawed. This morning's handwritten card, almond croissants, and chai lattes from the Laurel Canyon Country Store got me within shouting range of Masha's good graces, but she won't relax until I apologize to Glasswell.

"Hullo?" His voice, first thing in the morning, stops my pacing. It stops everything in the room. He sounds hazy, almost sweet.

"Glasswell, this is Olivia."

Ideally, he'll hang up now, and I can beg the silence for forgiveness.

But a grunt tells me he's still there.

I sit down on the nautical-shammed window seat, looking out at the broad expanse of sandy beach. A gray marine layer scarfs the sky, making the shore feel close and cold. It always amazes me how something so seemingly dense "burns off" into blue every morning. I tell myself to be like the sky, to let my inner fog dissipate into incandescent wisps, to clear the way for brighter things.

"Olivia who?" Glasswell says, the edge back in his voice.

Okay, so we're picking up our battle where we left off, but Masha needs to hear us making up.

I glance at the chaos of the suite. Masha's dress hangs in the closet, fresh from being steamed, but her veil is still a wrinkled mess. Her cousin's six Caboodles have exploded cosmetic detritus over every surface of the room. In the corner, my mom's hot glue gun heats up to affix popsicle sticks to programs so they can be used as fans—temps this morning are supposed to be five degrees warmer than expected. I still need to stuff the monogrammed favor bags with the back-ordered until-this-weekend needlepoint kits Masha is Instagram-obsessed with. Then I have to text the violinist, confirming I found the Acus amplifier she requested. And the caterer, to relay the coordinates where the Santa Monica City Council said he can park his pupusa truck.

If I can't have dignity on this call with Glasswell, I must insist on efficiency. Masha's mom and aunts are on the way to the bridal suite, and I need to get through this call before my audience increases in size.

"It's Olivia Dusk," I say evenly into the phone. "And I'm calling to"—wow, this is hard to get out—"ap-apol—"

"Are we on speaker?" Glasswell asks.

"That's big of you to say." I give Mash a thumbs-up.

"But Masha's in the room, right? And this call is the bride's condition for you to hold on to your reign of terror as maid of honor?"

"That's *such* a refreshing point of view."

"And perhaps a condition for your best friend walking down the aisle at all?" he prompts.

"You're funny." I laugh theatrically and point at the phone. "He's a riot, Mash."

"Well, as long as it's not coming from a place of sincerity," Glasswell says. "Do you mind if I record this? It's for your benefit. That way, when you go off the rails at the wedding, we can play this recording and save some time."

I laugh jauntily and say, "I don't think that will be necessary."

"Now, grovel."

"Well, Glasswell, I won't keep you—"

"Call me Jake."

"I should have welcomed you last night, not attacked you. For that, I'm sorry."

"How sorry, Olivia?"

"What's that?" I say. "You're sorry, too? Mash! He's sorry, too."

"*Awwww!*" Masha says. "See?"

I continue for her benefit: "He says he recognizes that he can often be an enormous—"

"Stop," Glasswell cuts me off before I've chosen the right insult. "I'm going to save you from yourself. Think of Masha, okay?"

I take a breath. He's not wrong. "Thank you."

"Now," he says, "is there anything else before I go get dressed?"

The idea of Glasswell rising from bed in a state of undress causes me to gulp, then visualize, then—

No. I recover.

"You and I," I say, "are on the same team this weekend. We're here for our friends. Let's not lose sight of that."

I look at Masha, who is nodding, satisfied. I smile at her. She beams back and I know that I'm forgiven. I commit to being better, kinder to Glasswell for the rest of the day.

"I . . . look forward to seeing you soon," I say into the phone.

I almost end the call before I realize he hasn't responded.

"You used to be a much better actor," he says, sounding suddenly less playful. "Don't quit your day job, Dusk."

As I pull the phone away from my ear, I hear Glasswell say, "Actually, do quit your day job. You can't drive for shit."

. . . . . .

NOON FINDS ME less composed and glamorous than I would like to be, but at least I'm heading for the wedding canopy, strappy heels looped around my wrist. Across a solid mile of sand, I've lugged gift bags, programs, a ring bearer pillow, and Masha's forgotten outfit change for the reception. When I finally release my burden behind the PA, I see Masha and Eli posing adorably for the wedding photographer. Less adorable is the conspicuous absence of Glasswell.

I reapply deodorant and exhume the melted remnants of my lipstick from its tube. Using my phone as a mirror, I've painted my top lip rather adroitly when Masha takes me by the shoulder, panic on her face.

"Don't worry, I got your clothes. And your something blue!" I fish from my purse the blue satin garter Masha left back in the suite.

"It's not that—"

"The glue is dry on the programs. They're down to fan your grandparents."

"Liv—"

"And the replacement extension cord for the violin magically worked," I gesture toward the band setting up behind us. "It isn't brown like the one that didn't work, but I think sound trumps vision in this equation—"

"Olivia," Eli cuts in. "Yogi Dan is lost."

I blink. "Who?"

"The officiant," Eli says.

This was Glasswell's *one* contribution today.

"What do you mean, 'lost'?" I say.

"Poetic, right?" Masha says, her hairline dotted with sweat. "The person supposed to guide us into the next phase of our relationship has no idea where he is. And if he's still not here when Babushka and her rabbi show up—"

"Easy, Mash," Eli soothes, putting an arm around her waist. "I'll handle Babushka and the rabbi."

"And I'll find Yogi Dan," I say, my eyes darting around the beach, which suddenly looks crammed with millions of people who aren't yogis. Well, this being Santa Monica, a couple hundred probably are.

"I've got him." A resonant voice slices through the tension.

I turn and face Glasswell in a tux. I try but find no fault in the sight of him. His barn door is sealed, his hair is styled differently than on his show, different than last night, and for a moment he looks like he did in high school.

"He's at a cannabis café called Milo and Lhüwanda's," Glasswell says, opening a map on his phone.

"On it," I say, swiping Glasswell's phone and tearing off toward the boardwalk.

"What the hell!" he says, and tries to grab it back. But my adrenaline high is far beyond his reach.

"This is my responsibility!" Glasswell says, catching up.

As soon as we're out of earshot from Masha and Eli, I do my patented Glasswell spin. "That explains why it's completely fucked!"

"You don't know what Yogi Dan looks like, let alone how to talk him down from Mars."

"And you do?"

"He's an old acquaintance," Glasswell says. "And very hard to book for weddings."

"All I know is he's the one piece falling through."

"If you want him to officiate the wedding, you'll let me handle it." Glasswell looks me up and down. "He'll take one look at your energy and migrate to another plane."

"Look back there." I point to the beautiful, beaded wedding canopy, to the electric string quartet tuning up, to the pupusa truck emanating aromatic steam. "I did that. Just like she wanted. And what did you do? You made her cry."

"You win the wedding, Dusk. Is that what you need to hear?"

"What I need is for you to let me fix this."

I don't waste time letting him answer. Life's too short for bullshit from men. I kick off the heels I'd just strapped on and run for the shortcut alley behind the next light-blue lifeguard stand.

I'm a quarter mile down the boardwalk when a gust of wind blows my carefully crafted hair into my face. I look and see Glasswell approaching on an electric rental scooter.

"Want a ride?" he says like he thinks he's James Bond.

"Pass."

"It'll keep you from sweating." He stops the scooter, looks at the top of my head. "And your hair will thank you for it."

I board.

My arms around him, a memory rises. The last time I had an arm around Glasswell.

It was the Tuesday after prom, when we posed for yearbook, each of us representing our class for Most Likely to Succeed. We were light-years beyond awkward, but the photographer insisted: Glasswell's arm around my shoulder, my arm around his waist. I could feel the heat of him, smell his eucalyptus skin, which made me wonder how my heat smelled to him.

That photograph exists in the multiverse somewhere. I've never seen it. By the time the yearbook was shipped to my house that summer, my dad had died, and I couldn't see much of anything. I'd made the shift from Most Likely to Impossible to Succeed.

Maybe we're all always one slight motion away from a different life.

"We're here," Glasswell says and leaps off the scooter.

I mentally reacclimate. Task at hand: find officiant.

Glasswell's three paces ahead. I follow close behind, pushing into the quiet café with a sense of catastrophic terror.

"Whoa, whoa, whoa," says the security guard as he stands up behind a midcentury modern Danish desk. He waves his hand from high to low as if washing a window. "You need to chill this *way* the fuck down."

"Dan the man!" Glasswell says, smiling at what must be Yogi Dan, seated at an immaculate zinc bar. He looks like a cross between Bob Ross the PBS painter and Vincent Price in *Theatre of Blood*. He wears a white kurta and has tied a sand-colored headscarf around his Afro. In one hand he nurses an espresso in a small mug decorated with sky blue fleurs-de-lis. In his other hand he holds a joint the size of an andouille sausage.

"What the hell are you doing?" I yell at Yogi Dan, who doesn't stir.

"Are you Jake Glasswell?" the security guard asks.

"Don't you know how late you are?" I shout.

The security guard points a finger at me and looks at Glasswell. "Is she with you?"

"*With* is a strong word," Glasswell says, "but I'm willing to take the blame."

"You can stay," the guard says, then hulks toward me, "but Calamity Jane needs to take her talents outside."

"I really hope," Glasswell says to me as I turn grudgingly to go, "that these lessons start sinking in."

Outside is like a dream, a slow-motion beach town in a late spring heat wave, while I'm trying to deliver the wedding-equivalent of a vital organ in a beer cooler.

The café door swings open and the two fools I'm waiting on stumble out, arm in arm.

"I'm so glad you made it," Glasswell says to Yogi Dan, his glassy eyes suggesting he thought we had enough time for a toke before the wedding. I'm furious, and also a little bit jealous. I'd actually love to chill this way the fuck down. But Masha needs me.

"Yogi Dan hasn't made it *yet*," I correct Glasswell. "And the bride is freaking out, so if the two of you don't mind . . ."

Glasswell puts a finger to his lips, opens my purse, and drops the remainder of Yogi Dan's joint inside.

Yogi Dan turns to me, eyes kind and sparkling. "That is one bold lip."

At first, I think he means my attitude. Then I remember my mouth was only partly painted when the Where's Yogi Dan scandal exploded.

"She's bold all over," Glasswell says. "May I present Olivia Dusk, maid of honor. A beehive best left un-poked."

. . . . . .

"FRIENDS AND LOVED ones of Eli and Masha," Yogi Dan says, a mere twenty minutes late, "we welcome you with gratitude."

I'm standing at the altar, still out of breath from our dash on the scooter back to the wedding site—me chauffeuring Yogi Dan while Glasswell jogged beside us in his sand-buffed black oxfords.

By the time we made it, the guests were being seated, Masha was hyperventilating in a corner, and Babushka's rabbi was circling the altar. When she saw us, Masha's eyes lit up, her shoulders relaxed, and she took her place with her dad. I cued the string quartet to start "The Ocean" by Led Zeppelin.

Now, as I look out at the friends and loved ones gathered, all is as it should be. I know each one of these eighteen guests intimately. And for all their bellyaching, the mothers of the bride and groom don't seem to mind that their bridge clubs and accountants weren't invited. They only have eyes for their kids, who only have eyes for each other.

You did it right, Mash, I convey with a light squeeze when she hands me her bouquet.

For ten minutes, Yogi Dan speaks about marriage's joys and trials. Before I know it, it's my turn to step forward, take the mic, and give a reading.

When Masha asked me to choose a passage, I knew immediately which one. It's from *To the Lighthouse* by Virginia Woolf, which we read together in AP English our senior year. She was falling in love with Eli, and we'd found these words to be impossibly romantic.

"'What art was there, known to love or cunning,'" I read, holding my paperback copy from the class, the pages detaching from the spine, "'by which one pressed through into those secret chambers? What device for becoming, like waters poured into one jar, inextricably the same, one with the object one adored? Could the body achieve, or the mind, subtly mingling in the intricate passages of the brain? or the heart? Could loving [make them] one?'"

As I pass the microphone back to Yogi Dan, I catch his eyes, a quick blaze of interest in them, as he says, "And now a reading from the world's best man."

As the congregation chuckles, I struggle for composure. I didn't know Glasswell was giving a reading. It's not listed in the program, unlike my reading.

He pulls out a King James Bible and opens it to a book-marked page.

"'Two are better than one; because they have a good reward for their labour. For if they fall, the one will lift up his fellow: but woe to him that is alone when he falleth; for he hath not an-other to help him up. Again, if two lie together, then they have heat: but how can one be warm alone?'"

Glasswell's eyes cut toward mine. I quickly look away. I wonder if this reading was his choosing or Eli's. I wonder what Ecclesiastes means to him. Is he religious? Does he believe in marriage? Does he even believe in love? Does Glasswell believe in anything beyond the life in his lenses?

And, perhaps most pressingly, was he naked when we talked this morning?

I stop myself from prancing down that tempting mental lane. I'm not jealous because Glasswell is successful and I'm not, but I struggle with how he glided to the top of a game I never really got to play. In high school, he wanted to be a journalist; *I* was supposed to entertain. When Masha told me the story of how Glasswell sat by a TV executive at a Tuesday afternoon Yankees game, struck up a conversation, and by the seventh-inning stretch had landed a seat in the writers' room of *The Late Show with Stephen Colbert*, no one but me could believe it.

I believed it, because that's how life works out for him.

The thing is, deep down, I know that if my dad hadn't died, if I'd taken a place at Juilliard, the odds are long that I would have become a Broadway star. Too much luck involved, too many things would have had to go exactly right. Still, it bothers me that I never even got to take my chance. That's how life worked out for me.

It's embarrassing to wallow in regret. Most of the time I don't even let myself imagine the alternate reality where my dad is still alive, where I went after every dream.

Except when I'm around Glasswell. Then I can't seem to shake the feeling that something better might have happened had I done things differently. I know I made my own choices. I can't blame my dad's death or my mom's heartbreak. But if I'd been bolder, more ruthless, if I'd gone to New York like I planned, consequences be damned . . .

What would have happened? Where would I be?

"Our maid of honor made a fascinating point," Yogi Dan startles me by announcing to the wedding guests.

I glance at Glasswell, intending to smirk triumphantly if he looks my way. But he's not simply looking my way. He's staring. At me. And I can't stop staring back. His gaze holds me in place, goose bumps rising on my skin, as Yogi Dan goes on:

"Olivia said *inextricably*, a gold-gilt frame for the union you dawn today. Your lives never will untangle after this ceremony. You are forever connected, *inextricably*."

Glasswell and I are still staring at each other, and it's gone on long enough to feel like a game of visual chicken. This time, I'm determined to win. Competitive heat builds in my core, so warm it's a little alarming. I feel my cheeks starting to flush—

I don't care how juvenile it is, I'm going to win this stare-down.

"You may kiss to seal your love," Yogi Dan says.

Wait . . . it's already time for the kiss?

The opening chords of the string quartet's version of "Just Like Heaven" begin to play around us. Light blooms in my periphery, but I don't blink. The ground beneath me shakes, but not even an eight on the Richter scale would make me quit this contest. When the guests erupt in applause that says the kiss is underway, I'm still staring at Glasswell, and he's still staring at me.

But something has happened. Something has changed. He's not shooting eye daggers anymore.

He's looking at me kindly. Affectionately.

He's looking at me like a man in love.

Chapter Nine

THE BLEAT OF AN ACCORDION STARTLES ME BACK TO reality. The notes are loud, aggressively festive, and too close to our party. The tune verges on familiar, accompanied by . . . is that a tuba?

My maid of honor instincts kick in—instincts I hadn't realized were lying dormant all my life. Whoever this random traveling klezmer band is, they need to find another celebration to destroy. Because they're drowning out the string quartet's version of "Just Like Heaven." It's supposed to play after the big kiss, as the newlyweds walk down the aisle.

It's hard to get my gaze back from Glasswell's grip, but I turn toward the sound of the accordion.

That's when I realize something is very, very wrong.

A moment ago, there were eighteen wedding guests seated in eighteen wicker folding chairs under a candlelit canopy.

Now, there must be two hundred and fifty people pressing against me on all sides. Most of them are my mother's age, and the decibel of their conversation hits me like a hurricane. Looking around in panic, I recognize Masha's third cousin, and I think that's our fourth-grade teacher Mr. Rayco who just pushed past me, making his way toward—inexplicably—a white vinyl bar beside the ocean.

Where did that come from? Where did any of this come from? All these people. All this noise.

Somehow, in a second, Masha's wedding . . . *changed*. Instead of the handmade silk gauze chuppah crowning the altar, there's a digital monstrosity strobing like a nineties rave. Instead of twine-tied bouquets of ranunculus in terra-cotta vases . . . black urns of long-stem roses flank the aisles. The aisles . . . which are no longer made of sand. Someone has slapped down an enormous dance floor. Silver bunting lines an expanse of bloodred folding chairs. Masha made it very clear her wedding palette was soft gold. I rub my eyes and slap my face, but the nightmare thunders on. Did someone slip a molly in my Pellegrino?

"I can fix this," I say. Because if not me, who?

But how? What even *is* this?

Deep breaths. First, check on Masha. If I'm freaking out, imagine what she's going through.

I turn toward her, ready to help . . .

But Masha isn't at my side. Neither is Eli. Or Glasswell.

I rise on my toes and squint into the writhing mass of bodies. I see her! Standing with Eli, *very* far away. She's overrun by relatives—or should I say party crashers, because there was never a moment when leering Cousin Jeffrey made the cut. A polite smile strains her face. My poor, poor BBS.

I collapse onto a folding chair. I plant my elbows on my knees, hang my head, and close my eyes. I take deep gulps of air. I pause, waiting to inhale.

A hand—warm and firm—touches the skin where my dress opens at the back. The feeling is electric.

"Hey," says America's sexiest voice.

I jump away. "What are you doing?"

Glasswell leans down to massage my shoulders. I freeze because . . . he's really good at it. Every now and then his chest rubs against the back of my head, the tops of my ears. There's something about his touch that finds a secret place inside me, like a hidden velvet pocket inside a favorite old handbag. Like something that's always been there but you've only just discovered. His lips are at my ear. I hold my breath in shock.

"You were right," he whispers.

His breath against my neck weaves through my body like a stiff narcotic. I can't help wanting more.

"Right about what?" I whisper.

That couldn't have been me. I don't speak in that throaty, sexed-up voice.

But that's definitely me tilting my neck to give Glasswell a bigger piece, in case he wants to whisper all over me again. I'm coherent enough to know I'll be embarrassed later, but that doesn't change what I want right now.

I set a goal: as soon as he answers my question, as soon as I feel one more rough brush of his stubble on my skin—then I'll pull away.

But not yet.

"That I'd cry during their vows," he says into my neck.

I don't recall having breathed a word about anything related to Glasswell's tears.

"Was it obvious," Glasswell asks, "all the way back here?"

What does he mean *back here*?

I look around. How *did* I get all the way back here during the most important part of Masha and Eli's ceremony? Maids of honor don't sit way back here. It must be Glasswell's fault.

I stand to face him, my eyes bright with accusations. But when they land on his, all my ire disappears, like someone opened a trapdoor inside me. Bitterness and rage dandelion away. What remains is a feeling for which I know only one word.

Home.

That's what it feels like to look at him. As crazy as it sounds.

Are we smiling? I think we're smiling. Now he's . . . leaning in . . . to . . .

Holy shit. Glasswell's going to kiss me.

Stranger still: it feels like we've practiced this pre-kiss pose a million times. I don't just mean his grip on my hips or the tangoing tilt of our heads. I also mean the chemicals amalgamating within me. I find myself softening, opening . . . for *him*. I'm so swept up that for several breathless eternities I forget to ask myself what the hell I'm doing.

This would be a waste.

His words from all those years ago return. I break away and catch my breath. When I'm not looking at Glasswell, and not touching Glasswell, and not being touched by Glasswell, I can see clearly. And what I see are tacky folding chairs, smarmy Cousin Jeffrey, a strobe light Morse-coding how wrong this wedding has become. Masha must be on the edge of passing out.

"I'm gonna check on—" I say as a caterer comes between Glasswell and me. He holds out a finger-smudged tray of gray stuffed mushrooms and sad crab cakes—the hors d'oeuvres Masha and I have choked down at all her cousins' weddings.

"Where did you come from?" I demand of the waiter. I point at the food in his custody. "This is *all wrong*!"

"Is that Olivia Dusk?" A whisper pricks my ears.

I turn toward the voice and find a woman I've never seen before. "Who the hell are you?" I say, which makes her and her friend laugh and turn away.

"What's their problem?" I ask Glasswell, not really wanting an answer, especially one whispered like an orgy on my neck. What I want is to find Masha, to snap my fingers and make this reception deception disappear.

"We can leave whenever you want," Glasswell says.

I laugh. *Leave* in the middle of my best friend's wedding?

"I'm going to find Masha."

Glasswell looks alarmed, like I've just said I'm going to strip down and run naked into the ocean. He intercepts me, his broad shoulders squaring off in front of mine. "I'm not sure that's a good idea."

"Yeah, well, neither was all that cologne." I motion for him to step aside.

"I thought you liked—never mind." He sighs. "It's her wedding day, Olivia."

I pat his shoulder. "I knew you could figure it out."

I scan the crowd for Masha. There. I exhale at the sight of her—an island of sanity in this paint-by-numbers storm. Thank god she looks the same—beautiful dress, vintage Temperley, loose ringlets I watched her cousin wind around a curling iron this morning. Her lips in Vice by Urban Decay, spotlighting her smile.

"She's swarmed," Glasswell says, looking at the crowd around her. This is true, and precisely why I need to save her. "You can email her tomorrow."

I whip my head around. "Did you say 'email'? *Tomorrow*?"

"You heard the rabbi," Glasswell says. "All that talk about Masha and Eli needing peace in their new life. It's important to them. And we should honor it. Tonight of all nights."

My mind hones in on one word, and it isn't *peace*.

Rabbi? The only rabbi at this wedding was the one Masha's babushka brought as her plus-one. And he certainly wasn't given a speaking platform. Doesn't Glasswell remember the mission to recover Yogi Dan?

"Where's the celebrity officiant?" I ask.

"Where is what?" Glasswell asks.

"Yogi Dan? Willie Nelson's little brother in pretzel form?"

Glasswell's staring at me, straitjackets in his eyes.

I look past him, past the entire mystifying scene. Off in the distance, I dimly discern the silhouette of Yogi Dan's afro gliding toward the parking lot.

I take off running.

"Hey!" I shout. "Yogi! Wait!"

Yogi Dan is hurrying up-beach, almost to the parking lot off PCH. Something is different. As I get closer I notice his attire—he's swapped the kurta and headscarf for a yarmulke, pin-striped suit, and tallis. But even though dusk has fallen, and even though this day's gone haywire, of one thing I am sure: that man is Yogi Dan. And he's got something to do with all of this.

"Yogi Dan!" I shout again, running harder. My voice, now that we're away from the klezmer band—is definitely loud enough for him to hear. But, like in the café, he doesn't look up. He completely ignores me. Right up until I pelt the trunk of his hybrid Honda Civic with a handful of sand. "Rabbi!"

He rolls down the window, leans his head out and smiles. "Shabbat Shalom."

"What did you do?" I demand.

He raises one shoulder and flashes a cryptic smile. "Life is mysterious. If I may make a suggestion: Go with it."

"Go with *what?*"

"The mystery. Or don't go with it. It's gonna happen, either way."

"What's going to happen?"

"The mystery."

"Are you fucking kidding me?"

"*I'm* not. The cosmos may be. Kidding, that is."

"That's it?" I shout. "That's all I get?"

"The imbalance of love results from a limited perspective," he says. "You need infinite subjectivity in your life."

"That's heavy," I say, "but I don't have time to wander the earth, contemplating its meaning."

"That's where you're mistaken."

I sigh and turn to see the ocean at sundown, purple as a Mission fig.

"Check your purse," Rabbi Dan says.

I look inside and find the joint Glasswell took from the café, just before the world went sideways.

"What do I do with this?" I say. "If I smoke it, will it take me back?"

"I doubt it," Rabbi Dan says. "But who knows?" Then he peels out, screeching from the parking lot onto PCH, narrowly missing several honking cars.

"Hey!" I shout, fumbling for my phone to take a picture of his license plate. Blurry. Useless. "Wait!"

"What was *that* about?"

I turn to find Glasswell, standing behind me.

"And where did you get that joint?" he asks.

"*You* gave it to me—never mind. I thought you wanted to leave," I say, dropping the joint back in my purse.

"Do *you*?" he asks. I don't know why he cares what I do. But ever since that look we shared during the ceremony, Glasswell has been behaving quite un-Glasswell-esque.

Tonight's almost-kiss comes back to me—his lips so close to mine, the heat of his hands, the startling way our bodies fit together, like we'd practiced it. I bring my fingers to my tingling lips. As much as it confuses me to admit it, our almost chemistry back there had been almost fire.

"Liv," he says my nickname with such tenderness that it makes me melt inside. "Hear that?" He cocks his head toward the reception.

I make out the rippling synth notes of the Talking Heads's "Once in a Lifetime," which Masha and I agreed ages ago is the GOAT dance song at a wedding. Suddenly I want to get back there, bounce around, and belt this song out. Get things back on track.

"Dare me to throw out my back again?" Glasswell says, holding out his hand.

"You do you," I say, walking past him.

Undeterred, he catches up and puts his hand in mine. "Thing is, I need someone to dip if I'm going to throw it out properly. And I choose you."

I look at his hand in mine and feel that shiver again. I look into his eyes. Instantly I'm smiling. Without wanting to.

"You're shaking," he says. "Time to call it a night?"

If I could speak to someone I trust, maybe I could get a handle on what's going on.

"That thing you said before," I say, "about emailing Masha tomorrow—"

"I'm sorry," he says. "That was cold. I know you want to make things right with her."

"*Right* with her?" Masha and I made up this morning. Surely Glasswell recalls torturing me when I called to apologize.

"Just . . . baby steps, you know?" he says. "And maybe not starting on the night of her wedding?"

"Thanks for the tip."

"Olivia," he warns, but I'm already gone. I need to find Masha. Now.

. . . . . .

BACK UNDER THE tent, I can see the wedding for what it is: the huge and impersonal factory-setting wedding I've been to several times before. The same DJ, the same catering company, the same florist as all Masha's cousins have had. Her family should own stock in this racket. I'm pretty sure those disco ball-shaped centerpieces are the ones Masha and I built in her aunt's garage for Pammy's wedding last spring.

I remember that day clearly. It was less than a week after

Masha had gotten engaged to Eli, but she hadn't told her family yet. She'd invited me to help with the centerpieces on the condition that I didn't breathe a word of her engagement. She left her ring at home, knowing that the second her aunts and cousins saw it, the wedding train would leave the station.

But the wedding Masha is having is precisely the one she wanted to avoid, the kind of wedding she feared would swallow her like a whale. How is this possible?

I watch Masha now with Eli, making the rounds on the dance floor periphery. She was clear in her wedding plans that she wanted to spend the bulk of this time dancing. But there's no room for getting down, besieged by all her aunts. The smile plastered on her face pains me. All teeth, no eyes. Those cheeks will be sore tomorrow.

"She's miserable," I say.

"Are you sure you're not projecting?" Glasswell counsels at my side. Somehow, this doesn't annoy me. I don't mind having him to bounce ideas off. I don't even mind when he takes me in his arms as the Talking Heads fade into Frank Sinatra.

"This isn't her," I say.

"What do you mean?" Glasswell asks, holding me close, Frank singing "I've Got You Under My Skin." A different kind of dizzy sweeps over me.

"I'm so confused," I say. "How did we get here?"

Masha. Glasswell and me. The Yogi-turned-Rabbi peeling out like a bail-jumping Buddha in the night. I'm starting to worry that no one's going to explain this to me. That even if they wanted to they couldn't.

"Sorry to interrupt," a girl I've never seen before appears before me. "Would you mind if I took a selfie with you?"

I step away and gesture that Glasswell's all hers. The girl laughs and says to Glasswell, "She's so funny!"

"Olivia doesn't do selfies," Glasswell says. "But she's happy to sign autographs."

"Cool, yeah," the girl says.

Glasswell reaches into his breast pocket, turns to me. "Do you want to use the Beast?"

Out of curiosity, I nod, and Glasswell puts a beautiful Montblanc pen into my hand. I glance at its inscription. *Olivia Dusk, Zombie Hospital.*

Zombie Hospital? As in the TV drama where exhausted, lovelorn doctors operate on the undead? Masha and I are addicted to *Zombie Hospital,* mostly because of its leading man, Miguel Bernardeau. But I'm not so big a fan I'd shell out for a fancy pen . . . right?

The girl fishes into her purse and pulls out a receipt. "Can you make it out to Janelle and write *Follow your dreams?*"

Glasswell gives me his shoulder to write on, and in a bewildered daze, I do. When I hand the receipt back to Janelle, a smile fills her face.

"TYSM!" She beams and bounds away.

"Glasswell," I say. "What the howling heap of hell was that?"

Instead of answering, he puts his arms out to dance with me again. I see Masha's parents, Yulia and Lev, a few couples over. I steer Glasswell toward them, until I can catch Yulia's eye. As soon as I do, I smile, ready to fall into the firm hug she's been giving me since elementary school. But when Masha's mother glances back at me, there's only cold vacancy in her eyes.

I suck in my breath.

"Yulia." My voice is intimate, laced with years of sleepovers and dinners. I need Masha's mother to validate my existence. She's a central character in the story of my life.

"Beautiful wedding, isn't it?" she says to me stiffly, then with a smile, "Hello, Jake."

Glasswell leans in to kiss Yulia, then to shake hands with Lev, who ignores me completely.

"I'm so happy for Mash—" I start to say.

"Everyone's been civilized." Yulia gives me a pointed look. "So far."

Glasswell swoops me away.

"Was that dig aimed at *me*?" I say to him. "Because that felt like—wait, there's Masha. Almost alone."

It's time to go straight to the source. I pull away from Glasswell and beeline for the far side of the tent. For my best friend, my BBS.

She's taking a sweet picture with her niece Adora, the flower girl, but as soon as she turns away, I open my mouth—

Masha serves me the hand with a side of death glare. "No."

I sputter. "No . . . what?"

"No to you. No to this."

"Masha!" My voice cracks with emotion.

"This is *my* day, Olivia," she says, her tone ferocious, non-negotiable. "You were invited because Eli is loyal to Jake, but you're not going to make my wedding day about you."

"I would never—" I break off and look at Masha's family

closing in around her. They look protective, wary. And not surprised.

"Why is everyone acting like this?"

"Because we know what to expect from you."

"Olivia has an early call tomorrow," Glasswell says, taking my arm, "we should probably get going—"

Since when does Glasswell speak for me in fights with my best friend? Since when do I have two fights with my BBS in the space of twenty-odd hours?

"This is all his fault," I point at Glasswell, who shakes his head at me.

He leans close. "No one's going to get that joke. Let's go—"

"Hold on," I say, "we're talking."

"No," Masha says. "*You're* talking. I finished long ago." And then my precious Masha turns and walks away.

Chapter Ten

I DRIFT LIKE FLOTSAM FROM THE PARTY AND WASH UP at the valet stand. The night is warmer here, pressed against PCH, hissing with cars. A streetlight hums overhead, painting me in tragic light. I take off my shoes, feet throbbing, lean against a brick wall, close my eyes, and implode.

My best friend just served me the kind of contempt I've only seen her give telemarketers. When I left the wedding tent, two of her cousins applauded.

If someone would just tell me what's going on, maybe I could fix it. But the only person interested in talking to me is Glasswell.

My throat constricts.

Masha's rage had a *fermented* quality, as if her complaint against me had been roiling for months. Far longer than last night's rehearsal dinner. What is happening?

"Hey."

"You again," I say to Glasswell without looking at him.

He sweeps me into a full-body hug—torsos, hips, ankles, hearts. I feel his pulse, calling and responding to mine. He feels . . . safe. I'm past the point of *How dare he*. My heart has become homeless. I need something to hold on to.

I release myself into Glasswell's arms and cry.

"It's okay," he whispers into my hair.

"She *hates* me." I shake with fresh sobs, realizing the words are true.

Masha. My ride or die of twenty years. The gentlest soul I know.

Through the curtain of my tears, I see the valet standing nearby. I don't usually care what strangers think of me, but I find myself wiping my eyes, trying to keep it together.

The valet clasps his hands behind his back. He keeps Glasswell and me in his peripheral vision, in the uniquely Angeleno manner of being one brunch table down from Zendaya and pretending not to care.

"Want a better view?" I ask the valet, stepping aside to offer him unobstructed access to Glasswell.

"I—what?" the valet stammers.

"Sorry," Glasswell says. "We've had a rough night."

"Do you have your claim ticket?" the valet says.

"I'm not even in line," I say, thinking of my poor LEAF all the way back at the hotel. "I stopped here because there was a wall to lean on—"

Glasswell looks at me. "It isn't in your purse?"

I wave him off. "I didn't park here. You go ahead."

He smiles. "I'm happy to drive you home, Ms. Dusk. If you'd like."

There's something in his voice that catches me off guard. A warm buzz spreads through my blood. Gently, he lifts my purse out of my hands. I watch as he opens the complicated vintage clasp—first the slide of pearl, then the twist of its gold-plated shell. It opens more easily in his hands than it ever has in mine. He reaches into the precise silk pocket—the one sewn under the label—where I keep valet tickets. And pulls one out.

As he hands it to the valet, my eyes fall on my phone in my purse.

"I'll be right back," I say to Glasswell as I slip around the corner. I swipe up on my phone's lock screen. I don't recognize the image—unknown mountain, unknown snow—but I can't worry about that now. I'm seconds away from my mother's soothing voice.

Lorena will know what to do. I tap my Phone app, then the star for my Favorites, but I don't see my mother's name. In her place . . . is Glasswell.

How did *he* get into my phone? I'll kill him. This is one step too far.

But it doesn't end there. I don't recognize any of my Favorites. Who are these people? Why does one of them go by "Eddie Redmayne"? There's a panic rising in me that I can't confront. Clues point in a direction very far from my world.

Stay the course. Call your mother.

I force myself to take a breath. I dial her cell.

"Hello?" It's a gruff voice. An older man's voice. Not Lorena.

"Who *is* this?" I say.

"Who is *this*?" the man says.

"Where's my mother?"

"Your *mother*?"

"Lorena Dusk! Why are you answering her phone?"

"I've never known a Lorena in my life."

"Well," I say, sobs returning, "you should. She's beautiful and kind and she has her own podcast—"

"You have the wrong number—" the man says.

"I produce the podcast," I say, starting to hyperventilate. "I don't read all the books like I should, but it's *our* podcast and it doesn't matter no one hears it and you need to put her on the phone *right now*!"

I look at the phone and see the man's hung up. I look past the phone, at the concrete, suddenly sensitive to its texture. I become dimly aware of my body's reckoning with how terrified I feel. I can't do this—whatever this is—without my mom. Without Masha.

It's only nine. I'll get a Lyft. I'll go to my old house. I'll climb the stairs and enter the ice locker Lorena calls a bedroom. She'll be wearing a silk robe with a thousand faceless people printed on it. She'll be wearing retinol eye pads and watching *The Thin Man* on TCM. She'll pat the empty side of her sleigh bed and I'll climb in. I'll give her the sign we invented after my dad died—one hand over the heart, one hand over the lips.

Hold me when I don't have words.

A car horn sounds. Glasswell idles at the curb in a red Jag. He rolls down the window.

"Did you fuck with the Contacts in my phone?" I say while the valet stands there staring, like this is a black box play for his amusement.

"Come on, Liv," Glasswell says, "let's go home." He pops open the passenger door.

I decide to call his bluff. It'll save me forty bucks on the Lyft ride to Lorena's. I slide into the car.

As Glasswell turns south out of the lot, I don't reflect on what a failed evening tonight was. I rifle through my purse, looking for my keys. "Should I put the address into the GPS?"

"You're really taking this role-playing thing to the next level," Glasswell smiles again, which doesn't make any sense.

My keys aren't in my purse. I'm about to tell Glasswell to turn around—maybe I dropped them in the sand—but then I see a set of keys in the center console, attached to a tan and green valet tag. I pick them up. And suck in my breath. There's the spark plug my dad gave me when I turned sixteen and got my license. The first key chain I ever had. Instead of my bent plastic Nissan key, this one holds a sleek black Jaguar fob. Along with several other keys I don't recognize. What I don't see— what I'm looking for—is the Magic 8 Ball chain bearing the key to my childhood door.

"Can you just drop me at home?" I ask Glasswell, curling into a ball.

"Where else is there to go?" he asks and squeezes my knee. His touch is brief, careless, but it sends the same sex wave through me as his breath did on my neck. I turn and find him watching the road like what he just did was nothing. But I still feel it in my toes.

Glasswell touches the navigation screen and sets our course. I watch the cross streets of my neighborhood populate the screen. I see the dot on the map where my house sits inside the labyrinthine hills of Laurel Canyon. I don't care how he knew my address. All that matters is I'm going home. We're thirty-nine minutes away. The traffic looks easy. I can make it.

Out my window the ocean is the same—original and

endless. The beach-blown narrow mansions are familiar, too, as is the curve that dips beneath an underpass and grasps the south edge of the 10, the mile-wide artery that will pump me almost home. Maybe it was only the wedding where everything was out of whack.

I make a mental inventory of the comforts I'll gather around me the second I get home. Box of frozen pizza bagels. Freezer-door bottle of Cazadores. Six and a half unseen episodes of *Stranger Things*. Softest of chenille pajamas, a Christmas gift from Masha. Gram Parsons in the green knit sweater he wears on chilly canyon nights.

If I can pile into my bed with all of the above, I will feel like myself. If I can make it to my bungalow, I intend never to complain about anything again.

Glasswell handles the screen again, cueing up a song. I'd rather ride in silence, but when the opening words of Whitney Houston's cover of "I Will Always Love You" come on, I'm too surprised to complain.

I remember Lorena used to blast it in her Volvo 240 wagon, driving Masha and me to baseball games when we were kids. I remember Glasswell following me out of prom when this song came on . . .

I try to roll down my window, but it's locked. I look at Glasswell. He reads my need exactly. The window unlocks, I open it, hang out my heavy head, and sing. I sing to Masha and Eli, to the moon and the universal ocean, to Lorena, and my dad, and that old man on the phone. I get to the second verse, and belt out the line where Whitney wishes her beloved "joy and happiness." But my voice breaks off before the next line.

The line that wishes them love.

Masha and I used to argue over what these lyrics meant. She claimed to find them profound. I thought they were funny, because they suggest that having love is more important than being happy. As a kid, I thought maybe I'd understand this line when I got older, but I still don't.

But then, Glasswell starts singing the line where I left off. His voice is a bright, surprising tenor. I stare at him. My eyes widen. Hearing him hit all the notes of *love*, then break into the stunning chorus—the meaning of the line finally lands.

That joy and happiness are temporary. That love is . . . all the time.

Where did this revelation come from? How did Glasswell's voice AirDrop it to my brain? More importantly, why does it feel like he's singing this, of all songs, *to me*?

That's when I know. The knowing curls up in my stomach, settling in for the long haul. This is bigger than a very bad night. Some piece of reality has been shaken loose. I'm not in the same world I woke up in.

But where the hell am I? How did I get here? Why am I with Glasswell? What do I do?

I want to ask him all these questions, but then again, I don't. I reach for the button to set "I Will Always Love You" on Repeat.

* * * * * *

WHEN I FEEL the dark, romantic curves of Mulholland Drive, I open my eyes and gaze over Glasswell's shoulder at the view. Mulholland is the highest street in LA, snaking the zenith of the

Hollywood Hills, offering alternating views of downtown and the San Fernando Valley.

When I was a baby and couldn't sleep, my mom says she'd get in the car and just start driving. Usually she'd end up on Mulholland. This road, above all others, soothed me, soothed her. She used to tell me that an Angeleno's never alone in pain or pleasure. And there's no surer way to know that than looking out from this old, audacious road.

There's no better time to drive Mulholland than at night, no better view than the Valley's distant, waving trees making house lights twinkle, the ground doing an impression of the sky. At the far edge of this dazzling expanse, the San Gabriel Mountains tear the horizon into sheaths.

Now Glasswell veers down the steep palm and pine-lined path that leads to Laurel Canyon proper. Soon, I see the Gothic wall sconces of my landlord's house and just beyond them, my near-invisible driveway. My body tenses with desire to get out of this car and be alone.

"It's right there," I say, indicating where to turn, but Glasswell's already missed it, like everybody does. My driveway's narrow as a needle's eye, especially at night. "Reverse!"

"Did you fall asleep?" Glasswell says, turning up the driveway after mine. The driveway that leads to the top of the summit. To the mansion up the hill from my backyard.

"No—" I start to say. But then Glasswell slows before vast gates and presses a button above the rearview mirror.

The gates swing open wide.

My jaw drops.

"What are you doing?" I ask. I point down the driveway, down the hill, down the far side of the wheel of fortune. "My house is . . ."

A smile begins in Glasswell's eyes. "Yes . . . ?"

I should stop talking. All the things I used to know have become question marks. Each new protest out of my mouth makes me sound more bananas. And Glasswell seems very confident that I don't live where I think I live. Where I woke up this morning, and every morning for the past three years.

He's still driving—there is so much driveway to drive up, I see for the first time. We approach a wide French-style fountain and a detached four-car garage. The garage door rises. There's a Porsche Taycan, a Lucid Air, and two Zero motorcycles inside.

"When did he buy this place?" I whisper as the knowing inside of me balloons. Still, I don't want to face what it's trying to tell me. I wouldn't know how to face it if I did.

On unsteady legs, I get out of the car and close the door. I breathe in the musty smell of the dark garage, which somehow is familiar. Though I've definitely never been up here, I feel like I've seen these rakes and shovels, these surfboards on ceiling-mounted racks.

At the door that leads outside, Glasswell turns back, waiting for me. "You coming?"

I need to see my bungalow. I need to know how deep this rupture with reality is.

"I'm exhausted," I say, "so I think I'll just . . ." I gesture toward the slope of hill that leads down to my hobbit hole.

"Crash on the hanging daybed?" he says dubiously. "I don't know. A lot of wildlife out there."

Since when does he care if I get scratched by a racoon? "Good night."

He blinks. "You're really not coming in?"

"Not even if I were blackout drunk," I say. Which I very well might be.

He sighs, rubs the space between his eyes. "I don't get it. But you know where to find me."

I watch him turn and walk toward the faux-Loire chateau.

Only after he's gone do I realize I don't know how to get out at the gate. I wander the yard, looking for the fastest route down. It's lush with laurel trees and jacarandas. Fanning from the pool is a vast deck from which it looks like you could take a running leap and hang glide to your massage appointment in West Hollywood.

An iron fence looped with twinkling lights lines the perimeter of the lawn. This fence looks over into my backyard. I've only ever seen it from below. I rise on my toes, hold my breath, and look down.

The lamp I always leave on in the kitchen casts a warm glow out the window. My heart swells at the sight, and I want to be inside, locking doors and drawing curtains. But I hear voices. Voices coming from my property. People sliding open my back door.

"Stop!" I shout. "Thief!"

They don't hear me, of course. The distance and the echo are too far. And quickly, I realize this is for the best, because now a woman emerges from my back door carrying—

A candlelit birthday cake.

The happy birthday song carries up the canyon. She places

the cake before a man, and a troop of guests applaud as he blows out the candles. Someone cuts the cake. They all sit down and eat. Leisurely. Like they own the place.

My gaze gropes around the yard and finds the furniture is different. There's a cold metal table instead of my warm teak one. A grill where my hammock used to be. Thick cotton maroon drapes where white lace curtains hung this morning.

A different dog runs across the yard.

My stomach twists. "Oh my God. Where is Gram Parsons?"

The birthday boy flips a switch that sends a white shaft of light through the canyon, illuminating the cliff twenty feet down the hill from where I stand. Trumpets blare—the unmistakable fanfare of a Twentieth Century Fox film.

They're projecting Gwyneth's *Great Expectations* on my cliff! But it isn't mine. Not here. Not anymore. That much is clear.

I spin away and fall to my knees. Across the yard, on the other side of the pool, I see Glasswell through wide glass French doors.

He's in a gorgeous kitchen, brightly lit. He's changed into a white T-shirt and black joggers. He's cooking something on a steaming range.

He lives up here.

And those birthday burglars live down there.

Where do *I* live?

The room next to Glasswell's kitchen is also lit, also exposed by broad French doors. It's a library—an exquisite one, lined with books on three walls. I see some expensive-looking leather-bound editions and some very cool art books, but my gaze is

WHAT'S IN A KISS?

pulled toward the top shelf of the far-left corner of the room. Something looks familiar.

Too familiar.

I squint. Are those . . . *my diaries*?

I let out a shriek and rush across the yard to get a better look. I don't dare go inside, but I don't need to. I'd recognize those books anywhere. It's not my full canon of color-coded journals, only the first five books I wrote. Eighth grade through senior year. Strange. I zero in on the fifth one—the pale-yellow edition I know I stashed in the glove box of my LEAF yesterday. Right beside it, serving as a bookend, is a framed photograph in black and white.

It's a couple in profile. They're dancing, the man dipping the woman in his arms.

I press my face against the glass and cease to breathe. Because . . .

The man in the photograph is Glasswell. The woman he's dancing with . . . is me. He's in a tux. She's—I'm wearing a white dress. We're smiling, gazing deep into each other's eyes.

"No. No way," I whisper, even as I know. Even as I feel it to be true.

I look down at my left hand and see a thin gold wedding band.

My knees buckle and I fall backward. Into the pool.

Chapter Eleven

SPLASH.

I sink like the *Star of Scotland* in the deep end of the pool.

Married?

My feet touch the bottom. I bend my knees and push off, shooting toward the surface.

To Glasswell?!?

Whose idea was this?

I break through the surface and gasp for air, my shock tempering the water's chill.

That photo of us dancing. The soulmate smiles we wore. The ring on my finger. And Glasswell's . . . ugh . . . *kindness* tonight. These are clues that tell a convincing story. Usually, I'm the kind of detective who ends up abandoning the mystery, but this one I can't deny.

I push out of the pool and lurch onto a chaise lounge. I find a plush towel on a side table, drag it over myself, and try to figure out whether the hysterical sound coming out of my mouth is laughter or a keening sob? Whatever it is, it's causing the canines of the canyon to respond.

How could this happen?

I twist the ring. There's no green stain on my skin beneath it. It's real. Why did it take me so long to notice? I do tend to forget to look for wedding rings before chatting up attractive strangers at bars—Masha's gotten on me for this before—but I really should have noticed the ring on my own damn finger.

Married.

In some surreal sense, this happened. Is happening. It's not just Glasswell up here living the high life. I seem to be living it, too.

But I am not a plaything of the gods. I am not an art experiment. I am Olivia Dusk.

So how do I get out of this?

I need to wake up. As far from here as possible. Because one explanation is that this is all a dream. An extended, torturous, traumatic dream. A thought edges my mind—something I'm supposed to remember, something I'm supposed to know.

Why We Dream was my mother's inaugural podcast read.

I curse myself for not quite having skimmed it. It was more of a mid-bagel glance. But I did listen to my mom describe it. The book said that every dream manifests the dreamer's deepest, unspoken desires.

I look at the house where Glasswell lurks inside. Agree to disagree, Michael Walker, PhD.

The French doors open and Glasswell shows his face. "Baby?"

I seize up in the chaise, grabbing more towels and pulling them to my chin.

"You still out here?" he says into the darkness. "Thought I heard a wounded deer."

The yowl I make now is every bit as feral.

Glasswell's head angles toward me. His posture grows taut. He crosses the yard at a clip.

"Did you . . . go swimming?"

"It was an accidental dip."

"You must be freezing."

I can barely speak through my chattering teeth. Glasswell springs into action, and is—right before my very eyes—stripping off his clothes. Down come the sweatpants. Off peels his sweatshirt . . .

Until he stands before me in a thin white muscle tank and tight black cotton boxer briefs. I can't even pretend I'm not ogling him. The man's muscles are gravitational, and my eyes are moons.

When Glasswell turns toward a towel rack, I gape because I've never seen an ass like that on a non-principal ballerino. And I've been looking.

"Olivia?" he says, and I realize he's holding out his clothes for me. "Put these on before you catch a cold. I'll hang your dress up."

"Uhhhh . . ." He expects me to strip. Like a wife.

From inside the house comes a beeping sound—a kitchen timer or a smoke detector or please God, an alarm saying *Wake up, this was only a dream.*

Glasswell looks toward the sound.

"I'll be right back," he says over his shoulder. "Take that dress off."

I do as he says—once he's inside and can't see me wrestle with the soaking sheath. I take everything off, dropping my underwear into the pile, trying not to remember traipsing around in it in Masha's suite this morning.

I slide into Glasswell's clothes, breathing in his eucalyptus scent. I feel the ghost of his body in the warm material. It feels like clothes straight from the dryer, except the dryer is a hot-ass bod. I'm in over my head.

I wrap my hair up in a towel and drag two fingers underneath my eyes, where running mascara must make me seem even more like wildlife. I drape the dress over the chaise lounge and study it for damage.

I remember Masha's hand like a stop sign in my face, the cold judgment in her family's eyes. I have nowhere else to go, no one else to call, no choice but to march toward this beast of a chateau with Glasswell inside.

I enter the sunken living room to notes of Fleetwood Mac. The house is massive, its surfaces all white marble and mauve leather, soft gray velvet. Does Glasswell really own this place? What kind of prenup do we have? And where did we find that sex-height marble dining table?

Oh God. Have I had sex with Glasswell on that table?

Of course I have. And probably everywhere else in this house. We're married. We must have banged a thousand times. A pleasurable tweak passes through me at this thought.

I scowl. Even my body is against me.

"Hey," he says, coming around a corner I didn't know was there.

I yelp in surprise. His eyes roll over my body so territorially I almost slap him. Then I remember he's not trying to be a creep. He thinks he's my husband.

"I love it when you wear my clothes," he says, his low growl feeling like he's got his hands on me. He steps close, blocking any chance of an exit with his heat, with his scent. "I know what you need."

I gulp. "You do?"

Slang sex words roll from his tongue. It's a lot of vowels and L-sounds, clearly something dirty.

"I don't know . . ." I say.

"You were begging for it last night."

My insides wince. High Life Olivia begs for it? She doesn't even know what "it" is!

"I'm pretty tired," I say. "Maybe I'll just crash out here—"

"Come on, I thought we'd go a little crazy tonight," Glasswell says, sotto voce. "And try it . . . with a chicken."

"Okaaay," I say to buy us all some time. Lots of people in the canyon keep chickens in their yards for eggs. I briefly flirted with the idea myself. As I look around for evidence of my husband's husbandry, I wonder just how crazy *is* this realm?

Sex stuff . . . with birds? I beg for this?

"Really?" Glasswell seems surprised. "You're into it?" Like a boy on Christmas morning.

He takes my hand and pulls me deeper into the room. Oh God. Something deeply perverted is imminent. He leads me to the vast sofa and sits me down. Instead of sitting next to me, he grins.

"Don't move," he says excitedly and disappears.

Help! What is it about hot guys that turns them into sexual freaks? Life's too easy, so they need to generate a challenge? Or is the problem too much success?

A moment later, a heavenly scent fills my nose. Glasswell's

headed back toward me. He's carrying a large wooden tray—of steaming food.

"Et voila! *Alouettes sans têtes*," he says. "I know your French side shudders because the dish is traditionally made only with beef, but you know, we've had that chicken sitting in the fridge."

I laugh, relieved to my marrow, and only a little concerned about my fading French comprehension skills.

"*Thank you.*" I hear in my voice the profound gratitude that Glasswell and I aren't into bestiality, but he takes my tone in stride. Like he does things like this regularly for me. Like I'm this grateful all the time.

I can't get my mind around how comfortable he is—in this house, in that kitchen, and most of all with me. This is clearly what he wants, not just in our wedding photo, but every day, every moment. Right now.

I don't understand what's happening, but I'm starting to see it could be worse.

I take the tray he's holding out. The dish looks like it could have come from the kitchen at my favorite French restaurant, Petit Trois. He filleted the chicken, pounded it, stuffed it with breadcrumbs and garlic, and rolled it into a spiral. Beside it lie two forks, two napkins, and two empty white wineglasses.

"Loire or Bourgogne?" he asks.

Before I speak, he reads it in my eyes.

"Loire. Great. Be right back."

How did he know—a second before I knew it myself? White wine from the Loire Valley is exactly what I want. It's what my mom likes to order on her birthday.

I run my hand over the mauve leather of the sofa, which

looks like it could seat forty guests. A flame flickers in the molded stone fireplace in the corner. A window-wall looks out on all that's lovely in LA. The plush white rug is straight from the showrooms I stare into while stuck on La Brea, coming home from Werner's restaurant.

Werner.

I wonder if we know each other in this realm. Should I call him? Could he help me? He's the least judgmental guy I know, and though I've never seen him correctly operate an elevator on the first try, he can keep a secret. I make a mental note to check my phone later for his number.

Glasswell returns with a corkscrew and a bottle of Sancerre. I want to know when he moved to LA, whether his show tapes out here. I want to know what I do with my days. I clearly don't Lyft in that fancy Lucid in the garage. But since I don't know how to broach these topics with Glasswell, I take the corkscrew and opt for wine.

He sits down next to me. His knee overlaps mine and his elbow rests on my thigh, and he's warm and he's firm and he makes no move to shift away. The length of his arm presses the length of mine, he looks at me, and smiles—that wedding photo smile, that forever-everything-entwined smile. He leans over and kisses me, halfway on my cheek and halfway on my eye, so casually it barely matters where it lands because there are seven million more where that one came from. It freezes me in place, because I can feel the love it's made of.

Which is scarier than anything else tonight. But it's real. It's here between us. And if I don't get away soon, I'll have to face it.

Glasswell picks up a remote, which comes as a huge, well-timed relief. In seconds something numbing will be on TV. In high school, if memory serves, Glasswell was obsessed with Premier League soccer. I'm ready to zone out, eat my chicken, banish all thoughts of marriage from my mind, and pass out on this acre of a couch.

When Glasswell opens the Bravo app and selects *The Real Housewives of Plano*, I almost spit out my wine. Glasswell watches *TRH*?

"I know," he says guiltily. "We said we were going to wean ourselves off this month—"

"We ain't weaning *shit*," I say and snatch the remote from his hands.

"Thank God," he laughs as I press Play.

We settle back on the couch, holding our plates in our laps. On TV, a real housewife is quoting Scripture, one hand lifted high in prayer, the other holding a margarita.

I take a bite of Glasswell's dish, and I can't help but moan. It's too good—hot and garlicky, tender and rich.

"You did not cook this," I say.

"The dish by which a real chef wishes to be judged," he says, with the air of pretension I haven't heard him use yet as my husband. That's more like it. It only took two hours for the old familiar snob Glasswell to return.

Then he winks and nudges me, like we're in on some sort of inside joke.

"Were you quoting someone just now?" I ask.

"My favorite wife," he says.

What? I'd never say that. Or would I, in this life? Has Glasswell turned me into an elitist snob? Is that the price for all of this? The two of us get along in this marriage realm . . . but I suck? Is that why Masha hates me?

"It's a complicated impersonation," Glasswell says, "Since you were originally quoting Aurora. Still, I think I nailed the nuanced layers."

"Yeah, that's what I heard," I say, my tone made of ice.

"What does *that* mean?" Glasswell asks.

"*What does anything mean?*" My voice breaks, and he reaches over, giving my shoulder a rub. In the exact place with the exact firmness that I like.

"It's been a hard night," he says.

"It . . . has."

"I know," he says kindly, softly.

He doesn't know. Something is seriously broken with my life. And my last brilliant idea for fixing it—going to sleep in my bed and waking up in the real world tomorrow . . . isn't possible. I miss Gram Parsons. The thought of him in his green sweater makes a lump form in my throat. Does he exist in this version of my life? Is he—I shudder—someone else's fuzzy little guy? I miss Masha—the Masha who doesn't want me dead. And my mom— whom I talk to so often it's like our phones are walkie-talkies.

I've got to get back to my life. I'm on the brink of tears. I don't sob or shake, I don't even wipe my eyes, but somehow Glasswell sees it. He puts his arms around me.

Now I start to sob.

"Should we go to bed?" he asks.

I'd love to go to bed. Especially now that I've consumed this anvil-heavy chicken and Sancerre. Besides, I imagine snob-Olivia's sheets have thread counts higher than the national debt. But wait . . .

Married people sleep in beds together.

"You go ahead!" I say. "I'm going to . . ." Roll down the hill and see what happens? ". . . take a bath."

. . . . . .

THIS BATH. IT'S like I've made a pilgrimage to a temple. The tub's been cut from a single piece of Carrara marble. Surrounded by candles and dozens of expensive potions, it's nearly the size of my old bungalow below. The tub sits in the middle of a large, glass-encased room. I look through the glass, toward the dark cliff's edge above my former home. I pick up the matchbook on the sink and light the logs in the marble fireplace in the corner. How many fireplaces does this house have?

I set my wineglass on the marble floor. I turn on the tap.

As the tub fills with steaming water, I take down three of Glasswell's sweaters from a retractable clothesline above. In real life, he wears suits, at least as far as we mere plebes know. But apparently in our house, he sports alpaca hoodies, handmade in Ecuador. I can't help running my fingers over them, picturing his shoulders in these corners, his muscles mixed with heat.

I pile the sweaters, dim the lights, and light a candle that smells like tomatoes growing on a vine. I dump in salts and oils and foaming gels and soon I'm sitting with my second glass of wine, submerged lavishly in bubbles, trying to clear my head.

I try to reason with the uncanny, to use the things I know are different here. I've got no Masha. No mother. Just Glasswell.

What I need is guidance, a combination fairy-apothecary, like Carol Kane in *The Princess Bride*. I need a sassy ethereal presence to put it to me straight, lay down the rules. What I've got is an evasive yogi-rabbi who vanished into the Pacific Coast Highway. But what would that stoner even say if I pinned him down?

You're here because you were an asshole to America's Sweetheart Jake Glasswell. Now accomplish these three tasks to prove you've learned your lesson, and I'll put you back in your real life.

That's what happens in these stories, right? The time-warped pay their karmic dues. Then they bound gratefully through the front door of their real home.

The thing is, I *have* learned my lesson. Glasswell is human. He is capable of being kind. I've been too hard on him. I made him into a villain, to preserve my own fragile sense of peace.

Now I'll do better. It's been painful and I've grown.

So, if anyone is watching, maybe we can skip ahead to the part where I go home?

I gaze out through the window at the one star you always see from this part of the canyon. It might not even be a star. Maybe it's Venus.

I make a wish. I'm ready. Someone just tell me what I have to do.

I remember the joint Yogi Dan and Jake gave me just this morning. I spy my purse, hanging from the closet doorknob. I can reach it without even leaving the tub. I dry one hand, stretch behind me, and open the bag's pearl clasp. I crank open the window next to the tub, light the joint on the flame of the tomato-scented candle, and take a tiny hit.

I cough, then lean back in the tub, closing my eyes, willing the weed to be magical, to take me home. It can even spit me out naked and stoned back at Masha's real reception and I could figure out the rest.

But I stay right here, extremely tranquil and a little obsessed with the geometric tile of the backsplash until my wineglass is empty and the bathwater is cold.

"I'm not stuck here," I report to the joint before putting it back in my purse. "There is a way back home. There always is. I just can't see it yet."

Maybe I have to smoke it in Santa Monica, on the beach where Masha was married? I'll make it my first stop tomorrow. I grab a towel, dry off, and decide, while I'm here, to sample the body and face creams in my voluminous collection. I slather on too much.

I enter my closet, large enough it can be entered. I laugh at the clothes I own. There's no sign of the chenille pajamas Masha gave me, but this plush jersey robe will do. Then I go to the bathroom door and peek out—

Glasswell sleeps in the glow of his bedside lamp, a book opened on his chest, reading glasses on his nose. I draw closer. Gently, I remove his glasses and place them on the table. He doesn't stir at my touch. I lift the book up, save his place, and clock the cover: *Branding Your Business in Ten Easy Steps.*

I squint at Glasswell, a lot confused and a little charmed. Does he still feel like he's finding his brand? Even after six seasons of his show? I study his face, innocent and calm. Handsome. I think about how cool he was tonight.

"Goodnight Glasswell," I whisper and turn out his light.

I pad down the hallway, searching for a guest bedroom. When I pass the library, I double back and enter the beautiful wood-paneled sanctuary. There must be a thousand books in here, but my eyes fall on my diaries. Maybe I'm my own fairy-apothecary. Maybe my words are the sky for me to fly home.

I find the pale yellow journal. Senior year. It's the last book on the shelf. My journals from age nineteen onward aren't here. I look on the shelf below—and find only travel guides. Brazil, the Philippines, Turkey, Budapest. I wander all around the library but don't find the other diaries. There should be ten more, including the magenta paisley-print book I'm halfway through filling this year. Where are the rest of my journals?

I pause before a framed diploma with my name on it. *Olivia Dusk, Juilliard Class of 2018*. I press my hand to the glass.

I went to Juilliard? And graduated on time? Which means I must have left for New York mere months after my father died. How could that be?

I grab the pale yellow book from senior year.

In one world, I know that this book, complete with its flailing twenty-seven-page prom diatribe, sits inside the glove box of my LEAF. Which sits in the parking garage at Shutters on the Beach. If it hasn't been towed.

In this world, maybe it tells a different story. Maybe it holds an answer.

Chapter Twelve

———

May 25, 2014

Dear Princess Di,

I awoke this morning as a girl. I write to you now as a woman. Seasoned, certain, alive. What changed?

Everything.

What changed it?

A kiss.

It was prom. You know that. I've been referencing it for pages. But I did not go into prom with stars in my eyes. I hardly expected a transformative experience. Unlike Masha (for whom prom presented a life or death romantic crisis), I'd written prom off as an eighties relic—monumental for Gen X drama queens, but just another festivity for me. I didn't shop for a new dress. I barely brushed my hair. The plan was chill: snag a limo, sway with my friends for a few hours, call it a wrap.

But then . . .

We interrupt this story to fall back on our bed and scream into a pillow.

Jake Glasswell. Jake and Olivia Glasswell. Olivia and Jake Dusk. Jake Dusk. Jake and Olivia Dusk-Glasswell. Olivia Dusk and Jake Glasswell invite you to celebrate their matrimony—

PILLOW SCREAMING.

You know what's crazy? Until last night, I didn't even <u>like</u> Jake.

I thought he was full of himself and way too competitive, and, generally, all up in my business. From baseball to debate to student council, the boy slid into nearly all of my extracurriculars. Only now I realize why . . .

Wow, I can't even believe the things I used to think about him—that his goal in high school was to one-up me at every chance.

It's like when you imagine high school all summer before freshman year, so clearly, it's like you're conjuring reality. And then the moment you step inside the building and see the actual lockers painted their actual soft serve shade of brown, the moment you hear the roar of the hallway and feel the crush of backpacks from all sides, the pencils jutting out like knives—what you <u>thought</u> it would be like vanishes in the high-beam headlights of the hard, oncoming now.

I love now.

The only way to love eternally is to love now.

And everything is different now. It's like I never met Jake before tonight. It's like we never spoke before Cupid swiped right on us on a curb outside the gym. I thought I was stepping out for air, but in the moments before Jake sat next to me, I looked up at the sky and felt something—

Like a promise.

Like an early warning of a soul-quake.

He came outside. He looked up at the stars. I looked up at the stars. While I was wondering if he knew the names and shapes of constellations, he sat down and started talking.

At first, I had my guard up; before prom, all I knew what to do with Jake Glasswell was compete. But something was different last night. The whole evening, our conversation had been natural, expansive. We talked about everything, from our families to our futures to what a hilarious disaster the Wednesday performance of *Romeo and Juliet* had been.

Here's where it got good:

Jake said: "If you'd been <u>my</u> Juliet—"

And I looked into his eyes and really saw him for the first time. I saw him in the role of Romeo. I saw me facing him on stage. And I wanted it.

"<u>Your</u> Juliet?" I whispered.

He blushed adorably. "If I'd been <u>your</u> Romeo. Is that better?"

<u>Why</u> hadn't he auditioned? What had made him look at me that day on the balcony and freeze? Our theater director had called out "Romeo, ascend!" but Jake just stared at me, shook his head, and walked out without a word. I'd always assumed he couldn't

imagine playing that love story opposite me, but suddenly I wondered: Was I missing something?

He put his hand on my cheek and I was born. I didn't have a cheek before Jake touched it. I didn't have a heart until it pounded right then.

"I know there's another world, Olivia," he whispered. "One where we . . ."

"Where we what?"

He tipped his head toward mine, so close his eyes filled my vision. I smelled his eucalyptus soap and felt his breath against my skin.

Then he pulled back. His eyes were still closed and he grimaced.

"This would be a waste."

"What?" I almost turned away. But then I thought about the stars crossing and uncrossing endlessly above, about the soul-quake warning I received right before Jake sat down. I thought about what was happening between us with our eyes. I took his hand and used it to push my fear away. "What could be a waste about this?"

As his eyes mapped my face I saw a hint of shyness enter them. "Two people get only one first kiss," he said. "Maybe we should work up to it, until you're sure—"

"You think I'm not sure what I want?" It almost made me laugh that he couldn't tell exactly how I felt. It was that obvious to me.

When he didn't answer right away, I showed him. I put my lips on his. I kissed Jake Glasswell. And kissed and kissed and kissed him. Softly at first, I got to know his lips. Then he kissed me back and everything got more passionate and ten thousand times hotter. His hand moved from my cheek to the back of my head, his fingers tangling in my hair as he locked his lips deeply in mine.

"Only one first kiss, huh?" I finally said with a gasp.

"That's what I heard."

"But what if the first one doesn't end?"

He shook his head and smiled.

"Let's find out," he said, then he leaned in to kiss me again.

Di: even though I'm here, now, writing this alone in my bedroom, I am still, in some realm, kissing Jake Glasswell. Always. Our first kiss hasn't ended.

I know it never will.

Chapter Thirteen

I AWAKE IN A COOL SILK COCOON, MY HEAD ON A down pillow so supple it might be alive. My nose detects the slightest calming notes of ylang-ylang. I'm not all the way awake, and yet I somehow feel replenished. As if I, an infamous insomniac, may actually have had a good night's sleep.

No tossing and turning until my sheets are 98 percent on the floor? No heat in my lap commemorating a late-night iPad rabbit hole? No recurring dream of being evicted and living in a tent by Henry's Tacos? Did I actually have deep and peaceful rest?

My eyes open.

Holy wow.

Out a giant window, a sliver of sun crests the eastern mountains, trimming the sky a dizzy pink. It's not rare for me to be up this early—but I don't think the sunrise has ever been the first thing I've laid eyes on. This is a revelation, a private box in the opera house of life. This is the kind of sunrise that makes a person want to seize the day.

I feel a feather-light caress on my left shoulder. I turn my head and see a man's hand on my arm, his finger drawing circles on my skin. I lie very still. I picture the arm that must be connected to that hand. I trace it underneath my back, my neck, coming out the other side to connect with an underarm, then a chest—

I turn my head and inhale.

Glasswell's spooning me. Shirtless.

And . . . ?

Yep. Pants-less.

Underwear-less.

"Aughhhh!" I shriek, leaping out of bed and taking the silk cocoon with me. This is a mistake whose implications I only realize once I'm standing up. Because I've left Glasswell— let's just say volcanically exposed. Things are lying everywhere. While I'm busy trying not to look, Glasswell also leaps out of bed.

"Whahappened?" He spins around, sending *things* flying everywhere.

Since he's not awake enough to notice that he's naked and—I'm *not* looking—also harder than a diamond, I pitch the comforter at him.

"Isitaspider?" he says, fighting his way out from inside the blanket.

I take the opportunity to straighten the pajamas I put on last night. "Hey, De Beers," I say to Jake, "how did I get here?" I point fiercely at the bed.

"You fell asleep in the library," he says.

Then I remember. The journal I'd fallen asleep reading . . . The kiss that never happened . . . Except . . .

I wrote about it in vivid, swoony detail, so explicit I can feel it in my lips and body, even now.

Our first kiss hasn't ended.

I know it never will.

After that, the journal was only blank pages. That kiss was the last entry I ever wrote.

What if I wasn't exaggerating?

What if there really *is* another world?

Where I *did* kiss Glasswell, and it *did* change both our lives?

Where I went to Juilliard.

Where we're married. Like this, right here.

"We need to talk," I say.

Glasswell—Jake—tilts his head. "What's up?"

"Remember prom?"

"Patient-Reported Outcome Measure?"

"I'm serious."

His brow lifts. He clocks my rigid body language. "You fell asleep reading your high school journal. I carried you in at about two."

A hazy memory surfaces—a scene I'd relegated to a dream. Jake lifting me from an antique library chair. Jake's arms like a sanctuary. Jake carrying me through darkness into this cloud-like room. Jake lying down next to me.

The silk cocoon wasn't the fancy comforter. It was him. His fingers on my skin. His nearness and heat.

How is it possible that the best sleep I've had in ages happened in *his* arms?

"Are you okay?" Jake asks, rubbing his eyes.

"Did we . . . move too fast? After prom?"

Jake runs a hand over his stubble, his eyes locked on mine. Just when I think I've slipped up and revealed that I don't belong here, he smiles. "I think it worked out alright."

But it didn't. Not for me, because I don't know what happened after that night. I'm missing miles of autobiography leading me to who I am. And I've lost my mom, my dog, and my best friend.

I turn toward the sun. Where does one dream end and another dream begin? How do you walk the line between fantasy and spin? In my real life, I told myself that better days were just ahead. That was fantasy, sure, but then . . . what exactly is this? I don't know who I am here. I don't know what I want.

What if everything I thought my life was is actually a dream I had last night? With Jake's naked body looped around my leg?

No. That life in the bungalow down the cliff was real. It was mine. It was hardscrabble, it was unadorned, but it was me. And I'm going to get it back.

But how?

I fall back on the bed and consider a quick, invigorating cry. But then Jake lands beside me, draping the comforter over us. He lays on his side, watching me with verdant eyes. He nuzzles his face in the crook of my neck, and oh boy, here it comes. When he exhales against my skin, it feels so good I could surrender everything. His breath holds me hostage. My cells rise toward him. I don't know how he does it, turns me on with just his breathing.

"Do you think we have time?" he whispers.

He can only mean one thing . . .

Morning sex.

The rest of him moves closer. Including the lumber he seems to have purloined from the Petrified Forest.

"I need to fuck my wife."

I see in his eyes he's not acting. He's not dreaming. He's not imagining I'm someone else. High Life Jake Glasswell wants me. In this bed. Posthaste.

And this absolutely cannot happen.

As I scramble to the foot of the bed, Jake's iPhone alarm goes off. He groans and rolls away but not before he takes a husband's squeeze out of my ass. The shock of his touch sends a lurid lash through my body, leaving me paralyzed.

"I'll make coffee," he says from the doorway.

It takes a full hot minute for the effect of Jake's touch to burn off. I know I've got to be out of this bed before he comes back, but I don't know where to go.

I think of Gram Parsons, who would be eating his Mexican breakfast about now.

"Hang in there, burrito brother," I say. "I'll find you."

My phone buzzes on the bedside table. I pick it up and see a full screen of notifications, none of which make sense. A volley of texts from someone named Ivy Riñata. A lot of alerts from *Deadline Hollywood*—who turned *that* notification on? Jake Glasswell's wacky showbiz wife, I suppose.

I tap the icon for my email, remembering how, yesterday morning when I woke up, the red bubble said that upwards of eleven thousand were unread. Today there are only eight. Six of them bear a variation of the subject line *Zombie Hospital*.

An ominous sensation grips my chest. I tell myself to breathe as I open one flagged Urgent, from a sender named Ivy Riñata.

Attached are today's sides. Remember call
was pushed to 8. I reminded A you asked to

leave by 6, but it may not happen. Peace and
love, ✗

Today's sides? Don't daily sides get sent to a show's cast and
crew? Does this mean I work on *Zombie Hospital*? An actual job?
That doesn't sound like me. But it does explain where I got the
fancy monogrammed pen.

I click the attachment, which opens a pdf labeled *Call Sheet,
Zombie Hospital, Season Eight, Episode 811.* Season Seven is airing
now—Masha and I had a watch party for the premiere—so they
would be filming Season Eight. And somehow, I'm a part of it.

I mentally peruse my résumé, guessing I'm most qualified to
do craft services, or maybe tutor actor kids on set. Then I remember the diploma hanging in this mansion's library with my
name on it. Juilliard. I went. I got the degree. Did I somehow
parlay that into a role on a long-running show? It's a far cry
from Broadway, but it is a slanted version of what I once said I
wanted.

I wade through the dense document in the email, searching
for my name, but before I find it Jake's back in the doorway,
bearing a breakfast tray.

"Uh-oh," he says, reading my expression. It makes me realize
how furrowed my brow is, how tense my jaw. "Rough day?"

"Do you know . . ." I pause. *What I do for a living?* I can't ask
that, and the fact that I almost did makes me realize something
alarming. I'm beginning to view Jake Glasswell as a confidant.
If Masha were on speaking terms with me, she'd be amazed at
the irony. She'd sing:

It's like Jaaaaake on your wedding day.

But Masha's not around to sing that. Jake is all I've got.

My stomach growls as he approaches with the tray. I would not say no to leftovers from last night, but when he gets near enough that I can see what he's carrying, my face falls.

A mug of black coffee, a mug of hot water with lemon, and a little glass bowl with six different kinds of vitamins.

"Breakfast, love," he says.

"That's not breakfast," I say. "That's a chemistry experiment."

"It's what Aurora recommends," he says, "and she knows of which she speaks."

"Don't say that name when you're the closest thing to punch." My eyes flash at Jake and to my relief, he laughs.

What is his relationship with Aurora in this realm? If he and I are somehow . . . married, then the two of them can't be dating. Are they non-boinking cohosts? Why does Jake subject me to her dietary whims?

Realizing that I'm too hungry to reason this out, I turn my thoughts to Winchell's Donut House on Melrose and plan to stop there as soon as I escape from here.

"You'll be off by six, right?" Jake asks.

I think back to Ivy's email. It said something about trying to get off at six. Do Jake and I have dinner plans? Where do we like to eat? The way he's looking at me makes me think it must be something more concrete than slurping noodles on the couch. Does he drag me to functions and red-carpet stuff? Does the Juilliard-pedigreed me know how to act at those things? Can I make that cocked-hip, half-akimbo pose? Or do I lurk in the shadows, furtively scarfing down canapés? Have we ever fooled around at a premiere?

That thought curls my toes and convulses my lower stomach. Which tells me I *can't* come back here tonight, to this man who needs to *fuck his wife*. Because his wife needs to figure her shit out before her husband busts out the handcuffs.

I rise from bed and try to center myself on two feet.

"I'm gonna need for us to have a fight!" I announce to Jake, because fighting is how we relate. Fighting with him makes me feel like me.

"I know," he says, and sighs.

"Don't *agree*! Fight!"

"I mean, I know why you're mad . . . you saw the new tooth-paste I bought. But you're murdering your enamel with that whitening stuff, and one of these days—"

"*This* is what we fight about? Toothpaste?" I look at him, disgusted. "You suck at fighting. You fight like a Quaker on ecstasy."

"Ohhh," Jake says, his eyes lighting up. He gives me a knowing nod. "More role-playing! Dr. Kenyon will be so proud"—he raises one eyebrow—"*Mistress Cherise*."

"What . . . no!"

Who is Dr. Kenyon? A marriage therapist? Of course, we'd need one! But why do we pay someone who encourages the use of dom/sub pet names? And who the hell's idea was *Mistress Cherise*? My stomach flips because I fear, instinctively, that it could have been mine.

"Sorry, I misunderstood," Jake says, crestfallen and confused.

I'm starting to feel bad for the guy. He didn't ask for any of this, and he seems to be genuinely trying to help. But he can't help me. We come from two completely different realities.

"Ohhh." His eyes light up again. "Ivy sent revised pages—is that it?"

Okay, so he understands me a little.

"And you're trying to get in the zone for a scene?" he says.

"Bingo," I say slowly.

"Then let's fight, Doctor. I'm here for it." Jake makes a grotesque face, lifts his arms, and plods toward me. "Me sue you for malpractice."

A genuine laugh bursts out of me, because . . . he's funny. The man just went *all in* on a disgruntled zombie bit before eight a.m., nailing all the nuances that make the zombies on the show so wonderfully campy.

In the real world, I pretend Jake isn't so comedically impressive. Because he hurt me. Because enough other people adore him. Because it's easiest to mask my pain with contrarianism.

But this morning, when Jake shines his spotlight directly on me, I can't help but drop my walls. I dissolve into hysterics, which makes him dissolve into hysterics, and for just a moment, when we're laughing, I forget that I don't belong here.

His arms come around me and his lips meet the top of my head, and he says in the gentlest voice, "Baby. You're going to be okay."

I push away, gasping for breath. "I've got to get out of this—"

"Show," Jake says, letting his arms drop to his side.

I was about to say *world*.

"I know," he says.

I laugh darkly. "You don't—"

"This isn't forever." He gives me a sad smile. "Let's just make it through the season."

He leaves the room, but his words linger in the air, reminding me of what I said to Gram Parsons when I picked up that last fateful Lyft shift. The one that led me to Jake Glasswell, the one that led me here. Whatever role I play on *Zombie Hospital* in this life, I don't like it either. And Jake speaks to me like I'm Gram Parsons.

I skim my emails for other clues and find myself clicking on the subject line of the last non-*Zombie Hospital* message.

Your monthly donation to Food Forward

I hurry to open it, because this is something that resonates with my real life. Food Forward is a charity that picks excess fruit from private properties and gives it to people in need. Mom and I have volunteered for the past ten years, picking apples and oranges in neighborhoods all over Southern California.

But the subject line confuses me. I've given a hundred dollars here and there for their annual campaigns, but I've never had the cash to be a monthly-auto-debit giver. I scroll down to the middle and my jaw drops. I give *ten thousand* a month to Food Forward?

I swipe to leave the email app and let my finger hover over my bank app. Anxiety twists my chest, as it always does when I get here. I click, let it do face recognition, and wonder why that works. How much of me have I imported across this cliff's abyss?

Then I see a very strange number in my balance. A feeling flows through me that I don't recognize.

Can this possibly be true? Just in case it is, I double my donation. Maybe I should triple it?

I knew Jake did well, of course, though I'm not sure I ever thought specifically about his finances. Still, something about this unexpected bank balance gives me the feeling I might be crushing it professionally, too.

A notification appears on my phone, sounding the same chime I have set in my real life for Lyft trips. But it's not a rider summoning my LEAF. Philippe's on his way here to chauffeur me to set. I have twenty-two minutes to get dressed and out the door.

I scramble into my bathroom, wondering how to dress for a life I don't understand. While I brush my teeth, I do what all Angelenos do when they find themselves in a social situation they can't make sense of. I consult IMDb.

I type in *Zombie Hospital*. The familiar TV still image pops up, and I scroll past a few actors I know are in the show, but I don't scroll very far before I see a headshot I do—and do not— recognize. Because it's me. Looking like I'm trying to seduce the glass off my iPhone screen.

It seems I've played the role of Dr. Josslyn Munro for seven seasons. The role Selena Gomez plays in real life.

There's a world in which this news would have made me feel elated, sending a triumphant trumpet blast through my soul. But standing alone in this strange bathroom, IMDb'ing myself, a wall away from a stranger who thinks he's my husband . . . I don't feel elated. I feel confused and fraudulent. On edge. Alone.

I think back to last night's wedding, to the guest who got my autograph, the valet who asked for a selfie. It does seem that I'm famous.

I open YouTube, type "Josslyn Munro" into the search bar. The hits are endless. The frames all show my face. I watch myself contort in outrage. I watch myself say Dr. Munro's catchphrase—"The Hippocratic oath applies to zombies, too"— in eighteen different ways.

It's cringey. It's shameless. It's . . . utterly absorbing. Most helpfully, it tells me what to wear. In each of the episodes I'm either wearing scrubs or some variation of a black T-shirt, leather jacket, and jeans. I grab the latter outfit from my closet. There's no time to shower, so I have to hope I'll get my hair done on the set. The thought makes me laugh. How in the world am I going to convince the people who work on this show that I have any clue what I'm doing?

One thing reassures me: Jake seems to think I can do this in my sleep. Maybe I can muddle through. It'll get me out of this house, at least. And on my breaks, I'll find out how to reach my mom and Masha. I'll sort out how I got here. I'll find my way back home.

And don't these Hollywood productions have huge spreads of elaborate snacks?

I swig the coffee, neglect the water, and stuff the pills into my pocket. Philippe texts he's three minutes away. I slink back through the kitchen, hoping to bypass Jake.

No such luck. He's on his laptop at the kitchen table, untangling the cords of what appears to be . . . a brand-new RØDE-Caster Pro 4 podcasting bundle.

Four microphones, four headsets, and a state-of-the-art pro-duction console . . . I've had this model in my online cart for over a year. It would have been a dream to record Lorena on such a machine. But even on Cyber Monday, the price tag was too big of a swing for me. Looking at Jake now, casually plug-ging jacks into holes, I feel covetous—until I remember that by California law, half of that console is mine. Besides, judging from my bank account, the Olivia and Jake who live here can afford a dozen RØDECasters. Jake probably got this model for free, a gift from the brand, because we live in a country where it's cheaper to be rich than to be poor.

But economics aside, what is he *doing* with it? Is *Everything's Jake* getting a podcast spinoff? The sight of this gear is making me homesick. Where is my mom? If only I could put those head-phones on and hear Lorena's voice coming through . . .

"What's all this?" I ask.

"I told you, right?" Jake says. "Ben's coming over this morn-ing to cut the new teaser."

"Right," I say vaguely, not wanting to reveal that I have no idea whether Ben is some assistant or, like, Affleck. With Jake, these things could go many ways.

He drops the mess of wires, rises from the table, and swoops me in yet another hug. It's strange how natural it feels to have Jake's arms around the small of my back. Without my knowing how, my own arms have found their way around his neck. For a moment I breathe him in and hold him back. Then he tries to kiss me.

I turn my head away so his lips land on my jaw.

Again—that shiver. Imagine if he'd hit his target.

"Great. Well. You cut that teaser," I say, pressing back to arm's length so we're holding each other like kids at a middle school dance, "and I'll just go out there and, you know, do my thing . . ."

"Knock 'em undead," Jake says.

I groan.

"See, that joke never gets old," he says with a wink that somehow makes my cheeks flush. "See you tonight, Dusk."

· · · · · ·

SITTING IN THE middle row of Philippe's Escalade, I see we have thirty-five minutes before we make it to the set. I open the sides from Ivy, who I'm realizing must be my assistant, and read through what must be my lines.

My character is the BFF to main character Dr. Summerlyn Mountjoy. I flip through the sides anxiously, trying to absorb my part. I haven't acted outside of a middle school classroom in almost ten years. Now, I'm going to fake it in a TV production. I will never be able to pull this off.

I wonder if Shraddha Kapoor plays Mountjoy in this realm, like she does in real life, because I always thought she seemed pretty cool. Maybe she'll take pity on me. Maybe we're already friends. I could really use a friend—

Lines, Olivia. Memorize them.

Luckily, there isn't all that much to my scene. I get a lot of haughty facial expressions, several one-word scoffs, and two places where I say, "I need to feel more undead inside."

As I practice committing to such a line, I find myself making a motion—one hand over my heart, one hand over my lips.

It's the old sign I used to make with my mom, right after my dad died. *Hold me when I don't have the words.*

I haven't needed to use that sign with my mom in years, but it's the second time I've reached for it since I got to this world last night.

It comes as an instinct, from a part of me I can't remember, but which also feels ingrained. Juilliard? Did they train me to learn lines by attaching true gestures and emotions to them? The answer ripples through me—at once reassuring and heart-wrenching.

In real life, all my dad's death did was break Lorena's and my hearts. In this life, it seems I learned how to *use* it.

But use it to do what? Masha and I always thought *Zombie Hospital* was pure escapist fun, but anticipating actually saying these lines makes me wonder how I've done something so un-challenging for six whole years.

The Escalade stops in traffic at La Brea and South Sixth. I look out the window and yelp at what I see. Eli and Masha are seated at a sidewalk two-top outside République. They have two carry-on suitcases by their table. They must be en route to their honeymoon! They're adorable, sharing an apple fritter, less than ten feet from my car.

Bliss fills my heart at the sight of my best friend. Then it's replaced by fervor. This is my last chance to clear the air with Mash before she leaves the country for a week.

I try to roll down the window. "Hey!" I tell Philippe, "can you please roll my window down?"

He shakes his head. "Your allergies, Miss O. Natural air not allowed until June."

"What?" I mean, I do get hay fever, but who gives a shit? I sigh and pick up my phone, relieved to find Masha's number in my Contacts. I dial, put it on speaker, and watch her. She sees the phone ringing, leans forward to see who it is.

"Pick up!" I shout, banging on the tinted glass. "It's Olivia! I'm right next to you!"

Contempt crosses Masha's face. My heart sinks as she shows her phone to Eli, who shakes his head in solidarity like, *Can you believe the nerve.*

For a moment it looks like she's going to throw the phone into the street, but Eli takes it from her, slips it into his pocket, and just like that, it's over.

The traffic moves. Philippe pulls away. I turn and watch through the back window as my best friend turns a new page in her life. And closes the book on me.

Chapter Fourteen

THE STUDIO GATE SLIDES OPEN AND THE ESCALADE drives through. After Masha dissed my call, I pleaded with Philippe to quit the GPS and take me to Santa Monica, to the site of last night's wedding. Because what was I doing, pretending to go to work in this life? How could I do anything except return to the scene of my reality schism and beg that beach to take me back where I belong?

Apparently, it wasn't the first time I'd begged Philippe to take me somewhere other than to set, and he was under strict orders to deliver me straight to a grid of anonymous beige square buildings in midcity LA.

He slows before a dark-haired early-twenties woman wearing glasses and overalls, her hair in a topknot. She doesn't wait for the Escalade to stop before she flings open my door and hands me a key on a metal lanyard.

"As requested, they changed the lock on your trailer," the woman says. "And Marty has five for you now." Her body vibrates with busy energy that will not suffer fools. She nods toward a nearby trailer.

I look at the tattoo climbing her forearm—a tendril of poison ivy. Peace, love, and Ivy emoji Riñata. My assistant.

I'd love to call my mom and say I've got an assistant, and that somehow kissing Jake Glasswell led me here.

Who is Marty? Hair and makeup?

"Thanks. Ivy." I glance to make sure I'm right about her name. She's unfazed as she raps on Marty's trailer door.

"Glad you survived the wedding," Ivy says. Before I can reply, before I can question whether I *did* survive the wedding, Ivy's skipping down the trailer steps and on to her next errand.

The trailer door swings open, and the redhead dressed in black with turquoise jewelry must be Marty. She squints at me with a trained, omniscient eye. She says nothing, but I feel like she can tell something's different.

She points me toward the chair. I sit and feel her gaze on my face, my skin, my eyes. Brushes glide swiftly over my skin, her body blocking my view in the mirror. She leans in to do my eyes, narrows hers, purses her lips. The confession—that I'm not myself, that someone needs to do something about it—is forming on my lips when there's a knock, and Ivy returns to the doorway.

"Is she ready?" she asks Marty, who squints at me once more, mists a spray over my face, and spins my chair away.

I sprint to keep up with Ivy through the lot, through stage doors, down frigid hallways, past crew members in cargo shorts and hoodies, ducking mics and lights, double-Dutching thick black cords. Finally, we stop on a set I've seen a hundred times on TV.

Inner squeal, outer cool as I take in *Zombie Hospital*'s cafeteria.

There's a long metal table in the middle of the set, two plates of food. This is where Dr. Mountjoy and my character like to gossip and relax.

A crew member approaches me with a surgical cap and gown. She begins to put them on me. While she's tying the gown, a middle-aged woman huddles close.

"I know," she says.

I meet her eyes, dark and intelligent. What does she know? Who is she?

"We experimented with your lines. You saw the sides. But network wants things status quo."

I nod. She must be the director. There's something I wanted changed that I'm not getting.

"Is Olivia here yet?" an impatient—and familiar—voice slices through the set. Aurora Apple charges in and stops before me in a matching turquoise surgical gown.

In this realm Aurora is Dr. Summerlyn Mountjoy. She's not on Jake's show. She's on mine. She's the star. I'm her sidekick. I exist to make her look good. Heat rolls up my spine like a warning, telling me that in this world as in my real world, I don't trust this woman.

At least, I find myself thinking, Jake doesn't spend all day with her.

"I need to talk to you," she says, grabbing my wrist and pulling me away.

I was obsessed with Aurora as a teenager. I was judgmental of her as Jake's cohost. But now a surprising emotion tightens my chest. Am I . . . jealous?

She moves closer to me. "What's wrong with you? Are you

still pissed about your lines? Didn't you see my texts? I really need—"

"Quiet on the set!" a call comes from the back of the room. There's a flurry of activity, quiet bodies darting everywhere. Aurora and I rush to the cafeteria table. A woman who must be my body double clears out of the way and I take her place, sitting across from Aurora under two key lights, a camera inches from my face.

"Action," the director shouts.

"So how are things with Spencer?" Aurora asks.

Instead of answering, I reach into my gown, look from side to side, and pour liquid from a flask into a plastic cup.

"Josslyn," Aurora says, "Don't. We have thirteen hours left in our shift."

"I found Spencer in bed with a zombie," I say.

"Again?"

"And right now, that same zombie is waiting for me in E 19. Bullet wound in her right breast."

"Do you want me to cover for you?" Aurora asks.

"Oh no," I say and take a long drink from my plastic cup. But instead of reciting my catchphrase as scripted, I decide to improvise. Using my imagined Juilliard training to *be in the moment*, I say, "I wouldn't miss cutting this bitch for the world."

"Cut!" the director says. She turns away and throws up her hands.

Aurora's irritated. Muffled laughter leaks out from the crew.

The director comes up behind me, leans down, and whispers: "We've discussed this, Olivia," she says. "If you want this life, you've got to say your lines."

. . . . . .

LUNCH BREAK FINDS me searching for my trailer while casually pretending to be on a stroll. I round a corner and slam into
gorgeous Miguel Bernardeau. His hair's wet, like he just stepped
out of the shower. But every other inch of him is firm.

"Hey, Liv," he says with a wink.

"Hi, Miguel," I say, surprised that I'm not more starstruck. I
wonder if my calm around my real-life celebrity crush has anything to do with my being High Life happily married?

By the time I finally spot my name next to a trailer door, I
feel my eyelids closing. If I weren't so tired from five hours of
pretending to be an actor, I'd be thrilled: my own trailer! But
right now I need to fall down on the softest private surface.

I unlock the door, step in, and dead bolt it behind me.

"Oh my God," I gasp. "I'm home."

In this trailer I find almost everything from my Laurel
Canyon bungalow—my childhood papasan chair, my lava lamp,
the framed poster of *Romeo and Juliet*, the vase I "sculpted" back
in high school, filled with a dozen of my favorite flower, the
humble pink carnation. I sink into the papasan chair and inhale.
It smells like home.

I sit up, a flicker of hope within me. "Gram Parsons?" I say,
but no jingling collar answers.

My gaze falls on the only thing I wouldn't have in my
bungalow—framed photos of Jake and me. It's strange that we
don't have any of these displayed in our house—only the carefully curated wedding picture in our library. The kind of photo
an interior designer would approve of.

The pictures here tell a different story. One is a photobooth strip of shots where I'm kissing different parts of Jake's face. One is us on the ferry to Catalina Island—the camera catching my straw hat in the process of blowing off my head. Jake is failing to catch it, hand high in the air, and we're laughing, my hair a disaster. Another photo has me straddling Jake's shoulders in an infinity pool with a volcano in the distance. There's one of us holding a koala, munching eucalyptus. In all of them we're laughing. We look happy.

I think of the moment in my journal, right before our first kiss, the moment when I'd gotten scared and almost turned away. But I hadn't. Somehow, instead, in this life I took his hand and pulled him to me. And that instant led to these photos. This laughter. Memories I don't have but Jake does.

Memories that made him fall and stay in love with me. I wish I could talk to the me who spent the past ten years with him. I wish I could know whether she's happy, whether she really loves him, too.

Realizing these framed photos must only be a fraction, I take out my phone and open my Photos app. I scroll through an endless montage of our love. I can't look at them closely, it's too overwhelming to see my blissful face: a laughing selfie in the produce aisle at Bristol Farms, a million of us hanging at the house, napping, cooking, dancing, hosting parties, enjoying life.

I swipe to the most recent picture.

It's the blurry pic I took last night of Yogi Rabbi Dan's license plate.

I text Ivy, because what are assistants for if not impossible assignments?

Me: Say someone needed to track a guy down using a photo of his plates . . .

Ivy: License or dinnerware?

Me: Strictly vehicular.

Ivy: California or out of state?

Me: Oregon.

Ivy: I'll hook you up by week's end.

Me: Seriously?

Ivy: My sister's a PI, remember? She still owes us for bailing her out of jail.

Me: Oh yeah . . . thank you!

Ivy: ✌🖤✂️

I've just texted Ivy the photo when I get a text from Jake:

Getting to Grauman's by seven. Excited. See you there.

Our plans for tonight are at Grauman's? As in the Holly-wood Blvd theater where every major movie premiere is held? I picture a brightly lit red carpet, a bland industry schmoozefest. I picture Jake in a tux, checking his watch, waiting for me—

I won't be there. Come seven tonight, I'll be on the beach in Santa Monica, using a magical joint to get out of Dodge. But if I *were* going to a premiere with Jake . . . what would I wear?

There's a knock on my door. Before I can answer it, I hear what must be a key enter the lock.

What the fuck. Ivy said I just had this lock changed. Who could possibly . . .

I watch the dead bolt pop upright. My door swings open and . . .

Aurora barges in, a straightened metal clothes hanger in her hand.

She picked my lock.

She sighs and collapses beside me in my papasan.

"I know," she says. "We need firmer boundaries. I'm working on it with Dr. Kenyon, thanks for the referral, by the way. But this is an emergency."

I stare.

Are we friends?

"Lily found out about Dustin and me, which is what I wanted, but I didn't want it *yet*, you know? I haven't had any time to prep my team and—don't say it, I know what you're thinking . . ."

She's still talking, luckily with no intention of pausing.

I look at her, then the photos of Jake and me. I'm used to thinking of Jake and Aurora as a pair, a symbol of everything superior to me.

I reach out slowly and put my hand on Aurora's arm. I'd like her to stop talking, to leave me to my ongoing implosion.

She looks down at her arm and draws in a deep breath. "Wow," she says, closing her eyes and resting her head on my shoulder. "That's really grounding. Thanks. So, you think I should·go to Lily's afterparty, wearing something I don't mind getting ruined when she flings Bordeaux in my face?"

"You read my mind," I say.

"You're brilliant," she says.

"You mind if I leave at six tonight?" I say. I'd like to get to Santa Monica before sunset. I'd like to get home—to my real home—by bedtime.

Aurora rises, nods, and blows me a kiss on her way out my trailer door.

· · · · · ·

AT SIX I'M totally exhausted. I've spent hours insulting and operating on a gray prosthetic breast.

I could rest up and hit the beach first thing tomorrow. I wonder if I could stay here and sleep in my trailer, the one familiar space I've found. Twilight's falling and I bet no one would notice. Except Jake.

What would Mom tell me to do?

Call your mother, her voice finds me.

I sigh and pull out my phone. I can't use the excuse of the mayhem of being on set to put this off any longer. I open my web browser and start to type her name . . .

Delete delete delete delete. My heart thunders, because there's only one logical explanation for Mom not being listed in my phone. Something terrible happened in this world and Lorena's dead.

I don't want to know that truth in any realm. I'd rather live with the uncertainty.

I shove my phone back in my pocket and walk quickly toward my trailer. I pass a woman I recognize. She was at the wedding last night, doing the Griddy next to Jake and me on the dance floor.

"Hey."

"Olivia, hi." She smiles.

"You were at the wedding."

She nods, points at herself. "Fenny."

"What do you do around here?"

"I'm the head writer."

I wince. "I really should know that."

"That's okay," Fenny says. "Occupational hazard. Aurora calls me 'Scribe'—"

"Well, Fenny," I say, "how do you know Masha?"

"She's in my book club." Fenny tilts her head. "How do *you* know Masha?"

My face must reveal that Fenny's question feels like a stab, because she quickly says, "Oh wait, you used to be friends, right? Like in middle school? And your husbands are friends now?"

My eyes fill with tears.

"Dude, you okay?" Her concern is just genuine enough, and I'm just traumatized enough that I let it all pour out.

"I'm having a hard day," I say through a heaving sob. "I'm not sure what I'm doing. Or why—"

Fenny laughs, looks around at the set. "Believe me, I know how you feel."

For a moment I wonder if this is a widespread problem, if no one's actually from here? Maybe we're all from other worlds. We wake up one day in this strange place with no visible escape, so we keep our heads down and try to blend in, flying by the seat of our unfamiliar pants?

"I mean," Fenny says, "I interned for Jez Butterworth! I dramaturged for Tom Stoppard! Now I've spent seven years in sweats on Skylark Lane, writing single entendres for a puerile doctor show."

"Ah," I say, seeing Fenny's complaint for what it is. "Good old art versus commerce."

"Everyone says how lucky I am, but I can't help asking myself," she pauses, before imitating David Byrne: "How did I get here?"

"How do I work this?" I talk-sing, vibing with her.

"This is not my beautiful house," we say at the same time, breaking into laughter.

"No one's *seen* me here yet," I confess.

She nods, smiling like she's trying to understand but doesn't quite get it, and that's alright. It makes sense that Fenny's friends with Masha. She's cool. Open.

"Are you waiting for Philippe to take you home?" she asks.

I was waiting for him, but now it hits me that Ivy would have instructed the driver to take me to Grauman's, the premiere. And I learned the hard way this morning that Philippe's not one to improvise on the road.

"I've got a thing all the way out in Santa Monica. I was just going to"—I smirk at the irony—"call a Lyft."

"I just moved to Venice," Fenny says, fishing her keys out of her bag. "It's a teardown and a long story, but probably near where you're headed. I could drop you on my way?"

Chapter Fifteen

A HALF AN HOUR AND THREE CONSTRUCTION-RELATED detours later, Fenny and I have traveled less than a mile toward Santa Monica. Now my second sunset in the High Life is softening the sky, and I'm nowhere near smoking that joint and vanishing into a wormhole on the beach.

"What the hell! No way," Fenny says. "This detour's taking me up to Hollywood and Highland?!"

I cringe. Hollywood and Highland is synonymous with gridlock. It's the Bermuda Triangle of LA tourist traps—the Walk of Fame, the Wax Museum, and worst of all . . . Grauman's Chinese Theater.

Where Jake is expecting me in less than twenty minutes.

"Do you ever feel like the cosmos is fucking with you?" Fenny asks me as we settle into a lane hemmed on both sides by orange cones.

"It's more than a feeling." I peer through the windshield at the standstill traffic, praying this detour will not take us directly past whichever red carpet my fake husband is on. I let my mind follow the worst-case scenario, glancing down at my jeans and leather bomber. I'm still in my clothes from set. Not dressed to be immortalized on Getty Images with Jake.

At least my hair and makeup are done?

No red carpets! If I need to duck down to the floorboard until we've passed Grauman's, I will.

Sirens sound behind us. All the cars in all directions with absolutely no place to go start honking. Fenny clutches her temples.

"I should have let you get a Lyft," she says apologetically. "I'm a little cursed these days."

"And I thought it was me," I say, and she laughs. I'm about to propose we bust out Yogi Dan's joint right here, and maybe I'll lay bare to Fenny my whole, preposterous story—when the people in the Volvo in front of us get out of their car.

And start walking toward the intersection.

"This is the first sign of a zombie apocalypse," Fenny says. "Believe me, I've done the research."

From behind us, more people emerge from their cars, passing us on foot. I can think of no good reason for this, save a zombie apocalypse, but it's happening.

I roll down my window, stick my head out, and hear the new single from Wet Leg being cranked somewhere up ahead.

"That actually sounds kind of fun," Fenny says, giving me a look, like *should we?*

The alternative seems to be sitting here until we're ninety-five. I don't have that much time to get back to my real life. We unclick our seat belts and exit Fenny's car.

We're a hundred feet and three dozen cars away from the busiest intersection in LA, and as we get closer, I see the problem. A food truck has flipped on its side in the middle of Hollywood and Highland. I rise on my toes to see what look like tacos . . . everywhere.

Fenny whistles under her breath. More people pass us on

foot. Everyone seems to be drawn to the scene, not by voyeurism, but by some force I can't put my finger on. It's a total clusterfuck, in a town famous for its road rage—and yet, somehow . . . the vibe is *good*.

SUVs have their sunroofs open, with kids hanging out the tops and laughing. Two women wearing big straw hats dance past me like they're in a Wet Leg video. A poodle with pink hair prances between cars, pausing for pets from the crowd.

"Olivia," Fenny says, taking my arm. "Isn't that your husband?"

I follow Fenny's gaze *up*. To a palm tree on the corner where my fake husband is perched . . . twenty feet in the air. He's not in a tux. He's in jeans, sneakers, and a hoodie. He's talking into a megaphone, though I can't yet hear his words.

He's not at a premiere. He's—

What *is* he doing?

A stunt for his show?

But I don't see a camera crew anywhere. Just a few people holding up their phones. I tap one of them on the shoulder—a teenaged girl filming the scene from the hood of a black Tesla.

"Excuse me?" I say.

She turns to me and blinks. "Oh my god, *Zombie Hospital* chick—your character is sus."

"Guilty," I say. "What's going on up there?"

"It's bonkers," she says. "So this taco truck got T-boned. The driver's fine, but the truck's on its side. My brother went up there to try to get it upright again. And my mom—" She waves at a woman weaving toward us, both hands full of foil-wrapped tacos. "Ew, Mom! You stole tacos off the *road*?"

"That man in the palm tree is *selling* them," her mother says, defensively. "To help clear the street!"

That man in the palm tree?

"That's Jake Glasswell," I can't help correcting her. "He's not selling tacos, he's—"

"He's the father!" a man in a nearby minivan calls out his open window. He, too, is unwrapping a taco he must have just purchased off the intersection.

"Excuse me," Fenny says, shooting me a quizzical look. "Did you say, 'the father'?"

"Apparently," a lady in a Porsche leans forward to chime in, "there's a woman in labor up there." She points. "Right at the light on Highland. She's having twins! And she can't get to the hospital until they clear the road. So *that* guy"—she points at Jake, still in the tree, still speaking into his megaphone—"he's the babies' father—"

"He's not the babies' father," Fenny corrects the crowd of strangers. She points at me. "He's *her* husband."

Now the crowd turns to look at me. Phone cameras swivel my way.

"It's Dr. Munro," people whisper. "*Zombie Hospital.*"

"Uh-oh," the teenaged girl says to me. "Did you, like, know about his baby mama?"

"No!" I say. "I mean, he's not even my . . . not really—" I break off, feeling my cheeks go pink. This is not the time or the place for truth. So I say the thing that's most obvious, most relevant. "He's *Jake Glasswell*, okay? Look at him! This is just some stunt for his—"

"Who's Jake Glasswell?" the girl asks her mom, who shrugs.

I'm about to sputter a laugh when I stop, a sinking feeling in my stomach. I push past these people and head straight for the man I swore this morning I would not return to tonight.

"Olivia?" Fenny calls. "You okay?"

"I'll be right back!"

It's not Fenny the cosmos is fucking with.

And suddenly, I can hear Jake, his smooth, warm voice amplified by the megaphone. It has a calming effect, even on me.

"All right, folks, get 'em while they last," he says, right as I reach the intersection and finally see the full situation for myself.

The sideways truck, its doors flung open. I see about ten men gathered around it, scratching their chins. And what must be a thousand foil-wrapped tacos splayed out all over the street. I sense the rush hour traffic, compounding in size exponentially by the minute.

"We've got carnitas," Jake's voice soothes from above. "We've got chicken mole. We've got a spicy shrimp, which I'm told is wild caught. It's wild to catch it here, anyway! We've got potato and poblano for you vegans out there. Don't be shy! All these delicious tacos are a steal at just one dollar each! Why? Because the City of Angels needs us tonight, to do our part, clear this road, and be on our way."

Smaller details come into focus as I look around. There's an uncanny order to the crowd. Are they being shepherded by hidden production assistants from *Everything's Jake*? Have they all signed waivers to be extras?

The line of pedestrians patiently snakes around the palm

tree where Jake is perched. When they reach the front, they gather tacos. They pay for them. Then they go back toward their cars.

"You'll see Enrique's Venmo handle right there on the truck," Jake is saying. "Don't forget to tip. He's had a bad day, but we're gonna make it better for him, right?"

"We love you, Enrique!" someone screams.

I shade my eyes with my hand to study Jake in his very bizarre element. He's working the intersection like I watched him work Oprah and that panel of *Everything's Jake* fans, but something's different about Jake right now. Maybe it's just that I'm witnessing it in person, not through a screen, but I can see a light inside him. He looks fully alive, the way I used to feel when I performed. Like my soul was wide awake, open to discover anything. *That's* why I wanted to be an actor. Not for money or fame, though it seems, in this life, that's what I got. What it seems I lost somewhere along the way . . . was this, what I see in Jake right now. He's having *fun*.

It makes me wonder. Maybe I was never meant to make it to Santa Monica tonight. Never meant to stand on a beach and— in all probability—fail to get back home. Maybe I'm meant to be right where I am, now. Maybe there's something here I'm supposed to see.

I study Jake. Who knows what this is all about. My mom would say: take the message, Liv, and then hang up the phone. I *want* to hang up, but—

"What's the message, Jake?" I ask aloud.

"There's someone special whom we all need to thank," he says, then points to an older lady in a hot pink dress standing below him on the sidewalk. "This is Elena, our volunteer salsa barista. She's visiting from Dallas, and she thought she was going to see *Hamilton* tonight . . . instead, she's here with all of us, helping out. So be kind when she ladles out your habanero sauce."

"Elena is everything!" someone shouts and Elena gives the crowd a laughing wave.

Fenny nudges me, suddenly at my side. "You clearly married very well," she says, nodding at Jake. "I'll go get us some tacos?"

"Uh-huh," I squeak. I think about how that teen girl and her mom didn't know the name Jake Glasswell. I think about someone else confusing him for the father of a pregnant woman. Even Fenny's comment confuses me, because it doesn't seem like she was referencing Jake's wealth or fame. It seems like she was referencing just *Jake*.

A niggling feeling creeps up my chest.

"And let's not forget our cause, everyone," Jake says into the megaphone. "The reason we're working together to expedite things. Give it up for Julie over here." He gestures toward an orange Jeep, just behind the light at Highland. I squint to see a very pregnant woman in the passenger seat.

"How you doing, Julie?" Jake asks.

Out her window, she calls something at Jake and gives him a weak thumbs-up.

"Julie's about to have a beautiful set of twins," Jake announces. "A boy and a girl. We don't know their names yet, but just as soon as we get Enrique and his tacos cleared, she'll be able to get to the hospital."

The niggling feeling is getting stronger.

"Julie's taking deep breaths, everybody," Jake says. "Let's all join her in taking a deep breath now."

I let my own chest rise and fall in a few deep breaths led by Jake. It helps. A little.

"You got this, Julie!" someone shouts across the intersection.

"Breathe, Mama!" a woman calls from a convertible.

"Julie, do you have another song request?" Jake asks the orange Jeep.

I watch him lean out a little further in the palm tree to hear her words. He nods.

"Julie would not say no to a little *Dirty Dancing* soundtrack, everybody," Jake says. "So can someone with a Spotify account *please* get these babies out of the corner?"

A second later, a beamer on the east side of Hollywood Blvd starts blasting "(I've Had) The Time of My Life." The taco line cheers, and by the time the song rolls into its first verse, it's a full-on dance party in the street.

On shaking legs, I move closer, into the intersection. I must stand out as the only person *not* dancing, because that's when Jake finds me in the crowd.

I stop walking in the middle of the street. I stare at him. He stares at me. A sense of knowing ripples through me, the answer to the questions just beyond my grasp.

His face lights up, like someone flipped a switch. I blink and feel a corresponding switch flip in me. He just saw me this morning, and expected to see me tonight, and still, it matters to him this much that our eyes have met, like I'm a touchstone for him.

I find myself thinking *that must be nice*. For him. For High Life Olivia. That seems like not a bad way to feel about your spouse.

But I am not his spouse. And I don't understand what's going on here. I raise my hands like *what the fuck?*

He grins. He waves. He shrugs.

Like he can't believe it either, but he'll roll with it. With anything.

And that's when I know. This isn't a stunt. This is a natural phenomenon. On the ground: an honest car accident.

And up in that tree? That's just Jake, being Jake.

With shaking hands, I take out my phone and google *Jake Glasswell*.

His ancient Twitter feed. A wedding website the two of us apparently made ourselves, which I'll have to look at later. A LinkedIn page announcing vaguely that he's a "writer/producer."

And then, scrolling down, I see a very basic website for a food truck.

Jake Au Jus, specializing in unusual French dip sandwiches.

I click the link.

Merde! We're closed, the landing page proclaims, next to a picture of Jake, waving from inside the kitchen of a small red truck. He's wearing a chef's hat and a goofy adhesive handlebar mustache that somehow makes him look even cuter. He's smiling, but I see wistfulness in his eyes. It hits me that I—or High Life Olivia—probably took this picture. But for what? Jake didn't actually have a food truck, did he?

I type *Jake Glasswell talk show* with increasing urgency as a man in front of me dips his girlfriend Patrick Swayze style.

It looks like there aren't many great matches for your search, the internet enlightens me. A heavy pit forms in my stomach as I confront an unsettling truth.

Jake is showless in this life.

He isn't famous. He's just Jake. Husband. "Writer/Producer." Failed French dip slinger. Megaphone-wielding Good Samaritan in a palm tree.

I watch him now, chatting with some people in line for tacos at the base of his tree. When Jake mentioned "the show" this morning, I leapt to the only logical conclusion: that he was talking about *Everything's Jake.* But if there's no show, what was that podcast gear for? Is "Ben" a real producer . . . or just a buddy Jake hatched an idea with? Are we looking at a Lorena-and-Olivia-level winging-it situation?

Further to that: Do all those dollars in our bank account . . . come from me?

I stare at him and all that charisma. What's Jake's deal in this life?

His fame, his fortune, his stratospheric success. Where is it?

What if, when we kissed at prom, it took *everything* from him? And all he gets is . . . me? That could never be enough.

A cheer sounds from the street. Startled from my thoughts, I see that the men have somehow righted the truck just as the tacos are cleared from the street. Elena is helping Enrique pack up the salsa bar. People are taking selfies with Jake in the background, with the truck, with Julie, who is doing Lamaze in the Jeep.

One of the men who'd been working on the truck runs to

the Jeep and hops in the driver's seat. Everyone applauds. I see that he's the actual father, that he lifted an actual truck out of the road for his wife and future children on the day they would be born. Their family will tell that story for generations. And Jake will be a part of it.

A police escort on a motorcycle finally reaches the intersection. Soon he's guiding Julie's Jeep across Hollywood Blvd. People are cheering, laughing, and some are crying as they make their way back to their cars. Fenny finds me in the mayhem, handing me a paper sack of tacos. She gives me a hug.

"You gonna stay with Jake?" she asks.

I look at him in the tree. He's watching me, and I know there's only one answer. "Yeah. Thanks for the lift, Fenny."

"I'll never forget it," she says. "See you on set."

The traffic jam unjams. And soon the corner is quiet, or as quiet as it ever gets, and I'm at the base of the palm tree looking up at Jake. I feel jittery with adrenaline, amazed, and brimming with questions about how we ended up here.

"Hey, baby." His unmegaphoned voice sends a shiver through me. "So that was crazy."

"Crazy," I agree. "And you were . . ." I search for the right words. I can't find them.

"I—"

"You—"

"Liv, I can't get down."

"What?"

"I need help. I'm stuck."

"Oh! You can't get down!" I forgot. Jake is scared of heights.

I think back to his public panic attack on *Everything's Jake*, the climbing wall. I remember Aurora talking shit at him from on high.

"Oh God," he says, sounding ill. "This is high school all over again."

"High school?"

"At least then I had the foresight not to climb the trellis," he says, like I should know what he means.

And then, I do.

The trellis. The set for the audition of *Romeo and Juliet*. Our senior year. I wrote about it in my diary. When I'd seen Jake take one look at me up on the balcony and flee the stage.

That's why he'd bailed. He was scared of heights.

"When I saw that woman in labor," he explains now, "I leapt before I looked."

I put my hands on the tree trunk, wishing I could take his place up there. "You did good, Jake," I say sincerely. "And you're going to make it down. Inch by inch. I'll be here."

He swallows. Nods. He holds my gaze, and I see it flow between us, that he can take my support for granted, that it alone will get him out of this tree.

A sense of power washes over me. It's a feeling I haven't known before, something warm and steady in my heart. For the first time since I landed in the High Life, I let myself enjoy a moment's well-needed peace.

"You can do it," I say gently. "Deep breaths. Just like Julie."

He cracks a smile, then gets still. We both take a deep breath, and Jake seems, suddenly, ready to try.

. . . . . .

IT TAKES HIM almost twenty minutes to descend the tree trunk. His face is pale and damp with sweat, and when he's four feet off the ground, he panics and drops. Right into my arms. We both thud to the pavement, laughing and only a little bruised. Jake helps me up. He wraps his arms around me and heat fills my chest, my face, my belly. Jake looks down at me and I look up at him, our lips inches apart.

We're going to kiss. We're going to do it. I feel like a firework near a lit match, on the brink of going off. Exploding. Lighting up the sky.

Something buzzes on Jake's watch.

He starts laughing, pulls away from me. And I'm a little let down. I catch my breath as he says:

"We can still make it!"

"Huh?"

"Ben's inside with Mark." He points at Grauman's theater. "They missed the whole thing with the truck, but they're saving our seats."

"What seats?" I ask. Who are Ben and Mark?

"For the movie!" Jake laughs and pulls two tickets out of his pocket.

I hold his wrist to read the tickets. His skin is warm and I can feel his pulse, racing like mine.

Grauman's Chinese Theatre. A revival of the Audrey Hepburn/Albert Finney classic *Two for the Road*, which I love.

We were never going to a red-carpet premiere tonight.

Because Jake isn't famous. We were going to the movies with a couple of friends. We still are.

"We'll have to scrap dinner until after," Jake says, "but if we hurry, we can make the opening credits."

Now I grin and wave the sack of tacos Fenny gave me, because sometimes the cosmos is kind. "I took care of dinner."

Jake grins and puts an arm around me. Together we walk toward the theater.

"Is this a perfect night," he says, "or what?"

Chapter Sixteen

I AWAKE IN THE COCOON AGAIN. THIS TIME, I'M ON MY side, facing Jake, who's still asleep. I take in his sculpted cheekbones, long eyelashes, and lips that could divest me of my secrets. Gazing at the muscles of his shoulder, I'm overcome with desire to reach out and touch him. I pin my hands under my back and let the sunrise sweep over his features.

It's not like I didn't know Jake was gorgeous before. But after last night, he looks different. I see the man behind the beauty, and he's kind, with depths I hadn't imagined.

What happened last night at the taco truck traffic jam was a shock to my whole system. The way Jake rose to the occasion, the way he helped all those people—who he simply *was*—it unraveled the threads in my Coat of Many Reasons to Hate Glasswell. The one I'd worn for a decade. The one I thought I might feel naked without.

This morning I'm beginning to entertain the possibility that I've been wrong about everything. Even—and especially—high school. Jake hadn't walked out of that *Romeo and Juliet* audition ten years ago because he'd seen *me* on the balcony. He'd walked out because he'd been scared to climb the trellis. I see now that he hadn't wanted to play Romeo for the star power or the attention. He'd wanted to be the guy who got to kiss me.

And I shut him down.

In one reality, Jake took the hint and backed off, coming close to but not quite kissing me at prom.

In another reality . . . I leaned in, and here we are.

Some version of Jake knew we should be *this* all along. But what can any of that teach me about how to get home?

That's the question I must keep in mind. I lost sight of it last night. Though thankfully I kept my wits enough about me that I went home alone right after the movie, while Jake and his friends went out for drinks. I saw the two of us coming home together, tipsy and tumbling into our marital bed.

And we can't do that.

Sex with Jake while I'm this mixed up would be a bad idea.

Is it an incredibly *hot* bad idea? Sure. Do I wonder how deep-in-love Jake moves in this large, luxurious bed? I'm only human. Are his abs so tight that he possesses the ancient Trojan musculature known as the inguinal crease between his torso and his waist? Ding-ding-ding.

But the danger signs flashing all around me are too glaring to ignore. Letting Jake *in* would alter everything, in ways impossible to predict.

When I heard him come home around midnight, I pretended to be asleep. In truth, I'd been on my phone. I binged all three episodes of his podcast, which is called *Clean Slate*. In the show, his cohost, a psychologist, shares current research on emotionally intelligent masculinity, which Jake rounds out with personal accounts of his struggles with his own father, who he lost touch with at eighteen. The episodes were gripping, and I heard the unspoken questions inside each of them—

Do I have the curse? Am I destined to repeat my dad's mistakes?

I heard how he's hurting and hopeful and vulnerable, just like everyone else in the world. I heard his gift for opening himself up for the greater good. He's talented, even when he isn't famous. But is he happy? Does he not sense all the *great* things he's missing in another realm?

After I listened to the podcast, I opened TikTok on a whim and started typing in *Hollywood and Highland*—

Hollywood and Highland Taco-Debaco autocompleted, and I clicked.

It led me to a video someone had taken while everyone was dancing to "(I've Had) The Time of My Life." The camera panned from the line of taco customers to the men working on Enrique's truck, to Jake up in the tree. The caption over the reel reads *Expectant Father Saves the Day! Clears Epic Traffic Jam for His Wife in Labor.*

I laughed at the mischaracterization of Jake's role, but I watched it ten times, zooming in on his perfect, charismatic smile, on his complete comfort guiding a difficult crowd to a happy resolution. Of course people guessed he was the father. Otherwise, he's just some random guy, too good to be true.

I was wide awake when Jake came into bed. Buzzing with questions about how this version of him never found the success baked into him back home. I acted like I was sleeping, but I didn't hate it when he wrapped me in his arms.

And I don't hate waking up in them now.

His eyes open like he heard my thoughts.

"Big day," he smiles. His gaze runs from my eyes down to my lips. "I refuse to be distracted by how sexy you are in the morning."

Something like a giggle leaves me. Not a sound I've ever made in front of Jake. I look down.

"Your mouth," I say, "seems to be writing checks your body can't cash—"

"You're right," he says. "My franchise is expanding into your territory." He pulls away, taking his smoking hot hard-on with him when he goes. I bunch the covers closer, feeling the chill of not being near him. Who keeps a room this cold?

In an effort not to see Jake naked, I roll over and grab my phone. What does "Big Day" mean in High Life-speak? Just how out of my depth and dignity will I be today? The "Home" calendar I share with Jake reveals that from 9:00 a.m. to 5:00 p.m., I've blocked out time for something I've labeled "Deck."

What does it mean?

On the bright side, I seem to have the day off from shooting *Zombie Hospital*. On the dark side, a whole day doing something mysterious with Jake, alone? Eight whole hours for him to see that I'm a fraud who only looks like the woman he married?

I can't let my guard down.

"Deck" *could* be showbiz-related, like the visual decks made to pitch a TV show. Maybe it's related to Jake's podcast? I do have a few budding opinions about *Clean Slate*'s intended audience and scope . . .

One certainty is we're doing "Deck" together. It's something he—and possibly we—are looking forward to.

"How much time do you need to get yours ready?" Jake calls from his closet.

When I don't answer, he pads back into the room—bare-chested, burnished muscles, cotton pajama pants slung low. Even if I'd had an answer, seeing him without a shirt silences me.

"Oh great, you're totally ready, aren't you?" Jake fills in my silence, cruelly tugging on a hoodie, which he somehow still manages to look like a sex god in.

What's gotten into me? It's times like these when I could really use a best friend or my mom to reason this stuff out.

"I'm close, I swear," Jake says, riding his own train of thought. "Just a few last finishing touches. Five minutes and I'll meet you, okay? This is going to be so good."

He laughs, taps the doorframe, and he's gone from the bedroom. I search my phone, but nothing in my text threads, emails, or Notes app offers any clue about Deck Day. I brush my teeth and stand inside my closet, letting Jake's casual attire inform my own selection.

Reaching for my sneakers, my hand rustles something that feels like a satin gift bow. I kneel down, parting a rack of sweaters to reveal a box marked *Deck Day*.

Jackpot?

The box is wrapped in paper printed with lipstick kisses. Is this a gift for Jake? I shake it. Something light shimmies inside.

"Olivia!" Jake's excitement rings through the house. "It's time!"

The opening chords of Journey's "Faithfully" blast through speakers built into the closet walls. I jump at the sound, then gather myself. I have to play along with whatever Deck Day is. I've got to fake it till I make it back to my bungalow downhill.

Through the bedroom windows, I see Jake outside by the pool. He's got a brown paper bag that looks auspiciously like takeout, his laptop opened to a Spotify playlist. Next to him stands a forty-pound sack of soil, several flats of seedlings, a power hose, and a clear Tupperware container full of rags.

Suddenly I see how simple, how literal—how non-sexual!— Deck Day is. We're passing our day . . . tending the garden on our deck. Together. Like married people do.

I smile, glancing at the gift in my hands, at Jake nodding in time to the music, at the food he's had delivered. I feel a pinch in my heart. Real Life me can handle High Life this.

I step through the sliding door to the backyard. When Jake sees me, he throws back his head and his arms and belts out the "whoa-oh-oh"s at the end of "Faithfully." Because I'm a Journey freak, it's impossible for me not to sing along. I harmonize as I pass the pool, going low when he goes high, letting Steve Perry carry us through the song's melodic peaks. It sounds so good it's obvious we've done this before. By the time the song is over, I've come to sway by Jake. We're endorphin-flushed and laughing.

He turns down the music. "Remember when we saw Steve Perry in the produce section at Gelson's?"

Nope. "Of course," I say.

"You asked him to sign your squash, but we didn't have a pen."

"Classic Steve Perry," I say. "What is it with that guy and produce?"

"Can I go first?" Jake asks, bouncing on his heels.

I have no idea what he's talking about. "By all means!"

He opens the brown bag with a snap of his wrists. "For the girl who once told Amy Reisenbach there's no better breakfast than a hot dog, I give you . . ." From the bag, Jake lifts three Styrofoam containers, lines them up on a teak dining table, and gently lifts their lids. "A breakfast buffet from—"

"Pink's?!" I finish his sentence, staring down at my real-life three favorite orders from the famous LA hot dog eatery. The Guadalajara—all those jalapeños! The Rosie O'Donnell—extra-long with sauerkraut! The Brooklyn—pastrami with Swiss!

I have a lot of questions about the conversation Jake just mentioned—starting with *who is Amy Reisenbach*—but I have to let that go. I've got to stay in the moment. That's not so hard. I do love the smell of mustard in the morning.

"I love this," I say without thinking, my eyes locking with Jake's. I feel the whirlpool between us pull me in. I drop my eyes to the food.

"I love *you*," he says simply. "And you're also going to love this playlist, which is all new, no repeats from Reseal the Pool Day."

"Better not be," I say mock-sternly, noting our enormous pool's waterproof flagstone. *We* did that? And also: He loves me?

Like it's no big deal.

"And now?" Jake asks, dive-bombing a kiss between my eyes.

I close my eyes and fold into him. The need for his affection is growing stronger and more real.

I step away, self-conscious. "And now . . . what?"

"What's in the box?"

"Yes! The box!" I look down at my present for Jake, every bit as curious as he is. I hand it over. "Knock yourself out."

His eyes dance across the wrapping paper. He exhales deeply. My man sure loves his Deck Day.

He shakes the box. "I can't wait."

"No need to."

"Okay." He smiles. "I'm going in."

Jake tears into the present like it's a conjugal visit. His eyes light up as he thrusts his hand into the remaining shards of the box, then withdraws his closed fist. He gives me a naughty grin. "You didn't."

"Are you surprised?" I ask, dying to know what I gave him. Cuff links? An ID bracelet?

Jake opens his palm and reveals . . . a pair of black satin boxer briefs.

"Oh God, they're butt-enhancing." He starts laughing, holding them up to his waist, and I see the various nips and tucks in the fabric meant to accentuate a man's parts. What the hell is wrong with High Life me?

"I told you I would only wear these on the condition that you . . ." Jake peers inside the box again and looks up at me grinning. "Aha!"

Looped through one finger is a black satin thong.

His and hers.

"Well, game on," he says, still laughing. "It's going to be a little distracting, but we can get it done."

"Hah!" I say. "I meant it as a joke. Obviously. We're not going to . . ." I gulp. "Actually. Wear these. While—"

Jake rips off his sweatshirt, along with his T-shirt underneath. He pulls the knot loose on his sweatpants.

Then, my God, he's naked, and the man is absolutely hung. Well before I've gotten a good enough look, he slides his new, ridiculous, butt-enhancing briefs up to his waist . . . letting his whole hot self tumble into the bulging satin pocket. The fabric clings to his thighs. I never knew male thighs could look so sensual, so curvy and compressed . . . now he's turning to give me a view of his sculpted ass. And just wow.

As I stand gawking, Jake says, "Aren't you going to put yours on?"

I'm so confused. We're really going to attempt manual labor undressed like this? Set aside the awkwardness of hauling sod with next to nothing on, set aside the potential for sunburn on sensitive skin—how will it be possible to focus?

How will it be possible to avoid having sex?

I know we're married, standing on our own secluded property, but I can't help looking anxiously around me. Jake's body is so obscene it must offend the trees.

"Your turn, sex bomb," he says and smacks my ass.

I nod, wondering if he can tell I'm hyperventilating.

It's basically a bathing suit bottom, I try assuring myself. *Albeit one fit for a Brazilian supermodel.*

And yet in this reality, *I* bought this thong and its matching counterpart for Jake. I was game to wear it. Game to let Jake *see* me in it.

My chest feels like it's on fire, and . . . funny thing: now would be a convenient time to change the underwear I have on. Because suddenly they're wet.

"Here goes nothing," I say under my breath. And then, under the cover of my thigh-length hoodie, I drop my pants, my cotton briefs. I step into the black silk thong.

Jake eyes me, hungrily, moving closer to tug on the sleeve of my hoodie. "Off she goes."

"But I . . . there's no top."

He chews his bottom lip. "I guess the person in charge of costumes should have thought of that. Or maybe she did."

I close my eyes. I slowly pull the hoodie up over my head. I stand before this very hot man in my insane thong and sheer white tank, feeling exposed enough for several female-produced soft-core pornos. I think about how if I take the next step and remove my shirt, that Jake and I may end up fucking into Tuesday.

I think about how if I *don't* take off my shirt, we'll have to discuss why. And perhaps he'll find the truth—

I whip off my shirt. I let it fall to the ground. I look up at Jake.

Goose bumps rise on my bare skin. As his eyes run over my body, my nipples pinch so tight I gasp.

"You're beautiful, Olivia," he says.

Then his hand is on my waist, strong and warm and firm. And his mouth is almost on top of mine, and I can't help closing my eyes, tilting my chin, and—

I hear a squirting sound. I open my eyes and see Jake . . . squeezing sunscreen into his palm.

"I don't want your fine ass getting burned," he says, his voice a rough whisper on my neck.

He takes his time rubbing the cool cream into my shoulders,

his hands slowly warming my skin as they massage circles down my back, across my waist, over the rounded curves where the thong leaves my palest skin exposed. I hold my breath and try to relax into how good his touch feels, how well Jake seems to know my body, how not-weird all of this is for him. I let him guide me through the experience of being cared for, being protected by him, which leaves me breathless and a little shivery.

There's something sweet about it, and many things sexy about it, and a wonderful dose of ordinary all at once. This, it seems, is our marriage in a nutshell. Hot and sweet and steady. And I think: this version of me sure is lucky.

When Jake's hands trace up my stomach, adding more sunscreen as they find their way to the sensitive skin of my breasts, I can't help moaning. I hear Jake moan, too, which may be the sexiest thing of all. The sound—one I've never heard him make—startles me back to reality. I take a step away, finishing the job of rubbing in the sunscreen myself.

"You okay?" he asks, as out of breath as I am. He tries again to put his arms around me.

I can't do this. It's too big. Not just the iron in his briefs, but all the implications. I put up a hand to stop him before he kisses me.

"Wait," I whisper.

"Must I quote Mistress Cherise?" Jake asks, his breath on my neck again, murdering my resolve. "'Sex is not to be avoided.'"

I know I'm meant to laugh at his Transylvanian-style Mistress Cherise accent, but as I look over the railing, down to the tree line of my real-life house, I say a little prayer for myself.

That I can make it through this day without surrendering to my desire for Jake.

"First, we work," I make myself say. "Then we play."

"I've never known you to be one for delayed gratification," Jake says, taking a step back, allowing me to catch my breath. "But you're right, it'll be hotter that way."

. . . . . .

AN HOUR LATER, Jake has hauled the soil across the deck, while I pruned our basil plants and weeded our budding tomatoes in their raised beds. We've had fun getting to know the power hose, made crumbs of the Pink's hot dogs, and I've committed myself to a long future of exhibitionism, which I had no idea was so exciting. I didn't know I could be this comfortable almost naked, let alone this aroused. And since no actual sex has been had, I haven't broken any cosmic rules.

Yes, there were moments when we first started, when I couldn't help wondering if my breasts looked weird from Jake's angle, if my bikini line was groomed enough for this thong— and by the way, *no* bikini line can be groomed enough for this thong. But every time I caught Jake looking at me, there was so much tender longing in his gaze—part comfortable possessiveness, part unknown thrill—that I soon let all inhibitions go. Which, honestly, I've never done while naked with a man before. Even while having some of what I considered very good sex, I've still been a whole lot in my head.

But I'm not in my head today. I'm in my body. My comfortable, titillated, nearly naked body. And it feels good.

Soon, we've made our way through a flat of tender seedlings, gently ushering dill and tarragon into nourishing new homes. The sun is getting hot, but every time I look over and see my High Life husband's spectacular ass—and see him checking out mine—I get a renewed burst of energy.

I pat down one last seedling into soil, moving in time to "Octopus's Garden."

Our sun-warmed shoulders kiss. It feels as if the whole deck is vibrating with desire. Jake hands me a damp towel to brush the soil off my hands and his elbows. Then, playfully, I brush some invisible soil off his pec, and he reaches around to brush a little off my left cheek. Then my other left cheek. He takes my hand, and we stand up and step into each other's arms. And it feels right. Too right for me to question. Too right for me to rationalize.

"Break time," Jake says, his voice a sexy growl.

Want fills my entire body, but then, I glance over his shoulder at the hill that leads to my home. My real home. I remember my goal and force myself to step away again.

"I was thinking happy hour?" I throw out.

Jake laughs and looks at his watch. "Already?"

"Do you like piña coladas?"

Jake raises an eyebrow. "I like making love at midnight."

"Perfect." I back toward the kitchen. "I'll go whip up a batch."

He looks at me sideways, laughs again.

"What?" I demand.

"You're seriously suggesting that you, Oliva Dusk, are going to walk inside our house, enter our kitchen, and 'whip up a batch' of piña coladas?"

"Um, yes?"

"What's the first thing you need to do?"

"Find the rum?"

"Then?"

"Crack a coconut?"

"You're adorable," Jake says and kisses me on the head. "I'll do it."

I should be happy to have some time to think, to have a little physical space from the man I'm trying to resist. I cross my arms over my chest, feeling somehow more naked now that Jake is gone. I need to find a way to wrap up Deck Day without wrapping my legs around Jake. Is it cruel to call my assistant on a weekend, to see if her sister found Yogi Dan? Where do nudists keep their phones?

Jake steps out from the sliding door, still wearing his briefs, now accessorized with an untied red silk robe. He has a second matching robe draped over one arm—for me. Genius. *That's* where nudists keep their phones. He's holding a tray bearing two frozen white cocktails.

I let him slip the robe over my shoulders, but leave it untied like Jake has done with his. After so long without clothes, the brush of silk against my skin is as erotic as everything else today has been. I really need a drink.

I take a glass from Jake's tray, sit down at our outdoor table, and drain my piña colada in a breath.

"Whoa there, tiger," Jake says, sitting next to me and taking a gulp himself. "But I guess we *have* been working hard." He holds my gaze and smiles. "So, now that I've plied you with alcohol, what should we do next?"

He asks this rhetorically, as if there is only one answer to this question, and the answer requires no words. Luckily the rum pumping into my bloodstream is giving me just the sort of courage I need.

"What do you say we play a game?"

"Which one?"

"Truth or Dare."

"All right." Jake smiles. "Truth."

How did we happen?

Why do you love me?

Where's my mother?

What should I do?

I can't ask what I really want to know. But I can start small with what I've learned in the past two days.

"When you think of . . . Amy Reisenbach," I say, hoping I got her name right. "What first comes to mind?"

Jake takes another sip, then looks at me with deep, complex affection. I want to linger in every layer of it. He's got me on the edge of my silk-robed seat, because somehow, I've struck close to the heart of our story.

"I was scared," Jake says.

Scared is not a side of Jake I've seen. I want to ask a million questions, but I force myself to wait, to listen.

"Don't get me wrong, I was ecstatic for you. Getting discovered by a network head right out of college, just for being yourself at a Yankees game?"

I stare at him, stunned, as he keeps talking.

"The luck required there," he says, scratching his head. "It stills blows my mind."

Does Jake mean what I think he means? The famous Yankee game where real-life Jake got discovered . . . *I* was the lucky one that day? *I* left the Bronx with the life-changing job opportunity? It's a memory I'm dying to access, unpack, and examine from different angles. But all I can do is hear Jake out.

"Good old Section 15B, Row 2, Seat 9," Jake says, in a haunted tone that confirms that in another world that seat was meant for him. I took Jake's seat at the baseball game, then I took his place in life.

"After that game," he says, "life looked so different from everything we'd planned. I'd just started at the *Times*—"

"The *New York Times*?" I balk accidently out loud.

Jake worked at the *Times* after college? Like the yearbook said he would?

He laughs, like I've made an old inside joke. "And you were beginning to audition on Broadway . . ."

Like the yearbook said I would.

"You'd gotten twelve callbacks . . ."

"But no offers," I fill in. It's just a guess, but Jake nods.

"And of course," he says, "your loan payments . . ."

"Right," I gulp. "Of course. Those. They were . . ."

"Huge."

What loan is Jake talking about? In my real life, there had been no loan to pay back, because there had been no Juilliard. Only a hard conversation with Lorena at the kitchen table two weeks after my dad died. I closed the door on my plans, and that was that. I try to imagine what I'd done differently here.

"So when Amy made you the *Zombie Hospital* offer," Jake continues, "we chucked it all, flew out to LA, and six years later, here we are."

"But *why*?" I blurt out.

"Why . . . what?"

"Why did you just . . . give up your dream? You had a great job—"

"I'd always wanted to learn to surf—"

"Jake. I'm serious."

"You know the answer, Liv," he says and puts a hand on my knee. "I didn't think of it as giving up my dream. I thought of it as an adventure. I told you, on the very first night we got together, that I believe when a person finds something they love this much, they should shape their life around it."

Jake did tell me that, but in the version I remember, he was speaking about my acting.

"I found you," he says today. "I'm *glad* I was naive about journalism out here, about the jobs I'd be able to get. Remember those two weeks when I was a paparazzo?" The squeeze of his hand sends heat up my thigh.

I laugh, but only because I know it's my cue to laugh. Jake worked for the paparazzi? That sounds awful. Completely dispiriting. How could he not resent me, after going from the *New York Times* to *TMZ*? The irony that this man, object of the paparazzi's gaze in my real life, *worked* as one, however briefly, here . . . it's too much.

"I knew then what I know now," he's saying. "That I'd found the most important thing. The rest of it I'd figure out, as long as I had you."

"You don't regret—"

"A thing," he says without a moment's hesitation.

It makes me think of how, just a few days ago, in my mother's garage, I'd used the same words about not going to Juilliard. I didn't regret it. Can it really be that Jake doesn't regret this life either? Can it be that when you love someone, no matter what life deals you, you still win?

"Besides," Jake says, "if I'd stayed a staff writer in New York, the podcasting world would have been deprived of all this." He spreads his arms and laughs.

I take him in, gorgeous in his robe and ridiculous briefs. I can't tell how deep his joke runs at his own expense. I wish that he knew what I knew, about the life he could have had if things had gone just slightly differently.

If he'd sat in Seat 9 at the Yankees game that day.

"Olivia," he says, almost but not quite reading my mind. "If *you'd* passed on *Zombie Hospital*, if we'd never come out to LA, you always would have wondered: What if I'd taken my big shot?"

I'm holding my breath because the parallels and missed connections are too insane to process. In this life, I pulled him away from the career he'd originally wanted. Now he's trying to find the job he's meant to have—and judging from last night, he's every bit as good at connecting with people as he is in Real Life—only somehow, he hasn't caught his break.

I can't help feeling this is all my fault. I can't help wanting to fix it. In this realm, I'm the only person who appreciates Jake's potential. And that feels criminal.

"I think this podcast is going to be good for me," Jake says. "I know you weren't wild about it at first, for obvious reasons ..."

He nods, and I nod back, like I have a clue what he's talking about. What reasons would I have for not wanting him to do a podcast?

I feel unmoored by all that I don't know about our recent past. I feel surprised by how much I *want* to know it, sad that I don't think I ever will.

"You have a gift, Jake," I say. "You know that, right? You have this way of connecting with people, of lighting up a crowd. Last night—"

"That was nothing."

"I'm serious."

"Thanks, Liv. You always see the best in me." He meets my eyes. He's not placating me, but also, he doesn't know the things I know. He hasn't seen the Jake I've seen.

He looks out across the canyon. "Maybe by the time our firstborn can talk, they won't have to say, 'Daddy's a bum.' They can proclaim, 'Daddy only has ten subscribers, but he's sure proud of that podcast.'"

"Sounds like a pretty judgmental kid," I say. "Maybe they should take a look in the mirror at the back of their car seat now and then."

Jake laughs, but I feel an enormous weight settle over me. I'm not staying in this life, but this version of Jake—this tender, open, dazzler of a man—*is* staying here.

And I'm not sure he's thinking big enough.

I decide that for as long as I'm stuck here in the High Life, I will do some good. I want to help Jake get what he deserves. Maybe not *Everything's Jake*, but some version of it—a career where he's celebrated for his charms, for his preternatural gift of connecting with people, of connecting them with one another. A vehicle that gets his gorgeous face and soul on camera, like they were meant to be.

The world I come from is partly powered by Jake Glasswell— by moments where he made someone's day brighter, someone's long-lost friend pick up the phone, someone's fiancée say *yes*, so many someones' lives a better place. And I'm going to bring it to the High Life.

"Hey, Liv," Jake says, startling me from my schemes.

"Huh?"

"Truth or dare?"

Oh great.

There's no way I'll get a truth right, so I say the dreaded "Dare."

Jake settles back in his chair with a smile. He presses something on his phone, and Marvin Gaye's "Let's Get It On" begins to play.

"Dare you to give me a lap dance."

I know I need to keep a safe physical distance between Jake's body and my own. But when he looks at me like that, his green eyes on fire—for me—I find myself slowly rising from my chair.

"Don't miss the chorus," he says as Marvin winds down the first verse of the song.

I step toward him, half clad in my silk robe, laughing and

fizzing with a nervous thrill. I stand with my legs on either side of his. He runs a hand up my thigh and I shiver.

Okay, fine, I want this man. I want all the sex there is from him. And I'm terrified, because he loves me, and to sleep with him feels like it would be cheating on the woman he believes he's married to. So I shouldn't. But I also don't know if I can stop myself, because goddamn, when I sit down he almost catapults me across the canyon. There's practically no way to adjust in his lap without coming.

He grabs my neck and pulls me close until we're just about to kiss, and this is *it*. The moment when I'll finally know what it was like, that bolt of lightning that changed our lives, the vital flashing root of everything.

My phone comes to life somewhere nearby. The ringtone is "Tossing and Turning" by the Ivy League.

Jake exhales a groan and says, "Let it go to voicemail—"

But I take this interruption as a sign and leap up. I find the phone in my crumpled sweatpants. I look at the contact photo on the screen.

Ivy. On a unicycle. Apparently at Burning Man.

"I have to take this," I say and run to the far side of the pool.

"Ivy," I say into the phone. "Did you match the plates?"

"Are you on a run? You sound really out of breath."

"No. I'm fine, I just . . . never mind. What'd you find? Who is he?"

"The car is registered to a T. Lennox of Eugene, Oregon—"

"Roger that," I say. So Yogi Rabbi Dan's real name is T. Lennox. I'll find him. I'll make him take me home.

I look back at Jake, at the beautiful garden on our deck, and I can't help feeling pride at our accomplishment. I can see that Jake's proud too, his bare feet tapping to Marvin as he surveys the job.

"Olivia?" Ivy's voice comes through the phone.

"What! Yes?"

"T. Lennox is Ms. Teri Lennox. A dental hygienist."

"Right," I say. "Eugene, hygiene, we all Gene for ice cream. Teri must have a husband or a brother—"

"Olivia, the car was reported stolen five days ago. I'm sorry. The plates are a dead end."

—

Chapter Seventeen

"THE HIPPOCRATIC OATH APPLIES TO ZOMBIES, TOO," I growl at a freckle-faced eight-year-old the following morning.

The kid stares at me for a moment, then his lip trembles and he erupts into sobs. "But he ate my mommy!"

"Cut," the director calls from behind her chair. "That was . . . convincing. Did I say that? I'm stunned. You're both free till after lunch."

Blushing with a bit of pride, I put a hand on the kid's shoulder. "You okay? Did I push too hard?"

"Lois!" the kid yells. "She's touching me again—"

"Olivia, please," the director says. "Buster's asked you several times."

I don't know why I'm relieved by this continuity with my High Life self, or why I was relieved yesterday when Ivy called to give me her bad news. Or why I felt relieved for the rest of the afternoon, laughing and dancing with Jake while finishing Deck Day, until we collapsed into bed, too physically exhausted to do anything but sleep.

I'm still going to find Yogi Rabbi Dan. I'm still going to make him take me home. This is just a temporary setback. But if I must endure more time in the High Life, so be it. Now that I have a vision for getting Jake's career on track, I'd like to see that plan get started. Then I'll feel right about going back, happy that in every version of the multiverse I know, Jake enjoys his just desserts. I can leave feeling like our two souls are karmically cool because of the kindness we shared here.

I head toward my trailer. I should go over my new lines for the afternoon. But the only lines I want to run are the ones I have for Jake. The story he told about us yesterday on the deck answered one question about the state of our careers but raised so many others about our life these last ten years.

What other curveballs did life throw at us? Why did we have our biggest fight, and how did we get past it? What was the best weekend getaway we ever took, and what was the worst? What do we write in our anniversary cards to each other? Where do we dream of retiring?

When Jake looks at me, I see the stored treasure of all the life we've shared together. It's in his eyes and in the words he whispers to me half asleep, and I can't help feeling jealous that I don't have some of that treasure myself.

Even if it isn't real.

"Bad boy! Bad!" a voice scolds inside my trailer. With trepidation, I open the door and see Aurora's back. She's crouched down near the floor and wagging a reprimanding finger at—

My legs go weak as I take in a tiny white terrier mutt with an underbite. "Gram Parsons?!"

Aurora whirls around and stands, scooping up the dog—*my* dog—in one hand. With the other she pats her newly short hair self-consciously.

"Okay, you hate the cut," she says, looking hurt. "I was going for Florence Pugh, not Gram Parsons—"

"No, the dog—" I hold my hands out. It's all I can do not to snatch him from her arms.

"Ugh, meet Tito," she says. "My awful sister randomly moved to Sun Valley this weekend and dumped this gremlin on me."

"I can't believe it," I breathe.

"I know, right? She doesn't understand"—Aurora gestures between us—"*we* can't be beholden to a dog. Our work is our life. And when we leave here at the end of each day, there's nothing left in the tank for some micro turd factory—"

"May I hold him? Please?"

"Be my guest." Aurora plants Gram Parsons in my arms. "Watch out, he pees."

I turn to mush feeling his warm weight. I dissolve in a storm of his kisses. It feels so good to hold my dog I begin to cry—silently, blinking madly because I don't want to explain it to Aurora. Not that she'd notice, anyway.

I scratch Gram Parsons under his chin, and he locks my hand there. I soften into his brown gaze, feeling a peace I haven't known for days, a peace that used to be available any time I wanted. But instead of making me homesick, a strange instinct finds my heart: I want to introduce Gram Parsons to Jake Glasswell.

"I'll take him off your hands," I tell Aurora.

"What?" she says. "Why?"

"I like dogs."

Aurora seems suspicious.

"And because," I say, "we're friends. And I know you have so much on your plate with, uh—"

"My birthday plans?" she whispers, touching fingers to her chest.

"Such a big event," I say.

"Thank you for seeing me." Aurora's now blinking back tears herself.

"I do," I say. "And you're enough."

Gram Parson's goes belly up in my arms.

"Should we get wasted tonight at Soho House?" Aurora sniffles. "Or you know what—I just joined the Mulholland Tennis Club. We could wear tiny skirts and sneak margaritas on the court."

"Let me check my calendar," I say, pulling out my phone until I can make something up. Then I see I really do have plans.

Baseball Playoffs vs. Cardinals. North Weddington Park. 6:00 p.m.

Jake and I play in a baseball league? Of course we're in the playoffs. I picture Jake in tight polyester pants and—

"Olivia?" Aurora snaps her fingers in my face.

"I can't tonight. I've got a baseball game with Jake."

She gags. "When are you going to divorce that loser?"

I stare at her. "What did you just say?"

"Oh honey, I'm kidding!" she coos. "I mean, I'm kidding if you want me to be." Aurora looks me up and down. "Because you know there are other teams that would love to have you ride their bench."

"You can stop talking now."

She waves me off. "You always get like this when I rag on Jake. I simply want the best for you. For you to know *real life*. Imagine combining your income with another big earner's wad—"

"Please leave," I say and open the trailer door. "Now."

"I appreciate your feeling safe enough with me to express your marital frustrations—"

"*I'm happy,*" I say with savage intensity. I'd only meant to shut her up, but the words feel true. I'm happy in my marriage to Jake Glasswell. Not the real me, of course, but the me who ended up married to him. She likes it. She has fun and feels safe. She sleeps well and eats well and laughs a lot and sends flirty texts for no reason and looks forward to what otherwise would be considered extremely tedious household maintenance.

She's in love. And she is stronger for that love.

"Okay, I'm out," Aurora says. "My sensual masseuse is waiting in my trailer."

I slam the door behind her, fall onto my papasan, and cuddle with Gram Parsons.

"Wag your tail twice if you know me from another life," I whisper in his soft, gray ear.

Lo and behold, he does.

......

DRIVING TO NORTH Weddington Park that evening, I'm feeling good. Gram Parsons is riding shotgun, and I'm about to play my favorite sport on the same field where I used to play as a kid.

I've left a message with Amy Reisenbach's assistant about setting up a lunch to broach the topic of Jake's career. I asked Ivy to call Masha's mother to get Yogi Rabbi Dan's contact info. Plans are falling into place. But as I head north on

Lankershim, my eyes fall on a billboard that almost makes me
flip my car.

I pull over and park beneath a huge ad for a podcast called
Call Your Mother. I stare at it. I blink. On the left side of the billboard is my mother's image, thirty feet tall and airbrushed. She's
wearing her favorite ombre mai tai outfit, complete with the
purple orchid behind her ear.

On the right side of the billboard is a woman I don't recognize. She's closer to my age, her hair is dyed the same shade of
red as Lorena's, and her outfit's accordingly mai tai'd.

"Mom, what's going on?" I dry-heave as I type the title of
the podcast into my phone.

There are 170 episodes. The show has over two million reviews.

Mom isn't dead. She's a star. And for reasons unknown, she
doesn't speak to me. What have I done?

My plans to stay in the High Life a little longer swerve from
feeling like an altruistic lark—leave the world a little better than
you found it!—to a miserable ordeal—face what a pariah you've
become!

By the time I pull into the parking lot at the field, I'm shaking. I've listened to the first ten minutes of Mom's this-world
podcast and I have to admit, it's genius. Instead of a review of
other people's thoughts, Lorena offers her own self-help, and
people call in from around the world to seek advice. She's as
masterful at helping strangers as she is at helping me.

"Where are you calling from, sugar?" my mom says in the
episode.

"Hot Springs, Arkansas."

"I once won a bundle on a pony in Hot Springs," my mom says. "What's your question, sweetheart?"

"I'm attracted to the preacher at my church."

"We've got a hot one here, Silver!"

Silver—that's the name of Mom's matching cohost—is me but better. She's quirky and smart, and she's on the mic as much as Mom. Their banter seems to charm their listeners as much as it infuriates me.

"Can I ask what this luscious lector looks like?" Silver chimes in.

"Luscious lector!" Lorena hoots. "Listen to our resident poet, Hot Springs! Have I mentioned Silver's been nominated for a *Pushcart*?"

How can Mom do this without me? How can she brag about Silver's success in the tone she uses to tell her mah-jongg friends about *me*? How can she be maternal to the world but not her own daughter?

The agony I feel at listening to Lorena dole out advice to other people on this podcast explains my apparent reluctance about Jake starting his own podcast. Suddenly, the very word *podcast* feels like an open laceration on my heart.

By the time I park at the baseball field, my anxiety is through the sunroof. I put my head in my hands and take Gram Parsons in my lap, so grateful he's found me in time for my moment of need. I feel ashamed that I've been so wrapped up in Jake, in my bizarro role on a bad TV show, in this strange life I've been try-ing on, that I neglected to confront what should have been ob-vious all along under the High Life surface.

That something is rotten here between my mom and me.

That Lorena isn't dead, that I'm dead to her. But where did we go wrong?

Kissing Jake wouldn't make my mom hate me, but some aftershock must have done it.

A moment from my conversation yesterday with Jake returns to me. Casually, he'd mentioned something about a loan.

A loan I had to pay back. A loan I'd taken out to go to Juilliard? That didn't happen in real life.

What happened in real life, after graduation, was my mom sat me down at the kitchen table for a talk. I knew what was coming. I knew our income had dipped after Dad's death. I was stunned when Lorena said she'd spoken to a realtor. She offered to downsize from her house to an apartment so she could help pay for tuition.

We sat at the table and cried. I was moved by her offer, especially after we'd spent senior year fighting about where I'd go to college. But I couldn't let her sell the house, couldn't even imagine leaving home so soon after Dad's death. That day, I decided to make family my priority for a while. I would stay with Lorena and grieve. Juilliard didn't allow deferrals, but maybe I'd try again in a year . . .

It didn't happen. I didn't regret it.

That was real life, but what happened here? I picture that same kitchen table conversation—only this time, I'm in love with Jake.

Did I leave home against Lorena's wishes? Did I take out a loan without her help or consent?

Did the distance between my mother and me grow instead of shrink? So that every misunderstanding began to feel like a snub?

Is that how, ten years later, the two of us are estranged?

"Olivia?"

I jump, wiping my eyes.

Jake's rapping on my window, wearing a jersey that reads *Yankees*, and baseball pants that fit precisely as I'd hoped. He's a little sweaty, a little grass-stained, and entirely delicious. I roll the window down.

"You're here!" He sounds amazed, excited, like he hadn't just seen me this morning. Like we hadn't spent all day together yesterday. He reads my expression and his face changes. "What's wrong?"

I sniff. There's no way to broach this topic here; all I can do is put Lorena out of my mind for now and remember that I'll be going home soon, where I can hug her and thank her for loving me.

"Allergies," I tell Jake, switching gears. I lift my special guest in my arms. "Meet Gram Parsons, your new mascot."

Jake laughs and shakes Gram Parsons's paw. "Where'd you come from, handsome?"

"I rescued him from a pound called Aurora."

"Did you name him?" Jake asks and takes me in his arms. Gram Parsons seems to enjoy this, too.

"It came to me from another realm," I say.

"We should take him to Joshua Tree," Jake says, "and let him commune with the ghost of his namesake."

I hug Jake back and look into his eyes. "How do you always know the right thing to say?"

"Practice," he says.

And there it is, a thousand layers of relationship history.

That Jake knows how to put my troubled mind at ease feels like a gift. I'll take it.

"This is a nice surprise," he says. "I didn't think you were coming."

I blink, confused. It's in the calendar. "You want to win, don't you?"

When he laughs, I frown. Am I not on the team? Why wouldn't I be on the team? Is that why I couldn't find any left-handed gloves or cleats my size in the garage?

"We're probably going to forfeit anyway," Jake says.

"For-*what*?" I say. "I'm not familiar with the word."

"Eli and Masha are on their honeymoon—"

Ding ding ding. There's the ugly answer. My High Life husband plays my favorite sport without me because my Real Life BBS cannot stand High Life me.

"And Vic called in sick. So we're down to eight."

"Sounds like Mudville needs a hero," I say, needing to channel my pain and confusion into something useful, something physical. I kiss my biceps and say, "Put me in, Coach. These pythons are ready to squeeze out some ribbies."

. . . . . .

DUSK IS FALLING and the field lights are coming on when the umpire shouts, "Play ball!" The scent of fresh cut grass is rich on the light spring wind, and I'm transported back to my youth, to my happiest days spent on these fields.

I'm playing catcher, which gives me a front row seat to Jake's deft pitching. I watch his muscles twist and tighten, hear the grunt that accompanies each exertion, the grunt that sounds just before Jake shows me what he's got. I'm sweating and not just because of the gear.

Gram Parsons jumps nervously at the first few balls coming his way. But soon he grows accustomed to the excitement, lies down, and takes a nap. I knew he'd be groovy. As in one world, so in the other.

The sting of Jake's ball whacking my glove hurts so good. We're flirting as we play, but we're also so in sync that it's three up, three down in the first two innings.

In the third inning, we're batting, two outs, and I hit a deep pop fly to center field. I run, hearing Jake cheer when my ball drops before the outfielder can reach it. I round first and slide in safe at second. My heart is pounding, my legs strained with the effort of running faster than I knew I could.

Jake steps up to the plate. My body is keenly attuned to his, watching the way his knees bend, watching the twist of his shoulders, knowing what he'll do before he does it. On his second pitch, the catcher drops the ball, and I take third. Jake grins at me from home. We can almost taste the first run of the game. When Jake swings at the next pitch, I feel it in my nervous system, the winning connection between us as he lines the ball into shallow right. They throw him out at first, but not before I cross the plate and put the Yankees up by one.

At the top of the seventh and final inning, Jake calls me to the mound for a huddle.

"What's the plan?" I say.

"You give me three more outs, then I make you come three times behind our favorite tree."

I look over his shoulder at what I can only assume is the

thick-trunked jacaranda he means. It does look sufficiently secluded, its branches reaching out for the LA River.

"That's," I breathe, "very celebratory."

Walking back to home plate, I'm nervous. I want what Jake
just promised.

But my mind is crowded with victories and failures, with
Masha playing on this team without me, with my mom making
a successful podcast with a more supportive version of her
daughter. With what I did to Jake when I sat in his seat at Yankee
Stadium.

How can he love the woman I am here?

Thwack.

The sound snaps me back to focus. It's a deep pop fly, almost to the fence. Our left fielder is running, but she'll never
catch it. It drops, bounces, and the runner is already rounding
second before the outfielder hits the relay at short. By then I'm
ready, blocking home plate, my glove open, waiting. The ball
sails toward me, and I'm poised perfectly to catch it, so I let myself glance quickly at the runner—just as he slams into me and
the ball finds my glove.

I close my glove around the ball and extend it toward the
runner, and I know I tagged him before I realize I'm also flying
backward, landing with a thud on the back of my skull.

· · · · · ·

"OLIVIA? OLIVIA!"

The voice is muffled, far away. It's familiar but I'm not
sure how.

Then the warm wet tongue I'd know anywhere. Gram

Parsons is kissing my face. I open my eyes and see his kind expression, and for a moment I think I might be home—in my
Real Life, with my real dog.

"Olivia."

I blink my eyes open and see Jake. He looks so worried, then
so ecstatic. His eyes are damp with tears.

"Thank God."

"Jake."

He lies down next to me, his head against my chest.

"Did we get him out?" I ask.

Jake laughs and wipes his eyes. "Yeah, baby. You clinched
the playoffs."

"Let's hit the jacaranda."

"I think maybe you should rest up first."

I reach up and touch Jake's face. He looks so emotional. I
need to reassure him.

I reach for the neck of his jersey. Now's the moment. I'm
going to kiss him. I'm going to—

"Olivia, do you know what day it is?" the woman asking me
the question plays third base on our team. Dr. Lindsay. She
takes my hand, the hand that was reaching to pull Jake in for a
kiss. "Don't sit up. How many fingers am I holding up?"

"Five of mine and three of yours—"

Fifteen minutes of questioning and examinations later, I
pass the test, but Dr. Lindsay isn't convinced she should leave
Jake and me to our al fresco congress. Apparently I was unconscious for longer than she's comfortable with.

She pulls Jake aside and I hear the two of them discuss my
pupils, about whether or not I should go to the ER. Mostly, I'm

watching Jake's face as he makes decisions about my care. It's nurturing to see him taking charge. If I weren't so tired and dizzy, this would turn me on.

"Olivia, I'm going to keep my phone on tonight, and Jake's going to stay in touch with me. If anything changes—vomiting or blurry vision—I want you to go to the ER. Hopefully by tomorrow, if you get lots of rest, you'll only have a headache."

I thank Dr. Lindsay, and Jake and I wave to the rest of the team as they file to their cars.

"Playoffs!" I call weakly.

"Do you want me to carry you to the car?" Jake asks once we're alone.

I glance around the field, beautiful and empty. I'm not ready to leave just yet.

"Can we stay awhile?"

He smiles and lies down next to me on home plate, propping his duffel bag under our heads. The stars are coming out, and Gram Parsons snuggles between us.

Jake fits his hand in mine. "Your one game and this happens. I'm sorry—"

I turn onto my side to face him. "This doesn't have to be a one-time thing."

"I'd love that," Jake says. "But what about your schedule? And . . . Masha?"

The mention of my best friend's name conjures immediate happiness . . . which one second later turns to pain.

But who says this fight with Masha has to be permanent? Who says I can't win her and my mom back?

For a moment, I can see it—this life but with its biggest

problems fixed, its gaping holes filled with love and laughter—
and I don't mind it.

"I'd want Masha to be comfortable, obviously," I say to Jake.
"More than that. I want to be friends again."

His smile spurs me on.

"Did I wreck things too much to salvage them?" I ask him.

He runs his fingers gently through my hair and traces my
features tenderly with his eyes. "You can fix it. I know you can."

I hold on to his wrist. "There are a lot of good things in this
life." My voice is a whisper, my lips a feather brush from his.

"Yes, there are," he says.

"And there are things that could be better."

"Always."

"I want to make them better."

"Anything you want," he says and leans in closer. "Everything you want, Olivia."

"Everything?" The question slips out. The suggestive tone
in my voice is involuntary. We're this close to kissing. One more
fraction of an inch, and my lips—

"Everything," he says, his hands gliding up my thighs.
"Well, everything but that."

"Huh?" My heart plummets like a rock in the LA River. My
hands and feet grow cold. I feel like I'm back on that curb at
prom and Jake's telling me this would be a waste.

"For twenty-four hours," he says. "Doctor's orders."

"No," I whine, though I'm relieved at the reason.

"No hard or sudden, rhythmic, pounding motions for
twenty-four hours."

I look at him with fury, then I laugh.

Jake's eyes light up playfully. He takes out my phone, sets a timer, presses go. He thumbs my lip, sending a lick of pleasure through me as he says, "When this goes off, it's Sex O'Clock. And I'm going for the record."

Coyly I say, "And which record might that be?"

"The one where you came five times in a single night."

"You better call Cooperstown," I say. "They're gonna want a witness."

Chapter Eighteen

I'M NOT ONE OF THOSE PEOPLE WHO PUTS A LOT OF effort into planning sex. Not the way I spent months at the mercy of the night Jake and I almost kissed, overanalyzing it to undeath. Never again will I torture my mind like that.

I'm not eighteen anymore. I'm a woman who knows what she wants, and what she wants is to fuck her husband of many years for the first time.

I do have one fear. There's so much baggage baked into Jake and me—there's his version of our relationship, there's my version, and there's this new version of the past few days. But if I'm going to get horizontal and vulnerable with Jake . . . won't he figure out that something's changed?

. . . . . .

THE MORNING AFTER my concussion gets off to a good start. I was told to expect a headache, but my pituitary gland seems to be secreting enough libido to blot out all other feelings. For breakfast Jakes makes an egg white, avocado, and tofu scramble, with creamy Groundwork espresso and homemade reverse osmosis soda water on the side.

Walking onto set I'm aglow with arousal, and I feel like

people can tell. I know I'm even more distracted than usual, but honestly, who could work under such conditions? Every time I glance at my phone and see our countdown—nine hours, eighteen minutes, and twenty-seven churning seconds—I imagine Jake watching the same countdown on his phone. I imagine him imagining me. Sprawled across a bed. For him.

I keep remembering last night, lying on home plate, under the stars, the slow drag of his fingers up my thigh while we talked. The touch of our chests as we turned to each other. The ache when he said we had to wait. I keep wondering how serious he is about breaking our record.

I can't believe a few days ago I feared Jake fucking me. Now I'm scared of what will happen if he doesn't do it soon enough. I feel like a violin string about to snap.

I haven't been here long enough to judge whether High Life Olivia and High Life Jake have a perfect marriage, but they may just have perfect chemistry. The kind that stays through all the work marriage requires. It's something I've never really known I could pull off myself. When things have gotten hard in my relationships, I've tended to say good riddance and suggest we both step back, usually for good. The reward has never seemed worth the hassle, worth the vulnerability and hope.

But something happened with Jake in this life and I never stepped away. Something signaled I could let go of my fears and stay. Something told me I could live the dream.

"You-need-to-let-me-treat-my-patient," I rush my line at the eight-year-old who's again in today's scene. Here's a tidbit you won't read in *The Hollywood Reporter*: Buster's not *that* good an actor that he can cry when I'm not pushing him too far.

"Olivia?" Lois says, stifling a laugh. "Let's try that again. Like you actually want to treat someone."

"Right," I say. "Got it."

Buster rolls his eyes.

"Places, everyone," Lois says. Then: "Action!"

"*You* need to let *me* treat my *patient*!" I scream, totally unhinged.

This time Lois can't stop her laughter. The crew is also amused.

"Let's break for lunch," Lois announces. She walks up to me and adds, "Why don't you go meditate or something."

Then I'm back in my trailer, with an entire hour alone with my sex-thoughts. How have I never thought to check our texts for dirty pics? I take out my phone, scroll backward through our exchanges, and sure enough there's a Christmas mistletoe dick pic that takes my breath away. I stare at it for ⅛ of a second before I click the phone to black.

This is not the way I want to experience him the first time. I want the real thing. Breaking records left and right.

I picture us back in that marvelous bed. I want to be there—need to be there. But in my fantasy, when I make my first reach for him—I freeze. He's going to notice something's different. He's going to feel that everything about me is new at touching him.

My mother's voice blasts into my thoughts, welcomingly unsolicited: *And this is a problem . . . why?*

Because he's slept with High Life Olivia thousands of times, but he's never been with *me*. And so, with seven hours, thirty-one minutes, and twelve seconds until Sex O'Clock, I decide to introduce an element of surprise. Something spicy. Something distracting—so that Jake won't notice that the thing that's new between our sheets is me.

. . . . . .

SEX O'CLOCK FINDS me sipping a dirty martini at Bar 1200 in the lobby of the Sunset Marquis, a place I've long thought is the sexiest lounge in town—low red leather booths and candle-light, potent classic cocktails, vinyl crackling through the speakers in the walls, and attractive, hungry people on the make.

I check my text for the thousandth time.

> Jake, this is Olivia Dusk. I hope this isn't too forward, but I got your number from a friend. She thinks we'd really hit it off. If you're not afraid of a blind date, I'll be at Bar 1200 at eight tonight.

He made me wait six excruciating minutes before those three reassuring text-dots appeared, followed by:

> See you there, Ms. Dusk. I look forward to making your acquaintance.

I'm wearing a black dress I grabbed at Bloomingdale's in the Grove on my way here. Tight, cinched, ruched, short—it's the kind of thing any straightish man on earth would like. I've dressed it up with bare legs, strappy red stilettos, and a chic lack of panties.

I've got on less makeup than I think High Life Olivia wears, and my hair's in a simple sleek ponytail, rather than the wavy blowout favored in the photos of actress-me online. So as I sit here, munching on the olive in my drink, and I catch a glimpse of myself in the smoked mirror behind the bar, I look more like Real Life me than I have since I arrived. As nervous as I am, this makes me more at ease.

"Olivia Dusk?"

I turn, and there he is in a crisp pin-striped suit that makes him look—for a moment—like Glasswell, the talk show host I used to love to hate. This connection makes me nervous, makes me wonder if I've made a mistake . . .

But then he smiles, and it's all there—the real Jake. The Jake I've gotten to know these past few days.

"You *are* Olivia Dusk, right?" He's doing a spot-on impersonation of someone starstruck and nervous. He even acts like he's blushing, like he can't find the right words.

"I could be," I say and look him up and down.

"I'm Jake. Jake Glasswell."

"Jake Glasswell," I say. "What a pleasure." I put my hand in his, expecting a shake, but he draws my fingers to his mouth and presses his lips to my skin—slowly, holding my eyes the whole time.

"The pleasure's mine," he says and slides onto the empty barstool beside me. He signals the bartender—"I'll have what she's having"—then spins toward me so our knees are overlapping. "I'm having the strangest sense of déjà vu," he says. "Have we met somewhere before?"

I twirl the toothpick in my drink and take a sip. "Maybe inside a bubble in Ibiza?"

"Where did you go to high school?"

"Palisades. Class of '14."

"What a coincidence," he says, narrowing his eyes. "Me too."

"Big school," I say.

"Enormous," he whispers, shifting to run his knee up my thigh.

"But I think I remember you," I say, teasing. "In fact, I'm pretty sure you used to be cute."

"Oh no," he says, but he recovers quickly, propping an elbow on the bar and leaning in to say: "In me thou see'st the glowing of such fire that on the ashes of his youth doth lie."

I swallow. Did this fine-as-hell man just quote a Shakespearean sonnet at me? I could kiss him. I could—wait. I remind myself of the game we're playing and try to project cool.

"You should take something for that."

He smirks, plays with the stirrer in his drink. "Didn't you play Juliet senior year?"

"That's right. While you were sliding past first base."

"So, you remember I played baseball? The truth is, I only tried out because the catcher was hot. But then, mysteriously, she quit."

"Maybe she was sick of wading through your fan club of sophomore girls to get to the dugout."

"Never happened," Jake says, "or at least I never saw them."

"That's why I quit debate, too."

"What?" He blinks. "I definitely did not have a debate fan club."

"No, but Mr. Saltzman thought you were the best. Before you showed up, I was the captain. Then suddenly, I was the co-."

I meet his eyes. "I was pretty mad at you for a lot of high school," I say, dropping my sex-growl, dropping the High Life, telling it like it was. "You were just . . . everywhere. And I thought, back then, that you were trying to outdo me."

"*Outdo* you?" He sounds stunned. "I was trying to be near you, to breathe the same air as you. I wasn't trying to compete with you. I was trying to compete *for* you. I was trying to get you to notice me."

"I noticed you," I whisper.

"And then there was that one night," he says.

"That changed things," I say.

"Prom."

"I thought you were going to kiss me on the curb," I say.

Jake flinches slightly, still trying to play the game, trying to inhabit the reality I'm painting—one where we didn't kiss, one where we parted ways. His face darkens as I watch him imagine it. His whole life if that kiss hadn't occurred.

"Not kissing you, Olivia," he says in an earnest, impassioned, breathy voice, "was the biggest mistake of my life. The only saving grace . . ."

There's a long pause while we stare at each other.

"The only saving grace . . ." I offer to him again.

"Is that if I'd kissed you at eighteen, I wouldn't have known what to do with you."

"What are you saying, Jake?"

"I'm saying that ten years later, I know *exactly* what to do with you."

My body thrums as I take Jake by the lapels. I stare into his eyes, heart racing, knowing—at last—that this is it. I lean in slowly, then all at once, and kiss Jake Glasswell like I should have done ten years ago.

When our mouths meet, I understand. The way his lower lip fits between mine. He tastes salty from his drink. He smells like a rainforest. His hands know where to hold me and how firmly. Though my eyes are closed, I *see*. How this kiss changed everything. How love launches ships and world religions. Kissing Jake Glasswell is that good, that right. Across every universe, in every distant crease of time, this is the kiss against which to judge all others.

We don't make it out of the bar before his mouth is on my neck, his teeth sinking into my skin, my hands all over him. We tumble through the lobby, crashing into a coat rack, not giving half a damn as we career past the front desk.

"Olivia!" a bright British accent calls. "Are you alright?"

I turn and see who dares interrupt us. "Not now, Eddie Redmayne!" I call and pull Jake's mouth to mine.

"Did you get a room?" Jake gasps. I take his tie and tug him toward the stairs that lead to the suites above the pool.

"Wait," he says, stopping one step beneath the one I'm on.

"What?" I almost shout because I can no longer wait. Not if he left his card at the bar. Not if he needs to grab some sort of contraceptive. Not if the hotel's on fire.

But it turns out the holdup is that Jake noticed the color of the panties I'm not wearing, and he needs to push me against the wall and put his hands and his mouth all over me. *That* I can stand here all night waiting for.

"Let's go," he says, and I'm seeing stars as he pulls me toward the hall.

Somehow I manage to find my key card, and then Jake lifts me up and takes me toward the bedroom, pausing in the living room to give Gram Parsons's chin a scratch.

"Hi, buddy," he says, and I love him for not questioning why I brought a dog to our tryst, why I couldn't leave him alone in that big house without us all night.

Jake throws, and I mean throws, me on the bed. The black dress with buttons running up the center becomes a shred. The rip it makes between Jake's hands is the hottest sound I've ever heard.

As I lie beneath him, fully naked, and his gaze holds mine, I thank God we waited. I pull him to me, yank his tie over his head, unbutton his shirt, and feel that first drop of hot muscled skin on mine. I can't believe we've only been married for five days. Because this feels like a lifetime of making love.

He drops between my legs and puts his mouth on me, gently tugging until I twist the sheets and scream. As his tongue finds every sensitive fold, I feel how well he knows me. Like he's the one who drew the atlas of my pleasure. He takes his time, letting me feel how much he likes this work, letting me sink into an ever deeper state of bliss. Then the pressure of his mouth changes, warm and wet and right there on the very center of my clit, and all at once Jake brings me to a gasping orgasm, the likes of which I've never known. And intend to know better from now on.

I lie in sweaty ecstasy as he comes up next to me, kissing a path up my side. We're still and basking, tracing shapes on each other's arms, and then I'm greedy to give him what he just gave me.

I decide not to worry that I don't know Jake's tastes like he knows mine. I'll make up for lack of expertise with overwhelming zeal. Which comes naturally when I'm face-to-face with his beautiful, beautiful cock. I can't believe he gets to keep this with him all the time. I trace my tongue around his tip, then I taste his full length, before pumping him with double fists and taking both of his balls deep in my mouth.

"You're amazing, Olivia," he says above me, and I sense what to do next. I take him fully in my mouth and suck firmly until he grasps my hair and pulls and lets out the sexiest groan I've ever heard.

"Wait," he says and pulls away moments before I know I would have tasted him. It's a deprivation I can't endure for long.

"What?"

"I need to be inside you. I need you. All around me."

"You don't have to ask me twice," I say, smiling at him, "but please do."

He mounts me, bringing the tip of his huge dick to my entrance. "I need your perfect cunt, Olivia. Can I have it, please?"

"Yes," I whisper, and then, as he thrusts all the way inside me, my whispers turn to screams. "Yes. You can."

My next orgasm erupts, and this time I share it with Jake. He comes with the deepest, hottest thrusts before collapsing on top of me. I lie there for a moment, in a haze of lust and magic, and everything feels new, like we're the first people ever to make love, the first people ever to inhale.

Jake pulls me into his arms, tips my chin and kisses me. Crazy after how rough we've just played that he can be so tender, that he can be so kind.

"Olivia?" he asks.

I nod, gazing into his eyes.

"Do you ever think how one thing could have gone differently and we wouldn't be in each other's arms right now?" He shakes his head to dispel the thought. But it's in the air between us. "Do you ever think how we might have missed all this?"

I nod, and then I kiss him so he won't see my eyes are full of tears. I kiss him until the air is clear of the possibility that Jake and I aren't here, right now, in every possible world.

"Room service?" he says.

"My kingdom for a Rueben," I say as he picks up the phone.

I snuggle up beside him, listening to him place the order, feeling his gorgeous hands trace warm circles on my skin, and there's one thing I know for sure: making love with Jake Glasswell has wrecked me for anyone else. Ever. He's wrecked me for just about everything except more of him, in perpetuity.

I'd laugh if I weren't so serious, if I weren't starting to realize what this means.

I can't leave this life. I have to stay here now, forever.

We haven't even tied the record yet.

Chapter Nineteen

"DO YOU HAVE ANY PLANS TO STOP BEING SO SECRETIVE?"
Jake teases the next morning as I hand him a matcha latte at the
Japanese teahouse on Wilshire.

We've been busy today, and it's not even noon. First there
was morning sex, then room service, then after-breakfast sex,
which stretched the limit of the Sunset Marquis's checkout time.
Then I told Jake there was something I had to do this morning
and asked him to come along for moral support.

We take our lattes to an outdoor table. There's a pull between us now. An alchemical shift has his fingers tracing my
forearm, has my eyes on the tight strip of denim over his zipper.

Somewhere around the fifth orgasm last night, upside down
in a hotel desk chair, I pledged my allegiance to the High Life.
Or at least, I decided to see if I could keep what's great about it
here—my relationship with Jake—and marry it with what used
to be great about my Real Life—my relationships with my mom
and Masha.

It was one thing to drop in for a visit to a world where I
wasn't tight with my mom, but I refuse to live that way long
term. I've never gone four days without talking to my mother.
I'm not sure the last time I went four hours. And these have
been hard, dramatic days. If I'm going to make it here, I've got
to make up with Lorena.

We finish our lattes. Jake and Gram Parsons head for the car, but I head back inside the teahouse and get another latte for the road.

"Looks like someone really got torn up last night," Jake says as I slide into the car.

"Someone did," I say, "but this latte's for my mom."

Jake stares at me. "Did you talk to her? Did she call?"

"No, but—"

A dark cloud spreads across his face. It's the face he made when I said I wanted to talk to Masha at her reception.

"What?" I ask, my chest tightening with dread.

"I should have known, your birthday's coming up," he says sadly. "Every year around this time, you talk about reaching out—"

"What stops me?"

He sighs. "Olivia, you know your mom—she's not—"

"Okay, I understand. There's history here—"

"That's putting it mildly."

"But something's different today. *I'm* different—"

"Olivia, you always have the best intentions, but—"

"Please, Jake. Will you come with me to try?"

. . . . . .

I TAKE THE wheel for the short drive to my mom's house. Feeling optimistic, I turn on one of her recent podcast episodes. A woman from Oklahoma wants to know if she should reconnect with an old flame.

"It depends," Lorena says, "on your reasons. Do you want the flame back because you're lonely?"

"I want the flame back because my town's population is eight hundred and seventy-two. Everyone else is taken."

"What are you doing talking to me? Run, don't walk, Oklahoma!"

I can't help enjoying the sound of my mother's voice, but Jake's knuckles are white on the armrests, his jaw clenched tight. He seems to be girding himself for ugliness.

But he doesn't know Lorena like I do.

"I promise you, Paula," my mother says to the next caller. "When your sister sees your minivan pull up, it will be hard to hold a grudge."

"Hear that?" I say.

Jake gives me an incredulous look. "Since when do you take Lorena's podcasts at face value? This is a woman who never once came to visit you in New York, who barely smiled or even spoke to either of us at our wedding—" He breaks off as I park the car. "Olivia?"

"What?" I say, unfastening my seat belt and looking through the window at my mother's house. The sight fills me with safety and warmth. The things he just said about my mom are painful, but they're only true in one world. Where I come from, our love is unbreakable, and that's got to count for something.

Jake watches me, waiting.

"Let's go," I say, opening the car door. Gram Parsons spills out and we cross my childhood lawn. I slide off my shoes, letting my feet sink into the familiar grass, thick and cool and spiky. I hatched a hundred dreams running through this grass.

"Olivia?" Jake says calmly.

"Jake?"

"Your mother hasn't lived here in years."

"Oh," I say, suddenly unable to breathe. "I know that. I just wanted some inspiration."

I swallow. I'm crushed and have no idea what to do. Where to go. Of course this isn't her house. Of course my mom moved on. She only lived in this duplex in the version of life where I held her back. When I left for college, my mother found her way on her own. She's famous now and good at what she does. She's vanished from my life.

I don't want to leave my yard, the orange tree still bearing the swing my mom hung for me twenty years ago. Looking closer, I see the painful signs that someone else lives here now. My mom would tend her flowers with far more love and care. Toy trucks line the porch. This is someone else's childhood now.

Tears prick the back of my eyes. I'm trespassing and can't move from this lawn. Jake puts his arms around me. I fall into him, holding on. Suddenly I can barely stand up on my own.

"How did this happen?" Emotion cracks my voice.

He sighs, like we've discussed this many times, yet somehow it still hasn't sunk in. "Your mom never got over you doing what any responsible adult would have done. It was just a simple loan . . ."

And just like that, he confirms all my suspicions. I see the whole thing played out as disastrously as I imagined. But it doesn't have to stay like this. I'm sure it doesn't.

Jake holds me close, looks in my eyes with an intensity that's almost too much.

"Your life was just beginning," Jake says. "You wanted to

go. You *needed* to go. And every lucky thing since then happened because we got on that plane to New York."

In Real Life, taking that flight was impossible when my dad died. But in this one, I took it. Because I'd kissed Jake.

And after last night, I understand how that would sway me. We're that good together.

"Maybe we should go home," Jake says. His voice is kind, but it's the wrong thing to say.

"No." I cry harder, tugging away from his embrace. Getting lost in Jake's spell—as I'd done last night—is what cost me my relationship with my mom. I suddenly see that if I'm going to do this, it's got to be alone.

I take a step away from him, backing against the trunk of a tangerine tree. I feel the bark against my shoulders, smell the fruit, and I know where to find her. It's Saturday morning, and the Santa Monica Farmers Market is three blocks away. She'll be volunteering at Food Forward.

"Jake, I have to go."

"What?"

"Take the car, take Gram Parsons, go home. I'll meet you there this afternoon. I'll explain everything."

"Olivia—" He sounds shocked and a little hurt, but he doesn't follow me as I take off running down the street.

. . . . . .

THE THIRD STREET promenade is a bustling pedestrian-only block with the biggest and most famous farmers market in Southern California. From artisan soaps to fresh dates to macro-biotic popsicles, they have everything you never knew you

WHAT'S IN A KISS?

needed. When I spot the Food Forward logo on a stack of boxes on a dolly, I follow it to a booth at the edge of the market.

"Rick!" I say to the founder of the organization. *Please know me, please know me, please—*

"Olivia," he says, doing a double take, giving me a worried squint. "Are you here about the glitch in auto-pay? We called your assistant. I really don't know how that happened."

"There was no mistake. I tripled the donation."

He blinks. "That's—wow. Thank you."

"Is my mom—is Lorena here?"

"She and Silver just left," he says and points toward the parking lot. He glances back at me, a note of worry in his face. "Green Polestar. But you didn't hear it from me."

"She's with Silver?" I ask. I knew they worked together, but weekend volunteering seems a little much.

I take off running. When I catch a glimpse of ombre tunic and matching harem pants, the word pours out of me, echoing through the parking lot.

"Mom!" The cry is all instinct, but it dies on my lips in a strangled yelp when I see my mother turn to Silver and adjust the orchid tucked behind her ear.

Suddenly I'm so jealous I want to tear this Pushcart nominee in half. Now they're getting into Silver's Polestar and already pulling away.

I hear a canine yelp and look up to see Jake's car squeal to a stop one foot in front of me. Gram Parsons sits in Jake's lap, his head out the driver's window.

"Get in, gorgeous," Jake says. "Gram Parsons wants to tail them."

We head north along PCH, Jake shadowing Silver's car as surfers in wet suits bob on distant waves.

"What do we know about this Silver?" I ask.

"Silver's not your problem," Jake says. "This is about you and your mom. Do whatever you can to tune Silver's false positivity out."

"Oh God, this is really bad."

Instead of a house, they pull into a parking lot. Is this the studio where they record their show?

"Mom," I call as she gets out of her car. I say it again, louder and more desperately. "Mom."

She whirls around, her eyes bright and so familiar on mine. I'm dying to run into her arms, but I manage to hold back. And it's a good thing I do. Because even though there's a moment of true love and joy on her face—it quickly twists into something else. Something I've never seen on her before, something I never fathomed could exist. Lorena is not happy to see me.

"What are *you* doing here?" Silver asks. "An unwelcome presence is a cancer on the world."

"Silver," my mom says, "don't."

I have to proceed as if Silver doesn't exist. As if it's just my mom and me.

Mom hasn't said a word to me. She looks at Jake, standing not quite at my side but solidly, supportively a little bit behind me.

"Hello, Jake," she says.

"Lorena."

"Olivia." Her face is like a stone.

"Mom," I say, letting my voice break.

"We're on in ten, Lorena." Silver's voice flows like poison through the chasm between my mom and me. "Strength is strongest when it's weak," she adds.

"Can I talk to you alone?" I ask my mom.

"I'm spreading a safety net for her," Silver says, "and it's made of razor wire that only cuts *your* soul."

"Olivia," my mom says my name and I almost fall over in relief. It's cold and angry, but it's familiar, too. She loves me, and she knows I love her. She has to.

"Mom," I breathe. I left the matcha in the car. I've botched this badly, but I'm here, as sincere as I've ever been. I love my mom. I need her. Surely, she must love and need me, too? "Can we please talk? I have some things I need to tell you. I—"

"I'm sorry," she says.

"I'm sorry too! I'm *so* sorry, and all I want is to make things right—"

"No," she says, "I can't do this—"

"Talk to me?"

"I can't."

"Okay, I'll wait. You're about to record. I'll wait here until you're finished and—"

"No," she says. Just no.

"What?" I whisper. "Mom." I catch my breath. I close my eyes. "I hurt you."

"And you insist on perpetuating it," Silver says. "Can't you let her heal? When a wound is always open it becomes a life."

Tears dampen my mom's eyes. I hate the sight of them, but . . . is this the crack in her veneer I need to make my way in?

I come close. I reach for her hand. It's cool and soft just like always.

"It's still me," I whisper from the bottom of my heart.

She whips her hand away and turns. "That's the problem, Olivia."

Then she walks inside the glossy building and is gone.

Chapter Twenty

I RUN MY HAND ALONG THE MATTRESS THE NEXT morning, seeking my husband's heat. We'd made love in the wee hours, both of us half asleep, and the memory of it is hazy and wonderful, like the luckiest kind of dream. This is the first time I've awoken in the High Life without Jake holding me— and it's the first time I've wanted him to. My body feels cadaverous, buried in the bed, and it takes me several seconds to remember why:

In the parking lot yesterday, Lorena looked at me like I was dead to her. I saw with my own eyes and felt with my own heart that my mother and I are estranged.

I want to go home. I want my mom back. I'll never take her love for granted again. I want out of the High Life. Except—

"Jake?" I say his name before I know I'm going to. I say it with an urgency I'm not ready to know I feel.

He appears in the doorway between our bedroom and the master bath, wearing a robe and bringing sexy back to brushing teeth. He smiles, toweling off his freshly showered hair like it's no big whoop to be so gorgeous. *Hey you*, my loins demand, *get back in bed where you belong.*

"Good morning," he says, wasting America's Sexiest Voice

on just me. Concern narrows his eyes and he sits by me on the bed. "You're still upset about yesterday."

"It's not just yesterday," I say, my voice cracking. "Has she hated me that much for ten years?"

"Olivia—"

"How did I let this happen?"

I slump against him and begin to cry, my shoulders shaking in his embrace. His arms are a comfort, but I'm so lost and scared. I don't know how to get home to my real world, where my mom calls me fifteen times a day and borrows my shoes without asking and clips comics from the paper for my refrigerator and texts me songs that suit my vocal range for the next time I karaoke. And likes me.

But when I do find Yogi Rabbi Dan, and I convince him to take me back to my Real Life, it will mean leaving this version of Jake behind.

A week ago it would have been an easy bargain.

I think of the ridiculous fun we had planting our garden together. The connection flowing between us, pitcher to catcher to pitcher on the mound. The magic of his skin on mine in the middle of the night. To say nothing of what he can do with his tongue. This week with Jake, I've experienced a level of intimacy I've never let myself imagine having with anyone.

Especially Glasswell.

And that's who he'll be again when I go home.

It hurts to think of that, and I wonder—could I make him love me in Real Life? Hah. That feels about as likely as making up with High Life Lorena.

Why can't I take him with me? Why can't I cobble together

my best life, picking and choosing the choicest parts like an interdimensional Frankenstein?

I don't know who made the rules, but it appears that no one gets it all—not Helen Gurley Brown, not Frankenstein, not Ebenezer Scrooge. Perhaps the purpose of this glimpse of parallel-Olivia is for me to choose. What matters most to me? What sacrifices am I willing to make?

Not my mom. Not Masha. I've been clear on that since Day One here. But now . . . how do I turn my back on Jake? He's too good—we're too good—to make that call just yet.

And . . . I'm crying again.

He kisses my forehead, dabs my tears with his fingertips. "Do you want to skip the party? Stay home and take it easy?"

I shake my head. For once, I know what he's talking about. Having finally wised to the Delphic powers of iCal, I'm equipped with the knowledge that Jake and I have RSVP'd to celebrate Aurora's thirtieth birthday.

Nothing fancy, just your basic chartered yacht to Catalina Island, which lies an hour off the coast of LA. Followed by your basic formal ball at the historic Catalina Casino. The basic Wrigley Mansion rented out for Aurora's guests. It's as over the top as Aurora—but it would be a lie to say I'm not tingling about another hotel tilt with Jake.

I want to see him in a tux, his hair wild from the ocean breeze. I want to dance in his arms as an orchestra plays Count Basie. I want to kick his ass at mini golf. I want to snorkel with garibaldis, share a waffle cone from Scoops, and muse about returning in the winter to read novels by the fire in a cottage within walking distance of the library.

Maybe it's frivolous, and maybe it will make leaving the High Life that much harder when the time comes for me to go.

Or maybe it will be the trip that convinces me to stay.

"We're still going," I tell him, running my fingers through his hair, breathing in the eucalyptus soap on his warm skin.

"Are you sure?" His mouth finds my neck, his tongue drawing the lightest line down my throat. "Because it could also be Sex O'Clock all day—"

"No," I say, laughing. "If we don't take a break, we're going to become conjoined. Then we'll have to pose for medical photos and have a painful operation—"

"We could join the circus," Jake says, slipping an arm around me.

"The clock strikes Sex O'Clock tonight at the Wrigley, after you wriggle out of your tux. Are you packed?"

"Yes." One kiss from Jake, one slip of his tongue between my lips has me ready to perish all thoughts of ever leaving our bed. I moan, then push him back a little to look into his eyes.

"Wait," I say. "Is this what we do?"

"Is *what* what we do?"

"Use sex to avoid our problems?"

He squints at me, confused.

"Not just parties we don't want to go to," I say, gaining steam, "but also this fight with my mom. Do you and I fuck to cope? We . . . fope?"

"Olivia, we're in love. We fove."

"Oh," my voice comes out a little squeak, far more thrilled to hear his words than either of us expected me to be. We're in love.

"If there's one thing I've learned from Dr. Kenyon and all the relationship podcasts I listen to," Jake says, "it's that married people having sex is *never* a problem."

"That's kind of my point," I say. "Maybe sex is a safe place for us to hide."

"But half the time we discuss our problems *while* we do it!" Jake says. "Remember last month when we had to decide on a new toilet for the half bathroom?"

"When you're having sex more often than not," I say, "things are bound to come up in the middle of it. Ding-dong! It's the FedEx guy! Let's have a four-legged race to sign for the package!"

"The way I see it, we've learned by now which problems are worth fixing, and which ones are better left alone." He says this tenderly, but it's a shock. Jake thinks my mom is a problem *better left alone.*

Before I can argue, he glances at his watch. "Let's leave here in ten so we don't miss the boat?" He doesn't wait for my answer—and it takes me a moment to realize he isn't being rude. He simply doesn't think I'll have more to say on this subject. There's a marital shorthand he knows and I don't.

As I head toward my closet, I think about how everything Jake's accustomed to is alien to me. The moments where I'm best at blending in are when it's just the two of us. But life isn't just one relationship—even when that relationship is as wonderful as ours seems to be.

A suitcase is spread open on my closet floor, half of it filled with Jake's clothes. I run my hand over his T-shirts, his socks, his red leather dopp kit.

I open the drawers in my closet, looking for clothes to add. As I dig around for a bathing suit, my hands find a stack of books buried at the bottom of a drawer. I take them out and spread them on the floor.

They're self-help books about repairing broken relationships with loved ones. Lorena and I reviewed a couple of these on her real-world podcast. In that realm I never dreamed of reading one for guidance in my life.

I flip through *Closing the Open Borders of Your Heart*. A year ago, I couldn't even open this one. I judged it as the height of woo-woo cheese. But High Life Olivia? She read the fuck out of this. And dog-eared dozens of pages. And highlighted things. And made notes in the margins.

Original wound = the mirror?

Don't expect infinity from an hourglass.

Häagen-Dazs can't satiate Mother Hunger.

Are these the ravings of a lunatic? Or simply another me grieving for her mom?

High Life Olivia may have *told* Jake that Lorena was a problem best left alone. But tucked away deep inside her closet, she was stockpiling self-help books like food in a fallout shelter. She was studying each one like it might be a map to guide her home.

• • • • • •

"WHAT ARE THE odds Gram Parsons gets seasick?" Jake asks later that morning as he turns off PCH toward the port at Marina del Rey. I feel the sharp stab of déjà vu. Another life ago, on the morning of Masha's bachelorette, I tried to parallel park into the same spot where Jake parks now.

I flash on my best friend's blindfolded face, her gleeful shriek when I pulled off the bandanna and she saw that we were going fishing. God, I miss her. If Mash were here, if she didn't hate me too, she'd tell me what to do about Lorena, about Jake. But Masha's half a world away in Sicily—and for the good of her honeymoon, I hope I'm the furthest thing from her mind. It's bad enough I was a stain on her wedding day.

When I realize Jake's still waiting for an answer, I hoist Gram Parsons in my arms.

"Seasick? This sea dog?" I say, pushing painful thoughts aside. "He was here a week ago, catching halibut with me and—"

I catch myself, break into silence. Jake gives me the same concerned look he gave me when I pulled up to my mom's old house.

"Gram Parsons will be fine," I say.

"Fine . . . *and* afloat," Jake says.

"What do you mean?" I ask as Jake reaches into the back seat for a small wrapped package.

"Don't laugh," he says. "Or do. But I'll feel better if he wears this." Jake opens the package to reveal a tiny life vest. Turquoise. With the handle on top that will make Gram Parsons look like a doggie briefcase. A near replica of the one I'd bought for him back home.

Tears prick my eyes, and I know it's ridiculous to cry over animal water safety, but the gesture speaks volumes about where Jake's heart is, and how naturally it syncs up with my own.

"Has anyone ever told you how wonderful you are?" I ask Jake as I clip Gram Parsons into his vest. A perfect fit.

I half expect Jake to make a joke, to bat the comment away, to kiss me quickly and move on, because there's a certain amount of goodwill that this marriage seems to take for granted, because there's a way to see this life vest as just an impulse Amazon purchase. But it's more than that to me, and Jake seems to hear this in my voice. He meets my eyes. He reaches for my hands. He takes the time to receive the compliment. Like a man.

Emotionally available. Hot as hell.

"Thank you," he says, and then he kisses me. His lips lock around mine and I pull him close, drawn to him on every level all at once.

"Let's fove," I whisper, gripping the lapels of his black jean jacket.

He laughs as a yacht horn sounds in the distance. "Let's catch this boat. But I'm going to fove you so hard in Catalina."

"Swear?"

As Jake rolls our suitcase across the marina parking lot, our immediate future looms into view. The yacht Aurora chartered looks like a skyscraper fell over in the water—all angled glass and brooding black. Topless waiters in tuxedo pants and bow ties glide around the multilevel decks bearing trays of cold champagne. Guests stream aboard like contestants competing for the most flamboyant hat. Across the yacht's hull the words *Wet Dream* are painted in cursive.

I find myself staring grudgingly at the scene, holding back on instinct. It's hard to be in public when all you want to do is have sex. And this crowd is such an obvious scene, I'm dreading wading into it. I find myself waiting for Jake to lead the way. But he's waiting for me. This is my High Life crowd, not his. With these people, he's more Mr. Dusk than Mr. Glasswell.

I feel him take a breath beside me. "We're really doing this?"

"It'll be fine," I say. "I mean, fun. Picture the hotel bed on the other side of that water."

Jake closes his eyes. "I'm there right now."

This yacht would fit Glasswell like a glove, but Jake is distinctly uneasy. I wonder what High Life Olivia knows about Jake's insecurity that I don't. And then I wonder if she *doesn't* know, if I'm picking up on it because of *my* real-life insecurity around this type of scene.

We climb the gangway and board the ship. In a lustrous white toga dress, Aurora stands at the stern. Her arms extended, she awaits my hug as Jake and Gram Parsons and I head her way.

"You bitches missed the caviar," she says, air-kissing me.

"But we made the boat," Jake says, less than enthusiastic. "Which is clearly the caviar of yachts."

There's zero chemistry between him and Aurora. She barely glances at him. In another life, they were inseparable—at least according to the *Daily Mail*. In any world, I've never seen someone look at Jake with such disinterest.

Even when I thought I despised Glasswell, I recognized it was obsessive. Maybe something inside me always knew it was a shallow form of fascination.

"You two are such *rebels*," Aurora says.

"How's that?" Jake asks.

Looking at Gram Parsons in his vested glory, Aurora says, "The invitations said to leave all furry bags of shit at home."

"Well, happy birthday!" I say. "Where's the bar?"

Aurora looks up at a second-story balcony. I take Jake's hand and practically jerk him upstairs.

The upper deck is crowded, overwhelming, the sun a spotlight on all the exposed flesh. Gram Parsons snuggles against me, making me want to lie down and snuggle back. When Jake's arm comes around my waist, I'm grateful.

I spot Fenny through the crowd, talking to Marty, the *Zombie Hospital* makeup artist. Fenny gives me a cheery wave. I gesture that Jake and I will head over to her once we get a drink.

But the line for the bar is long. We've barely advanced when the boat backs away from the dock. The wind whips Jake's hair, and I remember this was on my wish list for the trip to Catalina. So I take him in, how sweet he looks, and I kiss him.

The boat rocks us apart as it steers out of the marina, into open ocean. I stumble forward a step, edging into the guy in front of us in line. He turns around, and it's Michael Jinx—star of the recent action movie *The Luddite* . . . and one of Jake's celebrity friends in Real Life.

"Sorry, Michael Jinx," Jake says, self-consciously starstruck.

"No worries," Michael says, already turning back around.

It seems impossible they don't know each other here. That Jake is gulping, coming down from the excitement of interacting with a star.

All Jake has in this life is me.

And compared to what I know Jake *should* have, I can't stop asking myself: How am I enough?

"You should introduce yourself," I say in Jake's ear, and when he laughs me off, I press. "I feel like you two would be friends. Like you have the same sense of humor." I thump Jake on the shoulder. "You should invite him to come on the podcast."

Jake looks at me. "Is that a joke?"

"Or a stroke of genius," I say.

"He's here to party," Jake says under his breath. "Not to be accosted by nobodies."

"Maybe if you stopped referring to yourself as a nobody, you wouldn't be one," I say. "That came out wrong! You're not a nobody." My voice is rising to the point where Michael can definitely hear us, whether he wants to or not.

"Okay," Jake says, "I'm a *somebody*." He looks around theatrically, then looks back at me. "Big change!"

Gram Parsons whines, disliking the tone this exchange has taken. Jake takes him from me and pats his head.

"I agree!" I whisper. "You're just the kind of somebody Michael Jinx would love if given the chance. Believe me. I know these things."

"Maybe you hit your head harder than we thought the other day," Jake whispers back. "I have no idea what you're talking about."

"Think about it. Michael Jinx just did that Luddite movie whose plot hinged on the troubled father-son relationship. It's the perfect segue for your show. Just ask him. What's the worst thing that can happen?"

"Hard pass," Jake says, giving me a look. "New topic: What do you want to drink, if we ever make it to the front of this line?"

"What if fate put you in this endless line," I push on. "Directly behind your favorite actor, for a reason? What if fate wants you to stop wasting your talent by directing traffic jams in palm trees and making obscure podcasts—and start *using* it in places like *this*, on people who—"

"Who what?" Jake says, squinting at me. "Matter?"

"That's not what I mean."

"Feel free to clarify." There's irritation in his eyes. "You didn't seem to think I was wasting my talent last month when you ordered all that podcasting equipment."

"Well . . . I . . ." I start to say.

Gram Parsons tilts his head, warning me I'm in over my head. I don't know enough about last month to have this argument. I wasn't expecting to face off against a version of myself I can't remember. But why doesn't Jake want more for himself?

"I don't get it." Jake's voice is rising now. "All it takes is five minutes on a yacht with people who *matter*—"

Michael Jinx turns around to glance at us, eyebrows raised.

"Not you," Jake stammers apologetically at the actor. "I mean . . ."

"Actually," I say to Michael Jinx. "*Yes*, you. This is Jake Glasswell and he has a question." I motion to Jake, like *ask him*. I know it's a mistake, but it's too late.

Jake shakes his head, closes his eyes, and lets the moment awkwardly pass. The bartender hands Michael Jinx his drink, and he gives us a pitying look before disappearing into the crowd.

"What the hell was that?" Jake asks me.

"Jake—"

"I knew I shouldn't have come," he says as we make it to the front of the line.

"Cute pup!" the topless bow-tied bartender says to Gram Parsons. "What can I get for you—"

"Scotch. Neat. Double," Jake says.

I motion the bartender for the same. Jake puts a twenty in the tip jar. We take our glasses as Aurora clinks a fork against her champagne flute.

"On this, my thirtieth trip around the sun," she says, her voice cloyingly sweet, "I am so, so blessed to be surrounded by such *breathtaking* beauties—"

Jake groans audibly, causing people around us to look at him. I pull him around the corner of the deck.

"You don't want to be here," I say.

"I want to be with *you*," he says. "But I'm starting to wonder if you want to be with me. In whatever state of non-success I'm in."

"It's just that I've seen . . . I know what you're capable of—"

"You keep saying that, Olivia, and I truly have no idea what you're talking about."

"You said we know by now what to leave alone in our lives, but I disagree. You're a star, Jake, you don't know it, but—"

"Do you hear yourself?" he says.

"And I can't leave my relationship with my mother alone—"

"Says who?" Jake demands.

"Says the little girl inside me who wants her mom back." I swallow and meet Jake's eyes. There's a distance between us in this conversation that's making my chest tense with anxiety.

"You're the one who told me ten years ago," he says, "that our love would generate its own world, a parallel universe. That we could leave the pain outside our doors, that we could build a sanctuary just for us. I believed you, Olivia. And we did it. I don't have to interact with my toxic parents and neither do you—"

"My mom isn't—" I start to argue. But I'm out of my depth again. Jake knows more about the dark side of that relationship than I do, and suddenly I want to cry.

"I don't think we should talk about this right now," Jake says, his cheeks flushed.

"Hey now!" a female voice interrupts us and a hand squeezes my shoulder. "Had any hot dogs lately?"

I turn to see a blond middle-aged woman in a blue blazer with white trim and matching blue skirt. She's holding a fruity cocktail with a little rubber apple sticking out, and I have no idea who she is.

"Actually," I say, "I had three just the other day."

"*Three?*" The woman throws back her head and laughs. "That's my gal!"

She turns to Jake and extends her hand. "Amy Reisenbach."

I inhale a quick sip of scotch. The president of CBS Entertainment has just introduced herself to Jake. Lady Fortune, be a mistress of the sea.

"Actually, we've met," Jake says, sounding exhausted. He shakes Amy's hand. "I was on the other side of Olivia at that Yankees game. It's been a while."

"Of course! This is your husband." Her eyes narrow in thought. "My assistant mentioned something about . . ." Amy leans toward Jake. "Now I remember! According to Olivia, I should quit my job and knit mittens in Siberia if I don't make a lunch date with you to hear about your projects."

"My projects?" Jake shoots me a shocked look that gives me chills. So I sent one innocent email to one powerful woman's assistant. Why is he making this so hard? He's got the goods. He just needs exposure.

"Amy heard about the taco traffic jam," I say. "I . . . mentioned it to her."

"Her assistant," Jake says.

"Who mentioned something about a viral TikTok, was it?" Amy says. "All those tacos on the street. Insanity!"

"It was just a traffic jam," Jake says, shutting me down just when things were looking up. "Not exactly a passion project."

"But it could be!" I say. "Things develop that way, sometimes. Organically?"

"I don't understand what's happening here," Jake says, as politely as is possible through gritted teeth. "But I'm sure Amy's very busy."

"You could just have lunch," I say, catching a knowing nod from Amy.

"Don't worry, Jake." She winks at me and says, "I got my husband his start, too. This is what we modern breadwinners do."

I don't know where Jake's blood has gone, but it's not in his face. I've got to save this. Now.

"Look at this," I say to Amy, grabbing a martini off a passing tray to blunt the memory of what I'm about to do. Then I pull up the video—the one of Jake, with the megaphone, in the palm tree. It has half a million views.

"Get out of here," Amy says, truly engrossed. "Jake, you're a hero!"

And then we all watch the caption show up on the screen. *Expectant Father Saves the Day!*

"Oh my, are you *expecting*?" Amy asks, hand over her mouth as her eyes probe my body.

"Oh God no!" I say, almost spitting out my drink. I'd forgotten about that caption. "Someone assumed from the way Jake was acting, like such a hero, I mean. But we—the two of us!—are definitely not . . . no babies . . . no way!" I say and laugh. Which makes Amy laugh. Which makes us look at Jake.

Who does not laugh. He plants Gram Parsons in my arms, and says, "I think I'll go get another drink."

"Jake!" I call out as he disappears into a sea of gilded guests dancing before a DJ on the deck.

Chapter Twenty-One

"IT'S FINE," JAKE SAYS AS HE SETS DOWN OUR SUITCASE in the Bethany Glen room at the Wrigley Mansion. Nestled in the hills of Catalina Island, the gum magnate's summer "cottage" is Prohibition-glam, with dark green shutters and wraparound porches. Succulents frame views of the beach town of Avalon below. It would be the perfect place to spend a night with Jake, if I hadn't just betrayed him like a rum-drunk pirate on the sea.

"It's not fine," I say, taking a long swig of coconut water from Aurora's giant hospitality basket. I pass the bottle to Jake, who guzzles it. My martini and his second double scotch weren't the sanest of ideas.

"I get it. She's your boss, and getting pregnant isn't in your character's narrative arc."

Jake's giving me cover, and a wise woman would take it. But I didn't laugh when Amy asked about children so I can keep my stupid job. I laughed because the idea is preposterous. Maybe not to the Olivia and Jake who are actually married, but to me— the pop-up wife. The pretender. The woman whose longest, most intimate relationship is . . . these past six days with Jake.

As is evident by the yacht ride over here, I can't even pull off playing at marriage. I wouldn't dare play at motherhood.

I unhook Gram Parson's leash and flop onto bed beside

him, watching the Pacific meet the afternoon sky. Jake stands at the window and looks down at the sailboats bobbing in the harbor. Asshole boats with their obnoxious anchors. I used to have anchors, in my Real Life. Mom and Masha kept me bobbing where I was supposed to be. In the High Life I'm the *Star of Scotland*, a shipwreck generating sustenance and low entertainment. I don't do well shipwrecked. It leaves me vulnerable to dive-bys from the likes of Amy Reisenbach.

How did the version of me who married Jake survive this long without Masha and my mom? I've been here a week and I'm struggling, not to mention failing at the one good thing I have going here—my marriage.

A week ago, when I'd first awoken in the High Life, all I wanted was the familiarity of a blowout fight with Glasswell. Now that he's Jake—now that we're us—I can't bear to have hurt him. I can't bear it, because . . .

Because I think I'm falling for him. This him, in this world. Which I've got to leave.

Falling for him is the only explanation for my tenacious insanity on the yacht—for the physical need I felt for someone to recognize how magical Jake is. I know there's a world where Amy sees it. Where Michael Jinx sees it. Where damn near everyone sees it. I thought I could make it happen again. I thought it would be easy for Jake to get what he deserves. Then he could have something beyond me, and I wouldn't have to worry about not being enough.

This is a mindfuck on so many levels. I know Jake and I need to talk, but I don't know what to say. I can't go near the future children he wants to make with me. Jake and I have been playing house this week, but starting a family is too real, too big for me to pretend I know what I'm talking about.

Which is why my apologies this afternoon have been insufficient. Which is how we made it all the way to the hotel without having quite made up.

I want to make up. Because when things are good with Jake and me, they're really good. And when things are rough—as I've seen for the first time in the past hour—it paints a stark picture of the rest of my life here.

If I don't have Jake, I don't have anything.

"Are you going to lie there all day?" he says, picking up an envelope tucked in Aurora's hospitality basket. "Or are you going to read about the mandatory fun we're about to have?"

Is this how married people fight? They go at it for a while, then change the subject, knowing they can always resume the dispute when the mood strikes—because where are they going to go? They're together till death does them part.

"What should I do?" I ask Gram Parsons, whose kiss recommends fun.

I rise from bed and go to Jake, but he doesn't put his arms around me the way I've gotten used to this week. And though I'm desperate to feel our easy intimacy, though I crave the warmth of his skin where I put my cheek against his neck, I'm not confident enough to make a move. Instead, we stand chastely beside each other, reading the calligraphed schedule.

"Welcome to Aurora's Boot Camp?" I say, taking the opportunity to lean in a little closer. "Personalized especially for Olivia and Jake . . . Zip-lining at three, mini golf at four fifteen, submarine whale watching at five twenty-five. Is she serious?"

"Champagne sabering with the full group at six fifty-seven," Jake reads, flipping over the card. "In what world would we follow these orders?"

I wonder for a moment how Jake and Aurora endured each other in the real world. It looks impossible from this vantage point, high atop Mt. Ada on an alternate Catalina Island.

"Fuck it," I say. "We're adults possessed of free will. We don't have to do anything we don't want to."

"Really?" Jake looks at me with warmth for the first time since the disaster on the ship. "Even though Aurora's paying for all of this?"

"Our time is not for sale," I say, wanting to take the itinerary from his hands and rip it up. But something stops me. Free will hasn't worked in the High Life. In fact, each lunge at freedom backs me further into a corner. Nothing I do rectifies my wrongs.

Maybe I can't get Masha or my mom back. Maybe those wounds are too old and deep. But can't I at least repair what I broke on the yacht ride? If Masha were here, she'd tell me to leave bad enough alone, but she's very much not here. There is no calm hand on this tiller, no even keel to guide me beyond emotional icebergs.

In the name of *Everything's Jake*, I turn to him and say, "Actually, I really love ziplining. Can we start there and then quit?"

"Um," Jake says as a flicker of what looks like fear crosses his eyes.

Oh wait—he's scared of heights. Exhibit A, the palm tree incident. Exhibit B, the climbing wall clip, where I and the rest of the world saw him face this fear. His wife should know about her husband's single primal fear, and so it seems I've stepped in it yet again. I'm about to backpedal when Jake meets my gaze and smiles. Whatever hesitation was there a moment ago is gone.

He kisses me. "Let's go."

......

WE LEAVE GRAM Parsons napping diagonally on the bed and take the windy path toward town. I'm glad to feel a variety of clouds begin to part. The sun is bright, we're holding hands, swinging them slightly, watching two red-tailed hawks wheel at each other in the sky. The air smells like lemon blossoms, and we can hear the ocean lap against the rocky shore. By the time Jake and I reach Crescent Ave., I feel lighter, like I don't have to be the wrong thing in the wrong place at the wrong time.

The last time I zipped this line was during winter break of my junior year, when I tagged along with Masha's family for a Catalina New Year's Eve. I remember how free I'd felt zooming through the trees. How, in a way, I've been chasing that feeling ever since. That would have been the winter Jake moved from San Francisco, just before he started as the new kid at our school. I wonder what he was doing on the day I was zip-lining. Was he here yet? Was he in an airplane with the family he hates, leaving behind his friends, his life? Who was hardest to leave? As I felt my horizon widening that day, what was happening to his? Did my subconscious register the rumble of his jet as it squared up to land at LAX and I zip-lined like a bullet in the same sky?

These are things I'd know if I remembered spending the past ten years with Jake. They're things it's too late for me to ask about now. If I can't get home, if I end up staying in this life, I'll always be pretending to know more than I do. Which is my least favorite trait to encounter in other people. This prospect is so daunting that it hurts, a physical stabbing pain in my stomach that stops me in my tracks.

"Are you okay?" Jake asks.

When I look at him, my heart sinks. I missed out on getting to know him. I missed out on falling in love with him. I missed out on the moments that make life worth remembering.

I clutch my stomach, shake my head.

"Detour," Jake says. "You look hungry." He tugs my hand toward Scoops, the overpriced and delicious ice cream shop on Catalina's downtown strip.

I try to be a woman standing in an ice cream shop, deciding on a flavor. But it's hard. This life tends to show me that simple decisions have tectonic repercussions. Suddenly I'm paralyzed, staring at the menu like it's a list of all life's choices, and this is my one chance to do something right.

"Strawberry waffle cone for the lady," Jake calls across the counter.

"Did you just order for me?" It's hard to tell if I'm annoyed or turned on by this patriarchal display.

"We go through this every time," he says. "You stare at the menu for ten minutes, then you order strawberry in a waffle cone and proclaim it the perfect flavor. And we have a zipline to catch."

I know he's right, but what feels wrong is I have no idea what kind of ice cream *he* likes. Thus I re-enter my wobbly shame spiral . . . until it hits me that, actually, I do know. Rum raisin.

He's the one person in either realm who likes it. I know this from prom, that interdimensional colossus straddling both domains.

"Rum raisin," I proudly tell the teenaged Scoops employee. "Sugar cone."

Ice creams in hand, Jake and I stroll Crescent Ave. It crosses a tiny, touristy downtown full of rock shops and T-shirt stands, before winding around a rocky coastline. We pass the art deco casino, where big bands of the thirties and forties serenaded elaborate soirees in the world's largest circular ballroom. We pass the white umbrellas of Descanso Beach Club and its pebbly shore. It's still spring, too early in the season for peak summer crowds, so the town has a sleepy local vibe that makes me want to linger. It makes me want to make new memories with Jake, ones that I can access, too.

"Taste this," he says, through a mouthful of ice cream. "Maybe the best rum raisin ever."

"I'd rather bob for garbage in that trash can over there. I swear, if you make our kids like rum raisin . . ." I trail off, wishing I could snatch the words out of the air.

Where did *that* come from? And how can Jake seem so unfazed by it?

"Oh yeah, that's all you're going to eat while pregnant. Then you can partner with Baskin-Robbins and write *Dr. Josslyn Munro's Rum Raisin Pregnancy Diet.* You'll be a pariah in the medical community, but our kids will be biologically programmed. Master plan."

"Not going to happen." I mean it lightly, but it comes out with such gravity that Jake stops walking. He hears that I don't only mean his ice cream master plan. I mean all of it—the future as he sees it.

"Uh-oh," he says. "What's that look?"

"Jake, what I said on the boat—"

He groans. "I don't want to talk about it."

"I need to explain why I acted that way," I say. "And it's going to sound crazy. But at that Yankees game, Amy discovered the wrong person."

"That was *ten* years ago—"

"It shouldn't have been me," I say, my voice rising. "It was supposed to be you."

"What do you mean, 'supposed to'? According to what? Your imposter syndrome?"

"According to reality," I say. My mind hurts and I know I'm making things worse, but maybe that's a necessary stop on the way toward the truth.

"I care about Amy Reisenbach *almost* as little as she cares about me, so why are we talking about her?"

"Because you should care about her. Because she should care about you." I put my hands on his chest and look into his beautiful green eyes. I've stared at them in magazines for years. I can't keep them all to myself. It feels like I'm robbing the world of Jake and robbing Jake of the world.

"Doesn't some part of you feel it? Don't you know that your life was supposed to be glorious?"

"My life *is* glorious. I found you."

"You wouldn't say that if you knew what I know," I say. "I've seen . . . things you haven't. You were destined for a lot more than you're getting. With me. I'm not even supposed to be here."

"Is this a passive-aggressive way of saying you're not happy?"

"I'm not happy." What truth serum is in this Scoops ice cream? Suddenly I can't stop myself telling him as much of the truth as he might be able to hear.

He sucks in a breath and cuts his eyes at me. "Oh."

"I'm not happy with anything—except you. And I don't know if I'm staying or going, but if I stay—"

"*If you stay?*"

"Then I need to—I need the chance to help you get a piece of the life you deserve. And that's why we have to go find Amy at the zip line. So you can be the star, not me."

"Just because you don't think you deserve your success," Jake says coldly, walking so fast I have to run to keep up with him. "Because it's not up to Juilliard standards . . . because it cost you your relationship with your mother—"

"I told you that?"

The look he gives me makes me wonder how many rounds of this bout we've fought.

"I was raised by narcissists too, remember?" he says. "Your issues with your mother would have still exploded, even if you hadn't come to New York—"

"No!" I say. "That's the thing! They wouldn't have. I'd still have her. Same with Masha. If I hadn't left, if I hadn't gone to New York, if I hadn't been . . ."

I stop just before I say *with you*. But Jake knows me well enough to hear it in my silence.

"Things would be better if you hadn't chosen me? If you didn't work on a successful show that makes people happy? If you didn't have a loving husband? If you gave up your dreams to take on your mother's grief, which by the way is a ridiculous request for a parent to make of a child? Things would be better then?"

It's a complicated question. I want to tell Jake yes, and I want to tell him no, and I want to say the same goes for him—that his life would be better if he hadn't chosen me. But I can't say anything. I'm crippled by the ignorance of every small decision I don't know we've made. Every conversation, every argument, every thoughtless movement in the night.

"No wonder you can't imagine having kids," Jake says, turning to walk away. "Who would bring a child into a life they don't even want?"

. . . . . .

WE CLIMB THE rest of the way in silence, especially not remarking upon the incredible family of deer—a doe, a buck, and two fawns—that pass us, inches away, going the other direction, down the steep-inclined road. The doe locks eyes with me as she passes, and it feels like a sign that Jake and I should stop fighting and appreciate these moments. You don't get an unlimited amount of magical island interactions.

The zipline office sits beneath a canopy of trees. Awaiting us are five of the longest ziplines in California, looking out over the ocean. I recognize Aurora's stylist, and Miguel Bernardeau, who's tightening a harness around his young Spanish girlfriend's waist. And there's Amy, my mark, fastening her helmet. She waves like she's not groaning to see us again, lighting a little Olympic flame of hope inside me as Jake touches my elbow.

"I don't know what I'm doing here. I'm going to take a walk and meet you later—"

"Please," I beg him. "Please do this with me."

A woman with a clipboard approaches us. "Names?"

"Olivia Dusk and Jake Glasswell," I tell her.

"No," she says.

Jake spins on his heel. "Just the word I was hoping to hear."

"Wait." I grab the collar of his T-shirt. "Those are our names," I tell the woman.

"Not if you want to be on the three fifteen shuttle."

"I think the issue is we were supposed to be on the three p.m. shuttle," I say, "but we got a little . . ."

Divorce-y?

"But we're here now," I say. "Can we join the three fifteen group?"

"Under normal circumstances yes," she says. "But Ms. Apple has been quite specific about the schedule, and I'm afraid the shuttle is full for the rest of the day."

"It's a real tragedy," Jake says. "Somehow we'll have to find a way to carry on."

"Olivia!" Ivy sticks her helmeted head out of the shuttle. She clocks Jake's annoyed and my distressed expressions. "Is there a problem?"

"*You're* on this trip?" I say, walking to the van. "Why didn't you tell me?"

"You're the one who insisted Aurora put me on the list!"

"Oh yeah," I say. "Good thinking."

Ivy looks over my shoulder at Jake and lowers her voice. "What's going on?"

"We missed our shuttle," I say, "and now—"

"We're going to skip it," Jake finishes.

"Give me two minutes," Ivy says and pushes her way off the van. She pulls the woman with the clipboard aside.

Jake and I stroll a bit, walking past the ropes course, gazing at Descanso Beach below, then the mainland far off in the hazy distance.

"Great news!" Ivy calls, cupping her hands around her mouth.

I slink my arm around Jake's waist. "See? I knew this would work out."

"They have one more seat," Ivy says, her gaze on Jake then back at me. "For you."

"What?" I narrow my eyes at her.

"I'm sorry. I tried. They've only had one cancellation. It *would* give us the chance to catch up on some very pressing business. But I mean, if you want to, you can take my spot, Jake—"

"Oh no," Jake says, throwing up his hands. "I'll see you later, Liv—"

"Jake, wait—" I say.

"I'm scared of heights," he says. "I hate this kind of thing. You know that."

"I'll go with you. We can get more rum raisin."

"No," he says, his voice unyielding. He takes a breath, meets my eyes. There's love in them and a breaking point, the kind of thing married people learn to respect in each other. "Do the ride. I'm going to take a walk."

"Are you sure?"

"Shuttle's leaving," the clipboard lady calls.

"Have fun," Jake says. "I'll meet you at the champagne sabering."

I board the shuttle and slump onto a bench at the back of the van. This was supposed to be a shared experience.

Ivy squeezes onto the bench beside me. I sense that she's bursting with things to tell me, but experience seems to have taught her to wait out my mood.

"Thanks for getting me the seat," I say.

The shuttle chugs up a long and winding hill, past herds of grazing buffalo, until we're faced with staggering panoramic views of the sea. Across the steep canyon below stretch thick steel wires of sheer exhilaration. I tell myself Jake's happier wherever his walk took him than he would have been with his eyes jammed shut, zooming in a leather diaper through the sky. I tell myself that what I said earlier only came from good intentions, and that Jake knows that, too. By 6:57 we'll be cracking jokes about the size of Aurora's saber, then we'll be sipping champagne and dancing—our first time since Masha's wedding. This time, I'll enjoy it.

One by one the other zip-liners depart, screaming and laughing as they fly high across the canyon.

"Are you ready?" the guide asks me at the threshold. The drop is death-defying and my heart soars into my throat. I remember from years ago that it takes a leap of faith to lift your feet on this initial jump, to trust that the rope and wire are strong enough for the weight of all you've brought.

I could use a leap of faith. I take a breath—

And feel my phone buzz.

I inch backward, away from the edge. "I'll just be a second," I say to the guide who's waiting for me to go.

I unlock my phone. It's a text from Jake.

My walk led me to the ferry terminal, and I caught the last boat home. Let's take a beat and talk tomorrow when you get back? Have fun tonight. I love you.

Chapter Twenty-Two

I SKIP THE ZIP LINE, TAKE THE SHUTTLE BACK DOWN, and run to the ferry dock and confirm there are no more boats to the mainland tonight. I'm stuck here without Jake. Without Jake is the last place I want to be.

I stand on the dock and look across the lonely, foggy sea, feeling every inch of the three miles back to Los Angeles. I call Jake five times. Each one goes straight to voicemail. Either the ferry has no service or he doesn't want to speak to me.

Have fun tonight, he'd texted. How?

I love you, he'd texted. He's wrong. He doesn't know me.

I climb back to the Wrigley Mansion. The living room's ghostly quiet, and I realize everyone's getting ready for the champagne sabering. The thought of showing up for that is exhausting. No one will miss me.

I close myself in the hotel room, where the sight of Jake's earbuds and sweatshirt makes me slide down the door in despair. It's like he was raptured. He wanted so badly to escape me, he left his things behind.

Gram Parsons trots over and curls up in my lap.

"Thank you." I let him lick my nose. "You don't know how lost I'd be without you."

I take him out to use the bathroom on the front lawn of the mansion. Holding a plastic bag like a glove, I watch him poop under a sign that reads "No Pets Allowed."

"There you are," a familiar voice says.

"Hi, Ivy," I sigh even as I admire her blue-sequined formal dress. "Sorry I dragged you into hell with me."

"Are you kidding?" Ivy says. "I'm having a blast. You were right when you said not to call or text, or to take any calls or texts from you—it's much more fun."

"That feeling seems to be contagious," I say, disposing of the poop bag.

"Rough day?" Ivy asks.

I laugh, because what else can I do?

"Sorry about Jake," Ivy says. "But I have some other . . . not-great news. I called Masha's mother about that rabbi—"

"And?"

"Her dad took the phone and started speaking in what I think were Ukrainian expletives. Then he said the whole family would be blocking your number, and my number, too."

"You know, Ivy," I say, lifting Gram Parsons and gazing eastward toward my home in the waning afternoon. "That might be the best way to deal with me. Everyone should block my calls and emails. Then I'd know where I stand, and you wouldn't have to manage my expectations with phrases like 'not-great news.'"

"I just thought you'd want to know."

"Good night, Ivy."

"Good night, Olivia."

I decide to enjoy this bleak night at this exquisite inn I've always wanted to sleep inside. I'll take a bath and light a fire in the fireplace, then Gram Parsons and I will find something either very good or very bad to watch on TV. Once the party moves on to the casino, I'll have a Fisherman's Platter and a bottle of overpriced white wine delivered from Bluewater Grill.

In my Real Life, I'd call Masha or my mom. I think about the billboard I saw the other day—Lorena and Silver in matching mai tai outfits. I glance at my watch. It's six forty-five on a Saturday night, the hour when the show takes live calls. I realize that at this very moment, my mother is helping total strangers with their problems, while she couldn't care less about mine.

Wait . . .

I open a browser on my phone and pull up the website for her podcast. It's far sleeker than the site Mom and I talked about building in the real world. Silver has taste. And strong commercial instincts. I'm not not jealous.

I block the Caller ID on my phone and click the hyperlinked number on Lorena's website. I hear my heart pound as I hold the phone up to my ear.

"Call Your Mother Podcast Hotline, can you hold?" It's Silver.

Without thinking, I disguise my voice, giving myself a British accent with a slightly husky tone. "I can't, actually. It's important."

"Just a brief hold," she says with a chill.

"I beg your pardon, but I'm calling from London and it's very late, and I need Lorena's help."

"There are callers ahead of you."

"Tell her . . ." I start to say.

Tell her it's Olivia.

Tell her it's her daughter.

Tell her I'm sinking like a cinder block and I need my mom.

Tell her she's the only one who can help me.

"Tell her my many-eyed intuition led me to her starry night," I finally say, quoting a line from what I know is Lorena's very favorite self-help book.

"What does that mean?" Silver says.

"Just tell her. Please. Rather."

There's a pause on the line and I think Silver might have hung up on me. I wonder how many other accents I have in my arsenal, how many times I'll have to call back. And then the line clicks through and I hear the voice that's been the honey in my life's tea for almost thirty years.

"You've got Lorena, but Lorena hasn't got you!"

For a moment I can't speak I'm so grateful. Then, just before the words pour out, I remember to disguise my voice.

"Thank you very much *indeed* for taking my call."

"What's weighing on your soul, Many Eyes?"

"There's this man," I say. "He's been in my life for some time, but recently I've realized I can't live without him. The trouble is, I'm not sure any of it is real."

"I'm listening . . ." Lorena says. For a moment it's like we're curled up in her bed.

"Reality's a fantasy," Silver squawks.

"Silver," I say, "would you mind if we let Lorena speak for the rest of the call?"

"A chair missing a leg falls over," Silver mumbles. "But okay."

"You say the gentleman has been in your life a long time," Lorena says. "How did you meet?"

"In high school, ten years ago."

"High school sweethearts!" Silver says. "That's adorable. You hardly ever hear of those anymore."

"She didn't say they were sweethearts," my mom intuits wisely.

"We weren't," I say. "For a long time I thought I hated him. After high school, he seemed to get everything he wanted. I felt like I was sinking lower by the day. The one time we saw each other—at my best friend's wedding—was a disaster. And actually, that disaster is still unfolding."

I hadn't meant to tell this version of the story. I wanted to describe our lives as they have been in the High Life, to arrive at the rift I'm trying to mend in the world I'm in. But as I talk, I find reality and alternate reality are blending together. At first, I fear I'm botching the details of both stories into unrecognizability. But then I realize that what I'm doing is telling the truth of my heart. Not wholly here, nor wholly there, something harder to pin down. Something deep inside and ethereal.

"Tell me what's unfolding now," says Lorena.

"We reconnected, about a week ago. It's been odd and unsettling, but also beautiful. Much better than I expected. He's kinder than I knew anyone could be, especially him. And through him, I see myself in a different way."

I'm talking about our marriage, but I find myself thinking about our encounters in the real world, too. I read Jake wrong in the teahouse parking lot, and in my LEAF, and at the rehearsal dinner and the wedding.

"And the trouble?" my mom asks.

"The trouble is what I'll lose by saying yes to this relationship. Is there always a trade-off with love?"

"We all make bargains."

"But does it have to be so Faustian, so all or nothing and forever? How do you ever know if you're making the right choice?"

But I know even as I ask that losing my mother isn't a deal I can accept. That isn't on the table, because losing my mother would be losing my soul. The High Life has shown me what's possible in love. It's given me compassion for Jake at eighteen, when I let him hurt me. If I go home now and lose this Jake, I'll have learned how not to hate him. And I'll have learned how to love someone someday as completely as I've been loving him.

"Have you told him?" my mother asks.

"Told him what?"

"If I can hear how much you love him, I'm sure he feels it, too. That kind of love is strong. Don't sell it short. It can handle all your questions. Let him know what's on your mind."

"My biggest fear is that I can't stay here. With him. Or that I shouldn't stay, that he'd be better off without me."

"Those are very different things. Let's start with the first. Why don't you think you can stay?"

"I don't know if it's up to me."

"It's always up to you."

My eyes sting with tears. I want to believe that. "Thank you."

"If I may be so bold, Many Eyes," my mother says. "Are you scared of the relationship moving to the next level before you're whole enough to handle the level you're on?"

She knows me, even when she doesn't know it's me. "Recently, he's started talking about what comes next. You know, a family—"

"The big F word."

"You can't say *family* without asking, 'Am I?'" Silver says.

"Silver," my mom says, "please."

"I want to get it right," I say, leaning into all I feel. "I had a great mother. She was my hero. We used to laugh like crazy. She showed me it was okay to feel everything. She loved me through all my emotions, and I loved her through hers. She was strong. She was kind. She always seemed to know what to do. You only get one shot to nail it when you have a child."

"Oh honey, nobody nails it."

"You did."

There's a pause on the line. I can't take it anymore. My voice cracks and abandons all pretense of Britishness.

"Mom—"

"Olivia?" Confusion rings in her voice.

"Please don't hang up."

The line goes dead. Like a fool, I redial. And redial.

Busy.

"Aughhh!" I toss my phone hard at the wall. Then I scramble and dig it out from where it fell under the bed. I open my iHeart Radio app and pull up Lorena's livestream, but they've gone to a THC-infused soda commercial.

"What do I do now?" I ask Gram Parsons as a knock sounds on my door.

It's sunset and 7:06, which means everyone's downstairs toasting Aurora with sabered champagne. Did she send one of her assistants to drag me from the room? If so, they'll have to break the door down.

"Olivia?" a small voice says.

I stand, retie my robe, and drag myself to the door. Through the peephole I see Fenny. She's in a bathrobe too, her hair in the same towel twist as mine. She's holding her phone, lit up with a logo. I squint. It's my mother's podcast.

I open the door. She looks at me wide-eyed.

"Are you Lorena Dusk's daughter?"

. . . . . .

AN HOUR LATER, Fenny and I are in my bed, taking turns scratching Gram Parsons's belly. We've blown off the party in favor of room service and lots of wine. Two Fisherman's Platters and a large carton of fries are arrayed about us. *The Real Housewives of Albuquerque* is on mute, and we're polishing off a bottle of Pahlmeyer chardonnay. Fenny's smoking a joint from a twenties-style cigarette holder.

Even though the call with my mother ended badly, I've taken Lorena's advice to heart. To practice telling Jake the truth, I've decided to try it out first on Fenny . . .

Who's scribbling something on the hotel notepad.

"Are you taking notes?" I ask, leaning in a little blearily.

"I'm making you a Pros and Cons list."

"I like it," I say. "Old-fashioned."

"So far, under the pros of you staying in this life—I've got your marriage to Jake, your successful career, financial stability . . . Okay, and I know this item falls under the umbrella of marriage, but I'm going to make it a separate category, because it's truly remarkable: Five orgasms. Am I missing any-thing?"

I rack my brain. What else is good about this life? "That might be it. I mean, you seem really nice . . ."

"No offense taken," Fenny says, waving me off.

I can't tell if she's humoring my realm-jumping revelations because she's kind and trying to help me survive a nervous breakdown. Or if indulging the delusional cast is part of Fenny's job.

Or maybe she actually believes me. Which would make her either truly open-minded . . . or totally insane—probably a dis-tinction without a difference.

"Wait," Fenny says, crunching into a panko shrimp. "What about Gram Parsons?"

"He's in both lives."

She shakes her head in amazement. "You can't write this shit—not that I won't try, fair warning."

I gaze at her meaningfully. "I want you to have it."

"So what's better about your . . . real life?"

"I have Masha. And my mom."

"That's it?"

"That's everything. I'm broke and lost and I hook up with silly men, but I never feel hopeless about myself."

"Because you've got what matters—"

"A deep, lifelong connection with women who love me for who I am."

"Your wolf pack."

I close my eyes, emotional with how much I miss them. I try to summon the last time my mom didn't hate me, and the image

that comes to mind is Lorena in her studio, the day I'd cried
about Jake. She'd had the gyokuro waiting for me. We'd curled
up together on my beanbag chair. She'd given me strength, just
by being there, by reminding me there were bigger things to feel
than hate.

How did I ever hate Jake?

"There's one more thing I should mention about my Real
Life," I say, spearing a scallop with a plastic fork.

Fenny waits.

"Jake is famous."

"Come again?"

"He has the highest rated talk show in the country. It's called
Everything's Jake, and he does these absurd stunts, which I used
to think were ridiculous, but now I see that they're also profound. People quote him when they reconnect with estranged
family members. They come on his show and open up to him.
There are entire online forums of personal success stories devoted to thanking him. He . . . changes people's lives. I know
that sounds crazy, but it's true. Where I come from, you can't go
anywhere without seeing his smile, hearing his jokes, feeling his
light."

Fenny squints contemplatively. "I can see that."

"In this life we're happy together, but he's got a better thing
going in my Real Life than he has here."

"You're selling yourself short, Olivia."

"But it's true. I'm not enough. Not compared with that."

"Which is why you pitched him so hard to Reisenbach on
the yacht today?"

"Curveball, low and away."

"I could have told you that would never work. Things here are different from your other life. For a reason."

"How do you know that?"

"Because it's such a good story. And stories create their own logic." Fenny runs a french fry through ketchup. "And logic equals reasons."

"But we don't have an ending."

"That's because you're still in the middle."

"How should our protagonist proceed?"

"Hmm," Fenny says, taking a swig of wine. "If this were a script, I'd ask myself, 'What do the characters want and why?'" She hands me her list of pros and cons. "Why don't you weigh these, on a scale of one to ten, according to importance?"

While I get to work, Fenny rests her cheek on her fist and looks toward the TV, where a woman in turquoise jewelry dumps a pot of posole onto the head of her dinner guest.

High Life:
Marriage to Jake 10
Successful Career 1
Financial Stability 1
Pentagasms 5

Real Life:
Relationship with Lorena 10
Relationship with Masha 10
Jake's Success 10

"It's seventeen to thirty," I say. "Did I just make my decision?"

Fenny looks at my list, then at me. She nods. "The only question is how do you get home?"

"Multiple orgasms clearly don't work."

Fenny throws a piece of battered fish in her mouth and stands up. "Is there a man behind a curtain in this realm?"

I nod. "In my Real Life he was a celebrity yogi. But here he's a rabbi-slash-car thief. He married Masha and Eli."

"That weirdo from the wedding?" Now Fenny's pacing. "Surely you can find him."

"Nothing's worked so far," I sigh and look at the list again. "If I could shift any one of these factors, everything would add up differently."

"Such as—"

"If I could get Masha to listen to me. If I could get her to understand."

Fenny nods. "Then you could keep the pentagasm *and* your best friend."

"While I work on getting Lorena back, too."

"Two out of three ain't bad," Fenny says and pours the last of our chardonnay into my glass.

"But . . . how?" I ask, swirling my wine, lost in contemplation.

"Masha just got back from her honeymoon this afternoon," Fenny offers, taking out her phone and texting. "Let me see what I can do."

Chapter Twenty-Three

RIDING HOME ON THE *WET DREAM* THE NEXT MORNING, everyone's hungover, including me. The chill in the air and overcast sky has me focused on one scenario: double espresso in the hot tub on the deck. Gram Parsons and I slip into the head so I can change into my black bikini. I grab a beach towel and a coffee to take outside.

Last night, Fenny set a Tuesday lunch date for herself and Masha . . . which I will gently ambush. My goals will be twofold: try to get Fenny in the least amount of hot water possible, and see if there's any love left between my best friend and me. If there is, then the math I did last night shifts in favor of the High Life.

If Masha rejects me, I'll have to face it. I'll have to go back to the wild-goose chase for Rabbi Dan. I'll have to forsake Jake.

The hot tub is wide open, its jets on, steam rising into the air. I tie Gram Parsons's leash to the handrail. His tail wags within his life vest. I climb a step to the hot tub and throw my leg over the side. Just as I slip into the water, Miguel Bernardeau and his girlfriend appear on the other side of the hot tub in matching skimpy suits, also holding coffees, also climbing in.

"Ah," Miguel says, as if Gram Parsons had just licked the

rim of his espresso. "Olivia. I don't believe you've met my friend Lucia."

"Hi, Lucia," I say and give a little wave. She smiles and waves back.

"Great party last night," Miguel says as he reclines and closes his eyes.

"Yep." I sip my coffee and watch the massive wake behind us, then I gaze out toward Catalina, the condos of Hamilton Cove receding in the mist. I think about last night, about Fenny talking through my mess with me, waving her vintage joint holder in the hotel room. I think about the joint still in my purse back in Laurel Canyon . . . Then it hits me: If Rabbi Dan is anything like Yogi Dan, he might hang out at Milo and Lhüwanda's, the Santa Monica weed café. Maybe I can find him there.

Something in my periphery catches my attention. I look starboard and see a fishing boat gliding over the waves, out on a morning troll.

When the boat draws nearer, I make out the word *Tongva* on its hull. I blink, incredulous, and then, looking closer, I see a man and a woman on board, both wearing baseball caps. The man's cap has the Italian flag on it. The woman's cap features the three-legged symbol of Sicily.

I gulp.

Masha and Eli.

I stand instinctively. Fate has entered the chat.

"Are you alright?" Lucia asks in a Spanish accent.

"That's my . . . friend," I mumble and climb out of the hot tub. I unhook Gram Parsons from the handrail and pick him up, offering a prayer of gratitude for his life vest. The *Tongva* is very close—no more than fifty feet away, stern-by-starboard.

I find myself standing on the starboard railing, Gram Parsons in my arms. Behind me somewhere I hear Fenny shouting, "Olivia, no!"

Then all I hear is water, all around me. I surface in the cold Pacific with Gram Parsons bobbing beside me, and swim like crazy toward my best friend.

· · · · · ·

"WHAT THE HELL are you doing here?" Masha asks as Eli hoists Gram Parsons and me onto the *Tongva*.

"Surprise?" I try jazz hands.

"No," Masha says. "I'm jet-lagged, and your face isn't helping."

As Eli throws a towel around Gram Parsons and me, I recognize Brandy's "Sittin' Up in My Room" coming from a Bluetooth speaker. On deck cushions I see remnants of a galbi feast, crushed cans of PBR on the side.

"I like your style," I say to Masha.

"Where's Jake?" Eli asks.

I turn and look at the *Wet Dream*, where the crowd on the deck is now dispersing—all except for Aurora, who stands at the railing, her arms crossed, glowering at me.

"Jake's home," I say. "I think."

"Well, he can come get you," Masha says.

This is going to be about as hard as I thought. In my arms, Gram Parsons shakes off, getting dry.

"You have a dog now," Masha says. "There should be tougher laws on who's allowed to own animals."

"This is Gram Parsons," I say, extending his paw to shake hands. "He'd love to hear about your honeymoon."

"*Ugh*," Masha says and spins away. "I told Eli this was going to happen—"

"You told Eli I was going to swim from a yacht to your rented fishing boat on the high seas off of Catalina Island?"

"I didn't predict all the specifics," Masha says, "but I wasn't far off. Eli didn't believe me. I called this as soon as I saw the Instagram pictures of the baseball game. I knew you'd use the one week I'm away, on my fucking honeymoon no less, to weasel your way onto the Yankees."

"It was an accident—"

"How do you *accidentally* play baseball on your enemy's team?"

My eyes widen. "You are not my enemy."

Masha laughs at the sky like Captain Ahab. "Since when?"

"Since we were Broken Bone Sisters."

"Don't you dare use that phrase."

"Masha. Please. Let me tell you my story."

"I know your story, Olivia. It's in *Us Weekly* every month when I get manicures."

"You don't know this one," I say. "It's truer and crazier than anything I've ever said."

We look at each other, and her eyes look so much like my favorite person's eyes that it's hard to watch her look at me and see nothing of our lifelong happy bond. But even this Masha used to. Once upon a time, even this Masha was *my* Masha. We were the same pair of best friends, until I left for New York and we drifted apart and then, somehow, things between us got accusatory and defensive. But the longer we lock eyes, the closer I get to that flicker of connection, the inner flame of friendship that nothing can extinguish. Gram Parsons whines in anticipation. Masha swallows and looks at her phone.

"Five minutes. You can re-bait my hook—"

"Mash," Eli says warily. "You sure?"

I smile and hand Masha Gram Parsons, whom she allows to lick her nose before setting him down at his favorite place near the stern. On some level, in some realm, my dog and my BBS *know* each other. And in this simple exchange I can feel it. The way, every now and then, one life echoes another, like how a melody in a guitarist's hands was formed by fingers in another space and time.

"Where's the bait?" I ask.

Eli unzips his Los Angeles Ballet fleece, throws it to me. "I'll be in the cabin," he says to Masha. "Call if you need me."

In a Styrofoam cooler I find fresh skipjack tuna on ice. "Do you have any Party Skirts?" I ask.

"In the tacklebox," Masha says.

I thread the pink and purple bristles through the eye cavity of the skipjack. Then I hook the dead fish through the gills. Before I cast the bait into the water, I hold it up for Masha to see.

"Just like Lea Thompson in *Some Kind of Wonderful*," I say. The BBS have watched that movie sixty-seven times. Then I do my best Mary Stuart Masterson: "'You break his heart, I'll break your face.'"

"Liv, don't," Masha says.

"How was your honeymoon?" I ask.

"Great," Masha says, like she's answering someone at the DMV.

"I missed you." The words slip out, and I hear how obvious it is that I mean it. I see Masha hear it, too. Whether or not she wants to admit it, she knows me.

She sighs. "What's all this about, Olivia?"

Though I practiced my approach several times with Fenny, I find myself speaking from the heart.

"A week ago, at your wedding, something happened."

"I know," she says. "I could have handled that better—"

"That's not what I'm talking about," I say. "From what I've learned in the last week, I don't blame you for what you said at the wedding. For the past ten years, you and I have been living in two completely different realities."

Masha rolls her eyes at the ocean. "Here we go. The pressures of the rich and famous."

"Mash," I plead, badly wanting to take her hand, to seize her shoulders, to reach her somehow. "Please listen to me. Here's the thing. In the reality I've been living in, we're still best friends."

She sighs. "Olivia, if that's what you wanted—and sure, there was a time when I wanted our friendship back, too—then you wouldn't have dropped me when you left home. You might have made time for—"

"I'm not being clear enough," I say. "The Olivia you know . . ." I pause, unfamiliar with the details of how I dropped her. "Does the word *sucks* cover it?"

Masha nods.

"But I'm talking about an actually different reality. Like a waking dream, or science fiction. Where you wake up in a house you don't recognize and a life you don't understand. It happened to me. It's happening now. And where I come from? Where I really live?" I take a stabilizing breath. "It's not just that we're best friends, Masha. You're my favorite part of my life. I don't have a lot else there, but even if I did, you'd still be my favorite part."

She looks at me. "I don't understand."

"We get tacos at Guisados on Tuesdays and we go Christmas tree shopping at the crack of dawn on Black Friday. We see every Marvel movie in the theater, and we're saving for a trip to Egypt. The last time you went fishing was a week ago when I took you out on this boat and played this music and served this beer and ate these ribs. And when you reminisced about my dad, you let your eyes get misty, and I did too, and we both knew it wasn't so much about my dad as that whole era when our lives were laid out before us like wrapped gifts we could shake but not yet fully know. You caught a big ass halibut and it was awesome. You were happy and you were scared about your wedding. And I was your maid of honor, and you had this tiny perfect ceremony with eighteen people and a gold palette and a celebrity yogi officiant."

Masha's jaw drops. "That's the wedding I wanted."

"I know," I say as goose bumps fleck my arms. "And it was all going perfectly, until your officiant—"

She cuts me off. "No one believed me—"

"I know, your mom said if you went with a non-rabbi officiant, you'd rue the day—"

"Rue the day," Masha says at the same time.

"In the life I'm coming from," I tell Masha, "I pulled your mom aside in her backyard and spoke to her."

"What'd you say?"

"I said, 'The rue is due to you.'"

A smile teases the corners of her mouth.

"I don't understand," Masha says. "How did you know? I didn't even tell Eli. He couldn't have told Jake."

"Because I was there. I was there for all of it."

"No, you weren't. You were too busy. Too important. And you have been for a long time."

"I'm a Lyft driver, and a bad waitress, and a furloughed part-time drama teacher. I'm single and can barely make my rent. I know in your version of reality, that's not the Olivia you know, but having lived in her shoes for this past week, I really have to tell you that even that Olivia is not too busy and certainly not too important for you. For our friendship. She really misses you, Masha. All the time."

"What about Jake?" Masha says.

"What about him?"

"You said on the planet you come from you're single. When did you two break up?"

"We were never together. We're more or less strangers."

"That's not possible," Masha says. "I can maybe believe the rest, but I don't think there's a force strong enough to keep you and Jake apart."

"That's really nice," I say.

"I wasn't trying to be nice. I hate your relationship. It cost me my best friend."

"Masha, you know how in *The NeverEnding Story*, Bastian enters the book?"

"Yeah. The book needs him to kill the Nothing."

I take a deep breath, about to drop the most insane part of my hypothesis. "I think kissing Jake Glasswell at prom is my *NeverEnding Story*. And my Nothing."

"You mean—"

"In the life I've been living these past ten years, we didn't kiss. We actually got in a fight and I never spoke to him again—well, not until I saw him at your wedding last week."

"And then what happened?"

"I was standing before him at your altar—maid of honor, best man positions, you know. And your yogi officiant, who in this life is somehow a rabbi—"

"Rabbi Dan? Who married us? Hangs out at the weed café?"

I close my eyes. "That's the one. He did something. He said some words about lives being inextricably entwined, and the next thing I knew, I was in a different dress, a different life, in a marriage to a stranger—and I was a pariah at your wedding. In your life. My mom won't even speak to me." I start to cry. "I hate it here. I want to go home. But—"

"But you're in love with Jake," she whispers, tears streaming down her cheeks.

"But I'm in love with Jake," I wail. "So I've been trying to figure out how to stay. I thought if I could make up with you, and my mom—and let me just say, the attempt with my mom went twenty times worse than this, if you can believe it."

"I can . . . I heard the podcast on the way here." She sighs.

"So you're having to choose between true love—I mean, I suspect that's what it is, right?"

"The truest."

"And what you say is a true bond with your mother and best friend. It's an existential crossroads. I can see why you're here."

"There's one more thing about the other life."

"What?"

"Jake is very famous."

Masha laughs.

"No, he is. He could probably run for president. Most of the country is as in love with him as I am here, and I feel like I'm robbing them of the joy of him, robbing him of the chance to live out that amazing experience."

"Is he happy?"

"I have no idea. We're not in touch, so it's not like I'd know."

"Is he happy here, with you? I know what it looks like from the outside, but you can never really know."

"He's happy. Almost nauseatingly happy."

Masha leans over and pukes off the side of the boat.

"What was that?" I ask.

She makes a retching face.

"You don't get seasick," I say. "You have a stomach of steel."

"Had a stomach of steel," she groans and wipes her mouth. I hand her a PBR . . . which she holds and doesn't open.

"Hang on—"

Pale-faced, Masha smiles.

"How long?" I ask.

"Six weeks."

Ecstasy spreads through me and I scream. I throw my arms around Masha, who goes stiff. "Let go."

"Sorry, I forgot," I say. "You like to hug where I come from."

She looks at me sadly. "You really love me where you come from."

"Take the love you can remember from high school," I say. "Square it twice for every year since we stopped being friends."

"Go home, Olivia," she says.

"What?"

"What you just said—that weird math of love—it sounds really nice. I'm jealous that you have that. I'm jealous that you know an *us* with that history, that bond. Even if you and I patched things up—and I am going to have to sit with that possibility for a while—there'd still be this big decade-long gap that we'd be missing. There'd still be a whole lot of pain to move through. Which isn't an issue in your reality. Not to mention your mom. I know you have a lot of money, but your show . . ."

"It's so bad."

"Awful. I'm sure you can navigate a new career," Masha says. "That's the least of your worries."

"So that only leaves . . ." I can't even say it. I'm too sad.

"Jake?"

I nod.

"Listen, you've told me some crazy shit today, and I'm having to stretch my mind to accommodate it. And I can—actually, I really can. There's just one thing I can't imagine, and that's a world where you and Jake don't end up together."

I stare at Masha, wanting her words to be true. But it feels terrifying.

"Tell him the truth. Go home and tell him everything you told me. Bring him out on a boat and hold him captive in international waters until he believes you. It's not the worst move." She raises one shoulder. "Then you can start your romance that very minute. And it won't be tied up in this invisible darkness, like losing your mom and me. It can be pure and strong and whole."

"You don't understand," I say. "Jake is so out of my league—"

She waves me off. "Yeah, I'm not receiving that. And I don't even like you. I mean, I sort of like you. But I know love when I see it. You and Jake are the real thing. You'll make it on the flip side, too."

Gram Parsons crawls onto my lap, sensing a breakthrough. I rub the ridge between his eyes and smile at Masha. "You see, that is exactly what the real Masha would say in this situation—"

"Don't real-Masha me. I'm the real Masha."

"Got it. Yes." I nod and let out my breath. "Mash, do you think there's any chance that I could just stay here and work really hard at friendship with you, and you could help me—"

"Olivia, go home."

Chapter Twenty-Four

I FIND THE NOTE ON THE KITCHEN COUNTER IN OUR empty house. It's written on hotel stationery from the Hotel Fasano in Rio de Janeiro.

> Liv,
> Went to Zuma to clear my head. Packed your board.
> I'll be at our spot.
> Love,
> J
> P.S. Sunset's at 6:14.

What I'm not used to about marriage—at least this particular marriage—is that a person can be mad at their spouse and still want to see them. Jake and I haven't made up. I owe him several deep apologies for how I behaved in Catalina. Still, I feel between the lines of his note the undertow of his love.

It touches me and amazes me and stumps me (where *is* our spot?). And even though I've never mounted a surfboard in my life, I know I'll be there, wearing a wet suit and my heart on my sleeve.

I picture Jake writing this note: hips pressed lightly against the counter, one beautiful bare foot crossed over the other, sexy reading glasses on. I can see the way his elegant fingers held the pen. There's a ring of condensation on the marble countertop from his tangerine La Croix.

I look through the kitchen window, yearning to remember our stay at the Fasano hotel. I wish I could access what the shampoo smelled like, whether we had an ocean or a garden view. Did our luggage get lost? What carefree Brazilian clothes did we buy in the meantime? I want to remember making love at sunrise, on fancy sheets after a sultry night of samba in secret clubs.

But this stationery sparks no memories. There's no nostalgia in its fibers. I feel only blankness, a cold and empty hole. As good as it feels to be with Jake, I'm not a part of his past. I need to find Yogi Rabbi Dan and go home.

But first, one more sunset with my perfect husband.

I feed Gram Parsons and head toward the master suite to change. I want to pack this evening's beauty into my heart like a souvenir I can keep with me forever. One night away from him, and I'm so jittery to reunite I feel like I've shotgunned seven cups of coffee.

How will I make it if I go home? If I have to spend the rest of my life without him?

I face myself in the bathroom mirror. "Maybe I don't have to. Maybe I can stay." But not even my reflection looks convinced.

What if I never have another love like this? How could anyone ever have another love like this?

My limbs feel heavy as I rummage through my bathroom drawers for sunscreen. I still don't know where anything is in this house. The bottom drawer's track gets stuck on something, and when I tug it, it springs loose all at once—and a folded pamphlet flies out.

What to Expect After Your Miscarriage

"What?" I whisper, dropping to my knees on the bathroom tile. One hand clutches my womb in disbelief. The other shakes as I open the pamphlet. My gaze falls on fine print highlighted neon yellow. *After three months, most women's bodies are ready to conceive again.*

I cover my mouth with my hand. The pamphlet is stapled to a hospital discharge document with my name listed next to *Patient*, along with the words *ectopic pregnancy, emergency D&C*.

I had an ectopic D&C? The emergency procedure necessary to end a pregnancy that takes root in the fallopian tubes? And not even *this* I remember?

I couldn't feel it. I had no idea. It makes me ashamed of my cluelessness. I think of the couples counseling Jake mentioned us going to—I hadn't understood the reason for it. I thought starting a family was hypothetical, somewhere in the distant future. I had no idea about the loss we've already been through. The realization is so devastating, it makes me woozy. I search through other items in the drawer. A prescription for pain medicine from the time of my hospital discharge. A half-used box of maxi pads. An envelope with my name on it. Jake's handwriting.

I open it and pull out the homemade card, written on the back of a photo of the kiss from the balcony scene of Zeffirelli's *Romeo and Juliet*.

I touch my fingers to the lovers. I think of our kiss at prom, how young and naive we were, how brave we were to take that chance, to lean over the edge into a kiss that carried us all the way here.

> Dear Olivia,
> I didn't know I could love you more than I always already have. But when our hearts broke open last week, even more love came flowing in. We don't feel it yet, but we're stronger. And we're lucky. We have each other. We'll try again. Imagine all the kisses . . .
> Yours forever everywhere,
> Jake

The card is dated three months ago. *After three months, most women's bodies are ready to conceive again.* I pull out the only other thing left in the drawer. It's an opened box—an ovulation kit. Jake and I are about to try again. We're going to try to have a baby. This thought sends a beautiful shock wave of warmth through my body—even as my brain is flashing *Caution* . . .

Every cell inside me wants to make a family with this man.

But not like this. I can't do it here, because one day my child will want me to tell them stories of how their dad and I fell in love. And I won't have the answers, because I wasn't there. Because I don't belong.

I've been faking it as Jake's wife all week, but you can't fake motherhood. I can't get pregnant here. I cannot have a child. And I can't stay here and *not* have a baby, depriving Jake of the family he wants. It tears me apart to face that this, finally, is it.

I take a beach towel from the linen closet, find my key fob for the Lucid. I kiss Gram Parsons goodbye and walk to the garage. It's five o'clock on a sunny Saturday in April. I've been in the High Life for a week. The sun sits high in the sky, a little west of center. I feel it guiding me, tugging me along. If I leave now, if I follow the sun, I can meet Jake at Zuma in about an hour. We can surf, we can talk, we can watch the sun go down. He won't know it, but that will be goodbye.

I'm crying by the time I reach the bottom of our driveway. There's a woman there, putting her key into my Real Life mailbox. I recognize her as the birthday cake burglar. She's wearing sweatpants, flip-flops, her hair in a topknot. Thumbing a stack of bills, she looks lost in the thick of her life's own struggles. She looks a lot like I used to look when I lived there. I wipe my eyes and roll down my window.

"Hi," I say. "I'm your neighbor. Olivia."

"Sarah," she says and smiles. "Crazy how we all live on top of each other here, but we never see each other." She looks at me. "Wait, Olivia Dusk? From *Zombie Hospital*?"

"That's the one."

"I was just watching your show while I folded laundry. Like, your face is literally frozen on my laptop. LA's so crazy, right?"

"You know what's even crazier? I used to live in your house."

"Really?" She laughs. "Wait, you're not the photographer who only took shots of nudes in bathtubs?"

"I think I lived there . . . before that. Or something." I put the car in Park. "Can I . . . come inside for a minute, to see what you've done to the place?"

"Totally," she says and waves me in.

I mount the three steps to the little front porch, hearing their familiar creak. Sarah's stained them, but in another world, they're a garish green I've always kind of loved. I run my hand along the banister, knowing where its rough places are. Home-sickness washes over me, and I wonder if I'll ever feel at home again, if I'll always feel stuck between lives, between realities, no matter what happens, where I go, what I choose. I've glimpsed a world I can't un-glimpse. I've felt a love I can't un-feel. Now I must un-stay. I know what I have to do, and I can't not do it.

The front door still sticks. I step over the threshold, and even though she's got incense burning, underneath it I smell the familiar scent of the house, woodsy with a whiff of jasmine. I walk through the rooms, touching the wall where my bookshelf used to be, where I'd once stored the rainbow color-coded stories of my life. I walk into the kitchen, where through the open window, you can still reach out and pluck the herbs that grow at eye-level on the ground. I touch the cool, damp soil.

I was here. I'll be here again. I want to take comfort in this, but it makes me want to cry.

"What do you think?" Sarah asks. "Is it weird to be back?"

"I like what you've done," I say even as the details of her changes disappear. On some level, I'm aware the furniture's dif-ferent, and the paint and the curtains, but none of that is regis-tering now. None of it matters. What I'm experiencing is a woman's life in this home. It's a little hardscrabble, a little glam-orous, a lot cobbled together with love and optimism, with re-jection and doubt and pain. Just like it was for me.

I remember everything about my life when I was here, and I want it back. I want to stand on the solid ground of the choices

I made. I want to feel them in my bones when I lie down in bed, when I sit outside at my table and look up at the two stars visible in the LA sky.

But I want Jake with me, too.

"This place is quirky as fuck, but I love it," Sarah says. "Wanna see the back?"

I follow her outside, where days ago I attempted to primp for Masha's wedding on this very lawn. That life—that me—feels so close, and so uncannily out of reach.

"You put in a projector," I say, studying the machine mounted under her roof's eave. "I always wanted to do that."

"My boyfriend housed it in this weatherproof casing," Sarah says proudly. Then she pauses, her features hitching a little with anxiety. "I know the bedrock is technically yours—"

"Those flickering images are mine!" I joke.

Sarah laughs.

"No, it's cool," I say. "That's how it should be used."

"You should come down some Friday, if you want. We have a movie club. We're going through every Gwyneth Paltrow movie. This week is *Sliding Doors.*"

"I've never seen it."

"Oh my God! You *have* to see it. Gwyneth plays the same woman in two different realities."

"Kind of like now."

Sarah's eyes go wide. "Exactly! Look at you, standing in your former life."

"Look at me," I say. Tears fill my eyes.

"Are you okay?" Sarah asks.

"Here's something they never tell you about getting married, Sarah. Don't forget to tell your husband you love him. At least one time."

"I'll remember that," Sarah whispers, taking a step away from me.

We stare at each other for a freakish moment, and though I wouldn't say no to a hug, I realize we should probably be done here. That she's extended enough kindness to a stranger in one day. But it's hard to leave, because this is my house, too, and in my other life it's a sanctuary from a hard world. I don't know when I'll be here again or what I'll have to go through to get back. The only thing I know is what I have to give up.

Jake. Glasswell. My husband. The only man I've ever loved.

A LITTLE-KNOWN FACT about Malibu is that even though it covers twenty-one miles of stunning coastline, only a small portion of it faces west. So if you want to watch the sun skinny dip into the sea, Zuma is one of the only places to go. But as I wind down Kanan Road toward PCH, a storm rolls in from the north, complicating the sky with dense gray clouds.

I'm anxious about finding Jake. Zuma is huge and usually crowded. The times I've gone there to meet friends, we've always had to drop a shared pin to find each other. But Jake expects me to know. We have a place we always go.

I pull up a list of prior places in the Lucid's GPS—I scroll through Musso and Frank, North Weddington Park, the Bungalow at the Fairmont Hotel. But there are no coordinates for

Zuma. My next best plan is to drive along the coast until I find Jake's red Jag, then look for him nearby.

But as I turn onto the beach access road, a sureness comes into my body. It's in my fingers on the wheel, in my toes on the accelerator. It's in my hips and ribs and eyes. It reminds me of something I used to experience long ago, when I acted in plays—right around the time I'd get down on myself, thinking I could never learn my lines in time, there would come a moment when I'd step onto the rehearsal stage, and my body would click into some hidden gear. The lines would come, not merely matching the script, but with a depth of emotion I'd spent months reaching for. The role had arrived, a gemstone polished by bone-deep intuition.

Now, the same thing happens. I know where Jake is. I let intuition guide me to a gorgeous inlet I've never been to before in Real Life. And there, parked on the shoulder, is his car.

I get out and run barefoot toward the water. The spray of sand stings my ankles, and the cleansing scent of the impending storm fills my nose. I scan the waves. There must be fifty surfers scattered in the water, all in black wet suits and dripping hair.

My heart picks up because I don't have much time, and there's more I have to do, and I want as much as I can get with Jake before I go. I stop running when I reach a surfboard resting on the sand. It's a green and black Odysea longboard, and I recognize it from the ceiling rack in our garage. Mine. A wet suit is folded on top of it, held in place by a beautiful abalone shell.

I pick up the wet suit and a sense memory washes over me: the give of the material, the heft of its weight. In this world I've worn this many times, with confidence and poise. I'm only here for a little while longer. I can do this. I can go out in the ocean and get up on this board.

I think of Jake leaving the suit and board here for me. Of his faith that I'd show up, even during a difficult argument, because that's what real love is. I don't know what's going to happen when I leave here, but I do know—far better than I could have a week ago—what intimacy means. I'll never settle for anything short of this.

Which means I'll be alone for the foreseeable future. I'm headed back to a world where Jake is Glasswell, and he hates me. And he's ruined me for everyone else.

"You came," he says, coming out of the water, wet hair whipped back out of his face. His smile melts me. I drop the wet suit and jog toward him. Then I'm running, sprinting all the way into his arms. They catch me, lift me up, and hold me against his chest. I close my eyes and breathe him in, eucalyptus and ocean. I shudder with the relief this closeness brings. He spins me once then sets me down.

I've never known love like this. And I can't take it with me.

"We need to talk," I say.

"I know." His hand touches my face, my neck, my shoulder, the length of my arm. Goose bumps rise on my skin. They always do when he touches me.

But if this is the last sunset I get with Jake, I want it how we came here for it. I glance at my phone. Twenty minutes of daylight left.

"Surf first?" I say, and he kisses me. Like we've got all the time in the world.

"I waxed your board," he says, and I can tell this is something he always does for me, without my asking. It's so simple, so kind, so Jake.

I slip into my wet suit, grab my board, and follow him to the water. The first frothy step into the cold shocks my feet, but once I go further in, deeper out, the suit keeps me warm. It's drizzling, the horizon moody, only patches of clear sky peeking through, turning amber in the fading light. We wade until the water reaches our waists, then we climb onto the boards and paddle out, parallel to the waves.

I know where to stop. I know which size and shape of wave to seek, how to mount the board right before the wave breaks— like intuiting which music is right for your mood. I can't remember the last time I swam out far enough in the ocean for my feet to come off the ground. Yet I know I've done it recently in this world with Jake. I wonder if I'll get to keep this expertise, this fearless giddiness when I go home.

"This one!" I call to Jake and we point our boards toward the shore as the wave rolls toward us—

"Now!" Jake shouts.

I hear him laughing, and I feel myself laughing as I sync myself with the rhythms of the waves. There's a part of me that's terrified, and a part that knows exactly what to do, and maybe that's just life at its best, but I've only really felt it in this realm. I'm not going to forget what it's like.

I paddle my arms and plant my feet. I rise on the board until I'm moving as one with the ocean. Jake is moving in tandem with me, a grin on his gorgeous face.

Like all good things, it seems to last forever, and then

suddenly it's gone too soon. Our boards ride to a stop on the sand, and we're still laughing as we come together, wrapping our wet arms around each other, wet suits squeaking as we embrace.

Facing the last lambent rays of sun amidst the unexpected storm, I put all thoughts of the future out of my head. I focus on what's in my heart. I tip his chin to mine and kiss him like it's the first time and the last.

Chapter Twenty-Five

"TARANTULA," I SAY, POINTING AT THE CLOUD UNFURLING above the violet horizon. "It's a tarantula . . . ironing a bow tie—do you see it?"

Jake presses his lips to my shoulder. Kisses slowly twice. "If cloud-spotting were an Olympic sport, you'd be tested for doping."

I give him a sidelong glance.

"Because you'd be so dominant!" he says.

Moments ago, we saw the sea take the sun like a shot of tequila. Now we're warming up before the fire we've coaxed out of the least wet logs on the beach. We're snuggling and laughing, putting off having a hard conversation.

"Look right above the tarantula," I say. "There's a bear."

"Wearing a do-rag—"

I point at the shifting mass. "Now it's Mary Magdalene."

"Don't you mean Bear-y Magdalene?"

"God likes to play, too."

"But you're still winning," Jake says.

We're huddled on a blanket I imagine we bought from a beach vendor on a trip to Mexico I can't remember. Jake's got an arm around me, and my hands are in the pocket of his hoodie. Through the soft, worn fabric, I can feel the muscles of his stomach. I can feel his familiar heat. It's so comfortable, so casually intimate, but I'm also aware of how soon this spell will be broken. How soon I'm going to have to break it.

"You're not hungry?" Jake asks, nodding at the snacks he set out on the blanket. Popcorn, smoked almonds, and my new High Life favorite—Flamingo Estate dried strawberries, seasoned with a hint of chili pepper.

"I'm starving," I admit. "I'm dying for a strawberry. But I'm also really happy with the current placement of my hands."

Jake smiles at me, and flexes his abs for effect. Then he plucks a strawberry from the jar and brings it to my lips. I open my mouth, kissing his fingers in gratitude, then I lean toward his lips. The tangle of heat and berry on our tongues is blissful, and I could very easily go for a pentagasm right here. But Jake pulls away.

He looks up at the sky and lets out a long breath.

"Dad."

I follow his gaze upward. Are we still playing the cloud game? The shape above us is a solid gob of gray, decidedly less playful than the wisps shifting in the fading light closer to the horizon.

If I had been here, in this marriage, all along with Jake, if I had grown into us honestly, moment by moment, I'd know what he means. I'd know the contours of his struggle and what to say to support him in his darkness. I hate that I don't know. My silence feels feeble, disappointing, and it makes me want to tell him everything, starting all the way back at prom.

But I can't. Even if—against all odds—he believed me, it wouldn't change anything. I'd still be going home.

"I'm sorry, Olivia," he says. In his pocket, he threads his fingers through mine.

"*You're* sorry?" I say. "I'm the one who should apologize. The way I acted on the yacht was——"

"You were trying to help me get something I want," he says. "I overreacted because, well, you know why."

I look up at the clouds, wondering if I do. "Your father."

"I can't help my reaction against nepotism. Against not doing everything on my own. Accepting Dad's help would have meant turning into him——"

"Which you could never do," I say, realizing this is true. It's why Jake is estranged from his father, because he didn't follow the family path. He chose his own way—both in this life and the one I came from. The painful beauty of this dawns on me: his choice to strike out on his own defines him. It matters more than whether Jake has the fame and fortune he has on the other side.

"But *you're* not my father," he says. "And I should remember that you love me for who I am, not who you want me to be——"

"I do," I say. I take a breath. "Of course. But I still shouldn't have said that on the yacht. I did it because . . ." I rest my head on his shoulder. "When I'm anxious, I fixate on solving external problems that belong to someone else. Sometimes I'll even invent a problem, just so I can solve it. I used to feel like that was the only way I could steady myself, to be useful. But it also lets me avoid dealing with my own issues. That's what I did to you on the yacht. And I'm sorry. The truth is, I don't care what kind of job you have. Just like I shouldn't care what kind of wedding Masha has or what kind of podcast my mom has. I need to let that go. Not just here, in this life, but . . ."

"Where else?" he asks. I shouldn't be surprised by how closely he's listening, but I am.

"Everywhere," I whisper. "All the wheres in all the worlds."

When he nods it brings tears to my eyes.

"What I'm starting to see," I say, "is that when I start here"—I put my hand over my heart—"when I'm true to the people I love, when I show up for them honestly, that's when I get steady. That's when I feel right." I take my hand out of his pocket, cup it to his cheek, the way he once cupped mine. I see in his eyes that it feels as good, as reassuring to him as it felt to me. "I feel right with you, right now."

"I've felt right with you from the first moment I saw you," he says. And then a playful glint comes into his eyes. "My first day of school at Palisades, junior year."

"Oh, come on. That's revisionist history." I bump his shoulder. "It was definitely prom. Not a moment sooner. It was us on the curb, when I leaned in and kissed you—"

"First of all, as has been established, *I* kissed *you*."

"Wrong!" I make a buzzer noise, energized by this little spat. I've missed fighting with him. We're kind of awesome at it. "I have proof. Documentation in diary form."

"Yeah, well, I see your diary," he taunts, "and raise you one meticulously detailed Moleskine journal."

"You do not have a Moleskine—"

"Third drawer of my desk in the office. You think you're the only one who writes? My account goes all the way back to my first day at school, the first time I saw the first girl I'd ever fall in love with. And it includes the truth about what happened at the audition for *Romeo and Juliet*."

I stare at him, trying to gauge whether he's messing with me. I know which moment changed the course of my life, and it was that kiss at prom. It's the demarcation point between Real Life and High Life. That Jake had feelings for me *before* then doesn't seem possible. Yes, he referenced the audition when he was stuck up in the palm tree, but I didn't know enough then to believe him. I want to argue this point further, but then—if he really did keep his own written version of events, am I supposed to know about it? Have I *read* it?

I tell myself to stop worrying about what I'm supposed to know in this life. The details of our past aren't real anyway. Or at least they won't be when I go home.

"Jake?"

"Yes?"

"If we'd never kissed at prom, if you'd leaned away—"

"You mean if you'd leaned away?"

"If one of us had leaned away, and we never got together—if we spent these past ten years apart, where do you think you'd be now?"

He considers this a moment, staring at the sea. He takes a long time answering, and I can't tell if the question annoys him. But then slowly, seriously, he says, "I think I would be living far away from you. I think I would have needed that distance between us, thinking it would let me move on."

"New York?" I say.

"Probably." He nods. "But it would have been useless. I wouldn't have moved on. I'd probably be channeling all that energy into some job, who knows what. Maybe it would make me successful. But I wouldn't be happy. I'd be dating the wrong person and realizing right about now the relationship would never work in the long run."

"Why not?" I say.

Jake turns from the sea to fix his gaze on me. He takes my hand. "Because there is only one long run for me. There only ever has been one. If we'd never gotten together, if we'd spent these ten years apart, I'd be making my way back to you now. I'd do anything to get another chance."

I try to see him as Glasswell, getting into my Lyft at LAX. He's the same person, but he isn't. And as beautiful as his idea of us is—that our love is inevitable—I'm the one who knows it didn't turn out that way in Real Life.

"The question is," he says, "if we'd spent the past ten years apart, and I came to you and told you the biggest mistake I ever made was not kissing you at prom, what would you do?"

I swallow the sob rising in my chest. "Luckily," I say, "we'll never have to worry about that."

. . . . . .

"WHOA, WHOA, WHOA," says the security guard at Milo and Lhüwanda's, the weed café in Santa Monica. I remember him from the last time I was here, a week ago, back in my Real Life. He didn't want to let me in then, either.

I put both hands up. "I'm chill, okay?"

"We're only serving straight food today. No joints, no edibles."

"Why?"

"Because we're out of weed."

"You're out of *weed*?"

"It happens. Once I went to Taco Bell and they were out of tacos."

I spot Rabbi Dan past the guard, with his yarmulke and short sleeve button-down shirt, his silk tie printed with menorahs. He's sitting at the zinc bar, reading a mass-market paperback, eating a slice of pound cake.

"Hey, you're on that show," the security guard says to me. "Whose dumb idea was it to mash up—"

"I completely agree," I say. "*Zombie Hospital* sucks so bad everyone involved should be imprisoned. Thing is, I'm here to see that gentleman."

"Rabbi?" the guard calls. "This B-list celebrity with you?"

Rabbi Dan looks me up and down, chews his cake. "Depends on what she wants," he says.

"I want to talk to you," I say to Yogi Rabbi Dan "I want to go home."

Rabbi Dan wipes his mouth with a napkin and nods to the guard. "Let her in."

"Thank you," I say, sliding onto the stool next to him.

"Did you bring it?"

I open my purse to show him the giant joint Jake put there the last time we were at this café. Right before Masha's wedding, right before the multiverse swallowed me whole.

"You haven't smoked it," Rabbi Dan says. "You must like it here."

"I took one hit. Nothing happened. You said it wouldn't work, anyway."

"That was then," he says. "You'd just arrived. But your eyes say now you're a different person. You *believe*."

I wonder if the rabbi's right. I decide he is.

"Where's Jake?" he asks.

"He's on his way home," I say, picturing him when we'd said goodbye in Zuma. I'd held in my tears as he kissed me, until I was alone in my car. "We were just at the beach together—"

"One final sunset?" Rabbi Dan smiles.

"I told him I'd meet him at home but . . . what happens when I leave here? To this version of him? What happens to everyone when I leave?"

"That's not for you to know," Dan says. "It's not for anyone to know. You make your choice and surrender to the universe."

My eyes fill with tears.

Dan tilts his head. "May I ask why you want to leave?"

"Because it isn't real," I say. "And I know you're going to say reality is overrated—"

"Do I talk like that?"

"But history *is* real," I say with conviction. "Experience is real. All those moments are the basis for love, and I missed too much of what built our relationship in this life. I can't stay any longer. I have to go back."

"Oh," the rabbi says, looking concerned. "You do know, Olivia, there's no guarantee of a return trip. This isn't an airline. You might leave here, but . . ."

"What do you mean? I could end up in some third reality?"

"Or fourth or fifth or thousandth," he says. "So you need to be sure you really want to leave."

WHAT'S IN A KISS?

My mind flashes to Jake an hour ago at the beach. The feel of my hand in his pocket. I don't want to leave that. I don't want to leave him. And yet I'm sure I'm not supposed to be here. If I think about it any longer, I might change my mind.

"I'm ready." I take the joint out of my purse and place it on the table. "I'll take my chances. Let's go."

The rabbi lights a match and puts the joint between his lips. He inhales, a bit unceremoniously for my liking—shouldn't such a moment be treated with more gravitas?

"'S good shit," he wheezes and passes the joint to me.

I hold it between my thumb and middle finger. "So I take a hit and . . . leave this reality?"

"Not exactly," the rabbi says. "What did you learn while you were here?"

"I learned the value of my mother and my best friend—"

"But you already knew that."

"I learned there's a world where Glasswell and I . . . don't hate each other."

"Wow," Rabbi Dan says. "You haven't even left and the Walls of Jericho are going up."

"What else am I supposed to do? In my Real Life, Jake's a god and I'm a wad of gum stuck to the universe's shoe. I've got to toughen up if I want to survive."

"Or . . ." Dan says.

"Or what? Go back to my Real Life and tell Glasswell what I learned about us here? That we could be in love, and it could be so beautiful neither of us should waste another moment not trying to recreate it?"

Rabbi Dan laughs . . . and laughs, for a solid minute, banging a fist on the bar as tears well in his eyes.

"My point exactly," I say. "I think I'll take my chances with my walls."

"I'm not laughing because what you proposed is ridiculous," Dan manages to say. "I'm laughing because this weed is *bubonic*."

I sigh and hold up the joint. "How long is this going to take?"

Dan's eyes rove from me to the joint, then back to me. "You don't think that joint's *magical*, do you?"

"What *else* would I think? I've been carrying this around all week!"

Dan laughs again. "You're hilarious. There is no magic joint."

"Where *is* the magic then?!?" I yell.

"Hey now—" the security guard says, standing up behind his desk.

"I'm chill," I lie to him. "I'm fucking chill, okay?"

Rabbi Dan leans toward me, taps a finger on my chest. "You've had it all along."

"Then what the hell do I need *you* for?"

"You don't." Rabbi Dan shrugs.

"Damn it, Dan. Why am I still here? How do I leave?"

"How did you get here?" the rabbi asks in a far-out stoner voice.

"How did *you* steal a Honda?" I ask.

"Hey, hey," Dan says, throwing up his hands. "Tithing takes many forms."

"You are so infuriating," I say. Then I allow myself to consider his question. How *did* I get here? Masha's ceremony. Rabbi

Dan said those words about two people becoming inextricably entwined. Then I stared at Jake. There was a burst of light, a tremor in the ground. And that's when it happened.

"A light bulb is turning on in your mind," Dan says and smiles as if he's been waiting for this all along. "Right on."

Is that it? Do I need to don my maid of honor hat and make Masha's wedding happen a second time? Do I need to go out the way I came in?

"Can you meet me tomorrow morning at ten at Lifeguard Tower 28?" I ask Rabbi Dan.

He nods and we rise from the table, the deal struck.

"Don't forget to bring the joint," he says. "There appears to be a shortage."

Chapter Twenty-Six

I SPEND A SLEEPLESS NIGHT ALONE IN THE BRIDAL suite at Shutters on the Beach, attempting to recreate the details of Masha and Eli's Real Life wedding. By ten on Sunday morning, I'm dragging toward Tower 28 a chuppah made of plywood, hot glue, and lace.

I hear the beep of a large truck in reverse, and I look toward the sound. A tow truck pushes a red 2012 Nissan LEAF out of the Shutters parking garage. Somewhere deep inside I'm panicked and intrigued. But I don't have time to think on it more.

I'm wearing a golden shift that approximates my maid of honor dress. I'm barefoot and have painted exactly half of my lips red. I made four handwritten programs, one for every person I'm hoping will show up today. I affixed the programs with popsicle sticks. I bought a small bouquet of white and yellow calla lilies from the florist up the beach. I have a sack of take-out pupusas, a string quartet version of "Just Like Heaven" downloaded on my phone, a sunny sky, and a heavy heart.

"I recognize this maid of honor," a voice behind me says.

I turn to find Rabbi Dan making his way down the beach. He's dressed as his alter-ego yogi self—his Jewish novelty tie replaced with the unnecessarily sheer white kurta, his yarmulke swapped for a sand-colored headscarf.

"How do I look?" he says and spins like the sand is a catwalk.

"Like a man I'd drag out of a weed café so he could be twenty minutes late to officiate my best friend's wedding," I say.

"Where is everyone?" Yogi Dan says, scanning the quiet beach. "I've got a bris at eleven or a kundalini class at eleven thirty. Depending on how things go."

I check my phone, but there are no new messages. Jake hasn't written me back since last night, after we text-argued about my decision to stay in Santa Monica. He was shocked, then confused, then annoyed. He wanted to come meet me, said he'd pack a bag and bring Gram Parsons and be at Shutters in an hour. When I responded that I needed some time, that I'd explain everything today, he called. And called. I put my phone on silent, knowing that if I picked up, I'd end up spending the night in his arms, and I'd lose the will to do what I have to do right now.

If he'd called one more time, I probably would have caved. But he didn't.

Now I'm terrified I've blown it anyway. Terrified he won't show up.

"He'll be here," Yogi Dan intuits. "The wild card is the bride."

He's right. When I'd called Masha last night to invite-slash-beg her to come today, she'd sent me to voicemail. I was in the middle of leaving a long, ungainly voice memo when I got her text.

Masha: You're still here? Didn't I tell you to go home?

Me: About that.

Me: I may need a tiny bit of help.

Masha: Wrong number.

Me: Please, Mash. If this works . . . you'll never hear
from me again.

Me: I mean, you'll never hear from me in this realm. In
my world, I'm probably going to need an extended
girls' weekend to hold you close and parse this shit.

Me: Not your problem, sorry.

Masha: . . .

Me: One favor, Mash.

Masha: What

Me: Twenty minutes of your time.

Masha: When

Me: Ten am tomorrow. Lifeguard Tower 28. Bring Eli.

Masha: If I do this, you'll leave me alone? For real?

Me: Wear white.

"She'll be here," I say to Dan, willing it to be true. "We want the same thing."

"Everybody does," he says. "Some of them just don't know it yet."

Out of the corner of my eye, I see a familiar blur of movement. Even when she hates me, Masha still walks the same way: her dark, curly head tipped a little to the right, a slight bounce on her heels. I hold my breath in gratitude as she and Eli approach on the boardwalk, hand in hand. He's wearing jeans and a white polo—I'll take it. She's in a short white sundress printed with tiny yellow daisies. My palms sweat as I grip the improvised bridal bouquet. My hands need something to do so they don't fold Masha in a hug.

She and Eli reach a concrete divider on the boardwalk. I watch as Eli stops her, lifts her in his arms, and carries her, threshold-style, over the ledge.

"I can walk," she says, laughing. "I'm pregnant, not paralyzed."

"Why should you exert yourself?" he says, seeming reluctant to put her down even on the other side of the barrier. "You should save your strength."

"Save your own strength," she says. "Once we hit the third trimester, lifting me will tear your arms out of your sockets."

"Who needs arms?" When he kisses her, I let out an adoring sigh.

The sound of it reaches Eli, who looks up and takes in the chuppah. Then me beneath it. He rubs his eyes.

Clearly Masha hasn't told Eli about meeting me today.

"Morning." I wave innocently.

Before Masha even sees me, Eli's got her by the shoulders, turning her back in the direction they came.

"What are you doing?" she asks.

"I think I left the panini press on," Eli says, darting a glare at me.

"We don't eat paninis." Masha laughs, then follows his gaze to me. "Oh."

"Let's go, Masha," Eli says. "You know what the doctor said about stress."

My best friend slips an arm around her husband's waist. She lets her breath out, and I love her for doing this for me.

"It's okay," she says. "I didn't tell you why we were coming here because a) I knew you wouldn't agree to it, and b) the explanation is totally insane. Basically, Olivia needs a favor."

"And you said yes?" Eli asks slowly. "To what, exactly?"

"A vow renewal," I say. "It shouldn't take long."

"We got married a week ago," Eli says.

"It's never too early to reignite your love," I say.

Eli squints at Yogi Dan. "Rabbi? Why are you dressed like a yogi?"

"Actually," Dan says, looking at himself, "this is very similar to how the Essenes dressed during the Second Temple period."

Masha points at Yogi Dan, her eyes growing wide. She touches Eli's arm. "Do you remember when I told you about the wedding I actually wanted?" she whispers.

"The one Babushka would never agree to?" Eli says, then seems to grasp her meaning. "How does Olivia know about it?"

I take the opportunity to place the bouquet in Masha's

hands. She rotates the flowers in her palm, studies them closely. "Yellow and white callas," she says under her breath. Her gaze travels up to my dress. "Gold palette."

I nod.

"Is this what it was like?" she asks me. "Did I get what I wanted?"

"It was beautiful," I say. "Very intimate. Just your style. The chuppah was nicer and we had live music, but otherwise—"

"What's with your lipstick?"

"This wasn't your preference. I did it for continuity, and luck."

"And my babushka?" Masha asks. "She agreed to this?"

I hesitate before telling her the truth. "Not at first, but there was a brunch where we set some boundaries. I told her to check herself. We worked it out."

"You did that for me?" she says.

"BBS, Mash," I say, and when her eyes shoot toward mine and I see the distance that her mind has to travel to fathom the possibilities of our friendship, to feel as naturally giving toward me as I feel toward her . . . it makes my decision that much clearer.

"Let's just do this," she says.

"But what the hell *is* this?" Eli says.

"I think," Masha says, "the rabbi . . . yogi . . . Dan marries us? Again?"

"Actually," I say, "first, we're waiting on—"

"What exactly did I miss?" says America's Sexiest Voice behind me.

"Jake!" I run to him, kicking up sand and leaping into his arms. He catches me, kisses me softly on the lips. It's so good to hold him that I almost quit the whole plan on the spot. "Thank you for being here."

"What's this about, Olivia?" he asks warily, eyeing the chuppah, the flowers, my dress and half-painted lips. I see I'm not the only one who was up all night. In the High Life, it's agony for Jake and me to spend time apart. I hate that I'm trying to get back to a place where we don't see each other, don't need each other, don't care about each other. I hate that leaving him is the best choice I have.

"You didn't tell Jake?" Masha asks me.

"Tell me what?" he says. "What's going on?"

I press my hands to his chest and gaze into his beautiful green eyes. I'm going to miss this view. "Will you indulge me for a few more minutes?"

He sighs. "And then you'll explain what's going on?"

"I'll explain everything."

My hands shake as I pass out the programs. Yogi Dan's copy has a handwritten script on the back, the words he said the last time we did this transcribed to the best of my memory for him to repeat today.

"Stand here, please," I place Masha under the chuppah before Yogi Dan. "And you here, Eli." I place him next to Mash. The newlyweds share a glance, brows furrowed, but they don't move while I place Jake on the far side of Eli. Then I stand on the far side of Masha.

I take out my phone and cue up "Just Like Heaven," the song that would have played right after Mash and Eli kissed, if we hadn't skipped realities. I want to have it ready when the moment is right.

"This is the song I wanted to walk out to during the recessional," Masha says, incredulous, glancing at my screen.

"I know," I say. "And you will."

She squeezes Eli's hand, and the four of us face Yogi Dan, who meets Jake's eyes, then Eli's, then Masha's, then mine. The moment is right. I cross my fingers behind my back.

"Friends and loved ones of Masha and Eli," Yogi Dan says in a booming voice. "We welcome you in peace and love."

I watch my best friend and the man she loves in profile. I watch their faces as they hear the words they wanted spoken at their wedding. Masha's features soften as she listens. Eli's eyes fill with tears. And Jake—

I can't bring myself to look at him yet, though I feel him looking at me.

Then it's my turn to give my reading. I open my copy of *To the Lighthouse* and hear Masha gasp. It's not my original copy from AP English—my High Life mom would have donated that by now. I picked this one up at Diesel yesterday. The cover's different, but the words I need are the same.

"'What art was there, known to love or cunning,'" I read, "'by which one pressed through into those secret chambers? What device for becoming, like waters poured into one jar, inextricably the same, one with the object one adored? Could the body achieve, or the mind, subtly mingling in the intricate passages of the brain? or the heart? Could loving [make them] one?'"

Masha stares at me as I finish, a hand pressed to her lips. I get the feeling that beneath her fingers, she wants to mouth our code—BBS. But she won't. Not here. And it's for the best. It gives me something to look forward to.

"And now," Yogi Dan says, consulting his program, "a reading from the world's Best Man."

Jake looks confused. "Is that supposed to be me?"

I hand him the King James Bible, also new from the bookstore, and flip it open to the bookmarked page.

"'Two are better than one; because they have a good reward for their labour. For if they fall, the one will lift up his fellow: but woe to him that is alone when he falleth; for he hath not another to help him up. Again, if two lie together, then they have heat: but how can one be warm alone?'"

As he finishes reading, his eyes cut toward mine, and I realize I'm not wondering anymore about what these words mean to him. He is a man who believes in marriage and in love. I've been lucky enough to bask in that belief this week, but I have to step away from it now.

"Our maid of honor made a powerful point in her reading just now," Yogi Dan says, and I remember how the last time he said this, I'd felt competitive pride. I was trying to win. I was trying to make Jake lose. I didn't understand we could win so much better together.

"Olivia used the word *inextricably*, a gold-gilt frame for the union you dawn today. Your lives never will untangle after this ceremony. You are forever connected, *inextricably*."

I know what I have to do. I raise my eyes to Jake. He's looking at me. I knew he would be. What was once a shallow game of chicken is now a profound expression of love. How strange that both experiences ignite the same sensation in my core, that building heat, that tingling flush in my cheeks. Is this it? Is it working?

"You may kiss to seal your love," Yogi Dan says.

I break my gaze away from Jake to see Masha and Eli lean in for a kiss. I missed this part, once upon a time, and it's beautiful to see.

Except that when I look back at Jake, he's not looking at me anymore. He's looking at Masha and Eli, too. He's clapping, the way you do at this point in the wedding, and I realize in horror we're still in the High Life.

I grab Jake's shoulders, pull his focus to me. I stare into his eyes and will him to hate me, will myself to hate him.

"Liv?" he says.

"It didn't work." I turn to Yogi Dan.

He shrugs. "Try the joint."

"Seriously?" I demand. "That's all you've got?"

"What do *you* got, Olivia?" he challenges.

"I don't know," I mutter, feeling catastrophically alone. Until I look at Jake.

If Jake's claim about his Moleskine is to be believed, both Glasswells fell for me on the first day of spring semester, junior year. Almost at first sight. Both Jakes wanted to climb the trellis to meet me as Juliet, but shied away because they were scared. Which means . . . the annoyance I'd always assumed was haughtiness in my Real Life might simply have been Jake struggling to reach me, to know me, to get me to see him.

Which means . . . all those moments from Masha's Real Life wedding that I'd filed under Glasswell being a dick—from Lyft pickup to ceremony stare-down—was I wrong about those, too? The sureness of my answer solves something inside of me.

"Okay." I close my eyes. "Here goes."

I have to get this right. It's the most important thing.

"Jake." I meet his eyes. They give me courage I didn't know was available. I think back on our bravery at prom. "I know there's another world. One where we . . ." I pause, seeking the words, "could be as good as we are now. I've made a lot of mistakes in this world that have separated me from my mom and my BBS." I glance at Masha, whose nod urges me on. "But in that other world, where I come from, I've really only made one."

"What was your mistake?" he says, indulging me.

"I didn't kiss you the first time I had the chance."

He smiles. "Surely, there'll be other opportunities," he says in that sexiest voice. "You could seize the next chance, if it means so much to you."

I open my mouth, then close it. Is it that simple?

But in my Real Life Jake and I are galaxies apart. "I can't," I tell him truthfully.

He steps closer to me, tips his forehead down to mine and whispers. "I feel like you should try."

"You don't understand," I protest. "I'm messy. And you're—"

He touches a finger to my lips. "In love with you. Here. There. Everywhere. All the wheres in all the worlds. Always."

Tears fill my eyes. I kiss his finger at my lips. I take his hand and run my thumb along his wedding ring, while he still wears it, while he's still mine. I rise on my toes and press my mouth to his. And just in case it's the last chance I get to say it, at least let it also be the first.

"I'm in love with you, too. Everywhere."

The opening chords of The Cure's "Just Like Heaven" play

around us. Light blooms in my periphery. The ground beneath me shakes, then falls away.

For a moment everything is black.

"Jake?" I call into the darkness. This didn't happen last time. I'm supposed to still be staring at him under Masha's chuppah on the beach, just back in my Real Life, where we're not married, where I drive a Lyft, and he's a star.

But I'm not under any chuppah. I'm nowhere near a beach or Jake. Fear grips me as the darkness shifts and I blink in sudden florescent lighting.

I'm . . . in high school. Walking toward my English class. I look down at the bomber jacket I'd gotten for Christmas, at my skinny jeans and Converse, and I know it's the first day of spring semester, junior year. Rounding a corner in the hallway, my shoulder bumps someone else's. I look up and see it's him. Seventeen years old and gorgeous, and—didn't this moment *really* happen? Didn't I glare at Jake instead of realizing I should have fallen head over heels right then?

I know it now. So I take the chance. I smile. "Hi. I'm Olivia—"

There's another flash of light, another rift beneath my feet. Suddenly, I'm at the gas station near my parents' house, filling up my car. When I look over, I see him watching me. He grins. I grin back. "You go to Palisades," he says. "I'm new—"

Flash. A boy steps onto a darkened stage, facing me up on the makeshift balcony. I'd know the moment anywhere. Auditions for our senior play.

"So strive my soul," Jake says.

"A thousand times good night," I say, knowing I'm supposed to exit now, but I can't. I stand transfixed as he says his next line.

"A thousand times the worse, to want thy light—"

Flash. I'm on a picnic blanket on Mulholland, leaning in to kiss Jake first—

I'm in Masha's parents' basement, watching him lean in to kiss me—

I'm in the ice cream aisle at Ralph's, holding two pints of gelato as I wrap my arms around him and make the first move—

I'm on a boat, fishing with my dad and Jake and when my dad turns away for an instant, Jake leans over and shyly, quickly pecks me on the lips, beating me to it, much to my surprise—

I'm at prom, on a curb, and Jake says, *I know there's another world*, and I say, *Me too*, and we both lean in at precisely the same time—

Flash. I'm at my father's funeral. Jake's there, holding my hand . . .

I'm on a plane flying to New York, jubilant with excitement to see my long-distance boyfriend.

I'm on a plane flying to LA, counting the days until he'll visit me in two months.

I'm taking acting classes at night.

I'm standing backstage on the first day of *Everything's Jake*.

I'm on a ferry to Catalina with Jake, Masha, Eli, and my mom, to celebrate her fifty-fifth birthday.

I'm holding the keys to the first rental house Jake and I share in Laurel Canyon.

I'm on a couch with my feet in his lap, writing a lesson plan for my drama class at LAUSD.

I'm reading *Podcasting for Dummies*.

I'm at the mixer in my mom's garage, slurping gyokuro and

laughing with her and Jake as we discuss *Get Out of Your Inner Hero's Way*, which I think I finally read.

I'm standing at Masha and Eli's intimate gold palette wedding, gazing at Jake Glasswell, who's gazing at me. There's a hazy dreamlike quality to the moment that tells me I haven't landed where I'm going yet. That I'm here temporarily for a reason. I grasp that this wedding is happening because Jake and I just rescued Yogi Dan from the weed café. This wedding is happening because ten years ago at prom I ditched Eli to hang out with Jake. In a moment, the two of us will give our readings. Jake will win, and that's okay. I know something he doesn't, that we're on the brink of a brand-new world. I smile at him. I can't help it. It takes him a second, but then he smiles back—

Flash.

I'm back in darkness, seeing nothing, but knowing everything: I could have met this man a thousand ways. We could fall in love a thousand times, in a thousand places, with a thousand sets of circumstances. We could write a thousand different love stories, and the details would be different, but our hearts would be the same.

Here. There. Everywhere. All the wheres in all the worlds. Always.

"I love you, Jake Glasswell!" I sing out into the void with joyful certainty, just as light blooms again in my periphery, and the ground beneath me shakes, and Yogi Dan's voice says from over my shoulder:

"I now pronounce you husband and wife."

Chapter Twenty-Seven

"MASHA?" I SPIN TO FACE THE BRIDE. OUR EYES LOCK, and I can see the change in her immediately. It's all there between us—our history, our laughter, tears, and love. I'm back at her real wedding. I'm back where I belong.

"This is your wedding dress," my voice breaks as my fingers trace the tulle of her gown. "This is your wedding hair." With trembling hands, I pat, very gently, her bouffant. I look up at the canopy above us, lightly threaded through with ranunculus. "This is your gold wedding palette. And your eighteen wedding guests—"

"This is it." Masha reaches for my hand and squeezes. She's smiling, the only bride in history who would patiently indulge such an interruption at the climax of her wedding ceremony. "You good, Liv?"

Tears well in my eyes. I lift our clasped hands and press them to my heart. "This is your maid of honor."

Masha nods, biting back a laugh. "Last time I checked."

"What is she going on about?" Eli says in Masha's ear.

"Oh fuck," I gasp. "Did I just wreck your wedding?"

"Not yet," America's Sexiest Voice says in my ear. "But you're dancing near the edge."

Slowly, I turn to face Jake, and oh my God, he's gorgeous. I feel my body light up at the sight of him and it must be obvious that I'm glowing, but then—

It occurs to me that while I was on my kaleidoscopic voyage through every love story with Jake, I don't know exactly when I landed back in my Real Life. Specifically: was it before or after I publicly proclaimed my love for Jake at Masha's altar?

"Did I say anything . . . unexpected just now?" I whisper.

"As a matter of fact, you did." Jake smiles.

"I can explain—"

"Olivia," Eli cuts me off. "All you said was *Glasswell*. Can we continue? I've got a bride to kiss."

"But she said it with a lot less rage than usual," Masha says.

"I definitely detected a note of fondness," Jake says.

Jake's teasing me—a reassuring return to form, but there's more to it. Like, in some unconscious part of his mind, he knows what we're capable of feeling for each other, of being to each other.

Or maybe Jake is looking at me the way he always has, only now I finally see him. I'm going to have to find a way to show him. I'm going to have to take the reins. I'm going to have to—

Kiss him.

"This is what you get when you hire a *mumar*!" Babushka's rabbi calls out in the audience.

"Sometimes, Rabbi," Yogi Dan's voice interrupts my thoughts, "you have to go off script to find the meaning of the scene." He beams at Masha, then Eli. At Jake, then me. "Look at these lovebirds. Do we want to linger in the moment, or do we want to kiss the bride?"

"We want to kiss the damn bride," Eli says emphatically.

"While we're young!" Babushka bellows, making everybody laugh. My gaze is locked with Jake's again, but the competitiveness has faded, leaving in its place a tingling thrill.

Then the crowd is cheering, the string quartet is playing "Just Like Heaven," and Masha and Eli are walking by us, hand in hand.

"Damn it, I missed the kiss *again*," I say.

"Somehow I don't think you missed a thing." Jake's fingers graze mine, then pull away. "Sorry—"

"For what? I mean, no problem! I mean . . . I didn't mind." I palm my face in an effort to shut up. Taking the reins is going amazingly so far.

"What's going on in there?" Jake nods in the direction of the fireworks exploding in my mind.

"I'm just . . . happy," I say with a smile to prove it. "For Masha and Eli. You know."

"I do know," he says, innuendos in his eyes. "I'm happy, too."

Someone shakes my shoulder. "Maid of honor? Best man?" the stressed-out wedding photographer says. "I need you for a photo."

Jake follows me out from under the wedding canopy, where we pass Yogi Dan, who gives me two vigorous thumbs-up.

"Thank you," I whisper, pausing for a moment to unclasp my purse and pass him what's left of the giant joint before I go.

Jake and I walk down the beach toward the water, and as we pass Lifeguard Tower 28, I see a familiar silhouette. Upswept mop of red hair, orchid tucked behind her ear, face hidden by binoculars.

"I'll be right there," I say to Jake and the photographer as my heart soars out of my chest.

"Mom?"

"Shit!" Lorena ducks behind the tower. "I'm not here. You don't see me." She drops the binoculars and her guard. "I respect Masha's small-wedding wishes, but I had to watch my baby's BBS tie the knot. You look so beautiful, honey, and you did such a good job pulling all this off. I'm proud of you."

I throw my arms around her, holding tighter than I've ever held anyone before. "I love you, Mom. I love you so much."

"I love you too, baby," she says with deep affection, making no move to loosen our embrace. "You're my best. Now get back out there. Don't leave Jake Glasswell hanging."

I pull away, dabbing tears from my eyes. I want to see her face. "What do you mean?"

"I mean, before that photographer interrupted you, it looked like you were in the middle of something juicy. Squeeze it till the juice runs down your—"

"Mom!" I say. "We were only talking."

"You think I don't know? I'm your mother. I know. It's time you got wise."

I smile at her. "I'll call you later."

"I can't wait."

I spot Jake standing alone by the water. My heart picks up as I approach him. By the time I'm at his side, it's like a jackhammer in my chest.

"What happened to the photographer?" I ask.

"She was called away to take pictures of the mother of the

bride," Jake says, gesturing toward the wedding tent. He turns to me and I think he might be nervous, unless that's my nerves refracting off of him. "She said to stay here. While the light's good. She'll be right back."

"Oh," I say. It's true the light is very good on Jake right now. "So we just . . . stay here."

A small smile splits his lips. "We can handle that, right?"

I think of my mom's reassurance a moment ago. I think of Masha in the High Life, angry with me on a fishing boat, but sure that Jake and I were meant to be. I think of lying next to him on home plate, slightly concussed, and eating hot dogs on Deck Day in our underwear, feeling there was nothing sexier than potting plants right next to him. I think of us posing as strangers at the Sunset Marquis. I think of us on that curb at prom, and what we should have done.

"Can I try an experiment?" I ask.

He looks at me. "Sure."

"And if it goes horribly wrong, can I take it back?"

He nods slowly. "Yeah."

"Jake?"

"Olivia."

"I'm terrified."

"It's okay. Whatever it is—"

I kiss him. Simple, swift, tiptoes, and lips. No arms—a safeguard to ensure I'll pull away after half a second, because although I want to melt into Jake for the rest of ever, I also need to check the results of my experiment.

But before I pull away, his arms come around my waist and

draw me into him, close and firm. His lips part and pull mine in as his head tilts and his tongue teases and the multiverse's sexiest voice actually moans . . .

"Olivia."

The way he says my name, with his teeth nibbling my lower lip . . .

"Yes?"

"Don't you dare take this back."

And then my arms wrap around his neck and he lifts me up and kisses me like we've practiced it a thousand times before. Like we know all of each other's favorite things. And we do.

"I can't believe this," Jake whispers, his breath so amazingly hot against my neck.

"Can't believe what?"

"I fell for you when I was eighteen. That night at prom—"

"You mean at the audition for *Romeo and Juliet*? Or wasn't it earlier than that, on your very first day of school?"

He blinks at me. "You knew? All along?"

"It was kind of obvious," I tease, enjoying for once being the one who knows more than him. "Wanna know a secret?"

He nods.

"I did too."

"At first sight?"

"At first sight."

He shakes his head, amazed, adorable. "All these years, I've wondered about you, Dusk. I never thought you'd give me a chance."

"Life's funny that way," I say and kiss him again.

A whoop and then applause sounds from up the beach. Jake and I break apart long enough to see Masha and Eli, watching us, and hugging, and jumping up and down.

"Dude!" Eli shouts. "I can't believe you made a move!"

"Actually, I kissed him!" I call out proudly as they jog toward us on the beach.

"That's a plot twist I did *not* see coming," Masha says. "But I will drink to being surprised." She holds up a bottle of champagne, takes a drink, and passes it to Eli, who passes it to Jake. Who holds up his hand like a stop sign.

"Wait, this is important. We need to get it straight. Olivia initiated a peck, but that's as far as she was going to go. I'm the one who made the *real* kiss happen."

My jaw drops. "Don't come at me with what's *real*."

"He'll die on this hill, Olivia," Eli says. "We might as well go with his version. It's safer for the planet."

"She's not backing down," Masha says, coming to my side.

"I kissed that gorgeous liar," I say, taking a swig of champagne. "I know what's real in this world. And the next."

Jake's green eyes flash with that old competitive flair, and I realize we're not done fighting each other. You can't have a great story without conflict. Or great sex without tension. Maybe all great loves are inevitable. And maybe what Jake and I have done just now, with this latest of first kisses, is to kick our love into a higher life, where it was always meant to be.

ACKNOWLEDGMENTS

With interdimensional thanks to Tara Singh Carlson for your passionate intelligence and for knowing the portal was a kiss. To Laura Rennert for your valiant and razor-sharp style. To the tremendous team at Putnam: Aranya Jain, Sally Kim, Ashley Hewlett, Alexis Welby, Brittany Bergman, and Ashley Tucker— I'm fortunate to work with each of you. To Laurel Canyon, my twisting, twisted, and enchanting home. To the women who sustain and inspire me: the OBLC, the Naked Mushrooms, and the Wolves. To the bravery of my matriarchs. To Asherah. To Jason, Matilda, and Venice: There's no world where we don't end up together. And to you, my reader and my friend. Thank you.

What's in a Kiss?

LAUREN KATE

Discussion Guide

A Conversation with Lauren Kate

Excerpt from By Any Other Name *by Lauren Kate*

BOOK
ENDS

PUTNAM
— EST. 1838 —

DISCUSSION GUIDE

1. What was your favorite scene, and why?

2. A road-rage incident causes Olivia to reconcile with her father's death and reevaluate her plans for her future. Have you had a surprise incident or moment like this that pushed you to question your own situation?

3. Masha and Olivia are very close, yet have very different outlooks on life and life's what-ifs, especially when it comes to relationships. What is the difference between how they face challenges or fears in their lives? Whom do you relate to more?

4. How did each reality affect Olivia's relationships with her loved ones? Do you think she could have truly been happy in either reality without knowing what could have been?

5. There is one incident that changes the trajectory of Olivia and Jake's relationship. Is there a moment in your life that you look back on and think, *What if?*

6. Olivia's diary is color coded and categorized by different stages in her life. Do you keep a diary? Would you consider keeping one? If so, how is it, or how would it be, organized?

7. Liv's romantic history and her ideas of romance are informed by her mother's heartbreak over her father's passing. How does this speak to the idea of honoring and remembering past relationships? In what ways do the struggles of our pasts influence our futures?

8. Masha's wedding reception triggers Olivia's surreal experience of living in an alternate reality. In both worlds, she's made sacrifices for the people she loves. Have you ever felt like you had to choose between two things of extreme importance to you? If so, how did you make that decision?

9. What do you think the title of the book means?

10. How did you feel about the ending? Were you expecting Olivia to choose that path?

A CONVERSATION WITH LAUREN KATE

What inspired you to write *What's in A Kiss?*

Recently my children asked for stories about how my husband and I first got together. Sitting across the dinner table, each telling our version of meeting at a party under the stars on a tomato farm in Winters, California, I wondered what other paths might have led me to this life. Surely, if I hadn't gone to that party, some other force of destiny would have brought me here . . . right? I wanted to write a romance that would ignite no matter the circumstances. A love story that insisted on itself, even when it was impossible. I'm not sure I believe in soulmates, but I do believe that some loves are stubborn, with cosmic agendas.

Why did you choose to set this story in Los Angeles?

Before I moved to LA, I had strong opinions about all the things I wouldn't like about it. Then I landed in Laurel Canyon in the fall of 2009, and it was instalove. Los Angeles is a rousing city, pulsing with dreamers, stratospheric luck, and really good tacos. Its natural beauty shapes my days—even though I grew up thinking nature was a tree in a mall. Writing this book, I pulled from my daily experiences, my frustrations and pleasures, and the people in my life who actually are as open to the multiverse as Olivia has to be in this story.

Which was your favorite scene to write, and why?
The scene where Olivia goes from being beloved Maid of Honor to loathed Persona Non Grata at her best friend's wedding was a thrill to write. I seek chances to shock my protagonists, to turn them upside down and inside out in starkly tangible ways, so that I can know them more deeply.

Who was your favorite character to write, and why?
Olivia was my BAE in this book. Because the rift in her reality exposes two very different sides of her character, she felt familiar to me in a long-term way—meaning I identify with her in both my past and present selves. Once she's displaced from her real life and loses access to the people she's closest to, I knew it was essential to put her in conflict with characters who enrage and annoy her. Of these characters, I particularly enjoy Yogi Rabbi Dan.

Were Olivia and Jake inspired by real people? If so, who, and if not, how did you come to their characters?
At the start of the book, Olivia defines herself largely through her relationships with those in her inner circle—her mother and her best friend, Masha. In the first chapter, she says of Masha that "when you've been friends as long as we have, it's impossible not to see yourself—every aspect of your identity—in relation to each other." I based this on my relationship with my oldest friend Megan. One of my favorite scenes in the book is

between Olivia and Masha, in the alternate reality where Masha doesn't consider Olivia a friend anymore. Every time I worked on this chapter, it made me cry, and the novel is dedicated to Megan, whom I channeled for this scene.

For Jake's character, I saw his public-facing golden-boy persona—the one Olivia finds maddeningly fake—as a cross between Jimmy Fallon and Will Arnett. Both of these artists are great at what they do, and their toothsome schtick is very explicit. It's like there's no room for authenticity. When Jake's external success is taken away from him, I tried to write a character who's really that charming, that playful, that kind. The shocking truth of Jake's character is that he's not an act, and when he shines everything he's got on Olivia, she has to grow a bit to take it all in.

If the story were told from Jake's perspective, how would his alternate reality differ from Olivia's?

Jake's internal life is less frenetic than Olivia's. He's less conflicted about his desire. The story would still confront Jake's and Olivia's responsibilities to their actual lives, but we might get to glimpse the lonely side of fame through Jake's eyes. And we'd likely see more of Jake's relationship attempts with other women. We'd need to see him try to be happy with someone other than Olivia. Because Olivia gives Jake no choice but bliss.

Do you believe in a multiverse? What other lives are you living?

I know there's more to our existence than we can see. I like to imagine myself in endless other careers, geographies, eras. I think I'd always find the souls who matter most to me.

This novel portrays various types of love: familial, platonic, and romantic. How do you hope this book speaks to the roles of these different loves in people's lives?

Everything I write is a love story, and while I think romantic love is exciting, I find myself taking an increasingly expansive view. Familial love is cellular, ancient, and wise. Platonic love is butter in the skillet—it makes life glide . . . and taste better. We need it all. As much as we can get.

Olivia and Jake both experience feelings of loss and regret. Why did you choose to make them similar in this way?

Olivia needs to deny the existence of Jake's wounds so her own life makes sense. That's something you see a lot in LA—young lovers break up and one of them goes on to become rich and famous. Then the left-behind lover has to see the successful lover on billboards and buses. The left-behind lover's got to do something with that, emotionally. You can't fall apart every time you drive down Sunset Boulevard.

Olivia toughens herself up to survive, and it becomes a large part of who she is. She's used to fantasizing that Jake has no problems, no regrets. For her character to evolve, she has to be shaken out of that comfortable self-delusion.

Without giving anything away, did you always know how the story would end?

I did know how the book was going to end—I often know the ending and the climax, but I tend to be wrong about the moment just *before* the climax, the moment that tips the scales toward the story's destination. This book was no exception. I remember coming to a small scene where Olivia is home alone just before she makes the choice that leads to the book's crescendo. What she discovers in that scene shocked me as I wrote it. It touched me deeply. And it's connected to my original inspiration for this book—the details of my personal love story that I feel I owe my children.

With a successful career as a romance editor, and an engagement to a man who checks off all the boxes, Lanie's more than good. She's killing it. Then she's given the opportunity of a lifetime: to work with world-renowned author Noa Callaway. All Lanie has to do is cure Noa's writer's block and she'll get the promotion she's always dreamed of. Simple, right?

But there's a reason no one has ever seen or spoken to the mysterious Noa Calloway, and that reason will rock Lanie's world. When she finally tosses her expectations to the wind, Lanie may just discover that love *By Any Other Name* can still be as sweet.

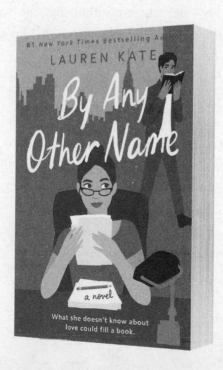

Chapter One

"PEONY PRESS, THIS IS LANIE BLOOM—" I SAY, BARELY getting the phone to my ear before the voice on the other end cuts me off.

"Hallelujah-you're-still-at-your-desk!"

It's Meg, our senior publicist, and my closest friend at work. She's calling from the Hotel Shivani, where, four hours from now, we'll be hosting a blowout wedding-themed book launch for Noa Callaway—our biggest author and the writer who taught me about love when my mom couldn't. Noa Callaway's books changed my life.

If experience is any guide, we're just slightly overdue for all our best-laid plans to go up in flames.

"No sign of the signed books. And no fucking pun intended. Can you see if they were sent to the office by mistake," Meg says, a mile a minute. "I need time to arrange them into a five-tiered, heart-shaped wedding cake—"

See? Best-laid plans.

"Meg, when's the last time you breathed?" I ask. "Do you need to push your button?"

"How can you manage to sound pervy *and* like my mother? Okay, okay, I'm pushing my button."

It's a trick her therapist taught her, an imaginary elevator button Meg can press in the hollow of her throat to carry herself down a few levels. I picture her in her all-black ensemble and stylishly giant glasses, standing in the center of the hotel ballroom downtown with assistants buzzing all around, hurrying to transform the modernist SoHo event space into a quaint destination wedding on the Amalfi Coast. I see her closing her eyes and touching the hollow of her throat. She exhales into the phone.

"I think it worked," she says.

I smile. "I'll track down the books. Anything else before I head over?"

"Not unless you play the harp," Meg moans.

"What happened to the harpist?"

We'd paid a premium to hire the principal from the New York Phil to pluck Pachelbel's Canon as guests arrive tonight.

"The flu happened," Meg says. "She offered to send her friend who plays the oboe, but that doesn't exactly scream Italian wedding . . . does it?"

"No oboe," I say, my pulse quickening.

These are just problems. As with the first draft of a book, there's always a solution. We just have to find it and make the revision. I'm good at this. It's my job as senior editor.

"I made a playlist when I was editing the book," I offer to Meg. "Dusty Springfield. Etta James. Billie Eilish."

"Bless you. I'll have someone copy it when you get down here. You'll need your phone for your speech, right?"

A flutter of nerves spreads through my chest. Tonight is the first time I'll be taking the stage before an audience at a Noa Callaway launch. Usually, my boss makes the speeches, but Alix is on maternity leave, so the spotlight will be on me.

"Lanie, I gotta go," Meg says, a new burst of panic in her voice. "Apparently we're also missing two hundred dollars' worth of cake balloons. And now they're saying, because it's Valentine's goddamned eve, they're too busy to make any more—"

The line goes dead.

In the hours before a big Noa Callaway event, we sometimes forget that we're not performing an emergency appendectomy.

I think this is because, well, the first rule of a Noa Callaway book launch is . . . Noa Callaway won't be there.

Noa Callaway is our powerhouse author, with forty million books in print around the world. She is also the rare publishing phenomenon who doesn't do publicity. You can't google Noa's author photo nor contact her online. You'll never read a *T* magazine piece about the antique telescope in her Fifth Avenue penthouse. She declines all invitations for champagne whenever her books hit the list, though she lives 3.4 miles from our office. In fact, the only soul I know who's actually met Noa Callaway is my boss, Noa's editor, Alix de Rue.

And yet, you *know* Noa Callaway. You've seen her window displays in airports. Your aunt's book club is reading her right now. Even if you're the type who prefers *The Times Literary Supplement* over *The New York Times Book Review*, at the very least, you've Netflix and chilled *Fifty Ways to Break Up Mom and Dad*. (That's Noa's third novel but first movie adaptation, meme-famous for *that* scene with the turkey baster.) Over the past ten years, Noa Callaway's heart-opening love stories have become so culturally pervasive that if they haven't made you laugh, *and* cry, *and* feel less alone in a cruel and oblivious world, then you should probably check to see whether you're dead inside.

With no public face behind Noa Callaway's name, those of us in the business of publishing her novels feel a special pressure to go the extra mile. It makes us do crazy things. Like drop two grand on helium balloons filled with floating angel food cake.

Meg assured me that when our guests pop these balloons at the end of my toast this evening, the shower of cake and edible confetti will be worth every penny that came out of my group's budget.

Assuming they haven't gone missing.

"Zany Lanie." Joe from our mail room pops his head inside my office and gives me an air fist bump.

"Joe, my bro," I quip back automatically, as I've been doing every day for the past seven years. "Hey, perfect timing—have you seen four big boxes of signed books arrive from Noa Callaway's office?"

"Sorry." He shakes his head. "Just this for you."

As Joe sets down a stack of mail on my desk, I fire off a diplomatic text to Noa Callaway's longtime assistant, and my occasional nemesis, Terry.

Terry is seventy, steel-haired, tanklike, and ever ready to shut down any request that might interfere with Noa's process. Meg and I call her the Terrier because she barks but rarely bites. It's always iffy whether simple things—like getting Noa to sign a couple hundred books for an event—will actually get done.

It will be a travesty if our guests go home tonight without a copy of Noa's new book. I can feel them out there, two hundred and sixty-six Noa Callaway fans, all along the Northeast Corridor, from Pawtucket, Rhode Island, to Wynnewood, Pennsylvania. They are taking off work two hours early, confirming babysitters, Venmoing dog walkers. They are Dropboxing Monday's presentation and rummaging through drawers for unripped tights while toddlers cling to their legs. In a dozen different ways, these intrepid ladies are getting shit done so they can take a night for themselves. So they can train to the Hotel Shivani and be among the first to get their hands on *Two Hundred and Sixty-Six Vows.*

I think it's Noa's best book yet.

The story takes place at a destination wedding over Valentine's Day weekend. On a whim, the bride invites the full wedding party to stand up and renew their own vows—to a spouse, to a friend, to a pet, to the universe . . . with disastrous results. It's moving and funny, meta and of-the-moment, the way Noa's books always are.

The fact that the novel ends with a steamy scene on a Positano beach is just one more reason I know Noa Callaway and I are psychically connected. Family legend has it that my mother was conceived on a beach in Positano, and while that might not seem like information most kids would cherish knowing, I was raised in part by my grandmother, who defines the term *sexpositive.*

I've always wanted to visit Positano. *Vows* makes me feel almost like I have.

I check my phone for a response from Terry about the signed books. Nothing. I can't let Noa's readers down tonight. Especially because *Two Hundred and Sixty-Six Vows* may be the last Noa Callaway book they get to read for a while. . .

Our biggest author is four months late delivering her next manuscript. Four unprecedented months late.

After a decade of delivering a book each year, the prolific Noa Callaway suddenly seems to have no plans of turning in her next draft. My attempts to get past Terry and connect with Noa have been fruitless. It's only a matter of time before our production department expects me to turn over a tightly edited—and nonexistent—manuscript.

But that's a panic attack for another day. Alix is due back from maternity leave next week, and the pressure will be on.

I'm flipping through my mail, waiting impatiently for Terry's response, knowing I need to get down to the venue—when my hands find a little brown box in the middle of the mail Joe delivered. It's no bigger than a deck of cards. My distracted mind recognizes the return address and I gasp.

It's the Valentine's gift I had handmade for my fiancé, Ryan. I unwrap the paper, slide open the box, and smile.

The polished wood square is pale and smooth, about the size and thickness of a credit card. It unfolds like an accordion, revealing three panels. In fine calligraphy is The List I made long ago. It's all the attributes I wanted to find in the person I'd fall in love with. It's my Ninety-Nine Things List, and Ryan checks off every one.

I've been told that most girls learn about love from their moms. But the summer I turned ten and my brother, David, was twelve, my mom was diagnosed with Hodgkin's lymphoma. She went fast, which everyone says is a mercy, but it isn't. It just about killed my oncologist father that even he couldn't save her.

My mom was a pharmacoepidemiologist on the board of the National Academy of Medicine. She used to fly all over the world, sharing stages with Melinda Gates and Tony Fauci, giving speeches on infectious diseases at the CDC and WHO. She was brilliant but also warm and funny. She could be tough, but she also knew how to make everyone feel special, seen.

She died on a Tuesday. It was raining out the hospital window, and her hand seemed smaller than mine. I held it as she razzed me for the last time.

"Just don't be a dermatologist."

(When you're born into generations of doctors, you make jokes about imagined medical hierarchies.)

"I hear there's good money in it," I said. "And the hours."

"Can't beat the hours." She smiled at me. Her eyes were the same blue as mine, everybody said. We used to have the same thick, straight brown hair, too, but in so many ways, my mom didn't look like my mom anymore.

"Lanie?" Her voice had gone softer and yet more intense. "Promise me," she said. "Promise to find someone you really, really love."

My mother liked overachievers. And she seemed to be asking, with her final words, for me to overachieve in love. But how? When your mom dies and you are young, the worst part is that you know there's all this stuff you'll need to know, and now who's going to teach you?

It wasn't until college that I was introduced to the writer who would teach me about love: Noa Callaway.

One day after class, I came back to my dorm, and the tissues were flying on my roommate Dara's side of the room where she and her friends were hunched together.

Dara held a half-eaten Toblerone out to me and waved a book in my direction. "Have you read this yet?"

I shook my head without glancing at the book, because Dara and I did not have the same reading tastes. I was pre-med like my brother and obsessing over my organic chemistry reader so I could move back to Atlanta and become a doctor like everyone else in my family. Dara was majoring in sociology, but her shelves were stuffed with paperbacks with cursive fonts.

"This book is the only thing that got Andrea over Todd," she said.

I looked at Dara's friend Andrea, who fell face-first into another girl's lap.

"I'm crying because it's so beautiful," Andrea sobbed.

When Dara and her friends left in search of lattes, I felt the gold foil letters of the book's title staring me down from across the room. I picked it up and held it in my hand.

Ninety-Nine Things I'm Going to Love About You by Noa Callaway.

I don't know why, but the title made me think of my mother's last words. Her plea that I find someone I really, really loved. Was she sending me a message over the transom?

I opened the book and started reading, and a funny thing happened: I couldn't put it down.

Ninety-Nine Things is the story of Cara Kenna, a young woman struggling to survive a divorce. There's a suicide attempt and a stint in a psych ward, but the tone is so brightly funny, I'd commit myself if it meant I could hang out with her.

In the hospital, Cara has only time to kill, and she does so by reading the ninety-nine romance novels in the psych ward library. At first, she's cynical, but then, despite herself, she finds a line she likes. She writes it down. She says it aloud. Soon she's writing down her favorite line from every book. By the day of her release, she has ninety-nine things to hope for in a future love affair.

I read the book in one sitting. I was buzzing all over. I looked at the chemistry homework I had to do and felt something inside me had changed.

Ninety-Nine Things held all the words I'd been looking for since my mother died. It spelled out how to really, really love. With humor, with heart, and with bravery. It made me want to find that love myself.

At the back of the book, where the author's bio usually is, the publisher included three blank pages, lined and numbered from one to ninety-nine.

Okay, Mom, I'd thought, sitting down to get to work. I wasn't sure which of Dara's friends this book had belonged to, but it was now undeniably, cosmically mine.

The beauty of such a large list was that it allowed me to weave between weird and brave, between superficial and marrow-deep and deal-breaker serious. In between *Enthusiastic about staying up all night discussing potential past lives* and *Answers the phone when his mother calls,* I'd written: *Doesn't own clogs, unless he's a chef or Dutch.* At the very end, number ninety-nine, I wrote, *Doesn't die.* I felt my mom was with me, between the lines of that list. I felt if I could pursue this kind of love, then she'd be proud of me, wherever she was.

I don't know that I ever *really* thought I'd find a guy who embodied my whole list. It was more the exercise of committing to paper love's wondrous possibilities.

But then . . . I met Ryan, and everything—well, all ninety-nine things—just clicked. He's perfect for me. Scratch that. He's perfect, period.

I fold up the wooden panels, tuck my gift back into the box. I can't wait to give this to him tomorrow on Valentine's Day.

Photograph of the author © Christina Hultquist 2018

Lauren Kate is the #1 *New York Times* and internationally best-selling author of nine novels for young adults, including *Fallen*, which was made into a major motion picture. Her books have been translated into more than thirty languages and have sold more than 10 million copies worldwide. She is also the author of *The Orphan's Song*, her debut adult novel, and *By Any Other Name*. Kate lives in Los Angeles with her family.

VISIT LAUREN KATE ONLINE

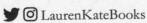

laurenkatebooks.net

LaurenKateAuthor

LaurenKateBooks